T0114987

# Liberty
## AND
# Justice
## FOR
# SOME

**A Novel By Ted Paulk**

iUniverse, Inc.
Bloomington

# Liberty and Justice for Some

Copyright © 2011 Ted Paulk

All rights reserved. No part of this book may be used or reproduced by any means,
graphic, electronic, or mechanical, including photocopying, recording, taping or by any
information storage retrieval system without the written permission of the publisher
except in the case of brief quotations embodied in critical articles and reviews.

This is a work of fiction. All of the characters, names, incidents, organizations, and dialogue
in this novel are either the products of the author's imagination or are used fictitiously.

iUniverse books may be ordered through booksellers or by contacting:

iUniverse
1663 Liberty Drive
Bloomington, IN 47403
www.iuniverse.com
1-800-Authors (1-800-288-4677)

Because of the dynamic nature of the Internet, any web addresses or links contained in this book may
have changed since publication and may no longer be valid. The views expressed in this work are
solely those of the author and do not necessarily reflect the views of the publisher, and the publisher
hereby disclaims any responsibility for them.

Any people depicted in stock imagery provided by Thinkstock are models,
and such images are being used for illustrative purposes only.

Certain stock imagery © Thinkstock.

ISBN: 978-1-4620-0661-8 (pbk)
ISBN: 978-1-4620-0663-2 (clth)
ISBN: 978-1-4620-0662-5 (ebk)

Printed in the United States of America

iUniverse rev. date: 3/22/11

Special thanks to John and Luann Carpino for
entertaining us for so long and so well.

Thanks to Sue, who worked for wine, for the technical help.

Thanks to friends and family for their support and input.

# Marcus Regan

My name is Marcus Regan. I had some bad experiences in Oklahoma while growing up in a suburb of Tulsa. The other kids made fun of me, especially the high school girls. They would catch me staring at them in class. I couldn't help it. I guess I was a funny lookin' kid in those days.

The fact that my mom and I lived in a shack over by the coloreds where it was no secret my mom turned tricks with any man, regardless of race, who showed up with some crack cocaine or meth didn't help my social status. She was content with getting high so she never asked for money from any of the men who drifted in an out of our house. They never stayed long. A few would bring some beer along with the drugs but none came with food. Seems I was always hungry, dirty and ragged. We lived on welfare checks, food stamps, and government cheese.

When I started high school, I was bigger than most of the seniors. I had matured before any of the other boys in my class. The fact that I had been held back in the fourth grade and again in the sixth grade might have had something to do with it. Hell, I was having to shave when I was a sophomore. I seemed to have a constant hard on and was unable to hide it in the thin trousers my mom made me wear. It seemed I was slinking around the school trying to hide my embarrassment over my protruding pants and my big nose the whole time I was there.

When Debbie, the cutest girl in class, caught me staring at her one day she'd said, "Don't look at me like that, Marcus. You're ugly as a mud fence and all nose." Funny how one sentence can stay with you for life. I've had a complex about my large nose ever since. I wanted to make her pay for her words. I often played scenes over in my mind; fantasizing of following her into the woods, ripping her clothes off, and fucking her so hard she would scream for mercy. I would have too, but she was always with her friends.

Although the girls giggled when they noticed my condition in class, I could tell they were also scared of me. After I finished school I wasn't able to stay away from the campus. I tried to get a job as janitor there but I don't think I ever had a chance. There was just something about me. Probably a good thing for the young ladies considering the thoughts that constantly went through my mind.

I got a job in the slaughterhouse for a little while. Other than the bosses, I was the only white guy that would take such a job. The place was full of Mexican and Niggers. Several of the workers there knew my mom, so I tried to ignore the looks they gave me. But then I got caught using a forklift to push a cow that had fallen and couldn't get up. I didn't know that was illegal until one of the Mexicans ratted me out to an inspector. I almost went to jail for something I didn't even know was against the law. I felt I had been singled out for no reason. All I got was the shit; no matter where I was. Everybody there did bad things to the animals, like using electric prods again and again when the animals wouldn't move or spraying the downed animals in the eyes with high pressure water hoses to make them get up and take their final steps to the bloody killing floor.

After I lost my job, I went back to hanging around the school. One day some of the jocks caught me trying to look in the window of the girl's locker room. They beat me up pretty bad. I hurt a few of them though before they got me on the ground and started kicking me. The principal called the police about me and I was warned to stay away from the school.

I moved to California right after that. It was back in the nineties and I chose California on purpose. I had to get out of Oklahoma because I knew I couldn't control my desire for those ripe young girls. I also knew if I was caught by the cops rather than the boys, and I was pretty sure that I would be caught someday, I would be facing some hard time. I knew that California is the state that hands down the most lenient sentences against those who would hurt their children…funny, huh?

I was proven right when I got caught for molesting my neighbor's daughter, Lacy, back in 2005. Lacy was considerably younger than the nubies, my word for nubile young ladies, those tender little darlings, that normally turn me on. I like them around fifteen or sixteen give or take a few months, before they get that grown up smell that most women seem to develop a few years after reaching puberty. The young ones smell like newborn babies…almost. Lacy was only eight years old that summer but she was handy.

The arrest wasn't really my fault. Lacy's mom, Andrea was her name; would let her little girl swim in their pool with nothing on. Lacy was physically mature for her age and that cute little naked bubble butt of hers was something to behold. There wasn't much of a fence between their backyard and the house that I had been renting for a few months, but there was a hedge I could sit behind and be out of sight. Andrea would take her top off and sunbathe while her daughter played. This did nothing for me as Andrea was probably around thirty with sagging breasts and visible stretch marks. She seemed to be in pretty good shape other than that, but I wished she would put some clothes on.

At that time I was working nights at the butcher shop in Chino. At least there were a few white guys that worked there too, so I had someone to talk to. No one knew about my mom out here. She hadn't seemed very sad to see me leave and I didn't shed any tears when I left.

I'd settled into a routine. After I woke up in the afternoon each day, I would often find myself sitting behind the hedge keeping an eye on Lacy. I tried to pass this off as putting myself in the role of guardian making sure she didn't get into any danger in the pool. I might be misstating the facts here a bit; watching her cavort in her yard while nude seemed to turn me on…a lot. I was disappointed on the days when Lacy didn't show.

I stayed out of sight, because I didn't want to disturb her or her mother. Sometimes the little nymph would see me and come over to the place where I was sitting. I would give her a piece of candy, I always kept a bag of jelly beans handy, and sometimes I would touch her. She didn't seem to mind and I wasn't doing any harm.

Well, her mom caught me off guard, with my hand thru the fence, and she was not as amiable as Lacy had been. A few minutes later the cops arrived and hauled me off to jail. They were pretty rough and when they put the handcuffs on me, they squeezed them so tight I could hardly feel my hands when we finally got to the booking area.

If it had not been for Bob Marius, it could have turned into a real bad experience. Bob, the lawyer, happened to be hanging around the jail waiting to see some other client of his who was in there on similar charges. We took an instant liking to each other…I had wanted to be a lawyer once upon a time, but I never went to college…we kinda bonded if you know what I mean.

He spoke really harsh to the cops and told them to get those cuffs off me right now. He then called a bail bondsman friend of his and got me out after a few hours. I'd hoarded some money I had saved from selling some stuff I had acquired, so I told him I would pay him when I could get to my stash. For some reason, the judge told me not to go back to my house. I could get someone else to pick up my stuff, but I had to stay away from Lacy's house. I didn't think that was fair, but Bob told me to be quiet and do what the judge said.

Two weeks later, I went with Bob to meet with the judge and a prosecutor at the arraignment. I had met with a shrink the week before because of a court order.

"Your honor, I would like to charge Mr. Regan with sexual assault of a minor in the first degree and ask for a maximum sentence," the prosecutor stated. The prosecutor, by the name of Jason Rolf didn't look too prosperous. His suit pants were wrinkled and too short. The coat he was wearing looked as if it had been purchased when he had been a lot lighter, the buttons strained and pulled the button holes. His shirt and tie both had coffee stains showing. I wasn't impressed with him and I don't think the judge was either.

"Hold on just a minute there!" my new friend and attorney, Bob said rather loudly. He was looking pretty spiffy with a suit that looked like it must have cost a thousand bucks and a tie that probably went for around a hundred. I was proud to have him representing me.

"Let's see if we can't reach some sort of agreement here. My client has never been arrested in California before and I would hate to see a rush to justice here. If we can take a few moments to review the circumstances, it appears that Mr. Regan was arrested and charged on just the word of the child's mother who didn't have a clear view of what was happening. According to my client, this was a total misunderstanding. He was merely responding to the child when she asked him a question. He was being polite and no unlawful behavior play took place." Bob paused for a breath. "What kind of guy do you think Mr. Regan is?"

I thought to myself, "This guy is really good." I almost believed him myself.

Jason Roberts, the prosecutor, pointed out that a state appointed psychiatrist had interviewed me and found that I had shown no remorse.

"Well of course he has shown no remorse," responded Bob. "He hasn't done anything to be remorseful for".

"Let's talk," Jason said, looking at Bob, "in private".

The two of them left the courtroom together and the judge said for the rest of us, a court reporter and a couple of other folks, to take a break. "The arraignment will reconvene in thirty minutes," he said.

A cop kept his eye on me while I sat there wondering what would happen next.

When Bob returned, he took me aside and said, "I cut a deal for you. Rather than facing twenty years, I got Roberts to agree to a five year sentence. You could be out in three if you behave yourself."

"Shit! I thought you were going to get me off with no time," I said, very surprised and upset.

"Come on, Marcus. You know you were trying to stick your finger where it didn't belong, to put it delicately, and her mom caught you. You didn't seriously believe there would be no penalty, did you? Seriously!" He was giving me a real stern look and I had to look away, it was an embarrassing moment for me.

"What if I don't take the deal?"

"I already told you, if you don't plead guilty, you are looking at twenty years or so at San Quentin. If you take the deal, we'll see that you are sent to some minimum security joint where you can work in the garden or the library or whatever interests you."

Thinking about that, and the way Bob laid it out, it didn't seem like such a bad idea to cop to the plea. "OK", I'll do it".

Three years later I was back on the street and man was I horny.

It didn't take long before I located a jogging trail along the coast overlooking the ocean. Made my dick hard just looking at the water and the girls running along in their little gym shorts and halter tops. The firm little boobies would bounce some but the firm cheeks of their fine asses didn't bounce much at all. It was heaven to be out among 'em again.

# CHAPTER ONE

# Jenny Meets Marcus

Her name was Jenny. She'd pulled into the deserted patch of dirt that overlooked the beach below and parked in her usual spot under a large pine tree. Her pink Focus was the only car in the sandy lot, but this was normal for this time of day, late afternoon, during the week. Most people were just getting home from work and getting ready for dinner or watching the news.

She checked the area without much thought of danger lurking; after all, this was *her* jogging trail. She'd been coming here for almost a year now, it was all perfectly safe. Before she got out of the car and locked the door, she placed the keys in the cup holder, knowing she would use the keyless entry access to get back in when she had finished her evening run. She started down the trail at a slower pace, warming up before she began to sprint.

She had just turned seventeen, exhibiting the innocent beauty that nature bestows on girls of that age. The new Focus had been her birthday present. Clad in running shorts and a tank top that showed her lithe body and long legs, she was indeed a sight to behold. He watched from the bushes further down the running path. He had arrived thirty minutes earlier in order to position himself in the best possible location; one that provided cover from any curious onlooker or Good Samaritan that might be passing by.

He had picked a spot just far enough from the parking lot where she started her run to allow her time to become slightly winded by the time she reached the secluded spot where he was waiting. It was at the top of a slight incline, but not so slight that it didn't cause the runner to experience some labored breathing by the time the hill topped out. He wanted as little resistance from her as he could get.

He had thought it out very carefully, stalking her for two weeks now; learning her routine; watching to see if she ever varied it; so far she had not. She would come here every Monday, Wednesday, and Friday without fail around five thirty. The sun was just starting to set on this fall afternoon.

He was breathing through his mouth to lessen the noise of his heavy breathing which was coming in fast, short bursts as he anticipated what was about to happen. He was having trouble getting air deep into his lungs, making him angry at this loss of self-control.

He had gone through almost this same exercise a year earlier in a wooded park two miles up the highway. After the passage of the year, the body of Becky, the girl he had raped and murdered, had yet to be found. The story of her disappearance was no longer of importance. News coverage of the missing girl had ceased months earlier.

He smiled to himself as he savored the idea that he had succeeded in getting away with the previous crime; playing the vicious assault he had performed on her over again in his mind and getting excited at the memory. He was too smart for them. He was determined to make no more mistakes like he had made with little Lacey. There were no witnesses in the area this time.

His armpits were sweating profusely and had soaked the tee-shirt he was wearing. He could smell himself and the testosterone reeking from his body. The smell excited him further. He felt the stirring in his loins as his erection grew harder. He wondered to himself if she would like it. Probably not, Becky hadn't. It didn't really matter though; it could only end in one way, just like last time.

As she came even with where he was waiting, he stepped out and hit her with almost as much force as his two hundred and twenty pound squat body could muster. He pulled his punch a bit; after all, he didn't want to kill her...yet.

She was dazed at first, knocked to the ground, lying in the dirt path, but as she became aware of what happened, she attempted to scream. He pulled a cloth strip from the pocket of the loose shorts he was wearing as he slipped them down around his ankles and then kicked them out of the way. He wrapped the bandage-like cloth around her head, covering her mouth to shut her up. He then dragged her into the underbrush and went to work on her. Other than his heavy grunting and raspy breathing, her muffled sobbing was the only sound in the deserted park.

CHAPTER TWO

# Introduction to Josh O'Brien

Josh O'Brien: It was 6:00 in the morning in Arizona as I watched the national news. I was getting ready to head out to the jobsite where one of my customers was refurbishing the old dam at Roosevelt Lake. I sold heavy construction equipment, the big dozers and other earth movers in and around Phoenix.

I also covered the copper mines around Globe and Miami which were located in Gila County. I'd been doing this for several years and found it to be the most satisfying work I'd ever done. I enjoyed the time I spent with the hard working men that made their living in the construction industry. "Building America" is how I jokingly described the activities of my clients. I knew that I had a part in making their business a lucrative endeavor for my customers.

Over the years, I'd earned a reputation for honesty and tenacity when it came to insuring that my customers were dealt with fairly. One of my several mottos was "Friend to all; fool to none". With the larger machines I sold priced at over a million dollars apiece, there was lots of room for manipulating deals. I avoided such tricks, preferring to deal fairly with all my customers who had learned to trust me, thus earning their respect and loyalty.

I could be counted on as a trusted friend who kept an open mind…most of the time.

Aside from work, I couldn't help but exhibit an unrelenting hatred against child molesters and men who hurt women. I'd experienced some beatings from a step-father who seemed to delight in beating both my mother and me. Mom was old school and refused to leave the asshole. She had married him right before my sixth birthday. When I finally gained some size and could defend her and myself, the man left. We never saw him again even though he left a son, Jody my little brother, behind as a reminder.

I never resented Jody and spent a lot of energy in looking out for him over the years. My love for him was unshakable and since I had to play the role of both big brother and father we were always close. At least something good came out of the union between my mom and the child beater...until that day.

I was away at college when I got the call from mom. It had happened when Jody was on his way home from school and had stopped at Alvin's, the little grocery store in town. Turned out a robbery was in progress as my little brother walked into the building; talk about bad timing. The owner, Alvin Cutler, was confronting a would-be robber who was wielding a baseball bat while demanding the contents of the cash register.

Alvin stood behind the counter. Furious at the boldly rude actions of the masked intruder, after all this was the South and Alvin's property was being threatened, the supreme outrage to this regional mindset; the proprietor grabbed a pistol from the shelf under the cash register and raised his hand firing. He emptied the revolver before he finally stopped squeezing the trigger. The robber ran away but Jody took a shot in the chest. He died on the way to the hospital. He was ten years old.

The robber and an accomplice were caught in record time as there were only four roads leading out of town. This turned out to be my first encounter with our justice system. Johnny and Jackie Riggs were the sons of HC Riggs. HC was a rancher who had a spread 30 miles away, over in Ellis Country. His holdings included over a thousand acres of good Trinity River bottom land. He ran five hundred head of registered Santa Gertrudis cattle along with a remuda of registered Quarter horses needed to work the cattle. HC was a good buddy of the county judge so a deal was cut.

HC hired a noted defense lawyer out of Dallas to handle the negotiations. At the hearing the conversation went thusly, "Your Honor, there was no deadly force used by these boys and no money was actually taken. If we follow the letter of the law, we have to admit that no crime was actually committed by these lads other than a few threatening moves. These young men have not had any run-ins with the law prior to this. We certainly would not want to ruin their futures by hasty judgments.

"Of course the death of young O'Brien is sad indeed, but the whole thing was just one big misunderstanding. Mr. Cutler thought he needed to defend his property, but he used excessive force. Under the circumstances, I believe the best course of action here is just to forget this unfortunate incident ever took place. My client, Mr. Riggs, has offered to pay for the boy's funeral and he has offered make a monetary donation to help the older brother with his college bills."

The judge concurred and that was the end of it. HC sent a check for $5,000 to me. I've yet to cash it. The death of my little brother left a bitter taste in my mouth along with a feeling of being robbed myself. In my own mind, I'm still searching for the justice that has been denied me since that awful day.

I believe in doing the right thing and I've expected the same behavior from others with whom I have dealings. In fact this has been my personal definition of integrity; "Do the right thing because it's the right thing to do". It's a simple philosophy that's proven easy for me to live my life by.

I'd majored in history and psychology in college and I tried to stay current. I watched a lot of network news, going back and forth between the major networks. Sometimes my wife, Susan and I watch the pundits on FOX just for laughs.

In the past, I've found Glenn Beck to be hilarious, up to a point. But lately, it only took a few minutes of Beck's "crazy bullshit" conspiracy theories that he pulled out of his ass, to make me switch channels to keep from throwing something at the TV. The message of fear and hate-mongering repeated over and over by the self-proclaimed reformed alcoholic and drug addicted Mormon had begun to wear thin faster. As Beck wrote his stupid conclusions on his grease board followed by slamming a red button that said *FACT* next the scary words he had scribbled, Susan and I would burst out in laughter. "And to think, some people believe this crackpot and his endless conspiracy theories!" I once said.

Susan replied, "They must but I sure can't understand it. A recent article in *Newsweek* revealed that he makes something like thirty million dollars each year. Besides his radio show and this fear-mongering TV nonsense, he hawks gold and survival food packages to the people he has frightened into believing that the end of the world, or at the least; the end of society as we know it, is near. He really knows how to instill paranoia in his viewers."

"Yeah, but what must he be telling his children and the rest of his family about what is happening in the United States? Does he try to make them as miserable as he does his viewers or does he just say, 'Pay no attention to what Daddy says on TV. It's just how I buy you all these wonderful things'?"

"I hadn't given it that much thought," Susan replied, "and frankly I don't really give a shit what goes in that cretin's home or head." That put an abrupt end to the discussion that day.

When we grew tired of watching depressing news, which happened a lot, we looked for a lighter slant on current events by tuning into the Comedy Channel. We enjoyed watching the Daily Show and the Colbert Report. Jon Stewart and Stephen Colbert were irreverent to all of the talking heads that practiced pomposity. These two sharp entertainers took no prisoners when it came to poking fun at pundits who took themselves too seriously. Beck, with his fake tears and hand wringing, was a frequent target.

Their writers seemed to hit the nail on the head time and again through humorous interviews and faux news reports, exposing the self-importance and hypocrisy of the many so-called public figures. Colbert and Stewart never ran out of targets and ammo, they just ran out of time. Thirty minutes, four days a week is not nearly enough time to cover all the foibles made the politicians and wanna-be leaders.

This particular Monday morning while I was finishing my coffee a more serious breaking news story came on that caught my attention immediately. Susan, in the other room, wasn't talking to me or anyone else for that matter, as the Cleveland Browns had gotten their asses handed to them the day before…again, and this was just a pre-season game. She was an avid fan, while I only watched sports to keep her company.

We watched the games at the local Browns sports bar where the banter among the boisterous fans would get really loud and crude in an especially exciting game. Browns fans are notorious for being loud and obnoxious; Susan was no exception. She would pass out insults to her own team when they made a stupid play or fumbled an easy pass as readily as she jeered the competition.

I'd say to her, "I think you Browns backers are all pissed because you can't be in Cleveland with the rest of the Dog Pound right now." She'd had season tickets when she lived in Ohio. Now in the Phoenix area it was often hard to find a sports bar that would show a game with her beloved team playing. This added to her frustration.

Susan could yell insults with the best of them, "Season ending injury", or worse yet, "Career ending injury" would often be her battle cry against the opposing team. She took her various sports teams seriously and she stuck loyally with them whether they were winners or losers. The last few years had been particularly tough on Susan due to the lack of success on the part of the Browns. She took each loss personally and would become depressed for a few days with each loss. Today was one of those days.

It was almost time for me to hit the road when the story came on that had stopped me in my tracks. It was a follow-up about the young girl, Jenny, who had been jogging in a park north of Los Angeles. She had gone missing two days before.

The reporter stated that her bruised and naked, body had been found this morning. She had been raped and savagely beaten before her attacker had cut her throat. According to the news bulletin, the short release issued by the police spokesman stated, "It's difficult to tell which had occurred first, the sexual assault or the murder. We can only hope she was at least unconscious while the assault was taking place".

The authorities already had a man in custody. A lady by the name of Mrs. Elmore, who was taking her German Shepherd for a walk, had spotted a man trying to break into Jenny's car. She'd yelled at him causing him to flee the scene in his own vehicle. The witness had written down the license number at the time, but had not reported the incident since the break-in had been foiled. She reasoned that since no crime had been committed, there was no point in calling the cops. Once the news story broke, Mrs. Elmore had put two and two together and called the authorities.

She had been asked as she was being interviewed if she'd been afraid to yell at the suspect, who later turned out to be accused of murder. She answered with a wicked smile, "My dog, Gustaf, who weighs around a hundred pounds, won't let anyone mess with me. I wasn't afraid to yell at the guy."

The owner of the suspect vehicle had been picked up at his home last night. The alleged person of interest in the case, Marcus Regan, was said to be a convicted sex offender who had been released from the state pen just over a year ago. He had molested an eight year old girl some four or five years before. Regan had been sentenced to five years for this crime, but had been released after serving only three years of his sentence. His early release was attributed to his *good* behavior while in prison.

The news anchor was saying, "A semen sample taken from the girl's body has yielded a DNA match to Regan. The matching sample in police files that links Regan to the crime had been drawn several years earlier, while he was in prison. At that time he was serving a sentence for having been convicted of committing a sex crime against a child."

The reporter gave some background about how the sample had been obtained. "All the prisoners in Regan's cell block had been ordered to give samples when the body of an inmate who had been raped and murdered was found in the showers. Regan was exonerated when he was found not to be a match, but the DNA sample had not been destroyed, much to Mr. Regan's chagrin.

"Regan's defense attorney, the renowned Robert Marius, is already trying to suppress this DNA evidence as self-incriminating. Marius has stated his client did not give his permission for authorities to take the sample; thus it should have been destroyed after the prison murder investigation had proven his client was not involved in that particular crime. Marius has further gone on record as noting that decisions handed down in prior cases support his argument that this particular piece of evidence is inadmissible."

Marius was shown on the screen shaking his fist while proclaiming angrily, "Furthermore, once this illegally obtained evidenced is tossed out, my client, Mr. Regan, will not be giving any DNA samples in the future. Self-incrimination will not be tolerated in the California justice system nor anywhere else in this country. "

What the hell does that even mean? It has nothing to do with the crime. The asshole's obviously guilty," I said out loud

Susan wandered in just in time to answer me, "Smoke and mirrors, dear. Cloud the real issue immediately. You know how it works."

As I continued to watch mesmerized by what I was witnessing, Channel 12 was starting to air some older file footage in conjunction with the latest story on the crime. A panel made up of several members of the press, was arguing about how a person with such a history as Marcus Regan could have been released back into society after serving such a minimal sentence for his crime against a young child.

A clip from the news station's archives was showing that at the time of Regan's release, one Jeffery Thomas, a social science "expert" hired by Regan's attorney, had adamantly declared that Marcus was a changed man since he had arrived at the facility.

"Mr. Regan has expressed remorse for his past deeds; therefore, justice would not be served by forcing him to serve any further time locked down, away from society. He has stated repeatedly that his incarceration was due to a terrible misunderstanding. He really was not found guilty of committing any crime. He was forced into accepting a plea agreement so he would not be railroaded into serving a twenty year sentence. We are depriving this individual of his constitutional right of liberty and pursuing happiness."

What Mr. Thomas was saying was not altogether the truth. During his sentencing phase for the molestation of the six year old, the state appointed psychiatrist had stated unequivocally that Marcus had shown no remorse whatsoever. The psychiatrist had recommended the maximum sentence be imposed against Regan. The detectives investigating the case had concurred with the psychiatrist. However; after conferring with Regan's lawyer, the prosecutor had asked for, and secured, a five year sentence for the defendant under a plea agreement.

At that time the prosecutor had told the judge, "Our office is inundated with these types of cases; my staff is buried by having to work cases presented by investigators making arrests and stacking on charges.

"Members of my staff, while being kept busy handling these trivial cases, are unable to pursue the more important issues before us. No one was really harmed by the accused in this incident; therefore this seems to be a reasonable request by his attorney, Mr. Marius. I want to handle this in the most expeditious manner possible if your honor concurs."

"Since the prosecutor's office has stated they are willing to accept the deal presented to the defendant, I can see no reason to deny this plea agreement," said the judge not bothering to take a recess to review the case before him.

The file film continued to roll as I continued to watch transfixed. I wondered to myself how the news program had acquired the tape so quickly. "In fact", Thomas had gone on to say, "I am confident enough in my judgment of this, Mr. Marcus's character, that I would have no qualms in allowing him to babysit my two young daughters. My wife might have a differing point of view on that, but I stand by my ability to judge this young man. I base this on my twelve years of experience spent working around the criminal justice system."

"Even this dumb son of a bitch can't be so stupid as to believe that his daughters would be safe with this perverted asshole!" I responded once again to the television screen. Susan quietly shook her head. She knew how upsetting these types of stories were to me. I tried to keep from taking these type of incidents personally, but I couldn't help myself. Each time, the pain was intensely felt by me as if one of my own family members had been violated again.

As the tape continued to roll, Thomas paused expectantly, making sure all was silent before he haughtily declared, "And it should also be read into the record that Marcus Regan has found God while serving his sentence. It turns out that prison has been a blessing to him by saving his immortal soul. Mr. Regan shared this information with the parole board at his latest hearing, going so far as to ask permission to pray for all who were present.

"I wasn't present at that moment but I can tell you Mr. Marius was. To hear him describe what took place was a moving experience indeed. All of those in attendance were moved mightily…some even to tears." Thomas added this tidbit as if this was the final nail to be driven in his grand testimonial as to why Regan should be released.

"You've gotta be shitting me!" I burst out again.

Susan walked by and said, "Are you going to work today, my dear, or are you just going to stand in front of the TV and yell at it?"

I didn't answer as the story played out. While I continued to watch there was still more self-serving bullshit being shoveled by Mr. Thomas, "In my humble opinion, my extensive educational background in psychology and social science, not to mention the law courses I have taken here in our superb California colleges, has made me a person to be acknowledged as having vast insight in these matters.

"I have been called on many, many times to testify on behalf of defendants as an expert witness. The record shows my judgment in these matters has been found to be without fault. I have never been taken in by chicanery on the part of any client under my watch in my entire career."

The effusive Thomas continued, "I am proud to tell you that I personally have been a major player in helping men; many of whom would most likely have remained captives in our unforgiving criminal justice system, obtain early release in recognition of their good works while they have been incarcerated. Most of them are responsible citizens today, working at respectable jobs in our cities and contributing to society as we speak. I say unto you that Mr. Marcus Regan is the real deal. You can take my words to the bank." Red faced and short of breath, Thomas finally disappeared from the screen.

There was a rumor going around in certain circles that later, when Regan's attorney had asked Thomas, off the record, if his words were sincere, the voluble *expert* had replied, "Are you out of your mind? I wouldn't trust that sorry piece of shit with my mother-in- law! Just send me my money please."

Later, when Regan had been released, there was some faint public outcry about his short incarceration, mostly by the mother of little Lacy, but this had been hushed up pretty quickly when a gag order was issued by the judge, at attorney Robert Marius's urging, in order to protect Regan.

The judge had issued the order along with a verbal admonition, "Having served his sentence, this individual has the same rights granted to any other citizen and will not be harassed under penalty of contempt of court.

I assure all of you; especially the members of the fourth estate, the fine and the jail time associated with violating my order will be severe indeed. You surely do not want me to make an example of you."

This five minute footage had been pretty much the extent of the coverage of the man now in custody. After his early release, Marcus had been quietly moved into state subsidized housing in a quiet neighborhood where he had resided in anonymity, until now. It was noted, as an afterthought, that the judge who had ruled in Regan's first case was currently serving on the Federal Court of Appeals.

The young reporter "on scene" outside the county jail was reading some statistics in front of the camera. "Marcus Regan is one of 92,000 registered sex offenders in California. This number pertains to men who are not in prison; except for the now incarcerated Mr. Regan of course.

"These frightful criminals, I guess I should say ex-criminals, are on the streets and in the neighborhoods of every city and town in this state. Regan is no exception to what has happened here. Most first-time child molesters have been granted early release due to 'overcrowding'; the prisons currently house around two hundred thousand prisoners, the majority of these have been convicted of some sort of drug violation.

He went on to cite a case now at the forefront of the news about how a killer scheduled to die the week before had been granted yet another stay of execution. "For example, while Al Brown was burglarizing a home he encountered and raped a fourteen year old girl who lived there. For this heinous crime he drew a sentence of four years. Yes, ladies and gentlemen, only four years.

"Upon his release in 1980, he immediately raped and killed a fifteen year old girl and then psychologically tortured her mother with several phone calls he made, telling where her daughter's body could be found. He followed this up with more phone calls revealing where her purse and other belongings had been deposited. Brown had been released over thirty years ago after serving a four year sentence for raping a teenage girl; this took place while drug users served their full sentences!

"This rape and murder happened 1980 in and yet Brown sits on death row today, quietly getting fatter off state provided food while his lawyers, at state expense, use every trick possible to delay justice. This man was convicted of a crime that is as horrible as any in recorded history. He was sentenced to death in 1982, I repeat nearly thirty years ago!

"Though sentenced to die this year, his execution has been postponed indefinitely; again, by a judge who now feels he must review the case in order to avoid a *rush to justice*, can you believe that crap?"

Someone must have yelled into his ear piece as he seemed to stop and listen for a moment before he continued. "Sorry, folks I'm so sorry, for my poor choice of words, but this really stinks!  I only mention this case to show as an example what is wrong with our system. I'll probably be reprimanded for being so blunt. We're supposed to only report unbiased news items but sometimes, as a father of two little girls, this is not always an easy rule to follow."

"Good for you," I said to the TV.

The reporter continued, "The California department of Corrections Rehabilitation is responsible for only about nine percent of these sexual predators.  The other eighty thousand or so perverts are pretty much on their own.  Somehow, this Regan character has managed to rape and savagely kill this young lady before he was arrested again."

"Son of a Bitch!" I exclaimed, "How many times does this have to happen before these asshole judges and lawyers start putting these creeps away for life; or better yet, execute the mother fuckers!" I paced around yelling at the TV. "Someone should kill that dumbass social science *expert* while they're at it!"

"Calm down, Honey," Susan said to soothe me. My interaction with the TV had gotten her mind off the Brown's loss at last. "You can't let this stuff upset you, besides you can't do anything to change the way things are. You're just going to give yourself a heart attack. "

"Well at least I' be out of my misery," I replied. "You know, if I were king," one of the things I would often say that caused Susan to shake her head, "The first item on my list of things to do would be to enact an irrevocable law stating that all child molesters would be executed the day after they were convicted. I don't give a shit about how connected they might be; diplomats, politicians, priests, or whatever."

"Sure, honey, you've told me that lots of times, just like you've told everyone else who would listen to you. We all agree with you, it's a good idea, but you will never be king so let it go. Besides, the ACLU and the crying hand wringers who are opposed to the death penalty would never let you punish a guilty man so speedily."

She added, "And there is no way the Catholic Church is going to give up their senior clergy just because they were accused of screwing a few altar boys."

"That's another thing. If I were king there wouldn't be an ACLU. They might have served a purpose once upon a time, like unions once did, but like the unions, they've lost their purity. That group should be disbanded and made to get real jobs. That brings up another point; I'd also make it a crime for lawyers to lie in court. Wouldn't that be novel?"

"But honey, where would you ever find a lawyer then?" she said with a laugh. "By the way, are we still on for dinner at the Goldwin's Saturday night? Amon's sister is coming for a visit." Time to change the subject; she must have decided this had gone on long enough for one morning.

Amon Goldwin, a good friend of mine worked for the Forest Service. We'd been friends for several years now. We met when I sold the agency three bulldozers to be used for fire control.

There had been a lot heated discussions between Amon and me about who should control the National Forests; the people of Arizona or Amon's self-appointed federal agency whose headquarters was located in Washington, D.C. I, ever against big government agencies that would control the public lands, argued again and again about how the people who used them should have more say in what happened to the forests, while Amon staunchly defended bureaucratic system.

We were having cocktails at Amon's house in Scottsdale on Saturday evening. The air was cool enough since the sun had gone down, and if it became too uncomfortable there was always the pool to cool off in. I was on his third cocktail when I said rhetorically, "You know, the Forest Service has become a bureaucracy run by a bunch old men who seem to be afraid of change."

Amon, a few feet away was just on his second drink. He was tending the grill where the steaks were just starting to sizzle. Sensing that one of our *discussions* was about to take place, he looked over at me and said with light sarcasm, "Really, why don't you enlighten me further?"

I recognized and respected the intelligence in Amon when we first met. We liked to try new, and sometimes strange, ways of looking at and analyzing controversial subjects. It was not unusual that we test our theories on one another before presenting them to a more diverse audience. Sometimes we really believed in our stated views, at other times, one of us would toss out a provoking comment just to get a rise from the other; poking the tiger as it were.

Amon preferred Toyota pickups to American made while I am adamantly addicted to the "Buy American" philosophy. I've been a Ford man ever since I could come up with the funds for a new vehicle.

Amon was an engineer whose thought process often baffled me. I knew several engineers, my newest step-father was one, and it seemed to me they inevitably over thought almost every decision they made from the purchase of a TV to choosing a shirt. He had theorized in response to my loyalty to Detroit, "I've given this a lot of thought and I've come to the conclusion that it is un-American."

I was almost beside myself when he hit me with this one. Raising my voice I said to him, "How in the hell can *even you* come up with such a dumb-ass statement as that?"

"Well, you have to agree that the quality of American cars has gone down hill steadily over the years. The competition from foreign manufacturers has put pressure on the American workers and manufacturers to produce a better product."

I acquiesced a bit by saying, "I have to give you that Amon, as far out as it goes. I think that might have been the case once upon a time, but damn it, nowadays our cars are as good as anything produced overseas."

"That's partially true, but most of the so-called foreign cars are manufactured here in the states these days, so it doesn't really matter that much what you purchase."

"Bull shit, the profit still goes back to Tokyo or Sweden or wherever the corporate headquarters are located." This was the type of banter that passed back and forth between us.

The talk returned to my comments about the Forest Service, so in answer to Amon's query I began to elaborate. "Well the agency appears to consist a plethora of narrow minded old timers who think that the younger generation and the general public have no clue about how to manage the national forests and should stay out of their business.

"This is the same body of entrenched old timers who refuse to acknowledge that it might be possible that they are out of touch with current and more acceptable practices advocated by new-age scientists working in the universities and the lumber industry. There aren't many new faces in the group as far as I can tell."

"Not everyone at headquarters in DC is old," countered Amon.

"You're probably right, but the old guys have the power and they refuse to relinquish it. It's similar to that new term "brass creep" in the military which works like the old Peter Principle. The tenured directors gain power and continue pursuing out-of-date practices which they think are tried and true. They've all reached their level of incompetence and are now making good wages without exerting a lot of effort; rocking the boat by taking chances on new techniques is not an option for them."

I watched Amon's face flush, but I didn't let up. "Your hardheaded old farts won't even take the free advice from Northern Arizona University's Forestry School. The university professors have told them time and again that controlled burns kill old growth trees as well as the young ones, yet year after year the skies to the north are filled with ugly, choking smoke from this outmoded method of forest thinning. Controlled burns also kill the squirrels and other small animals in the forests.

"The winter and fall air around the northern mountains is filthier than the yellow cloud that covers Phoenix most of the time. The city gets fined by the Fed's for poor air quality, while your group ruins our mountain air with no consequences. What's up with that?"

Amon replied, "What would you have us do? We can't let the forests burn so we have to do something."

I was quick with my answer as I knew many of the old time Arizona loggers personally and we had discussed the foibles of the Forest Service and it's out of date practices in detail. "Selective logging would be much more effective while, at the same time, providing work for the people in these small impoverished rural communities. It worked for years before the tree huggers became so powerful."

The differences of opinion expressed by wee two friends did not cause any lasting strong ill feelings between us, although the talk did become heated at times. We each merely thought the other didn't have all the facts. As Amon or I presented our argument, we were hoping, futilely it seemed that one of us would finally present an idea or a fact that would make the other stop and rethink his position. Ours was indeed a strange but stimulating friendship.

Our discussions were not limited to arguments about work, often encompassing a variety of such things as politics, illegal immigration, and criminal punishment. Once a topic had been talked out, we willingly moved to another that was just as convoluted and multi-faceted as the prior one. We'd been known to hit on as many ten subjects at a sitting.

This particular evening the discussion seemed to stay focused on some of the Forest Service's practices and rules I considered to be too heavy handed. Amon, who was younger than me by ten years, acquiesced to me on this count, "You are right about one thing Josh, change and the adoption of new ideas does come slowly to the bureaucrats…but you have to admit, it's not limited to the Forest Service."

I nodded in agreement as he added, "Seems like it's been going on for centuries the old men in all walks of life, once they reach a certain age and mindset, have made a mess of many things. I'll never forget Viet Nam and the draft of the sixties. What a fucking nightmare that turned out to be, fifty-eight thousand dead Americans, countless wounded both mentally and physically. Throw in the four million Vietnamese civilians who were killed along with the million ARVN combatants who died trying to fight American imperialism after kicking the French invader's asses. That American embarrassment was started by a bunch of old fuckers who wouldn't fight if they had to. Maybe in two or three more generations, we can get it right."

"We just recently had the same kind of mess with Cheney and Rumsfeld invading Iraq. I heard that Cheney had five draft deferments in the sixties and all of a sudden, he was an old war horse figuratively leading the troops into battle," said Amon.

"Yeah, I guess on the list of shortest books, "Combat Charges I Have Led" by Cheney would have to rank in the top ten."

Having won a small concession from Amon, I just had to make one more point, saying matter of factly, "If most the Forest Service administrators had their way, the whole damned forest would be closed to everyone but themselves and their friends."

"Oh Josh, you know that's bullshit."

"Do I? More than half of the Forest Service roads are closed between Labor Day and Memorial Day. You can't deny that now can you?"

Amon looked at me, thinking for a moment and then reminded me of a day trip we had recently taken together. "Have you forgotten when we took that drive on the Forest Service road in to Calf Pen Canyon?"

Calf Pen Canyon is located on the top of the Mogollon Rim north of Pine and Strawberry, two hours from Phoenix. The setting is beautiful with big oak trees interspersed with aspen and Ponderosa Pine. From late spring through fall when the snow comes, the ground is covered with wild flowers and lush mountain grasses. Small New Mexico Locust trees fill in the gaps between the larger plants. Grasses for deer and elk grow in the open areas. Above the canyon itself, which is located below the Rim, the vista goes for miles, encompassing several mountain ranges including the Matzatzals and the Sierra Anchas. The Tonto, Coconino, and Apache-Sitgreaves National Forests are all in view from that one vantage point.

He had me there as I said, "Yeah, I remember; how can I forget... that abandoned campsite looked like a landfill. We filled four big trash bags with beer cans and other garbage. It sure put a damper on that trip while at the same time opening my eyes. To think that someone could spend time in that beautiful spot and then just leave all their trash behind; I can't imagine anyone who would do such a thing would be in the forest in the first place."

Amon continued to push his argument, "Well, it's human pigs like the ones who left their garbage behind that cause my directors to want to lock the gates. It's not as simple as you would like to make it. Of course the forests are there for the people, but if the people refuse to take care of these beautiful places, and trash it like what you saw, what choice do we have?

"The Forest Service just doesn't have the manpower to go around cleaning up these sites. What you saw that day is only one example of the hundreds of similar fucked up campsites. Can you see my organization's side in this? Do you understand why they believe they are the guardians of our national forests?"

I wasn't quite so cocky now, remembering how that lovely spot had been desecrated, "Just as in everything we encounter, there aren't any easy answers are there? I'll try to cut your guys a little more slack; but that doesn't mean I agree totally with all of their Big Brother style policies."

"Who's Big Brother? What's Janis Joplin got to do with it?" joked the young forest ranger.

Lucinda, Amon's sister who was visiting from San Francisco came from inside the house to join us beside the pool. We made small talk trying to avoid anything controversial, for a change. Lucinda, a lawyer, had worked for the state of California's penal system, one of my favorite targets, for five years.

This very intelligent, professional lady's job was to try to find any evidence, or lack thereof, that would allow inmates sitting on death row in San Quentin to have their verdicts overturned. This was supposed to insure that no innocent person would be executed by the state. I know this procedure is carried out in every state but California and Connecticut seem to have developed it into a costly science of gigantic proportions that vastly exceeds what is required to insure the *innocent* convicts on death row don't suffer an undeserved execution.

I, of course, had taken issue with such a policy and I made it painfully clear upon my first meeting with Lucinda. This had occurred the year before when Amon and Betty had gotten married.

Shortly after being introduced, Lucinda and I had quickly gotten into a small but heated discussion about our differing views on the death penalty, but since we were at her brother's wedding, we had quickly agreed to disagree and moved on to the festivities at hand.

Amon and Betty's late spring wedding had taken place in the high desert, west of the little town of Rye. No fancy cathedral or huge wedding gown or tux for these two; just North Peak, part of the Mazatzal Mountain range, looming over the small group of celebrants.

Amon and Betty loved the outdoors and the location seemed an especially fitting place for them to exchange their wedding vows. The ceremony itself was performed under a huge Saguaro cactus. White waxen flowers bloomed on the tips of the several huge arms of the cactus that provided ample shade for the bride and groom. The smell of wild flowers was complemented by the sight of the bees buzzing around them.

The only down side, a minor one, was the wedding party had to watch out for rattlesnakes. A large diamond back was herded away with the help of a shovel pulled from Amon's truck. I'd offered to shoot the big reptile, but the happy couple was adamantly against such an unneighborly act, after all it was the snake's home, on their most important day. Finally the toast to the newly weds with cold champagne that had been brought along in an ice chest capped the beautiful yet primitive moment at the mountain's base.

Although I'm happily married to Susan, as we stood around the pool in the twilight, I couldn't help but notice how good Lucinda looked in the skimpy two-piece swim suit she was filling out just right. We men will always look at good looking women just because we can. Seeing me staring at Lucinda, Amon joked, "You do realize that's my baby sister you're leering at, don't you?"

Caught off guard and slightly embarrassed, I replied "Sorry, but you have to admit she does make an excellent argument for erecting a monument to the man who invented the bikini; even if she is your sister."

Amon and I had about talked ourselves into being quiet for a moment. I decided not to resurrect my arguments about capital punishment this evening. I decided to just enjoy the night and the company, while sneaking an occasional glimpse at Lucinda. I smiled as it brought to mind President Jimmy Carter's words in his Playboy interview so many years before, "I have lusted in my heart".

It was kinda hard for me to remain silent on the subject of capital punishment in California because my sense of justice was still unable to fully comprehend what purpose this job of Lucinda's served. It seemed to be a terrible waste of money and manpower, or woman power, in Lucinda's case, to try over and over again to postpone or even overturn the punishment of convicted murderers.

I had to admit that California wasn't quite as screwed up as Connecticut though. Once a felon is sentenced to death in that state, the court assigns two attorneys plus an investigator to go over the history of the individual, all the way back to his childhood.

Anyone who had any meaningful contact in the life of the inmate must interviewed to see if some thing, no matter how insignificant, could be used as a reason for his later behavior that had landed him on death row; anything at all that might be construed as a reason to justify overturning the conviction.

All this information must then be written up and reviewed by yet another committee. The process takes years for each capital punishment case to be finally completed before the sentence can be carried out.

The subject of automatic appeal and the intensity of effort put forth by individuals in trying to overturn the verdict had come up more than once in past conversations with my friends who were not acquainted with Lucinda. I'd voiced my discontent concerning this "crazy" practice more than once. "Seriously, there are people who do this for a living and are paid by the state. This is their only job.

"The true irony of this, and what pisses me off the most, is that the victim's families are paying Lucinda's salary, through their taxes. This, to me, is beyond all intelligent understanding."

When I paused to consider it all I would think to myself, factitiously, "God bless California and the crazy sense of justice the state and others like it pursue. It's too bad the victims don't receive the same kind of support in their quest for closure."

When we got home after the lovely evening with the Goldwin's Susan said to me, "I'm proud of you for your constraint in not pissing Lucinda off about her job tonight. You were the perfect gentleman. "

"Whatever do you mean, Sweetie?" I replied with a smile. There's always Facebook I happily thought to myself.

# CHAPTER THREE

# Fun with Facebook

Josh: I did allow myself some fun when it came to discussing the controversial subject of the death penalty on Facebook. One of the continuing dialogues on Lucinda's page centered on a website dedicated to abolishment of the death penalty altogether. One emotional lady appeared on the website almost daily crying about the way the poor criminals were treated. Of course I considered it my duty to mess with her misguided postings.

Her name was Dorothy; she had recently written that some *unfeeling fiends* in California were trying to pass a new law that would make the first offense for the molesting of a child punishable by death. She couldn't begin to express her outrage strongly enough. "This is so unfair to the "victim".

The victim to whom she referred was not the child who had suffered as you would first think, but the "victim" to her way of thinking was the asshole that had molested the child. "He would have no chance for rehabilitation," was the gist of her argument, "It would be tantamount to murder. Such a waste of a life."

"How many children should one be allowed to molest before severe consequences are imposed… two, four, ten? Give me a number that will work for you, Dorothy" I wrote sarcastically in response to what I considered a totally stupid entry by this naïve individual.

I'd read another posting from someone connected to the ACLU citing "cost" as a reason to abolish the death penalty. This *scholar* argued that since death row inmates must be housed in individual cells rather than sharing a cell in the general prison population, the state was running out of room. If they weren't sentenced to death, they could be housed with the other prisoners, two per cell.

"Yeah then they could butt fuck each other all night long,' I posted in the comment space and paused, but only for a moment, I hit the 'send comment' box.

I thought about it and then added, "I can offer a solution to the overcrowding problem. Speed up the execution process. The mandatory review, put in place by your lawmakers, takes over twenty-five years to get through the appeal process in California.

"Even in Texas, the state that carries out more executions than the rest of the states combined, it still requires more than a dozen years to exhaust all appeals. I would suggest that the voters and lawmakers get off their asses and pass a law that would limit the appeal process to six months, even a year if you must, but you, the people, should set a reasonable deadline for carrying out these sentences. As it stands now these appeals can run into the next two decades while costing a fortune to feed and house these hundreds of convicted murderers.

"Twenty to thirty individuals are sentenced to death each year in your state and yet no sentences are carried out. These freaks are killing a whole bunch of you each year. While you seem so concerned about *their* welfare you are missing the point, which should be that your own personal safety is at risk. Only thirteen of these convicted killers have been executed since 1992. From 1978 until 1992, no death sentences were carried out due to some brilliant Supreme Court decision. That decision was finally overturned after eighteen years and yet the prisons are overflowing.

"One out of one hundred prisoners sentenced to death have been executed in the last thirty years. That's one percent. There are currently around 690 inmates on death row in California getting older and sicker. They are taking up more and more room and costing more and more money to house and medicate. It's been over nine years since the last execution took place in California, although the disgusting and terrible crimes against children increase monthly."

I kept typing, "I guess another answer would be for the state to stop incarcerating so many of your citizens for marijuana violations. You would then have room to house the more serious felons, such as rapists and child molesters, for longer periods." He sent this one to *all* his Facebook friends, not just the anti-death penalty group.

Over the next few days there were dozens of derogatory replies posted on the website that condemned my insensitivity toward prison inmates. Hell, I hadn't yet gotten around to telling them that I think we should be harvesting organs from these prisoners. I was sure to start a riot with that sensible idea.

After I relayed the input from Dorothy's Facebook entry to Susan, she had responded, "I'm surprised to hear that so many women are opposed to severe punishment for rape. I can understand in this penis driven society, where the laws are mostly made by men, how these lawmakers fail to realize the pain, guilt, humiliation and degradation suffered at the hand of a rapist. But women at least should be able to commiserate with the female victims of these atrocities. Even unwanted touching from someone I *know* gives me the creeps. Rape would be so much more humiliating than I even want to contemplate."

I've known that the death penalty in California is "an empty promise" for a long time. This was not a term I'd coined, but I did find it accurate and was envious that I hadn't come up with it on my own. I'd heard these words invoked quite a few times before, usually by grieving and angry family members of a murdered victim. Most recently it had been invoked by Jenny's father in a televised interview on the *Today* show.

In point of fact, Dorothy's recent statement was totally misleading. Raping children is not an offense punishable by death in California. It seems some 'humanitarians' would prefer to see the criminal be treated less harshly than his victims. It is their belief that the unfortunate and often misunderstood offender can and should be rehabilitated through social workers' efforts.

I remembered when, as a child growing up in Texas, any rape, not just that of a child resulted in the death penalty for the perpetrator. "What the hell happened?... Oh yeah, the increased hordes of lawyers graduating from the new and expanded law schools over the last twenty or so years has added to the legions of lawyers trying to justify their existence and it seems that everyone wants to be a fucking lawyer these days."

Of course, to be realistic, I have to acknowledge, the indiscriminate execution of blacks for raping, or being accused of raping, white women in Texas and in other Southern states didn't help the cause after the sixties. A lot of atrocities were committed against minorities by white radicals in the name of protecting their women up 'til then. This practice had to cease of course, but the pendulum seems to have swung too far the other way. It's certainly not about race anymore.

This started me wondering, so to satisfy my curiosity, I checked the numbers out and found there is something like two hundred law schools in the United States. UC Berkley alone had around eight hundred law students enrolled in 2008. No wonder the courts are backlogged. These kids are scrambling for any kind of case. Most of them must be like starving, hyenas fighting over every bone.

On Sunday Amon and his wife Betty had joined Susan and me to watch a Diamondback's game at Chase Field in downtown Phoenix. We were having drinks at Alice Cooper's bar, Cooperstown, next to the stadium before the one o'clock game. It didn't take long, during our normal banter, for the conversation to turn to Lucinda and her job at San Quentin.

As I sat nursing my beer I looked across the table at Amon with a sly grin and asked, "Have you talked with Lucinda lately? Tell her I asked how Scott Peterson's doing these days. Are all his needs being met?"

"Fuck you, Josh. You know she doesn't like the guy." Amon knew I was just being an asshole.

"Yeah I know, but that's all I could come up with on short notice."

"Bullshit, you think about what you can say to annoy me all the time. By the way, for your information, Peterson is the only guy on death row that has his own attorney that is not paid for by the state."

I couldn't let that one pass. "What an upstanding citizen he is to face his responsibilities like that."

Amon didn't defend his sister's job but he did stick up for her, "Lucinda feels very strongly about what she does. I have to respect her for that."

"Oh, hell," I said to him, "I respect her dedication to her job and I can't fault her for having her own principles. I just wish she would use her talents for a different purpose. She'd make a hell of a prosecutor. I'd be her biggest fan."

"I'll tell her you said that. It will probably change her life," Amon replied sarcastically causing all of us to have a good laugh.

"Yeah, like she gives a shit what I think. No matter how much Lucinda and her friends might wish it, these men cannot and will not be converted into responsible citizens. Not one of them is going find the cure for cancer or invent the car that will run on water, if given the opportunity.

"These are hardened and cruel criminals who would have no compunction about hurting the very people who would set them free. If they got the chance, believe me, Lucinda, Dorothy or their other friends would be beaten, stripped, raped, sodomized and tortured before being killed. These are not the sweet, handsome young men with a bright future, portrayed by Hollywood. They are Scum!"

Amon seemed to be deep in thought for a moment, gathering his defenses. Then he said to me," What about the ones on death row that have been found to be innocent after further investigation, Josh? It seems to be happening a lot these days with men who have served long sentences and then proven to be mistakenly jailed. Don't they deserve all the leeway they can get in order to prove their innocence?"

The question seemed rhetorical so I remained silent as he continued. "Have you heard about the Willingham case in Texas? This man was executed in 2004 for supposedly burning his home and killing his three young daughters. Since his death at Huntsville, it has been discovered that the Governor of Texas ignored or dismissed an affidavit that could have proven Willingham was not guilty. It now appears an innocent man was executed because of a failure on the part of the state to fully investigate the incident…worse yet, it appears evidence was suppressed that would have freed him. "

He had a valid point and I had heard about the Texas case. "OK, I'll give you that much. In cases where there is doubt, the accused should be allowed to use everything available to prove his case. And there's no fucking excuse for law enforcement personnel or the governor to suppress evidence that would prove a person's innocence. However, when the evidence is irrefutable such as when DNA of the accused found under the victim's fingernails for example or the presence of his sperm in the torn vagina of a young girl, the asshole should be executed right away."

"Oh honey, please! That's so disgusting," intervened Susan. She gave me the look that let me know I was overstepping the bounds of good taste. I'd done it enough to know what she meant. "Let's change the subject, please! You're beginning to sound like a broken record. Who's going to win the game tonight?"

"Probably the Padres," I replied. All three of my friends then gave me the look.

"You big asshole!" laughed Susan.

After the game was over and the Padres had beaten Phoenix 6-1, I ventured, "Let's go to El Charro and have a drink and a burro." It was time to lighten up.

El Charro, my favorite spot in the East Valley, was one of the oldest eating and drinking establishments in Mesa and had the best green chili burros around. It also had the darkest bar and the coldest beer. It was a good place to go and drink and discuss *intelligently* how to solve more of the world's problems. The more beer that was consumed, the easier the solutions came.

"That sounds great!" said Betty. "I love their bean dip and chips better than the burros."

I quipped, "Too bad, this is Sunday, remember? Only salsa, no bean dip on the weekends."

"Damn! Oh well, chips and salsa and cold beer are pretty hard to beat."

# CHAPTER FOUR

# Josh's Trip to Page/Lake Powell

Josh: The following week I went on a fishing trip to Lake Powell. Located three hundred miles north of Phoenix on the Arizona and Utah border, the lake is one of the jewels of the west. It brushes up against Monument Valley on its eastern side. Huge multi-colored and rain stained sandstone rocks and mountains surround the clear bluish green lake formed by the Colorado River with sandstone monoliths scattered along the lake's edge. The sandy beaches could be compared with any tropical island as to cleanliness and pristine beauty.

The fishing trip had been planned for over a month and I looked forward to getting away from the city for some clean air and no depressing news stories. I was joined by a couple of my customers, Duke Hill and Ray Farmer, who each had their own construction companies. I took along Bill Alcala, one of my co-workers to round out the crew.

Duke and Ray were two of my favorite people, but these two had proved to be such fuck- ups when they were drinking in a public setting, which was constantly, that when we hooked up I tried to take them places where they couldn't get in trouble or at the least create a major embarrassing scene. A few hours spent with these two in a bar in Phoenix could be exhausting and sometimes dangerous.

Gloria, a regular on these trips, was in the back seat between Ray and Duke. She was always very quiet, in addition to being anatomically correct for the most part; sporting pink nipples on her perky little breasts.

Gloria was a very expensive mannequin with a blonde wig and a pretty smile. She had been *kidnapped* by Duke while he was remodeling a Dillard's department store in west Phoenix. The only article of clothing she was wearing was a cute little Greek fisherman's hat which Duke had purchased for her especially for the lake trip. Gloria could be counted on to generate a lot of laughter when we would set her in one of the raised fishing chairs on the thirty two foot fishing boat that Duke kept at Wahweap Marina, located just north and west of Page.

From a distance, she looked like a real lady sitting tall in her chair; fooling fishermen and tour boats alike. The joke never seemed tiresome to us guys. Time and again, fishermen would cruise by as if by accident, trying to appear nonchalant while peering at her. It was amusing to us as we watched the expressions on the gawker's faces change when they realized what they were seeing. Sometimes Gloria was in a swim suit, but most of the time, after a few beers, she would somehow wind up naked. Beer would make her clothes fall off, as the lyrics of the country song about tequila went. Everyone in the SUV except Gloria had a beer in hand as we neared the last hundred or so miles to the lake.

I was trying to think pleasant thoughts as I drove northward on highway 89 out of Flagstaff, toward the Navajo reservation. Willie Nelson was singing about how he couldn't wait to get on the road again and the mood was light.

As we headed north, I was hoping that no State Highway Patrolmen or Indian Police were watching too closely from behind one of the numerous clay mounds scattered along the highway. I wasn't sure if the unclothed Gloria was entirely legal, but I knew these cops had no qualms about writing citations for open container violations. There were four such violations waiting for discovery in the truck at this very moment.

The cops would also be on the lookout for any other money making infraction they could write up for that matter. Even though the governor, who was up for election in the fall, claimed otherwise, the state of Arizona was broke and it was no secret the order had been given to the State Police, "No warning tickets. Remember your time is our money". The trip to Page on State Highway 89 was an adventure in itself, just in evading the various law enforcement agencies, due to the competition among them on who could write the most citations. In addition to State Police and Indian

Police, there were also the County Sheriff's deputies to watch out for at either end of the reservation.

Ray rolled down the window and threw his empty bottle at a sign bolted to a huge rock that stated, "YOU ARE ENTERING THE NAVAJO RESERVATION, A SOVEREIGN NATION. OBEY ALL OUR LAWS. ENJOY YOUR VISIT". The bottle hit dead center and burst in pieces. Shattered glass flew all around the sign landing on the pile of old glass that formed a mound there at the base. It seemed this had been a target for bottles for a long time.

I yelled, "Jesus, Ray, cut that shit out! You wanna spend the night in the Tuba City jail? These Navajos won't take that kind of crap on their reservation; especially from a white man." By the pile of broken glass scattered around the base, known by the local whites as "Navajo pottery", it was evident that Ray wasn't the first person to use the sign as a target for his beer bottle.

"Sorry, I couldn't help myself. This sovereign nation shit tends to piss me off." Ray didn't look that remorseful. He'd grown up in Tonto Basin where there were still real cowboys and fist fights were frequent at the Jake's Corner and Punkin Center Bars. He resented authority more than any man I'd ever met.

Even when Ray was still a teenager he was big and strong for his age. He spent his free time hanging around the hard drinking grownups in the Basin and managed to get in more than his share of the fights there. He won so many of these encounters that the locals finally refused to fight him so he took his skills to the bigger cities where no one knew him. He did like to fight, maybe because he never lost.

I tried to change this unacceptable behavior by comparing his performance to amateur racing. "You know Ray; it's not fair for you to beat these guys up. It's like showing up for the high school drag races in a Corvette and racing guys in their dad's Fairlane. There's really no competition; you're kind of a bully, you know?" He didn't seem to understand my point, so I finally quit trying to change him. I just didn't go to bars with him, if I could help it.

The talk continued about the Indian's plight on the reservation. "Well we did our damndest to take their best land away from them," remarked Bill

Alcala, who had been pretty quiet up until now; "You gotta admit, the land around here isn't for shit."

"With the help of Kit Carson and his boys, this is what they have left." quipped Ray.

"Canyon DeChelly out of Chinle is pretty nice, and don't forget Monument Valley but those are about the only places on this reservation that is decent."

The countryside soon began to take on the features of a barren moonscape. Before the first moon landing the astronauts had trained nearby to get a feel for what they would encounter when they landed in outer space. Primitive shelters called "stands" that sold Indian beads and rugs were scattered along the highway, some close together, others standing alone. Most were manned by children or women in native costume, bright red, purple or green velveteen blouses and layered long skirts reaching to the ground.

Crudely hand lettered signs advertised their wares. These were placed against the lean-tos, which had been constructed from old scrap lumber, cardboard, sheet metal, and brush. Handmade rugs hung from the horizontal poles that held the plastic tarps or plywood roofs. The fragile structures looked as if they could fall down at any moment  One sign in particular caused a chuckle as we read what was printed on a large sheet of tin, 'FRIENDLY INDIANS'.

It was about that time the guys were starting to become bored from the ride and lack of anything that would catch their attention. I steered the talk to my favorite subject of late. Being the most sober as designated driver, I started the conversation by saying, "It's a proven fact that most inmates on death row will die of old age. I spent a lot of time researching this just to see if I might have been wrong. The facts are there for California, Texas, and any other state you would care to check out."

I remarked that rescinding the death penalty in California was hardly an issue. I repeated what I had told to Amon to see what their response would be. "Do you guys realize that only one out of one hundred, a mere one percent, of the convicted felons on death row in California will actually get the needle they deserve? I posted that info on my Facebook page the other day and all hell broke loose. You know, I wouldn't be surprised if Scott Peterson were to outlive me!"

"Well the son of a bitch should, he's about twenty years younger than you," said Duke, "and a hell of a lot better looking."

"A hell of a lot dumber, too," I replied.

I was on a roll now; I had a captive audience who agreed with me about how to dole out punishment to child molesters. But as I warmed to my topic my audience was beginning to doze off.

"Serial killers might be considered as candidates for the death penalty, but this not always true either. The fact is, Charlie Manson is still alive and still comes before the parole board each year for his hearing on obtaining his freedom. How long will it be before a bunch of bleeding hearts on the board see him and think, "You know, I believe Charles has paid his debt to society," or maybe, "I've been told he studies his bible every evening. Besides, he didn't really kill anyone per se. He was never placed at the scene of the crime where Sharon Tate and the others were found.

"At the hearing, the fact that Sharon was young, beautiful, pregnant and butchered will not be mentioned, of course. It was so very long ago. Ol' Charlie looks so repentant except for that fucking maniacal stare and the homemade swastika tattoo between his crazy ass eyes." I dwelled on this maybe a little too long saying, "I'll bet we could find a 'Free Charlie' website out there if we took to time to check it out."

I paused to take drink from my Coors, only my second so far since leaving Flagstaff, before I spoke again. "I had an epiphany on my walk the other day. I was thinking about when I had jury duty and the witnesses were sworn in. They placed their hand on the bible and swore to "tell the truth, the whole truth, and nothing but the truth". I realized that the whole swearing in ceremony in our judicial system is one big fucking lie."

"You seem to have a lot of epiphanies these days," Ray said, trying to poke me.

Unperturbed I continued, "We all knew that we weren't going to hear the truth and definitely not the whole truth, and most especially, "nothing but the truth". There would be the lies and the objections from one side or the other anytime someone tried to tell the truth. This is how justice is achieved in these United States, pretty much in the world for that matter. You just can't get justice through the justice system. Come to think of it, the name itself, "Justice System", is an oxymoron."

As we neared the big trading post at Cameron along the edge of the Little Colorado River, I was distracted from my story momentarily when two Navajo men drunkenly staggered onto the highway with their thumbs out, trying to catch a ride. They could barely walk and then they fell down together as I swerved to avoid them. I checked in the rearview mirror to make sure they weren't injured, but didn't slow down. This was not an unusual occurrence on the rez.

I'd seen the same shit on the reservation in Wyoming many times. It's a sad fact but there was nothing I could do for them, so I continued my lecture. "I saw an interview with the lawyer for this six foot two, two hundred pound plus lacrosse player that killed his girlfriend at that college in Tennessee last week. The 'student' had kicked his girlfriend's door down and then he beat her head against the wall until she was dead. He left her lying in a pool of blood where her body was later found by friends.

"I swear; I could not believe the defense attorney's initial remarks. 'It was a case of self-defense for my client,' this piece of shit emphatically declared with a straight face. 'There was a scuffle and he had to defend himself. It was an accident.'"

I was getting agitated while talking about what I'd witnessed and thinking of what the lawyer was saying. "There was no sympathy at all for the poor girl who had been beaten to death; only these insultingly ridiculous reasons for why his client acted as he did. One of you sorry fucks, give me another beer. I need to wet my vocal cords."

"You could give them a rest, professor," Bill said, handing me a cold one.

Ignoring the obvious sarcasm, Josh went on, "It's like a contest with these asshole shysters. Their egos are so damned inflated; God knows why, that they feel they must win their case at any cost. To hell with the innocent victims and their families, 'so long as I get my client off'," seems to be their mantra." I was getting more heated up as I vented my frustration.

I must have talked too long because Duke finally spoke up. "I'm getting tired of this conversation, Josh. What else have you been up to? Any new girlfriends? Don't we get to talk about anything other than man's inhumanity to man when we're with you? Are the fish biting at Powell?"

I decided Duke was right. It was time to give it a rest, but I continued to ponder how so many innocent victims can be abused time and again by so many bad guys who are rarely severely punished. Justice just seemed harder and harder to find these days.

The CD player switched to a new disc causing the Dixie Chicks to start singing about how they felt like hell today. "I feel real ashamed of myself every time I hear those girls sing," said Duke.

Ray said, "Why's that? I think they're great."

"Oh, I think they are some of the best, but remember the shit they got for saying that Bush wasn't their kind of President?"

"Sure, who doesn't? The rednecks went crazy smashing and burning their CD's, so what?"

Duke paused, and then said, "Those young ladies were the first Americans to speak out against the ignorance of that man. They had some balls, but at the time I kind of felt like the rest of the nut cases. It was only later that their words proved to be prophetic. What the fuck was he thinking when he invaded Iraq? I was part of the mob, led by Limbaugh and the Southern evangelists, who let some talking head tell me what to think."

I looked over at him and said with a smile, "At least you climbed out of the darkness and now you see the light. Hell, I voted for Little Bush the first time. How could you not like a guy who wore boots, lived on a ranch in South Texas, and used a chain saw? Too bad he had the IQ of an eighth grader."

"Why are you insulting eighth graders?"

Ray ventured, "If it hadn't been for that J. Edgar Hoover lookalike; Rove, Bush would still be governor of Texas. Doesn't take much to do that job; shake hands, eat barbecue, and approve school text book changes that deny evolution and refuse to mention slavery."

"Don't let my mom hear you say that;" I said, "or my sister either; they both think Bush was the greatest president we ever had."

"I'm still amazed that the man was opposed to stem cell research," ventured Bill. "That alone should have invalidated his credibility.

We were now heading up the big hill toward Page and away from Marble Canyon and Lee's Ferry. This part of the drive always reminded me of taking off in an airplane, due to the steep grade. We climbed up over three thousand feet while driving a distance of less than five miles. To the west Navajo Bridge could be seen where it spanned the Colorado River just south of Lee's Ferry. The panorama stirred memories in me causing me to reminisce, "Did I ever tell you guys about the eight pound rainbow I caught above Lee's Ferry on my four weight fly rod?"

Everyone in the vehicle seemed to groan at the same time. "About a dozen times", they said in unison.

"Alright, already. Like you really care about fishing. Duke; you're already too drunk to fish and we're still a half hour away from the lake."

"Get off the criminal shit and just drive for a while. I can remember when all you did was tell jokes. I would laugh my ass off about how to keep a dog from humping your leg; even if it was the most disgusting thing I ever heard." said Ray.

"The internet killed the art of joke telling," I said. "I used to know hundreds, but now I just read them, laugh and forward them on. Later I can't even remember the punch line."

In the distance, to the northeast, the towers of the coal fired Navajo Generating Station on the edge of Lake Powell came into view. This was the last leg of the journey, from Phoenix. We all breathed a sigh of relief, looking forward to unassing the vehicle. All in all it had turned out to be a good trip so far; no tickets and no wrecks.

When we got into Page we just had to stop at the Windy Mesa Bar for a quick drink and to stretch our legs. It was a tradition and we had to honor it. This time it didn't take long for Ray and Duke to get into a fight with three workers from the power plant. The locals had seen Gloria sitting in the SUV when they pulled into the parking lot. At first these idiots had been excited, thinking she was a real woman. When they walked up to the vehicle and peered in, it only took a few moments for them to realize she was a nude mannequin. Feeling like they had been made to look like fools, as if Gloria had anything to do with furthering that observation, they entered the big tin building that was the bar. They came in with attitude.

Bill and I had gone to empty some beer from our bladders, leaving Duke and Ray standing at the bar. They were the only two in the bar other than the old bartender who was washing glasses at the side sink. The three guys from the power plant bellied up and proceeded to make some rude remarks about Gloria.

Looking at Ray and Duke, the guy the others called Fred spoke up," Who's the bimbo in your car? She ain't got very big tits, does she?" This was said with an intimidating malicious grin. Ray and Duke couldn't help but notice the way Fred's mouth was filled with gaps where teeth had formerly been. The remaining few were badly stained, tobacco juice maybe. He was wearing dirty, coal-dust covered jeans and steel toed boots. His shirt looked like it had never seen soap, but then so did so did Fred. Coal dust filled the lines in his face and the large pores in his nose and cheeks.

"You lose those teeth because of that smart mouth of yours? You'd think with so few left to care for you could keep them cleaner," said Ray. "If you fuck with me you'll lose the few you have left and I'll make that face of yours even uglier than it is now. Even your boyfriends won't recognize you." He shot a glance at the other two, giving them a wicked smile. Fred was not pleased with the homo inference.

Ray along with Duke, had taken Fred's remarks personally of course, as they had ridden with Gloria sitting between them during the whole five hour trip. After all their adventures together she was like family. Fred lowered his head and charged wildly but was flattened by Ray's first punch, an upper cut to the mouth. True to his word, Ray had knocked out two more of Fred's teeth; may have been an improvement.

Since it was only three against the two of them at first and now the odds were even, Duke and Ray easily kicked the shit out of Fred's two side-kicks. They didn't seem to have too much heart for the fight after seeing what had happened to Old Fred. When Bill and I returned from the men's room, all three of the would-be pugilists were on the floor in various states of defeat. Fred was out cold and the other two were sitting under the pool table looking too frightened and shook up to venture from their new found shelter. I looked at the smiling bartender who was leaning against the wall.

"Can you give us a few minutes before you call 911?" I asked anxiously, not wanting my buddies to spend the night in the Page jail.

The smile did not leave the bartender's face as he replied, "I didn't see nothin'. These guys are always bullying someone around; looks like they underestimated your friends. I'll make the call after I'm finished getting some bottles out of the back; that is if they're still layin' here when I get back. I think I need a smoke break right now."

"Thanks", I said as I laid a twenty on the pool table. I then hustled Gloria's defenders out of the bar and back on the road before the cops arrived. We headed across Glen Canyon Dam and down to the marina at Wahweap. We hurried to get Duke's boat on the lake before anyone started looking for us. There weren't a whole lot of fish caught on the trip; a few skinny striped bass and a few fat largemouths, but we four friends…and Gloria, made up for the lack of fish by the amount of beer that was consumed along with the stories that were told. I even managed to remember a few jokes.

# CHAPTER FIVE

# The Move South

Josh: I'd been married to Susan for almost ten years. She was six years younger than me but I didn't consider her a trophy wife, even though she was pretty damned cute. She seemed wise beyond her years and I respected her uncommon common-sense. When we first met, she'd just started her new job at my company as an executive secretary to the Sales Manager. I was immediately taken with her bright smile and her sparkling hazel eyes. Just passing her in the hall made me smile. She gave off good vibes.

During the first weeks after her arrival whenever I happened to see her around the office, I would start singing, "You are the sunshine of my life." I just couldn't help myself. She just brought that song to my mind. Not the version sung by Stevie Wonder, but the original from the early sixties sung by Sacha Distel while he was pursuing Bridget Bardot, with only an acoustic guitar for accompaniment. Sweet and simple.

Her initial response to my uninvited off-key singing to her was, "Fuck you, Josh, get away from me" because, as she later told me, she thought I was making fun of her.

But I had persisted in getting to know her better; finally convincing her that my feelings were genuine. Something about her just seemed so right, full of humor and wit when we were together. Within a year we were married.

Where she really excelled, I often reflected, was her capacity for seeing things as they really were. There was no bullshit getting past Susan, either on the news or in conversations with others. She could hold her own in any argument; usually succeeding in making her point clearly and intelligently. She learned early on that most of the salesmen were in their positions merely because they were men. It didn't take her long on the job to learn the ropes. Soon she understood the sales department functions better than most of the men with whom she worked, but since she was a woman in a construction business, there was no chance in hell that she could aspire to being anything other than an administrative assistant.

She instinctively knew how to handle men and she could usually get me to calm down with a few choice sentences. But lately the almost daily reports of murder and rapes of innocent children was causing me to be more upset and for longer periods of time. I seemed to dwell on the depressing events that were occurring way too often.

This was the first marriage for both of us, although we had been in other somewhat serious relationships in the past. We had learned a lot about give and take from our previous experiences. We were both strong willed and didn't always agree, but we would listen to each other's points of view… most of the time. Although from time to time the house would echo from our heated "discussions".

Susan had been raised Catholic and had attended Catholic school through the eighth grade. Because of the strong church influence, she believed most rules and laws were there to be obeyed. My life experiences had led me to pick and choose which laws were valid, applying to me, according to my whims and views of society. I was a rebel with a cause, so to speak. Susan strongly believed in hell, while I couldn't imagine that God would create such a place.

"You're going to hell for your lack of beliefs," she would tell him.

"There's no such place," I would laughingly tell her. The arguing seemed to strengthen our relationship; at least up to a point.

Susan and I lived Mesa which was a suburb of Phoenix. Until a few years ago the city had been inhabited mostly by Mormons and snowbirds; retirees who ventured to the desert from the northern states during the winter. Lately, however, an influx of new businesses and the accompanying younger employees from other metropolitan cities had lessened the religious and conservative influence on this East Valley community.

Clubs and restaurants were springing up everywhere giving the city a new atmosphere. It certainly wasn't Scottsdale or Tempe, home of Arizona State University, but it had cast off some of the hard-shell ideas that had been the hallmark of the community only a decade earlier.

I had moved to Arizona from Riverton, Wyoming where I'd been employed as a police officer. The city would later be the setting of the story, "Broke Back Mountain". The story was then made into a movie and in winter the place seemed about as dreary as it had been portrayed on the big screen.

Riverton had a population of around twenty thousand people; half of whom were transient oil field rough necks and construction workers from Texas and Oklahoma. This comprised a rowdy population to say the least. I had moved there from Texas after finishing my tour in the Army and then completing college.

I'd seen a picture of the Grand Tetons and decided I needed to visit what I considered to be the most beautiful mountain range on earth. Riverton is located between the Shoshoni and Arapahoe Indian reservations in the middle of Wyoming. I stopped on my way through to visit some cousins of mine that were living in the quaint little western city and I liked it immediately.

After spending a few days with them and getting to know the area, I decided to stay a while. It wasn't in the Grand Tetons, but it *was* close to Jackson Hole and it was set in the Wind River Valley...how could you not be moved by such a name? This visit had taken place in August; the weather was perfect especially after the summer in Dallas. Although I was warned him about the winters, I couldn't imagine the cold could be that bad.

It didn't take long after joining the police department for me to discover that alcoholism and suicides were a way of life in this beautiful but harsh country. Winters were long; the first big snow, more than I'd ever seen at one time, in my life, happened on Halloween night. That same snow and more of it would still be on the ground come Mother's Day.

The construction workers and the cowboys that frequented the many bars were constantly fighting each other or among themselves if no one else could be found. I lost several shirts while trying to quell fights. The police uniform and the badge didn't command much respect in the middle of a bar brawl in this rough little frontier town.

"If you can whip my ass, you can take me to jail," was heard more than once in the course of a busy Saturday night. The standard fine for resisting arrest in Riverton was thirty five dollars and four dollars court cost. This was not much of a deterrent for the rough and ready crowd that inhabited the bars. I did this for almost two years.

The worst, or at least the most unpleasant calls to which I responded and dreaded, was when I would get a call to either of the two *Indian* bars in town, The Blue Bird or Lapier's. The big Arapaho or Shoshoni Indian men, it seemed they all weighed over two hundred pounds, would drink until they passed out. More often than not, they would pass out in the bathrooms and nothing could wake them. The other drunks would come in and piss all over whoever was passed out. By the time to call came for the police to send an officer, the comatose man would be soaked in urine or worse.

Removing the huge Indians from the small filthy bathrooms was a truly degrading and disgusting job. While the removal was taking place, usually involving two or three officers to manage the heavy job, the bar patrons would make derisive remarks while laughing rudely; forgetting that they most likely had been in the same drunken situation themselves in the not so distant past and would be again in the near future.

I decided to make a career and a location change shortly after a particularly heartbreaking incident. I received a call from the dispatcher directing me to accompany Faye Dyer, the local social worker, on a visit called in by the elementary school office clerk. Faye, not sure of what she would be encountering, asked for a police officer to accompany her.

The report was that several children from the same family had come to school through the snow, without shoes or jackets that morning. The temperature had been hovering around ten degrees for the last week and crusty, month-old snow covered the ground. Arriving at the small apartment, Faye and I discovered three dirty children alone in the house.

The only furniture in the place was a ragged recliner sporting a torn and filthy cover.

The stench of gas fumes from the free-standing butane stove in the middle of the room caused our eyes to fill with tears immediately. The ceramic grates that help absorb and deliver the heat were missing from the stove, rendering it pretty much useless as an appliance for fighting the extreme cold. The children, two boys and a girl, ranging in age between six and ten were crowded together around the stove trying to keep warm; more by body contact than by the sorry excuse for a stove.

In the flimsy apartment the wind could be heard whistling in around the cracked window panes that were covered in ice. There was no food to be seen in the doorless cabinets, nor did there appear to be any adult present. Faye quickly took in the situation and started trying to put the frightened children at ease while my police uniform and gun seemed to increase their fears. As they huddled ever closer together, the naked fright in their eyes reminded me of scared feral kittens.

Faye, noting the children's discomfort quickly spoke to them in a friendly tone, "Children, this is Officer O'Brien. He won't hurt you. Where's your mom, David?" she asked the eldest child. The school had supplied her with a list of the children's names and ages. There was no father's name to be found in the children's files.

David started to cry, causing him obvious embarrassment, since he was supposed to be the man of the house. "I don't know, I think Mom went to California with a friend. She hasn't been home in a few days." He suddenly paused, realizing the implications of what he had just said, and then hastily added, "But she should be home anytime now, probably tonight in fact." This was not the first time he had met social service workers and he was being loyal to his mom and protective of his little brother and sister. He didn't want to leave this crumby apartment for some unknown place. His greatest fear was that he wouldn't see his mom again.

"Officer O'Brien and I are going to take you to a warm home where some nice people will take care of you." Faye assured them all.

"No," cried young David, causing the younger two children to burst into tears, "I have to wait for my mom. She's coming back soon. She told us to wait here for her."

"David, you know I can't leave you kids alone like this. You all need some food and a warm place to stay. You don't want your little brother and sister to freeze or starve do you?" Faye spoke reassuringly. "Believe me, when your mom gets back, I'll tell her where you are. She then muttered something only I could hear, something about a "worthless bitch", the last two words being all I caught.

I had to admit that Faye was a real pro. She had the kids and their school books packed and ready to go in only minutes. She had gathered the few articles of clothing she could find and put those in a plastic bag. The promise of food had caused the frightened children to reconsider, as they had not had anything to eat for several days.

"David, you are the best big brother I've ever seen," said Faye; he beamed at her words though he still wasn't thrilled about leaving.

The children were quickly loaded into the police cruiser and delivered to an elderly couple, the Ellsworth's, Jenny and Ben; old time ranchers who volunteered their time as foster parents. The couple lived in an old log house on the outskirts of town where the children were welcomed warmly, both physically and mentally.

The roaring blaze in the huge rough stone fireplace seemed to help put the children at ease as Mrs. Ellsworth set the table with fried chicken, mashed potatoes and gravy. The wonderful yeasty smell of home baked rolls filled the kitchen causing our mouths to water. Faye had called Jenny earlier in the day to give her a heads up. Mrs. Ellsworth was from the old school that believed the best thing for kids was a big meal. She loved to cook and she was wearing a huge smile as she watched while the children devoured the meal she had prepared. Reluctantly Faye and I left the children and the heaping table behind.

"You want to grab a Big Mac and some fries?" I jokingly asked Faye.

"No, I think I'll just go home and have a bowl of soup. This has worn me out," Faye replied. The job had taken a toll on her this day as she told me she often wondered why some people bothered having children.

This had turned into a rewarding night for me, but it had also been heart breaking at the same time. I came to the conclusion there must be something better; arresting drunks, wrestling other drunks, breaking up husband and wife fights, and seeing how badly children were being mistreated ate at me. The pay had been twelve hundred a month when I started a year and a half earlier. When I left I was drawing down sixteen hundred. "I made more money in the army than I did at that job," I would tell my friends later. It was time to move on. I moved to Arizona and started my new life, working as a construction equipment salesman. I had needed a change and I got it with that career move.

I hadn't lived in Mesa long when I was surprised to hear the chief of police and the city attorney make a well publicized joint statement concerning burglaries in the city. The Tribune had reported that one in five homes in the city was broken into each year and the people were getting tired of it. Most crimes of this nature were going unsolved, creating an even greater sense of frustration among the citizenry. At council meetings people were threatening to take the law into their own hands, defending themselves with guns, no less.

This talk caused the Chief and the City Attorney to issue their joint statement. The attorney did all the talking while the Chief stood by his side nodding at the end of each sentence, "Any homeowner who shoots a burglar in this city will be prosecuted to the full extent of the law. We will not tolerate such unlawful vigilante-like behavior from the public.

"It is the job of Chief Garcia and the officers of his department to handle such matters. If you should happen to have an encounter with a burglar in your home, call 911 immediately. Do not, I repeat, do not try to take the law into your own hands. I will make you very sorry if you do. Unless your life is in imminent danger, and you'd better be able to prove it was, there is no excuse for you as a citizen to take someone's life."

As a former cop from a rough area I immediately thought, "You jerks must be out of your minds. This is an open invitation for every criminal in the Valley to come to Mesa." It wasn't long before I was proven correct. The headlines in the Tribune stated that the number of burglaries in the city had doubled in the three months following the joint announcement.

When the City Council met for the next monthly meeting, the chamber was filled to overflowing with agitated citizens demanding the resignation of the two men who had brought about this sorry situation.

Several people, who had been victims of burglars, took the podium to declare that the response time, by a uniformed officer, to a 911 call was fifteen to twenty minutes; too late to catch anyone. Faced with this info which was backed up by radio logs subpoenaed by a private lawyer who had been hired by a group of concerned citizenry, the council asked for, and received, the resignations of the two clowns who had made such an idiotic public statement. As I had predicted, the public announcement had been an open invitation to plunder the city's neighborhoods.

Once the resignations had taken place and the former law enforcement officials had been replaced with men who espoused a more realistic point of view; one that supported the homeowner being allowed to protect his property, the burglaries had gone back down to the previous level, but a few burglars had also been shot in the interim. The homeowners involved in these incidents claimed self defense while the new Chief and City Attorney concurred.

Susan had moved to Arizona from Huron, a small city just outside of Cleveland; hence the strong and unswerving affection for the Browns. She'd taken a job there as a police dispatcher after finishing community college. She, too, had grown tired of the long, harsh winters and the cold winds blowing off Lake Erie. Her sister, Peg, who had moved to Arizona a couple of years before encouraged her to move west. After one of the coldest winters on record, she accepted Peg's invitation. She was immediately hired by the same company that employed me.

Although we didn't much care for labels, both Susan and I considered ourselves to be *Independents*. Not "Independents" as the party affiliation goes, but "independent" meaning free to choose what we considered to be important. We refused to be categorized, often leaning toward liberal thinking in some matters; mostly in areas where individual freedoms were at stake and, though less often. We were conservative in other matters especially when it came to the death penalty; both sharing the idea that rapists and murders should be given an early opportunity to see God.

While I railed against crooked lawyers, soft judges and sex offenders who received what I considered way too lenient sentences, Susan had her own issues with the way women were being treated these days, especially in the heavy construction industry where she hit the glass ceiling on an almost daily basis.

"This company is so penis driven it is infuriating. Some of these lazy assed sales reps, especially the old farts who still believe a woman's place is in the home, want me to look up all their information for them. Despite their air of male superiority they still expect me to type and prepare their quotes for them. I think they spend most of their time on the computer looking at, and forwarding the pictures of nude women their buddies have sent to them. I'm surprised they can wipe their own butts. They make three times the money I make and work about one tenth as much as I do."

I had to agree, "I know you're smarter than most people there, including me, and you are one hundred percent correct; women have very little chance to move up in this crowd. I hate to say it but you'd have a better chance at climbing the career ladder in the military than you do here."

We agreed on most controversial subjects, for instance neither of them could understand why marijuana had not yet been legalized, since pretty much every politician currently serving in office had been, or still was, a fan of the weed.

I had laughed when Clinton claimed he had not inhaled, but then he also claimed he never had sex with 'that woman'. Obama admitted to inhaling, asking the press if that wasn't the purpose, after all. Susan and I continued to be amazed that not one of the elected hypocrites in state or national government had the balls to introduce the legislation that could stop the drug war, and raise millions in tax revenue.

One afternoon I had told a disbelieving old timer at the American Legion, "It's public knowledge that marijuana is not only the largest cash crop in California, it's the largest cash crop in the United States; bigger even that cotton, or tobacco; bigger than the value of corn and wheat combined. The estimated value is somewhere between fifteen and thirty billion, with a B, dollars per year."

"You gotta be shitting me," the old veteran said.

"Nope, over twenty three million Americans smoke the stuff every day."

"But I just read where pot is a gateway drug to heroin and meth. The Chief of Police was quoted in the paper just last week."

Another elderly lady chimed in, "I heard in that in California, the number of automobile accidents doubled when they legalized medical marijuana."

"Pardon my language, but Lady, that is a load of shit. Alcohol is much more dangerous than pot. By the way Sandy, can I have another Dewars?" I directed my request at Sandy the bartender.

"Then why don't they legalize it?" the old guy challenged.

"There's way too much money being made by keeping it illegal. Do you think Al Capone's boys welcomed the end to prohibition?" I asked rhetorically. "Hell no, they didn't, and neither did law enforcement. Repeal of prohibition killed the golden goose for Capone *and* prohibition agents. Legalizing pot will do the same to the cops and dealers today. In this instance the two groups are working together to hold on to their jobs by insuring that it is not legalized."

Later at home, I said to Susan, "These guys in office now; these current politicians are children of the sixties. They've been smoking pot for years. I was sure that when they came to power they would act to get these antiquated laws thrown out. Between the multitude of drug enforcement officials and law enforcement guys and the drug lords, there is just too much money being made on both sides. Ridiculous!"

Susan concurred, "There are over a million of our young people in prison in this country for marijuana offenses. Thousands of Mexicans are being killed below the border due to the drug wars. In Juarez alone, it seems there are hundreds killed each month. In one fell swoop this mess could end tomorrow. Why is it so damned difficult for our so-called leaders to reach an intelligent conclusion? The facts are right in front of them every damned day and yet they refuse to take action."

"You're preaching to the choir, my darling. I never heard of a politician that didn't love a new tax, but pot will be the first time they have missed the boat." I had mentioned this more than once when discussing the marijuana conundrum. "I guess that are just too many lawmen and bureaucrats at the trough that make a good living in pursuit of these would be criminals."

As she listened to my tirade, Susan lit a joint, inhaled deeply and then said, "Don't forget that the religious right and their bunch don't want us to do anything that will make us feel good; damn this is good stuff. Even if a group of politicians were for something as radical as pot, they are not going to risk their careers to make it legal. The former governor of New Mexico came out for legalizing marijuana but couldn't get it passed."

I said, "I know; I saw him on the Colbert Report the other night. He said that if term limits had not kept him from running for office for a third term, he would not have had the guts to come out in favor legalizing it because, even today, such a cause is a career ending choice for a politician. He did state, as we already know, that it would save billions of dollars and thousands of lives lost in the drug war; twenty eight thousand killed in Mexico in the last four years!"

Susan added indignantly, starting to feel the effects of the joint, "The cancer patients can't even get medical marijuana in most states, even though it's proven to help people who are terminal by increasing their appetite and giving them an opportunity to get high and feel better.

"That's pretty damned cold, but, in their self- righteousness and undeterred pursuit of their own ends, these hypocrites don't seem to care. Politicians and cops claim to serve God and their fellow man, but these are some hard sons of bitches. George Bush and his evolution-denying followers were even against stem cell research. You see what you're dealing with here, don't you?"

"Still not right, the FDA refuses to even test marijuana for medicinal purposes. They need to pull their heads out of their asses. Let me have a hit off that please. If the pharmaceutical companies could figure out a way to corner the market, pot will be legal the next week," I muttered.

Susan nodded in agreement, enjoying the mild high she had going from the marijuana. "That's probably why the AMA hasn't come out in favor of using it as medicine; no money in it for their members yet."

"Speaking of pot, I see they arrested Willie Nelson again last week."

"Yeah, great detective work." She took another hit.

"I would like to see some focus placed on taking care of the real criminal element," I said, feeling disappointed in the way our law enforcement agencies work. My mind wandered back to the incident that had taken place in Vermont a few years back where a local judge had sentenced a thirty-four year old man who had been found guilty of continuously raping an eight year old over a period of several years, to sixty days. There was some problem with the prison not having a rehab program for sex offenders who molested children, so he was released, as his "rights were being violated". On his nightly show, Bill O'Reilly had raised so much hell about this ridiculous decision that public outcry caused the judge to revisit the case and give the defendant an additional three years in prison.

The revised sentence had then conversely created a huge cry of "Foul" from the defense attorney and his cohorts who said the judge had no right to do this. The defense went so far as to say that the public had no right in shaping sentencing.

I thought, "Three fucking years for multiple rapes on a child! What can be done to put these guys out of commission?"

I'm the kind of guy who likes to think about different ways to find a solution to a problem. As I considered the way the laws seemed to be heading I thought, "What if it was my child that had been hurt or killed? What would I do?" Lately, when I was not concentrating on work, strange thoughts of vengeance would fill my head; fantasies of torturing and mutilating the scum who preyed on the innocent and the weak.

I heard about how child molesters didn't usually fare well in prison and I believed this was most likely the case. Rumor was that the general prison population was made up of a lot of bad dudes that had their own particular code of honor; such as it was. There was a pecking order and child abusers were on the lowest end of the totem pole. I hoped this was not an urban myth. It just seemed to make sense that any man who had fathered a child would not be sympathetic to a child molester. There were a lot of fathers in the penal system, I was sure.

I also knew there were gangs in the prisons and each gang had a leader. It was also rumored that some people on the outside were forced to pay protection to family members of the gangs, so *their* relatives, not affiliated with gangs, were not molested on the inside. As I considered this, the thought crossed his mind, "This might have positive possibilities."

I'd been mulling this idea over and over since my earlier outburst to Susan while viewing the initial Marcus Regan story that had been so publicized the month before. The latest update on the case was that a plea agreement had been reached whereby Regan would not be sentenced to death but would receive two life sentences. Susan and I watched the sorry story together as it was unfolding.

While searching for Regan's latest victim, after she had been reported missing by her worried mother, the police had discovered the body of yet another girl. It was discovered that Regan had murdered this young lady the previous year. Had he not killed his second victim so close to where he had committed the first murder, the police would probably never have found the remains of little Becky. Regan had agreed to plead guilty to both murders as part of the deal that would keep him off death row. He placed a much higher value on his own life than he did on the lives of the two young girls.

Regan's lawyer, Robert Marius, had found an "expert witness", Dr. Henry L. Jameson, to testify in Regan's behalf. Marius wanted to avoid a trial which might result in a sentence of death for his client. Such a case, concluding with the death penalty for Regan, would have an adverse effect on Marius personally. The revelation of his actions could easily result in bad publicity for him due to his prior role in getting his client a lighter sentence. He wanted to avoid that at all costs. Plus he didn't think Regan would stand a chance of not being convicted and it was most important to him to not lose the case.

Jameson, *the expert witness*, had earned a Bachelor of Science degree in psychology from a small state school in Alabama. Later he had received his M.A. and PhD from a university located somewhere on an island in the Caribbean.

Jameson had long competed with the famous Dr. Harry Chong for the opportunity to testify, always for the defense, in high profile cases. In legal circles both men were known to testify to just about anything requested of them just so long as the fee was sufficient or the publicity great enough to make it worth their time. There had been bidding wars between the two in the past. As of late, there seemed to be enough demand for their testimony they were both kept busy with various trials and no longer had to outbid each other for cases.

Of course, if anyone on the jury was familiar with Jameson's history, the potential juror was summarily dismissed for prejudice. In this case where there was no jury present, as it was merely a hearing to obtain a plea agreement, *Dr.* Jameson's testimony appeared to be superfluous, but he showed up anyway at Marius's request; just in case he was needed to seal the deal. Marius wanted to influence the court as much as possible and this judge was known to be in awe of professional witnesses with doctorate degrees…in any field and from any university.

Jameson arrived for the hearing wearing his trademark blue silk imported suit that was just a tad too tight across his broad posterior. The added padding around his shoulders that should have balanced the look of the suit failed to produce the desired effect, giving him a comedic air. His thinning hair was combed over in such a way as to try to mask his balding pate, much like that senator from back east that looked so silly at his news interviews.

This style did not work well for the good doctor either, as evidenced when a breeze caught his head just right, causing the thirty or so, ten inch long strands that made up the right fringe comb-over; fall down over his left ear. When this occurred he looked even more ridiculous and ill at ease. He would try to push the strands back in place and pat them down but with little success. He was such a perfect caricature of what a buffoon should look like, that it was hard to believe the prosecutor or judge would ever consider his testimony as valid. In spite of all this, he had made a successful career, if you could call it that, by his role as a purported expert in many areas.

When called to take the stand by Lawyer Marius, Dr. Jameson had testified that Mr. Regan could not personally be held responsible for the rapes and murders of the two young women, as he was bipolar and had suffered from ADD since childhood.

Jameson was passing himself off as an expert in the field of mental illness at this particular hearing. He told the state prosecutor, "The mood swings experienced by the accused were not his fault. He has willingly confessed and has shown extreme remorse for his actions. His parents were both alcoholics causing Mr. Regan to grow up under hopeless conditions; the state should have protected him long ago. The state from which Mr. Regan hails bears the brunt of responsibility for the deaths of the two women"

As we watched the story unfold, I said to Susan, "The dead girls have suddenly become 'women' and the state is to blame. Asshole! Marcus has been smiling for the TV crews and had shown no remorse at all for his actions as far as I can tell. I think the fact that the cops had Regan's DNA and he knew it, cinched the deal and left him no choice but to confess. He had to strike a deal that eliminated the chance of being executed."

"Doesn't he kind of remind you of the cop from Illinois that murdered two of his wives? He has that same shit-eating grin that appeared on his face every time a camera was placed in front of him."

"You're right, Josh, maybe murderers all have that same creepy look, sort of like a Down's Syndrome stamp, my apologies to those poor unfortunates for the comparison."

The words had barely left her mouth when the newscaster suddenly compared Marcus's case to that of Scott Peterson. "Marcus loves the attention. He will do well in prison and will probably develop pen pals just as the Peterson has. There will probably even be a few proposals of marriage made by some of the women who correspond with him." This made me think of Dorothy and her Facebook entries about the poor prisoner victimized by society since childhood.

The father of the dead girl was shown saying, "I hope his remaining days are a living nightmare."

I said to the TV and to Susan, "I hope so too, but I doubt if they will be while serving in a California prison. Isn't there something someone can do to for retribution, no matter how insignificant?"

At that moment reporter thrust a microphone in front of the Jenny's father's face and asked, "Can't you find it in your heart to forgive Mr. Regan? After all he had a terrible upbringing and will be spending the rest of his life in confinement."

"Forgive my ass! I would cut his throat myself if I could get at him. There is not forgiveness for such an evil individual. There's no closure for me and no satisfaction in knowing that he will spend his life in prison. It won't bring my little girl back." He could not hide his anger or his sadness as he motioned for the reporter to back off.

The broadcast story came to an end with the announcement that Regan would serve his term at Farmstead State Prison.

# CHAPTER SIX

# I Propose My Plan

Josh: Even though fall was just around the corner, the thermometer in my pickup was reading one hundred and five degrees as I parked outside the Oak Barrel Lounge in Mesa. As far as company trucks went, my Ford F-150 was pretty nice. At least I had air conditioning, but the Phoenix heat was hard to combat no matter what the vehicle was.

As I stepped out of the truck, the melting asphalt in the parking lot sort of squished under my boots; the heat radiating up into the soles of my feet. The palm trees and bougainvillea surrounding the bar were drooping, as if they were panting. I was thinking of the cold beer waiting for me inside the dark bar that had even better air conditioning than my truck. It was five-thirty, happy hour, and I was meeting Lloyd Packer who was already inside.

I parked next to his truck which was under the only shaded area in the parking lot. I could see that he must have gotten off work early. As his sales rep, I was usually was the first one at the bar since I didn't often have equipment to check out at the end of a shift. Lloyd's the equipment maintenance superintendent for H&L Construction, one of my biggest accounts. We make it a point to meet for drinks and sometimes dinner a couple of times a week. We have a chance to catch up on business without being interrupted by someone wanting a free Cat hat or some other distraction.

As I entered the cool darkness of the bar, I could hear familiar voices, a little louder than the other patrons, arguing. I walked up to the table where Lloyd was sitting with Lynn Walters, an H&L job superintendent, who was also a good friend of mine, I could overhear them arguing as usual, "It's a lifestyle choice, I tell you," Lynn was saying, "They choose to be cock suckers!"

"Bull shit! Why would anyone choose to do that?" Lloyd responded.

"Sounds like a heavy philosophical debate going on here, lads," I said as I took a seat.

Lloyd looked up, "Hey Josh, sold any cutting edges lately?" A question he would ask when he wanted to mess with me. Everyone one knew that my prices for dozer and motor grader edges were the highest in the state. He then responded to my remark, "Hell yes, it's a heavy subject. This dumb prick thinks gay people choose to be queer instead of being born that way."

Lynn was only in his mid thirties but his mindset was that of a man from the nineteen-forties, which would make him about ninety years old mentally. Damn, but he was hardheaded, a true anachronism. He had been raised in the little mining town of Ajo down by the Mexican border, where he lived in company housing provided by Phelps-Dodge until he finished high school. After graduating he then moved to Tucson where he worked in construction. A few years later he was transferred to Phoenix to oversee H&L's jobs in the northern part of the state. Since he thought like an old conservative, Lynn was always fun to screw with.

Never one to be without an opinion on just about anything controversial, I pulled out a chair from the table and said without waiting for an opening, "Let me tell you my experience on the subject." It never took long to pick up the thread of the conversation with these two guys. We had been friends for several years and had "discussed' and argued about all kinds of issues. We seldom changed one another's minds, but that didn't keep us from talking things to death.

"But, first things first, Brenda, bring me a beer please, I'm dying of thirst." Brenda was already headed toward our table with a tray laden with cold beers; she knew us well.

I continued, "I know this guy, Shawn Roberts, from Nebraska. He's a gay man and we were discussing this very topic one day, so I asked him if he thought his life style was a choice. I was pretty sure I knew the answer, but why not get it from the horse's mouth, so to speak?

"He looked at me and said, 'Josh, I come from a small, rural Nebraska town filled with redneck farmers. Do you think for one moment that I would choose to be gay in a place like that? Do you have any idea how hard it was for a gay teenager to grow up under those conditions? I couldn't get a date and was shunned by most of my peers. There were lots of fights and I had to learn to win, otherwise I would have had my ass kicked on a daily basis.

"'I even tried to date girls, thinking I might be able to change, but that didn't work either; it would be like you trying to date a guy. I couldn't do it. I left town and moved to Denver as soon as I was old enough. Trust me, it's not a choice.'"

I continued, "You guys might be interested in this fact I read the other day about the *Don't Ask, Don't Tell* policy practiced by our military. More than fourteen thousand gay servicemen have been discharged in the last fifteen years while 66,000 are currently serving on active duty while living a lie. How much sense does that make? The pentagon just finished their year long study on the effects repealing the DADT policy and turns out seventy percent of the members of the military think it should be repealed."

Lloyd and Lynn had both listened without interrupting, highly unusual for these two and for once I felt like I might have changed Lynn's mind until he said, "Aw, hell, your buddy's just one guy. There's thousands of them cocksuckers and carpet munchers out there. I believe Mike Huckabee. He said on Fox that it was definitely a choice as did the head of the Mormon Church."

I answered incredulously, "Jeez, I can't believe you still get your information from Fox...*and* the Mormon Church? Fuck me to tears! You sound like John McCain or Mitch McConnell. First they said they would follow the General's recommendations on DADT, but then they flip flopped on that after the Secretary of Defense and the Joint Chief's of Staff recommended doing away with the outdated rule.

"I'll tell you what, Lynn. I'm willing to back my convictions with good old fashioned money. I'll bet you that in spite of Senator McCagainst and all his old cronies who never spent a day in the military while claiming to be experts, that this "Don't ask don't tell" bullshit law gets overthrown this year."

"Talk's cheap; how much do you want to lose?" Lynn said. I had his interest now as we wagered on just about anything at anytime.

Keeping it light I said, "A hundred at least, just to make it interesting."

He got a greedy look in his eye. I could tell he thought he had hooked a fish right here in the bar. "Five hundred dollars would make it even more interesting don't you think?"

"Done; DADT will be repealed under this president. Lloyd you're the witness. Lynn, my boy, we have a bet. Let's shake on it." In our crowd, shaking on a bet was as binding as if we had drawn up a legal contract so we shook hands; each of us already counting our money. I was pretty sure that there were enough good, intelligent men in the legislature to finally stop persecuting our soldiers for their sexual orientation.

I had served with several gay soldiers; men and women, in Desert Storm. I hadn't felt

in danger of being molested or hit on during my service with these troops. Most of my gay comrades seemed to possess superior intelligence and energy. I had to admire their work ethic.

A major flaw in the DADT policy affected me personally in Iraq when a friend of mine who was up for promotion was outed by another NCO. The guy who did the outing was trying for the same slot as my friend. My gay comrade didn't tell anyone about his sexual preference; he was told on, and was subsequently discharged from the military. A flawed policy indeed that damn sure needed a major overhaul. Hell it wasn't really an issue anymore except in the minds of a bunch of old politicians and career soldiers that hadn't quite entered the new century.

I didn't figure there was any point in pursuing this topic any further so I turned to Lloyd and asked, "How's your highway job going? I see you beat me to the bar today. Is the work ahead of schedule?"

"Hell no; spotted owl's got the job on hold up on the Mogollon Rim," he said unhappily.

"Do what? Not more of this endangered species shit! Didn't we learn anything from that fucking snail darter fiasco? After holding up a major dam construction project for years, it turned out that there were hundreds of them living in pretty near every body of water in the South."

You couldn't tell by looking, but Lloyd had graduated from University of Arizona Engineering School at the top of his class in 1990. He appeared disheveled and wrung out from the heat as he looked down at his scuffed steel toed boots and oil stained jeans, before answering, "Some kind of ornithologist expert from Berkeley came out to the job with an EPA guy and a group of kids that call themselves the Center for Biological University, whatever the hell that is. The Berkeley dude claims he can talk to the owls with a whistle that he sells on the internet for twenty bucks. The group escorting him around swore he had gotten answers from spotted owls five separate times while they walked the job."

He took a drink from his bottle of Coors, and then continued, "I asked how they knew it wasn't the same fucking owl following them around. They didn't bother answering me. One little cutie I had been admiring gave me such a go to hell look that I knew my big mouth had turned my chances of hitting it off her into a lost cause.

"When I asked the professor to call one of the owls up for me, he told me he had a plane to catch and they all left; but not before shutting down the job. So now the work has been put on hold, the equipment parked and the men sent home while our lawyers and the lawyers of our client, the Arizona Department of Transportation, are rushing around trying to get the order to stop work rescinded.

"Thousands of western loggers have lost their livelihood over these fucking birds and now they're coming after us construction workers. Once upon a time, in order to placate the tree huggers, the loggers proposed leaving small stands of trees every few acres for the owls to nest in. The question was posed by one of the naturalists, 'But how will the owls get from one grove to another?' I shit you not! I had this picture in my mind of the owls walking along the ground from one stand of trees to another with wings tucked in tightly around their bodies, hopping over the downed limbs between the patches of trees, looking like penguins. You know, I've lived in Arizona all my life and I've never seen a spotted owl."

I had to add my two cents, "I said the same thing a while back to my friend Amon, who works for the Forest Service. His reply was, 'That's because they're endangered; there's not many left. That's why they need to be protected. '. How do you respond to that kind of logic?"

Lynn, who had been listening and nodding spoke up, "My job along the Verde River just got shut down because they found some kind of endangered toad, Chiracahua Leopard frog or Hopi Tiger frog, somethin' like that. I've never heard of this one before either, and I've fished damned near every stream in northern Arizona over the past twenty years. Another one of those Diversified fellas you mentioned claimed he saw one hopping across the right of way. Looks like the animals are winning."

"Amon would say that it's about time. He thinks there are too many humans and not enough animals."

"Funny kind of friend you got there Josh," said Lloyd.

"Well, Amon certainly has a different view about things. He figures the people in the world are infringing on the animal's territory. He thinks the buffalo should still be running free."

"Maybe he and his group should drink some of the kool aid those guys in Rancho Santa Fe took and make more room for the animals he feels we're crowding out. They can have all the squirrelly opinions they want, just quit interfering with my way of making a living. I've got girlfriends to feed."

"Come on, Lloyd, everyone's got a right to their opinion. Besides Amon's pretty cool for a government-working tree hugger. Just last week Susan, Amon, and his wife Betty and I were coming back from a road trip to Bisbee when I took a detour through the San Carlos Apache Reservation. When I pointed out the mesa where the Apache peridot mine was located, he insisted on taking a look. I explained to him it was off limits to us white-eyes, but I couldn't change his mind. Now you have to understand, we had a pistol in the glove box, several bottles of opened booze and a lid of marijuana in my SUV."

"Aren't those all forbidden items on the res?" asked Lynn.

"That's not the half of it. When we got up on top there was no one around, it being a Saturday when all the peridot miners go into Globe to sell their stones. The mine is just a huge hole in the ground where the stones are dug by hand most of the time. The tribal leaders are very protective of the mine operation but it was unguarded that particular day.

"Occasionally one of the miners will rent a bulldozer from me for a day or two and rip the rocks bringing more peridot to the surface but it's mostly hand labor up there. The peridot looks like green ice crystals clinging to gray lava-like stones. These are chunks of rough stone weighing about five pounds apiece after they have been ripped by the dozer."

"Get on with your story, Josh," said Lloyd. "I've been to the mine and I know what it looks like. After all I was raised just down the road from there in Safford."

"I've never seen it," said Lynn. "I've just seen the jewelry for sale at the Indian stores in Scottsdale."

"OK, as I said before I was so rudely interrupted, when we arrived at the mine there was no one around. It's kinda creepy up on top of that mountain looking down on the town of San Carlos, capital of the reservation and home to a bunch of bureaucrats, Indian and white alike when you throw in the BIA and the FBI. You know Geronimo lived there for a little while before escaping to Mexico. These people at San Carlos are his descendents and they still are mad at the white man.

"You can see for miles from up there. There's only one way in and that's a rocky road up the side of the mesa. I told Amon we needed to boogie before the Indian police spotted us. I could picture my Expedition being confiscated and me going to jail for all the illegal shit I had on board. Well, I'll be a son-of-a-bitch if Amon and Betty didn't hop out and start loading peridot covered stones into my truck just like excited kids gathering Easter eggs.

"Amon would have lost his job with the Forest Service if we'd gotten caught, not to mention the fines and jail time we would all be facing. I finally got them all rounded up and back into the truck before any Indian Police showed up. On the way down from the mesa top, Amon and Betty had the balls to roll a joint and smoke it. What could I say? My wife, sweet little Susan, took a couple of hits herself." At least I had given Lloyd a clearer picture of my friend who worked for the federal government.

"Alright, so he's a great guy, but it's this kind of thinking that's killing the construction industry here in Arizona and throughout the West. There's room for animals, birds and us; if the activists didn't go to such extremes."

"Amen," said Lynn, "Dozens of communities that were once thriving are now welfare centers in northern Arizona. Have you been through Eagar or Springerville or Happy Jack lately? Logging equipment is parked and rusting in the old lumber mills. Those are just a few of the depressed cities in Arizona that I'm familiar with. Who knows how many others there are all over the West because of owls and what-not? The good thing though is you can buy a summer cabin up there in the mountains mighty cheap now."

"Lucky we got a couple of wars to send the youngsters to since the work's run out," Lloyd muttered.

Tired of beating up the Forest Service and the military, I changed the subject to the one Susan and I had discussed earlier. "Did either of you see happen to see on the news where that perverted ass-wipe from California pled guilty to raping and murdering those two girls? He made a deal with the prosecutor so he wouldn't have to face the death penalty, Marcus Regan's his name."

"Yeah, I saw it and it makes me sick at my stomach. I guess it doesn't matter much about the death penalty in California though," said Lynn. "When's the last time someone died in San Quentin, other than from old age?" The question was rhetorical.

"At least nine years, I believe it's been since they gave a killer his due," chimed in Lloyd.

I looked at them and took a chance, "I want to toss something out to you guys. I know it sounds crazy, but I'm really getting sick of these fuckers that molest and kill innocent children and I want to do something about it. Not anything that will send us to jail, but I really want to send a message."

They both looked at me with questioningly. Lynn had more than once called me a "Know it all son of a bitch," only partly in jest, and I had surprised them on occasion by knocking the shit out of some mouthy bastard that had rubbed me the wrong way. In other words, sometimes my behavior was a little unpredictable. I passed it off as part of my Irish ancestry and being raised in the South.

I was in court only last month for punching a blowhard for calling Susan an "ignorant fucking bitch". We were sitting in the American Legion where she and this guy were having a disagreement about politics and it got kind of extreme. Now I can tolerate a guy disagreeing with my wife, she does let her opinions be known, but I won't allow that kind of insulting remark to go unchallenged.

I smacked him in the mouth without even giving it a thought. Surprisingly, instead of fighting back as I was expecting, the asshole called the cops on me. The funny thing though, was when I showed the judge the police report where the *victim* admitted that he'd called her a bitch, the fine the court had imposed was suspended.

My real problem over that particular deal was with Susan. She told me "I can take care of myself. I don't need you hitting someone for arguing with me." She was pretty pissed about my reaction to the crude remark that had been directed at her. I tried to tell her about honor among men and having to protect their women and stuff like that, but she refused to understand. I even quoted from an old English poem, "I could not love thee dear so much, loved I not honor more." She wasn't buying it. Guess she didn't have the same poetic background as me.

As a last resort I just told her, "It's a man thing; we just can't let assholes speak to our women that way."

"*Our women?*" apparently she didn't care for that either, so I did the smart thing and just shut up.

Anyhow back to Lloyd and Lynn; from the look on their faces, I could tell this might be one of those times when they figured I was overreacting. But they waited expectantly to see what I had come up with this time, so I began. "I've given this plan a lot of thought lately. This isn't something I just pulled out of my ass, but this Marcus Regan deal has really pissed me off and I'm ready to see what I can do to make these assholes think twice before they act." I took a drink from my beer before continuing.

"I've gone online and looked up some cases where similar crimes have been committed. We have some child molesters that are serving time right here in Arizona. They are at the state pen in Florence and also at the prison facility in Buckeye. That's where those two cons held that female guard hostage and raped her continuously for a week while the whole state watched helplessly.

"Remember, after they finally surrendered, one of the motherfuckers was even sent back to serve his sentence in his home state in the Minnesota, per his request? The governor actually made the deal with these guys while they were in prison holding the hostage; the same governor that is now in charge of Homeland Security of the United States. I tell you guys, that incident made me ashamed to live in a state that has such a bunch of balless incompetents in charge of our penal system."

"I think you're getting off track, Josh. Why would you think a female governor would have balls?" said Lloyd, "Come back to us."

"OK, sorry, I've got a couple of names of guys I think would be excellent candidates for our venture. My first choice is Avery Logan. Ten years ago, he raped a fourteen year old girl then shot her in her vagina with a twelve gauge shotgun; figuring to destroy any DNA evidence. She lived, but you can imagine what her life must be like. Logan's currently serving twenty to life in the state pen at Florence. The way I see it, he needs more to occupy his mind than the fond memories or raping a young girl. I'd like to have a hand in giving him something more serious to ponder; maybe even cause him to experience some regret, if not for the girl he mutilated then regret for what the other cons might have done to him…make it real personal. "

"That bastard should have his balls cut off with a jagged edged knife," said Lynn, listening a little more intently now, his interest piqued. "I'm not saying I'm in on the deal or that you have a chance in hell of pulling this off, but just in case you do make sense, just what would your plan be, and where do we fit in if we can agree on something?"

"We'll approach the wife or brother of one of the gangbangers or Aryan brotherhood guys that's serving time in the same prison. We say that we are not telling anyone to kill or maim anybody. What we *are* saying is that if we see on the news where a certain child molester met an untimely death or crippling accident while serving his sentence, you, the family member would receive an anonymous cash donation. We'll call it Death Insurance rather than Life Insurance. When we see such a story about Mr. Logan, an agreed upon amount of money will be delivered in a brown paper bag to a predetermined site."

Lloyd laughed out loud, "Are you fucking nuts, Josh? We don't know any gang bangers or white brotherhood members or their families…or have you been holding out on us?"

"No, I don't know anyone on the inside either, not yet but I'm working on it." And I had been. I had discussed just a tiny bit of my idea with Guillermo Rodriquez, the owner of GR Concrete in South Phoenix. Bill, as he asked me to call him, and I had a long history together; I had given him some good advice when he was first starting his business back in 1995. He had come into our dealership to buy some construction equipment. He didn't have much money, but he had landed a big job as a subcontractor at one of the Indian casinos. The specs for the job required that he have three backhoes and a small loader on the job site within a week. He wanted to get the units he needed using the job as his collateral.

Anyone who's been around working men, as I have for years, could tell this was a good person who could use some help. I felt a bond between us and acted on it.

I told him that obtaining equipment didn't work that way, and I went on to explain that I could lease the tractors he needed to him with an option to purchase whatever units he would be able to use on other jobs when he finished his current job.

All the rent he paid would apply to any unit he might later decided to purchase, and if by chance, he didn't do as well as he thought, he could return whatever units he didn't need when he finished the job with no penalty. He liked the deal I put together for him so we made it happen. This, his first big job, led to a series of bigger jobs. He sent one of the tractors back, but purchased the others with the equity he had built up. Today, Bill owns one of the bigger concrete construction companies in the county. He figured he owed a lot of his success to the help I had given him when he first started.

He trusted me and I, in turn, trusted him. I hadn't given him any of the details of my plan about Logan, just that I needed to talk with the wife or girlfriend of someone, preferably a guy with influence, who was doing hard time at Florence. Being Latin, he understood the concept of vengeance and I led him to believe it was a personal matter…which in a way it was.

His first response was typical of my rough talking construction friends, "What's up, you looking for some Mexican pussy from some mama whose old man is in the pen? I don't think that's a very good idea, Amigo. The families of these guys are comprised of many hermanos and vatos. You could wind up with you cojones nailed to the door of your house; especially you bein' white and all."

"No, no, Bill, nothing that dumb. Susan would nail my balls first if I tried something like that. I might be able to put a little cash in a needy lady's pocket and she only has to deliver a message." I gave him just enough details to satisfy his curiosity without telling him anything that might incriminate either of us.

"I'll get back to you, my friend," he was less suspicious now but still doubtful of my intentions. "This may take a few days, but trust me, I'll check it out. Can I mention that you are a gringo?"

"Well, yeah. I can't really pass myself off as anything else, but tell whoever you talk to, that I'm one of the good ones."

He laughed at that and shook his head. I was waiting for him to get back to me while I was shooting the shit in the Oak Barrel with the guys.

"Speaking of the details," Lloyd said, back in the conversation now, "what do you think will really send a message and make others take notice, in a kinda subtle way of course? Have you given it any thought? How about some mutilation…I've always been more afraid of blindness. I think that losing my sight would be like dying. What if 'our friends' on the inside were to gouge out a couple of Logan's eyeballs? Might be easier to pull off than a murder; might also make it easier to find a willing accomplice on the inside."

I was happy to see Lloyd getting into it and I really didn't care if it was mutilation or murder, the plan was just being discussed and I was flexible. Either one suited me fine, just as long as it was something other than a cushy jail cell for the asshole over the next twenty or so years. I was hungry for some pain to be dished out to those scumbags who were accustomed to causing the pain.

I looked at my watch and knew it was time to go. As I stood up, Lynn asked, "Are you out of here?"

I smiled at my two buddies and said as I walked away, "If I appear to be getting smaller, it's because I'm leaving."

"Very funny; call me tomorrow," Lloyd yelled.

# CHAPTER SEVEN

# Josh Strikes Out

Josh: Lloyd and I spent the next several weeks mulling over what the plan would be and how it would shake out. Lynn had been absent from our most recent meetings in the bar. His job had restarted after a professor from ASU was brought in, at a substantial consultant's fee, and pronounced that the frog that had been discovered on the job at the Verde River was not an endangered species after all.

Lynn had laughingly told us it was a "Commonus Bullfrogus" which fooled us for about ten seconds, so we wouldn't be seeing him for awhile as he had to get back up north and "build America".

Lloyd and I pressed on with the plan, "Who on the inside was most likely to accept the role as the one to mete out punishment to these types of creeps; gang bangers or Aryans?" This was the first problem that needed to be solved. I hadn't mentioned my conversation with Bill Rodriquez yet. I was still waiting for him to get back to me with a contact person.

He called a couple of times to update me, saying, "I'm having more trouble than I anticipated my friend. My friends still are distrustful of gringos. The ones I have spoken with think this might be a setup. There are so damn many undercover cops these days who are trying to make a name for themselves. Entrapment means nothing in the courts anymore. If a Mexican agrees to do a crime, he goes to jail; regardless of what enticements led him to break the law."

I wasn't expecting this much resistance at first, but I could see why things were not coming together. I told Bill, "I hear what you're telling me, but please keep trying. You know I'm not undercover and I do have the money. Your people understand revenge almost as well as the Sicilians. Explain that I am seeking retribution for a wrong done to my family. "

Since Bill was running into difficulties, I didn't see any point in closing all the other doors by implying that I already had a plan. If Lloyd could come up with a better idea, I was all for it. However; his work started getting in the way too.

Since his job on the Rim was still halted due to the spotted owl controversy; not even the esteemed ASU professor could get anyone off their ass on that topic, the owls were sacrosanct in tree hugging circles, Lloyd had been moved on to the construction site of the new state-of-the-art Nisso Auto Proving Grounds that was being built in the desert west of town.

 The end of summer heat had been intense and was adding to the short tempers at the job site. I had been out to see the project a couple of times. The activity at the job resembled an ant bed, what with all the Japanese engineers, who did not speak English, swarming over the jobsite.

Lloyd had his hands full trying to keep things running smoothly since his guys didn't speak Japanese. The client, Nisso Automotive, had sent its engineers to New York City where they made actual plaster impressions of various streets there. They wanted these impressions reproduced in detail on the Proving Ground tracks in Arizona. No short cuts were allowed, every crack and bump had to be identical to the original street imprint, and this was driving the American contractors crazy.

"They need an artist, a sculptor or someone like that, not a simple old construction worker Lloyd carped." This had kept my friend out of town and out of contact, other than construction business, with me for a while.

A week passed before we finally met up at the Oak Barrel again. Lloyd was surprised to see several bandages on my face, "What the hell happened to you? You look like hammered dog shit!"

"Thanks a lot, Pal. Since you were so busy trying to make a living and build America, or a New York street as it were, I decided to try out our initial plan alone. As you can see, it didn't go so well…got the shit kicked out of me and thought I was going to die for a minute."

"Yeah? I'm waiting." I could tell he wasn't happy with me. For once he was serious as he kept looking at my beat up features.

"Well I went down to the south of town, over in the *Avenues*, to present my plan to a senorita. I got her name, Alisa, and number, from a friend of mine. The number was a phone booth and I had to call at a certain time. I was told that her old man's serving time at the state pen at Florence and she could use some money since she had two babies to care for. Seemed like the perfect contact for me, babies and all. Figured they, her and her old man, would like the plan…justice for crimes against children being the objective here. I had a thousand in cash in a paper bag and was ready to make a deal. She seemed pretty happy with the proposal I made to her over the phone.

"I explained our plan to her, no names except for that of our intended victim, Avery Logan. Then I told her what he had done to that little girl. She seemed sympathetic to our cause as I explained, just a simple life shattering injury for the guy. I suggested the blinding thing, as you and I discussed, but I had to be careful, I didn't want to gross her out or scare her away. She seemed OK with it and insisted that I show up with some earnest money. Since I had gotten her name from Bill, I didn't suspect anything would go wrong."

Lloyd ordered a beer from Brenda, the pretty cocktail waitress that usually waited on us. There was a mild flirtation going on between the two and when the small talk between them was out of the way I ordered a Dewars and water. I was in the mood for something stronger than beer today. Brenda, wearing a black short skirt, walked away, wiggling her tight little ass in a provocative manner, distracting Lloyd for the moment, me too for that matter.

I told him, "That reminds me, you know how the guys are always bragging about the pretty women they've taken to bed; I say big deal, anyone can screw a pretty woman, it takes a real man to screw a fat ugly one".

"You should know," he replied without pause.

With the important tasks out of the way, the checking out Brenda's ass and ordering more drinks, Lloyd turned his attention back to me. I continued, "I set up a meeting with Alisa at the southwest corner of South Park. It was just after dark and there was a big oleander hedge by the picnic table and ramada where we were to meet. In retrospect, I reckon I wasn't being too smart. I had the money with me, totally confident that I was in control of the situation."

Lloyd took a long drink from his beer, looked at me in a funny, hard kind of way, and said, "You've gotta be shitting me! You're in South Park alone with this Mexican chick you have yet to meet and a thousand dollars in cash…and it was dark to boot? Let me finish the story for you, you got robbed and beat up, the end. Oh, and one more thing, there's no way you're gonna call the cops to report the crime because your explanation about why you were there with a bag of cash would be pretty hard to sell."

"You forgot the two guys with the chrome plated semi-auto Colts. But other than that small item, that's about the way it went down. One hit me with his big pistola a couple of times, took the bag of cash with a smile and said, 'Adios, Mother Fucking Gringo. We don't expect you to come back here messing with our chicas anymore.'"

Who'd he think he was; some kind of Mexican Bruce Willis? I was pretty pissed later, but at the time, I must say, I was happy just to leave there alive, even though I left my dignity there too, along with the cash. At least, Alisa didn't witness it all. She just disappeared. I think she might have been in on it," I said with a smile that hurt my battered face.

"You reckon?" Lloyd was smiling too.

"So much for going the gang banger route. At least if we find some Aryans or bikers we can all speak the same language."

"Maybe you should find another cause. This thing seems to be snake bit and you haven't even got it off the ground yet."

I took a long drink from the tub of iced scotch and water, checked out Brenda's ass again and said, "You may be right. Do you need any cutting edges for your motor graders at the Proving Ground?"

He laughed and said, "Sure, send me a truck load out to the jobsite tomorrow. That should cheer you up."

"I'd feel better if you ordered a new D9," I countered.

# Chapter Eight

# Golf is My Game

My name is Noah Beebe and no one can touch me. I'm more Teflon than John Gotti. They tried to get me after it happened, but she had it coming. She got just what she deserved. That bitch Natalie thought she was too damned good for me. I showed that white cunt and her queer bait buddy. We'd had a couple of dates and I was really digging her, but some reason she didn't feel the same about me. Was it because I'm a black man? Hell, I'm famous, she should have been happy to kiss my ass and take care of me. Didn't need her dissin' me to the magazines and shit. I don't take that crap from anyone.

Did she think her white shit didn't stink? Well, you sure could tell it did after I finished cutting her up. Natalie and her faggoty friend, Bernie, mother fucker! He's probably the reason I got off so easy, they still hate queers, even in California, although no one will admit it...that and the Mr. Charlie hating bunch that my defense team put on the jury.

I had to pay out the ass for those rich white guys, but they all came through for me...except for that one honky white bread shyster that wanted to *play fair* and not use the "race card". Race card my ass...use anything that could work for me. Use my age, I'm too old, too feeble to do such a thing. Alibi...I was out of town, "doubt" that was the trick, create doubt in the minds of those dumb ass jurors.

The jury really wanted to believe me and the defense seemed to do all they could to work for me too. For that matter I couldn't have asked for a better pair of prosecutors either; and the judge, wow! God does watch out for fools now don't he? It seemed to take forever to get through that trial, but I made it home free.

That stupid fucking detective that testified under oath that he never said "nigger" was unfucking believable. Even my mama used that word. Did he think I might give him some dough for that performance? Well, maybe I did and maybe I didn't. One thing I do know for sure, there was a lot of cash changed hands that year. Left me close to broke. Lucky I got that pension coming in every month. Love that pension...even the judge says no one can touch it but me.

I don't care much for Georgia and all the crackers here, but the golf course is good and Natalie's family can't touch my money. I miss the weather back home, but that second trial awarded the rest of my money to Natalie's family. I ain't givin' that up just to stay in California. Pisses me off that the Wallace's got the money for my book, should have published it here. My Black People still love me, now more than ever since I made a fool of the white man's laws. As a matter of fact, so do those young blonde white girls with the long legs and big tits. I can't help it that the girls seem to keep falling into my bed; life is good.

# Chapter Nine

# The Trip to Augusta

Ken Wallace: I watched him pull up to the country club in his new freshly waxed bright red Cadillac Escalade. I'd heard he always drove a new Cadillac these days. The old vehicle, the white Tahoe, which he had made famous after the murders he committed, *slaughters,* actually, was way beneath him now. The wheels on the Caddy probably cost more than the old Tahoe did when it was new. The valet greeted him deferentially, "Good morning Mr. Beebe. You lookin' pretty sharp today, Sir, but then you always do." Beebe handed the fawning kid a folded bill and watched with self-satisfied pride as his car was driven away from the curb.

Beebe was wearing some kind of foreign shoes that I thought were pretty ugly, but you could tell they were expensive, not the same as the Italian jobs, whatever the hell they were called when the pictures of them had been entered into evidence at the trial, but they were still obviously expensive, all soft and shining leather. I thought to myself, "The uglier some things are, the more expensive they seem to be." His whole wardrobe, just to play a round of golf, was way over the top. But I didn't really give shit what he was wearing today, I was going to mess it up for him pretty soon…around the seventh hole, I figured.

You see, a few years back, five to be exact; he got away with killing my daughter and her friend. You might have seen it on TV. Pretty much everything except the actual killings have been shown over and over again.

I've hated him for what he did and I've hated the sorry assed lawyers that got him off. To this day I hate the prejudiced jury, the inept judge and the piss poor prosecution that set helped set him free. But most of all, I have hated myself for not having the guts to make him pay for the way he butchered my little girl. That is, until now.

You see, I was at my doctor's office last week for my annual check up. The usual tests were run and I was expecting the usual results.

When Dr. Armstrong's nurse, Jan, called to advise me that the doc wanted to see me about a follow-up, I was caught off guard. "What's up?" I bantered. "Do I have some kind of STD? You know I quit fooling around after I met you."

"Just doing my job, Mr. Wallace," she replied. Her response was strange in itself, since she had called me "Ken" for years. Even though I didn't see her often, she was usually good for a few laughs, but she didn't sound too happy right now.

"OK, when should I come in? My schedule is pretty loose now that I've I retired."

Since my daughter's murder, I always say "murder", not "she passed away" or "she died", I haven't done much except let my hatred build. I'm consumed by it and have been since I first got the call from the police.

"Mr. Wallace?" the voice on the other end of the line had asked on that fateful day. It was around five o'clock and I had just gotten home from the office. I go in early and leave a little early if I can, just to beat the traffic.

"Yes," I answered.

"Mr. Kenneth Wallace?"

"Yeah, that's me. Folks call me Ken. What can I do for you?"

A woman's voice said, "I'm afraid I have some bad news for you, Mr. Wallace. Can you come down to the police station on Main and Broadway for a meeting with Detective Garcia as soon as possible?"

I was getting upset in a hurry. "What's this about?" I asked, while all kinds of the wildest fears ran through my mind...was it my wife, was it my daughter, my son? I was starting to panic.

"I'm afraid I can't tell you anymore until you get here. Can you come down, Sir? We can send a car by to pick you up if you want."

"No, I'm on my way," with a quaver in my voice. What the hell could be going on!

When I arrived at the police station the only parking space available was a handicap spot near the front entrance. Without hesitating I pulled into the space, jumped out, and ran into the building. The desk sergeant seemed to be waiting for me, even though we had never met. "Mr. Wallace?" he asked.

I nodded and he pointed toward a door to the right. "Detective Garcia is waiting for you in there, Sir."

There were too many "misters' and "sirs" flying around; it's been my experience that cops were usually pretty curt, up to the point of being rude, especially when they were in their own environment. I knew things were not right and my fear was palpable. I walked thru the door and was met by a guy wearing a knit shirt, jeans, with a .38 snub nose on his belt. "Detective David Garcia," he said as he extended his right hand. I reached out and shook it, but absent mindedly, a reflex, I waited, expecting the worst; I got it. "I've some bad news for you Mr. Wallace; your daughter Natalie has been killed."

Wow! Just like that. No sugar coating it, just a flat out, "Your daughter has been killed". I got real dizzy for a moment and my knees sort of seemed to go weak but I recovered and steeled myself. I had been expecting something bad ever since the dispatcher called but I wasn't ready for this. I couldn't let myself believe that Natalie, my beautiful Natalie, was gone.

"What happened?" I managed to say, my legs were still like butter. "What the hell happened?"

I found a chair with someone's help and sat down in it before I fell. As Detective Garcia gave me the details, just some, not all, I started to cry. She had been cut and stabbed, slashed several times, resulting in her death. I would later learn she was close to being decapitated. Her long time friend, Bernard Gardner was also dead at the scene; Natalie's home in Brentwood. Detective Garcia had no further details for me other than there was a lot of blood and I should not and could not see her body at this time.

Investigators were still at the crime scene and there was no point in me trying to go there.

He asked if there was anything else he could do. "No, I've got to get home. My wife will be getting there soon and I have to tell her in person what has happened to Natalie." I walked out of the office in a daze.

When I got to my car, there was a parking violation citation under my windshield wiper. What a world! I grabbed the paper, furiously crumpled it and threw it on the ground. A uniformed officer was standing on the sidewalk. My actions caught his eye as he gave me a scowl, "Hey who the hell do you think you are throwing shit on the ground in front of the police department? You want me to write you up?" he spoke in an angry authoritative voice as he continued to glare at me with his hands on his hips…true cop style.

"Fuck off, asshole," was on the tip of my tongue, but I realized that wouldn't help the situation, I needed to get home. So I quietly replied, "Sorry officer, I wasn't thinking straight." I picked up the offending paper and got in my car. I sat there for a moment seething at all that had just taken place. The drive home is still just a blur in my mind.

I could go on, but you've heard the story played out too many times already. The "alleged" killer, God how I hate that word "alleged", hired a group of hot shot attorneys who stacked the jury with sympathetic jurors… not sympathetic to Natalie, of course. They were able to turn the mass collection of incriminating evidence around to their advantage.

The defense said it was the victim's fault. Even though their client, Noah Beebe, was innocent, whoever killed her probably had justification. Natalie was too beautiful for her own good. That she had lived too wild a life style was implied at first then flaunted in bold letters on the front pages of the gossip rags. The paparazzi had made my daughter a public figure because of her relationship with Beebe, and the tabloids had painted her as a money grubbing wannabe. It was hard to find a sympathetic audience for her in the press.

The judge allowed this circus-like material to be admitted by the defense team day after day, while the prosecution made feeble protests that were not upheld. The most outrageous part of the trial, of course, was when the detective in charge of the case claimed that he had had never used the word "*Nigger*" in his life. Not only was there a legion of witnesses paraded before the jury to refute this; even by his co-workers on the force, but evidence was presented by the defense whereby he was recorded on hours of tape saying "Nigger" over and over. Hell, he used the word more than Mel Gibson or Michael Richards!

As the trial ground on, the prosecution team, an inexperienced duo, became worse than useless with their continued fumbling cries of "I object" being overruled by the judge, who was obviously in awe of the "Dream Team", as the myriad of lawyers hired by Beebe came to be known. On the other hand, the judge was just as strongly unimpressed by the State's representatives.

Natalie's friend who had been murdered with her, Bernard, was portrayed as some kind of pervert and received no sympathy whatsoever from the court or the jury. The list of "expert witnesses", all paid handsomely by Beebe, seemed endless. Their statements concerning everything from the way blood splatters to how long it takes a bloody sock to dry seemed to me to be a load of horse shit, but the jury seemed to buy it all; no matter how asinine.

The defense team left no stone unturned in order to prove Beebe's innocence. DNA evidence was shown to be unreliable, even though the lawyer who debunked DNA at Beebe's trial went on to later become famous for freeing convicted felons by using the same DNA tests he formerly denigrated at the trial as unreliable.

When Beebe was found to be innocent on all counts, the city went wild. I threw up. I couldn't put it out of my mind. It consumed me during my waking hours and kept me from sleeping at night. My wife left me and I gave my notice to retire after thirty-five years with the same company. I was fucking useless and had no purpose left in my life, except to hate Noah Beebe. As I said earlier, the trial had ended five years ago.

I arrived at Dr. Armstrong's office at the appointed time. It had been the day before when I talked to the nurse and made the appointment. I must say that I was concerned a bit, but not too much. I did some exercise, went to the gym and walked a couple of miles each day, so I felt pretty healthy for a man in his early sixties. That's pretty much all I had to do to stay busy lately. I was eaten up by the depression over Natalie's murder, but I tried to keep functioning normally, the best I could.

Jan told me the doctor would be with me shortly, as she showed me into an exam room. "Should I undress?" I asked with a nervous grin.

She didn't look me in the eye as she responded in a low voice, "That won't be necessary Ken. Doctor is just going to have a consult with you."

"He couldn't do it over the phone?" She left without answering me.

As I waited for the doc, I started to wonder what this was really about. Should I be worried, frightened, or what? I was getting nervous, to say the least, experiencing all three emotions at once.

When the doctor came in he was looking like someone had just killed his puppy, really somber. "What' up, Doc?" I quipped half-heartedly, trying to lighten things up.

"Ken I got your test results back. We can do further testing if you like, but it appears you have cancer, Stage Four, and it is questionable if any treatment will work at this point." I was glad I was sitting on the exam table or I might have fallen down.

"Damn, Doc, that's some heavy shit! You couldn't have softened the blow just a little?" The news had not quite sunk in yet, but it was starting to.

"There's no easy way to say this Ken, no softening the blow. I'm being as honest as I can be with you, my friend. We can start chemo right away, today even. We need to get you checked into the Cancer Treatment Center. How is your health insurance? Besides the bullshit of the disease, this can cost an arm and a leg, you know."

"Slow down, Doc. I've got to think about this. From what I've read, and I have read and seen a lot since my friend, Clay, just went through this last month. I already knew that   Stage Four is pretty much a death sentence. Chemo did no good for Clay, other than make him sick as a dog during the last four weeks of his life."

I was remembering visiting Clay and the constant pain he had endured before he died. His body had slowly shut down; he couldn't take a leak or defecate as his body filled with the poison of his own fluids. It was a horrible sight and a horrible death he experienced. It didn't take long for me to reach a decision as I had already decided before it became personal that I wanted no part of what I had seen Clay endure. I'd made my choice, after watching Clay; before I learned I was sick. It seemed ironic that I had just recently made this decision. Maybe Clay had sent me a sign.

"Your information's correct, Ken. Treatment consists of lots of chemo, maybe radiation. There are some experimental drugs out now, but they would make a horse sick. On a scale of one to ten, your pain will be about eleven. The hair loss and other side effects will be nothing compared to the sickness and pain you will have to endure." The more Doc talked the lower he spoke. I could tell he was holding himself together with some effort. We had been friends for years; before Natalie's murder and he had been a real comfort to me after her death.

"What's the alternative?" I responded. "What if I don't want the treatment? I mean I know I don't "want" it, what if I don't take it? How much longer can I function as a normal human being…you know get things done without assistance?"

"Maybe a month or two, three max. I can get you some good pain killers that won't affect you physically or mentally for a while. But once the cancer really takes off, it's only a matter of time. It's up to you, of course. Ken, I can't tell you what to do. Kevorkian tried that and went to prison. You already know that it's not something to be taken lightly, whichever course you choose. Take a few days to think about this and then let's talk again. I am so terribly, terribly sorry to have to give you this news my friend." There was some watering up going on around Doc's eyes and I could tell this had not been easy for him.

I thanked him, gave him a little hug, and walked out without looking back. Jan gave me a sad look as I passed her desk, but I couldn't find the words to ease either of our burdens or make the situation more bearable. I pushed open the door and went out into the sunny afternoon.

The first thing I did was to stop a Circle K and buy a carton of Marlboro Reds. I had quit smoking ten years ago, but I figured, "What the fuck?" Damn things were seventy-six dollars a carton! How could anyone afford to smoke these days and where could they smoke if they had the money? No smoking signs were everywhere. I lit up. I got dizzy at first, but then I got that old feeling, the nicotine rush. Welcome back old friend, you can't hurt me now.

As I puffed away, I realized that I wasn't frightened by the news Doc had given me. I even felt somewhat elated…nothing could touch me now. A weight seemed to have been lifted off my shoulders. I had been so lonely for so long…Natalie's death and the departure of my wife. I thought of Natalie, maybe seeing her again, if there was indeed an afterlife, and then it hit me…Noah Beebe…Beebe, you've about played your last round of golf. I went home and packed my bags.

Before leaving town and heading to Augusta, where it was national knowledge that Beebe played golf almost daily; this according to MTV and other news stations, I had to wrap up some business. I emptied my savings account, sold my stock, all for cash and put the money in a fireproof box. I called Goodwill and told them to send a van as I wanted to donate a houseful of furniture and clothing that I needed removed from my apartment immediately.

I had given the house to my wife when we split and then I moved into a small studio. I wasn't interested in dating or entertaining so I had no use for anything big or fancy. My place was within walking distance of the bar where I spent my evenings, a good thing, as I was rarely in any shape to drive when I left there.

I kept to myself. Everyone there knew my story and they knew I didn't want to discuss it. Since I was pretty morose most of the time, I didn't spend a lot of time visiting with the other patrons. I kinda listened to the others sometime, but I had heard most of the stories before and the only escape I had was to drown myself in the booze. Sounds funny when I think of it, I tried to keep fit by exercising each morning, but when evening came around, I headed for my old friend, Johnny Walker.

I took the box of cash to my son's house. Don answered the door and invited me in. I handed the package I was carrying to him saying, "Put this box in the closet and don't open it under any circumstances until you hear from me. I locked it just in case you get too curious. I'll give you the key when the time's right."

Jokingly he asked, "What'cha' got in there, Pops? Is that a brick of pot or a pound of cocaine you been holding out on me? Maybe some old porn flicks?"

I was serious when I answered, "Never mind what it is, it's a surprise but it is also our secret. Don't even tell Misty until I give you the OK.' Misty was Don's wife and she was quite a beauty along with being a bit more savvy than Don. Not that he wasn't a bright kid, after all he did design bridges, it's just that Misty was exceptional, in all departments. She also taught philosophy at the university.

"I'm leaving town for a few days. I need a little vacation. I haven't been out of the city since...well, you know," I told him while avoiding looking him in the eyes. I didn't want to give him any clue of my illness nor of my mission.

"Great, Pops. I've been worried about you for a long time now. Ever since you and Mom split up, you've had me concerned. Glad to see you're going to get out of your rut. Where're you heading? Fishing up in Wyoming, I'll bet. Up around Dubois where you took us when we were kids? Wish I could go with, but I'm covered up at work. Anything I need to look after while you're gone?" He seemed pretty happy for me and I played along.

Back when Don was twelve and Natalie was fourteen, we spent a week in Dubois fishing the Wind River and the surrounding streams that fed into it. We fished the small lakes in Whiskey Basin where I taught them how to fly fish along with teaching them all the knots associated with the sport. At first Don wasn't very happy when I told him we must always "catch and release" the trout.

"That's why we use barbless hooks, I had explained to both of the kids."

Later Don smiled as he released a beautiful twenty-four inch rainbow back into a deep hole in Dinwoody Creek. He had landed the trout after a glorious ten minute battle. Watching it swim back into the current and rest behind a boulder in the stream, he remarked, "Thanks for the lesson Dad. I feel like he is an old friend now." We had such a wonderful time that summer. I had always planned to return one day with them; try to recapture that carefree time of their youth, but we never did. I looked away so he couldn't see the tears welling up.

"Right," I answered, "Gonna go chase some fat trout but I gotta run right now," I said, not trusting my ability to keep it together much longer. I gave him a bigger hug than usual, we have always been a hugging kind of family, and a kiss on the cheek and then I was gone.

I had already packed; the Browning Sweet Sixteen, the shotgun that had been my father's favorite, was stashed in the trunk. I had removed the plug, so it could hold five shells. I had also packed the box of high velocity number four shot for the sixteen gauge. I figured this load would suit my purpose quite nicely. The number four shot was enough to destroy a joint, but not quite enough to blow the entire limb off. Well I hoped that's the way it would work. If not I didn't really give a shit, as Joy Behar would say, "So what? Who cares?" I was ready to inflict some damage on the asshole who had murdered my baby girl.

I packed a few golf clothes and put my bag and clubs in. I removed enough clubs to allow the shotgun to fit in the bag easily. I even made a cut in one of the head covers so it could slip over the stock and make the shotgun look like just another wood. I was feeling pretty pleased with myself overall. I couldn't quite shake the sadness of telling Don goodbye. He had no clue of what was actually taking place and he didn't need to right now. I hoped that when it all shook out he would be able to absorb it and appreciate what I had done.

I went to the drugstore and picked up the prescription pain pills Doc had called in for me. I didn't want to see him face to face again, so I had called Jan and asked her to make the call to Walgreens. Right now I wasn't feeling any ill effects of the disease that was supposedly killing me; or was it the disease that had given me a new lease on life, I wondered to myself.

I headed east with Janis Joplin telling me to take another little piece of her heart on my "Cheap Thrills" CD. I had purchased the album originally on an eight track, then once again on cassette, and now I had her on a CD...Sony and the other electronic guys had been systematically robbing me every few years what with the changing technology in music sources they kept updating and making smaller. I told myself, "You sound like an old geezer. Just enjoy how much easier it is now. Those eight tracks were a pain in the ass."

I had driven east on I-40, crossing the Arizona state line about one hundred and fifty miles back, when I reached Williams. I was getting pretty road weary and decided to pull over and spend the night there, taking the exit ramp into Williams proper. Old Route 66 runs through the middle of town and the refurbished shops looked like something out of the past. I could almost visualize the old cars and trucks loaded with people full of hope and their belongings headed for California I found a parking space across the street from a quaint looking place called Cruiser's; no problem finding a parking spot. I walked in and smiled at the bartender. Cruisers was a fifties style diner so I ordered a fifties style Johnny Walker on the rocks.

This was Wednesday evening and a menu board outside said "Playing tonight: John Carpino, 7:00 'til 10:00. "My kind of hours," I thought to myself. A tall young man dressed casually in loose jeans and a tee shirt; I supposed it must be John, was setting up his speakers in the corner in the outside patio, right next to the sidewalk and the street.

He was being assisted by pretty lady with long black hair. She appeared to be of Mexican decent and she kept flashing the prettiest smile at the man she was helping. I found out later that she was John's wife, Luann. Besides acting as his roadie, I learned she accompanied him on some of his songs.

Surprisingly, smoking was allowed in the patio area; I had become a two pack a day man in no time at all, so I took a seat, lit up a Marlboro and sipped my scotch. After the day of driving this seemed to be just what the doctor ordered.

When John started playing "Brown Eyed Girl", I was taken back to another time, what with the sun setting, creating an incomparably beautiful Arizona sunset, and the old Coca Cola signs and other memorabilia all over the place. I had had a few scotches and was so mellow; I put all the dark thoughts of what had recently happened and what would soon happen, out of my mind.

John played a lot of his original songs about Arizona and the Southwest, "New Mexico Bound" and "Just Drive On" were especially good, I thought. He was taking requests so I asked if he would sing "Saint of San Joaquin", one of my very favorites, by John Stewart. He said with a bit smile, Sure, it's one of my favorites too, but you have to sing it with me."

"Why not?" I answered, I know most of the words and I'll hum along if I can't remember them all." I climbed up on the small podium and joined him in what, if I say so myself, I figure was the best rendition ever performed of that great love song. The crowd, mostly Europeans in town to visit the Grand Canyon, seemed to think so too; the applause was long and loud as we finished our duet. "Not bad for an old geezer," I thought to myself, not really concerned about the true quality of the performance. I'd had a blast.

I was getting ready to go find a motel room and turn in. I noticed that John was selling CD's of songs that he had written. I bought a couple, tipped him twenty dollars and said, "Man you are so much better than I was expecting for a town in the middle of nowhere. I really enjoyed your music. This has turned into a special evening for me."

He smiled that great smile again and said, "Thanks, I enjoyed singing with you." I headed across the street to retrieve my car and find a place to bed down for the night. For some reason I was not the least bit hungry, but I was feeling the scotch and it was warm and soothing in my gut. It had been an outstanding evening. Williams, Arizona, who'd a thought it?

The next morning I had breakfast in a western styled cafe that had a lot of pictures of Bill Williams lookalikes hanging on the walls. There was an old photo, maybe from the twenties, of a group of men in buckskins and coon skin caps. One of the men had a mountain lion cub on a leash. The cub didn't look very happy. "Weird," I thought, looking at the picture and wondering what had happened to the cub.

My appetite seemed to be diminished lately. I wondered if it was my cancer companion starting to work. I still felt as strong as ever though, thank God, so I took a walk down Old Route 66 before I resumed my journey to Augusta.

For a moment I thought about heading over the see the Grand Canyon since it was so close, but then I decided it would be best to get back on track. I stayed on I-40; I like the northern route for the scenery much better than I-10, although it might have been a few miles shorter. "What difference did it make if I arrive a day or two later?" I thought to myself, "The end will be the same."

East of Holbrook I needed a pee break so I took the exit to Sanders and got out to stretch my legs, use the john, and get a coke. As I was getting back in the car a young Indian approached me and asked if he could catch a ride to Gallup. I said, "Why not? I could use some company."

"My name is Joe Yazzie," he said without putting his hand out. I stuck mine out and he hesitated before reluctantly giving it a halfhearted shake. "I'm a Navajo and I got to get to Gallup to see my parole officer." He spoke in halting English in a funny kind of way.

"Anything serious?" I asked, wondering if I might have screwed up by letting him in the car.

"Naw, I just stabbed a guy a few months ago at the rodeo in Window Rock. It was self-defense and we was both drunk, but I got to check in with the government man every month or they put me in jail."

He didn't offer anything else in the way of conversation for the next half hour, so

I decided to break the silence, "Yazzie, huh? Isn't that an unusual name?"

"Shit no, there's hundreds of us named Yazzie. Begay is another real common around here; it's like you white people named Smith or Brown."

"Be Gay? You gotta be shittin' me. What happened to the great Indian names like Geronimo for Cochise?" My attempt at humor fell flat.

Joe didn't seem to be even mildly amused as he answered with a straight face, "They were Apache. We Navajo are the *Dineh;* 'The People'."

As the mile markers flew past at the rate of about one every forty-five seconds, Joe slowly opened up a little and regaled me with tales of how the white man had fucked over the poor Indian for the last couple of hundred years. All the good land had been taken from the tribes and they had been placed on worthless high desert on the Navajo reservation. He referred to it as "The Rez".

"Don't you have the Peabody Coal mine up here supplying jobs and paying the tribe for the coal and the water it uses?" I knew a little about the Indian plight, but I also knew they got a monthly check for Uncle Sam for being a tribal member; also any one of them could go to the university of their choice at no cost to the student if they put out a little effort.

"That work is hot and dirty or cold and dirty, depending on what season it is." Joe was looking at me with a bland expression, revealing nothing.

"Stoic," I thought to myself. "Lo, the poor Indian," where was that saying from? I remembered some kid painting a picture of an Indian in grade school and the teacher asking, "Who's that?"

The kid answered, "'Lo', the poor Indian". I thought it was funny at the time. It seemed even funnier to me now as I remembered the incident.

Joe talked very softly and slowly, stopping after each few words, making it difficult to follow all that he was saying, "I tried it for a few weeks once… workin' at the mine…but I din't like it. The foreman was a white man… and he din't like me. Said I kept showing up late for work. I would tell him I was on Navajo time. He tol' me the coal mine worked on a different time," he said with a rare chuckle. "He fired me after only a week."

We were entering the Gallup city limits and it was about time. Mr. Yazzie had worn me out with his low talking rant about how the white man was to blame for all the troubles suffered on the rez; from rampant alcohol abuse and drugs, to the thieving tribal chairmen.

Yazzie had told me, "One chairman right after the other; they loot the tribal bank accounts and then go to prison. They all get caught so easy because of the clumsy ways they try to steal from the tribe. Most of the time, some thieving white man, usually a lawyer or a land developer is trying to show the chairman how to get away with it

"A while back Chairman McDonald was behind the sale of the Big Boquillas Ranch, a few miles out of Flagstaff. He sold it to some lawyers in Phoenix one day for a couple of million dollars. The lawyers sold it next day for many millions more. Know what the chairman got?" Without waiting for me to answer, he says "Coupla new Beamers, you know those little cars from Europe, one for himself and one for his son, Junior, one silver and one blue I think they were. A week later, they were driving them all around Window Rock, the capital of the Navajo Nation for everyone to see.

"The McDonalds' only got a few thousand dollars themselves but some of the others, the white lawyers, made millions on the deal. Some guy testified against the chairman and got to keep four million dollars with no time in jail; I think he was a white man too. That's what I mean, our Indians," Joe pronounced it 'Indins'," are too damn dumb to even pull off a shady land deal …but we reelect them as soon as they get out of jail. Today McDonald is one of our local heroes. The white man has ruined our leaders with their offers of bribes to make money for themselves."

I couldn't help but notice that even in this flagrant rip-off by the Tribal Chairman, to Joe's way of thinking, it was the white man's fault. We'd reached Gallup so I pulled off the interstate onto the frontage road to allow him to get out without getting run over. As he was getting out, I asked him, "Hey Joe, you ever hear of Drew Carey?" He looked at me quizzically and shook his head. "Drew is a famous white man and philosopher from Ohio. He said you Indians should have fought harder."

He didn't seem to find Drew's remark as funny as I did the first time I heard it, but as I said before, I'd heard Indians didn't have much of a sense of humor. I pulled back onto the ramp leading up to the interstate hoping to make Amarillo before dark. As I looked in the rear view mirror, I could see Joe giving me the bird and mouthing insults, "Ungrateful redskin," I smiled. "Drew was right; your ancestors really should have fought harder."

The next couple of days were spent driving and thinking. I was enjoying looking at the different scenery as I headed east; after the desert and the mesas, there was the flattest land I had ever seen as I neared Amarillo. It reminded me of being on the ocean, only there was no water; the horizon was miles away. Soon I was into Oklahoma; it didn't take long to cross Texas when you went through the Pan Handle on the interstate. Soon everything was green, grass and trees and fat cattle grazing. It almost lulled me into forgetting what I was planning to do, but not quite. I was going over in my mind how I could pull it all together. By the time I got to Memphis and turned south on I-55 toward Augusta, I was ready.

I had a golf membership that allowed me to play out of state in addition to playing at the local private courses. My club had a reciprocal program whereby I was able to visit the best country clubs and play their courses while their members could play on ours. I only played occasionally these days, mostly with Doc, just to get my mind off the mental anguish I carried with me constantly.

That fateful day I arrived at the club in Augusta I went into the pro shop. I bought some balls and some tees and wandered around the club house grounds. I got a cup of coffee from the kiosk and sat down to wait. Sure enough, Noah was on time and meeting a couple of other guys…no body guards as far as I could tell. He appeared totally at ease and unconcerned for his safety. Arrogant prick! No one else approached him as he made small talk with his party.

I had loaded my clubs, along with the shotgun, onto a cart. Taking my time, I nonchalantly took the cart path down to the seventh green. I was making sure no one noticed me. I didn't expect anyone to be suspicious, but I didn't want to take any chances.

I had scoped out the course and even played a couple of rounds the previous two days to see what would be the best course of action; locating the perfect spot where I could ambush the asshole and do what I had come to do without interference from some innocent do-gooder.

I had played a couple of rounds with some older fellows I met who were retired and looking for new blood. For old guys, they were damn good golfers and I lost a couple of hundred bucks to them, but it was money well spent. They filled me in on all the details about Noah that I needed… what time he arrived, who he usually played with. He was a celebrity, after all and my questions didn't seem to arouse any suspicions. I was using an alias so no one recognized my name. Since Beebe was a frequent guest, I was sure everyone at the club was familiar with his story…and mine.

I stood in the trees watching the group approach. There were two other players with Beebe. In the distance, I thought I recognized Reverend Sharpton and Reverend Jackson. The first was a strange looking little guy, his long hair greased back with what appeared to be about a pound of pomade. If it hadn't been for the grease, I might have thought it was Don King, but *that* hair is unmistakable.

The thought crossed my mind, "What kind of church let's you still be a "Reverend" after your girlfriend has given birth to two of your illegitimate children; this happening while you're married to someone else?" I was surprised at myself when I realized how my mind was wandering at such a critical moment. I was just minutes away from pumping a few shotgun rounds into Noah and here I was musing about Jesse's sex life. "Stay focused!" I told myself.

The taller fellow, the one that I thought might be Jesse, had just hit the ball and it was lying closest to the green. It was Beebe's turn next, he addressed the ball slowly, confident in his ability, then hit a flawless drive straight for the pin. Now he was closest.

"I hope you realize how lucky you are, Beebe. The last stroke you will ever make, the one you will always remember, was a real beaut."

I waited until all three men were on the green and then I drove the cart right up onto it with the shotgun across my knees. They looked at me aghast, at first more because I had violated one of the cardinal rules by having a cart on the green *and* disturbing their play, rather than the threat I posed with the automatic shotgun in hand.

As they all had drawn closer, I could see that I had been mistaken about the other two guys with Beebe; neither of them was Jesse or Al; "Too bad, it would have been fun scaring the shit out of those two".

"You and you get lost, now!" the words more like a growl coming out of me. My throat felt constricted and I was suddenly breathing faster than normal, my heart was racing a bit, but other than that, I was OK. About that time Beebe recognized me and I could see the light come on in his eyes by his changed expression…surprise then anger at first, becoming fear. He could see, by the automatic shotgun in my hands, that the world as he knew it was about to change…and not for the better.

"Don't leave!" he yelled to his departing partners. "Don't you motherfuckers dare leave me here with this crazy white son of a bitch!" Noah's eyes were getting wild now, trying to figure out how to gain control of the situation. He was accustomed to being in charge; evaluating the situation quickly, calculating, trying to make the fifty yard run into the end zone.

"Not this time, you murdering cocksucker!" I didn't hesitate; I shot him in the right knee cap as he bent at the waist and started toward me. Damn, he was fearless; at least, I had to give him that. I knew he was fast and I was not about to give him a chance to tackle me. He went down, just like I thought he would, so I shot him in the other knee just to make sure he stayed there.

The shots were loud and I could see players out on the adjoining fairways looking anxiously to see what was happening. What remained of Noah's former threesome were on their way over a hill. I could see the funny looking one driving the cart as fast as he could while the other guy that looked like Jesse, was punching numbers, probably 911, into his cell phone.

"I hear you love this game," he had rolled up in a ball with his arms wrapped around his ruined knees. Bones and cartilage were showing white against the bloody mess. Beebe's eyes, wide and white, looked like they would pop out of his head at any second. Kinda like the old movie caricatures of the scared black man. I pushed the silly image from my mind.

"I loved Natalie much, much more. I don't see you playing golf anytime soon, Noah. In fact, I can't picture you on a course again…ever."

"Mother fucker, you white mother fucker," he kept gasping through clenched teeth.

"That the only word you know? I always heard what a smart nigger you were and yet somehow your vocabulary now seems so limited." The obscene "N" word, "nigger" is not a word that I use lightly or often, but it seemed so right at this moment.

Beebe had curled up into the fetal position when I shot him twice more; once in each elbow, the pellets also scattering into his abdomen and sprinkling the front of his thighs, little holes. He jerked violently and then seemed to pass out while still moaning. I walked over to him, placing the barrel in his crotch from behind, trying to figure out my next intended target. I'm pretty sure the last shot blew away his genitals and part of his colon…saved the best for last.

The shotgun was now empty; I laid it on the grass. I went over and sat down on my cart and waited. I could hear the sirens in the distance. For the first time, I felt a sharp pain hit me in the gut. "Thanks for waiting," I said to the unseen killer that was lurking inside my body. I hadn't felt this complete in a long time. I felt no remorse and no pity for the blubbering man lying in the grass; in fact I felt a warm feeling of satisfaction; a feeling I had not experienced in years.

# CHAPTER TEN

# George Washington Brown Introduces Himself

GW Brown: Steve Martin described my plight best years ago when he said in the opening scene of his movie, "The Jerk", "I was born a poor black child". I sure was born into poor surroundings, South Augusta, tar paper shacks, just a tad better than the scenes from Tobacco Road. If Erskine Caldwell had chosen black families for the protagonists rather than the now famous poor white trash characters, Jeter Lester and Ty Ty Walden, I could have seen myself and my family in every one of his stories. We were something like *poor black trash*. Wonder why that term never took off, it's always been poor white trash…maybe being black was considered trash without saying so in the South of the Sixties.

My mama, Lucille Brown; boy did she marry badly, in more ways than one, named me George Washington. Up until the first day of high school, I had been pretty proud of my famous name but after a couple of quick and painful encounters with some older wise ass bullies, I quickly became GW. No periods, I didn't need the grief that name created. How was mama supposed to know that the father of our country had been a slave owner? She was probably thinking of George Washington Carver, but no one else was.

Mr. Brown, my father, left us shortly after my twelfth birthday, Lord, isn't that trite story about worn out by now? "One day I came home from school and he was gone. No note, no nothin', just gone." I found out later that mom had caught pop in bed with her younger sister, Erline.

Now I must say in Pops' defense, Erline was a sight to behold. A tall gal with legs up to there and she did like to show them off. Hell, I was only twelve years old and she was causing me to have some pretty wicked ideas, what with those shorts she wore around the house along with skimpy the tank tops and no bra.

Erline had moved in with us when her boyfriend kicked her out. She had only been staying with us in our little apartment for a short time when Pop took off. Auntie Erline left the same day Pop did. My little sis, Sally, and I were left alone with mom to try to get by as best we could.

I'll skip the stories of my early years; you can still see them on the news every evening. Only the names and faces have changed, "Young black man arrested, suspected, incarcerated, beaten, mugged, whatever. I'll take the story up again in the early fall when I turned sixteen. That was the day I came home from football practice a little early; Coach had let us go because the temperature had climbed to over one hundred and the humidity was about the same. Coach was pretty careful about overheating the football team, obviously ahead of his time considering the recent incidents of players dying on the field during practice under the tutelage of overzealous coaches.

I could hear Sally, who had just celebrated her thirteenth birthday the week before, screaming, "No, no, please Fox, no!"

Now Fox was my mama's new "friend". He was a strange looking Negro, if you know what I mean; what we called a *redbone*. He had red hair, no shit! Red hair and a kind of yellowish pall to his skin. He was tall, but he wasn't big or very strong, kinda pinched chest and narrow shoulders. He seemed to have a cigarette in his mouth at all times, causing him to cough a lot. He usually wore an undershirt exposing his skinny arms, and he kept his baggy slacks up with red and black suspenders. Folks all called him "Fox". I guess because of his red hair, but then it might have been because of his beady eyes and long pointed nose. He really did look like a fox; mean and sneaky.

I didn't much care for Fox, but my mom seemed to like him. At least she kept him around, even though, in the three months he had been here he'd never worked nor tried to help out in any way around the house. I was suspicious of the way he would check Sally out when she came in wearing her white tight shorts. I told her they were too short and too tight, but what sister ever listened to her older brother? She had just started to mature and had a nice round butt, not that I noticed in a sexual way, but it was hard to ignore, even a brother couldn't deny the fact that she was filling out. I was feeling more and more protective of her as she matured.

Her chest was starting to take on the look of a young lady also. I could see that she was changing into an attractive young lady. I could also see that Fox damn sure noticed, too. When I caught him sizing her up, I would give him the skinny eyes. He'd look away pretending that he hadn't been checking her out, but he had my attention; we both knew what was going on in his mind. Although I was only sixteen and not as tall as Fox, I was a lot heavier, muscle not fat. I played right tackle and was one the biggest players on the senior varsity team at Lakeview; a school with a reputation of fielding tough players, with a full trophy case to show its success over the years.

Sally's cries were coming from Mama's bedroom at the back of the walk up apartment. The door was closed and I hit it running. The flimsy sliding bolt had been slipped into place; originally to lock out an inquisitive kid I suppose, but it splintered as soon as I hit it with my shoulder.

"Help me, GW!" cried Sally. Her blouse was torn and she was trying to hold it to her chest to cover her little budlike nipples. She was frightened and embarrassed at the same time. I only glanced at her for a moment and then took it all in. Fox was standing over her with his pants around his ankles along with his underwear. He had an erection going on, sticking out of his red pubes. I can't believe I remember that insignificant detail; that and the sweat that covered Fox's face and soaked his stained undershirt.

The window was usually open during hot weather to catch any breeze that might be stirring here on the second floor, since there was no such thing as air conditioning in our place. I didn't hesitate or wait for an explanation, none was needed, nor wanted by me. I hit him low, caught him on my right shoulder and tossed him out the window all in one motion. I could hear him screaming as he fell through the air and then I could hear him continue screaming, so I looked out the window. He'd landed on the picket fence, well it looked like a picket fence but it was made of rusty steel posts.

Fox was bent at a funny angle. Both his head and his feet were touching the ground on opposite sides of the fence, but his back was astride the fence, appearing broken. He continued to scream.

What was really amazing to me was that as he was flopping around and screaming, the son of a bitch still had an erection. Yep, there it was standing at attention surrounded by the patch of bright red pubic hair. I had to give him some credit for keeping it up under the circumstance, but what the heck; I was sixteen so my dick was hard all the time too. I thought to myself, "Maybe that's why Mama keeps him around."

It wasn't long before the cops began to arrive followed by an ambulance a few minutes later. Taking only moments to access the situation, the cops responded in the usual manner; *arrest the black kid*. I was cuffed and taken into custody which consisted of being thrown into the back seat of a black and white, while being hit a few times just to let me know who was in charge.

I could still hear Fox's screams through the windows of the cruiser. The plastic covered seat was hot, sticky and smelly and the heat was overpowering. The Plexiglas panel that separated the front of the car from the back cut off any air circulation. Cop cars in Augusta in those days were like our apartment, no fucking air conditioning.

I sat sweating and waiting to see what would happen next. The paramedics were trying to strap Fox to a board, but they couldn't seem to straighten his back enough to make everything fit. I smiled to myself, "That's what you get for tryin' to fuck my little sister, you red headed Mo Fo. How you like that?"

Upstairs, my little sis had managed to get her blouse back in place while trying to explain to young cop why I had tossed Fox out the window. He made a few notes, took her name and then hauled my black ass down to the station. Wouldn't you know it?

Mama came to see me when she got off work. "Why'd you do that to my Fox!" it wasn't really a question, more of an accusation the way she spat the words out. I had imagined she would be happy I had saved sis since she had gotten so upset at Pops for screwing Aunt Erline; boy was I mistaken. That's when I first realized that you just can't figure out what makes a woman tick.

"Your main man Fox was trying to put part of himself in my little sister," was my surprised reply. "I don't think I need to tell you what part that was."

"Sally's fine. Fox was just foolin' around. He wasn't gonna hurt her. He told me before that he wouldn't never hurt a chile." She was sobbing now as she took a handkerchief out of her bosom to wipe her runny nose.

"Mama, you can't believe that!" I said, but I wasn't sure if she was even listening to my fumbling words or the meaning of them; I guess she wasn't, the way things turned out.

Since Mama refused to file any charges against Fox, plus she had told Susie to keep quiet, and Susie always minded Mama, I was charged with felony assault and moved to a cell with a bunch more juvenile delinquents, that all reminded me of myself.

When my Lakeview High coach, Hampton, "Hamp" Michaels, got the word that I had been jailed, he started making some phone calls. Lakeview had the biggest, baddest football team in the county. For the last four years, the team had won the state championship, trouncing even the biggest schools in Atlanta.

Hamp had played college ball and came close to going pro but the color barrier had been stronger in the days when he was a young man. He had faced reality and become an assistant coach at Lakeview where he had worked his way up to head coach over the last fifteen years. He'd resigned himself to his fate long ago and always had made the most of what life had to offer. "A man is as happy as he wants to be" was one of his mantras.

Hamp had his cap set on winning the championship again this year and I was one of the main keys to this goal. William, a friend and teammate of mine had talked to Susie. She told him why I'd thrown Fox out the window. After William came to Hamp, the coach was relieved to know there had been justification for my actions.

In the South, in most any town or city, big or small, football is the great equalizer. Over the years many institutions of higher, and lower, learning have lost their credentials due to fudging the rules; paying players or their parents to switch schools among other things. Sometimes blatant and sometimes more subtle, rules were often pushed aside to put a winning team together.

Coach Hamp had always played by the rules, but he did have a following of prominent citizens who had attended Lakeview, played ball there, and relived their youth vicariously by helping support the team in any way they were able. If they bent the rules a little, they never let Coach know.

It was through this group, headed by Judge Bailey T. Albritton, that I was placed in a foster home. By a great coincidence, Joe and Judy, my new foster parents, were also named Brown and were avid football fans. Through their support and guidance, I made Coach Hamp proud and went on to be awarded a football scholarship at Ole Miss, where I, believe it or not, went on to study the law. I would later laughingly brag to friends, wisecracking, "I graduated Magna Cum Loud", but deep inside I was extremely thankful to all who had helped me.

"Show a little class there, Lawyer Brown," William, still my friend, would chide.

As the years passed and my practice and reputation grew, I prided myself of being a man of integrity. As the Southern author who wore the white suits, would say, I was "A man in full," but my definition was to define myself in a good way. "Full" meaning that I could look at my life and work with pride. I didn't have to compromise in my own mind to justify my actions. I would often wonder how some of my colleagues could tell themselves or their families, "I am doing the best I can for society."

I would represent a client only if he was honest with me. If he was guilty, he would have to say so. Then we would present whatever extenuating circumstances were available in order to receive a lesser penalty, or even to have the charges dismissed if the mitigating circumstances so justified; however, if I felt he was guilty, but lying about it, I would toss him to the curb.

Everyone deserves a fair trial, as granted by the Constitution, but nowhere in said Constitution does it state that lying should condoned, warranted, or winked at. The charge of perjury, in my opinion, should be levied at every infraction; that would be true justice.

What had happened to my little sister; who by the way, went on to attend college and become a successful teacher, has always had an influence in my view of how to conduct my business and my life. I guess I owe a reluctant"thank you" to my mama's red headed boyfriend, Fox for turning my life around and putting me on the road to success.

When Judge Albritton's successor, Judge Shelby, approached me with Ken Wallace's case and told me that I had been requested by the defendant, I didn't have to spend much time considering what I would do. I was surprised that the case was pro bono, but I suspected Mr. Wallace had his reasons. Later, I found I had guessed correctly when he told me of the mission that he had assigned to his son and daughter-in-law. I have been successful in my practice and didn't really need the money anyway.

As had the rest of America, I had followed the case of Wallace's murdered daughter, Natalie, followed by Noah Beebe's mockery of my legal system. The fact that Noah was a black man, coupled with the fact that he was living in my town never did set well with me. A lot of better men than me had risked so much to improve the plight of the black community and here was this clown putting us back in the *dark ages*, by his selfish actions.

Ken, as Mr. Wallace asked me to address him, dropped a bombshell when he let me know he was dying of cancer and had less than three months to live. I asked," What *can* I do to help you, then? This case will never reach the courts before your demise, to put it bluntly."

"I know I won't make it to the trial, but I also know that you are known in Augusta as a man of integrity. As my attorney I would like for you to allow the people out there to hear Natalie's story one more time before I die. I want you to help show that she was not the terrible young woman that Beebe's defense team made her out to be."

I was most happy and flattered to carry out his wishes. I might add that Beebe was never the same. He couldn't wipe his own ass, what was left of it anyway, after Ken's visit.

# CHAPTER ELEVEN

# My Dad by Don Wallace

Don Wallace: They arrested Dad in Augusta. He was charged with attempted murder, even though we all knew that if he had intended to murder Noah Beebe, he could have done it. The charges were immaterial anyway. Everyone soon knew he would never live to stand trial, and public sympathy was on his side; a dying man avenging his daughter's horrible murder was the stuff of hero movies.

The prosecutor was relieved to find out the case would never go to trial. Dad had revealed his condition, but only after getting a promise from the judge and the prosecutor that his condition would not be revealed until he was ready to make it public. Relieved by his sad news that let them off the hook, they readily agreed to his terms.

I wanted to travel to Georgia to see him immediately, but he would not allow it. "The past is the past," he told me over the phone. "You must move on," he said emphatically, and then he instructed me to open the box he had left at my place before he left for *Dubois*.

There was close to a million dollars in cash in the box. There was also a letter:

> *Dear Don,*
>
> *You have been my cherished and beloved son. I don't know what I would have done without you after Natalie's death. I know it has been hard on you, and it's going to be harder still in the next few months.*

*I chose not to tell you that I have a terminal illness because I didn't want a lot of fuss made over me. Besides it would have been such a downer and I have been depressing enough to be around the last few years. The good news, if there can be such a thing at a time like this, is that this illness also freed me to carry out my revenge against Beebe. I have nursed this hatred of him for so long. By the time you read this, if all goes well, Beebe's golfing days are over and my time too is near an end.*

*I put this money aside for an endowment to be made at the university where Misty teaches. I want it to be anonymous, so none of Beebe's lawyers can get their hands on the money through some kind of lawsuit. The endowment will be for a scholarship program that encourages ethics in the practice of law. I'm not sure how this can be done, but Misty is smart enough to figure it out. The endowment will be in Natalie's name and if invested correctly, the money should last for quite a while.*

*Should the university balk at instituting such a scholarship program, divide the money between the humane society and St. Jude's. I would have given some to you, but I know you don't need it and, given the current circumstances, you probably wouldn't want it anyway.*

*The conditions concerning recipients of the trust funding should contain, but not be limited to the following (You and Misty can add any additional conditions you may deem appropriate):*

*The applicant must sign a pledge stating they will not defend child molesters, rapists, murderers, or anyone charged with crimes that harm other defenseless human beings.*

*An exception would be only be allowed if some publicity seeking prosecutor was trying to make a name for himself by going after someone who is obviously innocent; e.g., that arrogant asshole in Italy that has relentlessly pursued and ruined the life of that young American girl.*

*It will be left to your discretion as to whether the exception is valid. I want it stated in ironclad terms, that any deviation from the rules will result in the recipient repaying, with interest, all monies received.*

*The purpose of the endowment is to instill budding law students with unquestionable integrity, before they enter the legal profession. Hopefully this may make some small change in the attitude of the next generation of attorneys, steering them away from the practices of today's money grubbing litigators.*

*This may be hard for the university to accept. Misty, if your school won't accept these terms, try to find one nearby that will. You must have control over the program. If my proposal fails, and there is a good chance it will, the old bulls don't like change, then use the money to take care of the children and the animals.*

*Love,*
*Dad*

"What do you think about this," I asked Misty, handing her the letter. She had gotten her Ph.D. in philosophy two years ago and was teaching at City University. Dad thought she walked on water, but then, so did I.

She was wearing those high dollar jeans that I liked so much, showing off her long legs and cute butt, although for once, I wasn't too distracted by the sight. I was concentrating on the business at hand. She was certainly easy on the eyes, but not just another pretty face, as I often told her; she was a lot more intelligent than me.

She read it once and then read it again, trying to take it all in. "At first glance it seems OK, but I'm afraid there are going to be a lot of people, especially the old professors, as Pops pointed out, that aren't going to like the conditions attached to accepting the money.

"Pops," Misty always called Dad "Pops", "probably thinks this is a large endowment, but the university might consider this chump change, especially when it comes to adding guidelines; the good ol' boys tend to think someone is pissing on their shoes, propriety and all. I'll make the effort though for Pops and for Natalie."

Dad's arraignment was held a week after his arrest. He refused to meet with the first court appointed attorney, insisting on, and getting George Washington Brown, LLC. I guess he finally wanted his fifteen minutes to get his side of the story out to the public.

I first learned about this turn of events while watching Lawyer George Washington Brown, his real name by the way, being interviewed by one of the celebrity-chasing talk show hosts on FOX.

My buddy, Pete Stephens, had called excitedly, "Turn on FOX news right now. I'll talk to you later!" I wondered at that, since Pete was not the kind of lame brain that normally watched that channel.

I tuned in to see what Pete wanted me to see. There was this big black dude stating that his client, my dad, had done what any self-respecting man would do. He had taken his own revenge, since no one else had been able to do so. He was saying, "I'm a man of the law, but if someone had cut my child's throat the way Beebe had slashed Natalie Wallace's, and got away with it...well, let's just say, I would've probably done the same thing; only much sooner."

I'd been calling Dad each day around two o'clock, Georgia time, since his arrest. That seemed to work best, Sometimes I would reach him, but not always. So far when I had managed to get through, he wasn't too communicative. He seemed more interested in how Misty was coming with the endowment proposal. "These things take time Dad. You know Misty will do her damndest to get this wrapped up."

We hadn't discussed his illness or his state of mind. He seemed OK over the phone, so why push it? "Are they treating you alright out there? Bubba making any moves on you in the shower?" I joked.

"No one messes with me since I have my new reputation. Don't you know that now I'm a famous bad ass? Haven't you been watching the news?"

"Sure I have. Speaking of that, what's the deal with this George Washington Brown fellow? I saw him just by accident this morning. He looks to be a pretty good guy, but he sure is black. It seems strange to envision a black attorney in Georgia of all places, taking a white man's case against a black celebrity."

"Oh that," he replied. "Just felt that I had to try one more time to set the record straight for Natalie, and the court won't let me near a microphone or a TV camera. Mr. Brown is an exceptional individual. I checked him out before requesting him to represent me."

When I saw Brown on the talk show, he appeared to be a giant, but then the talk show host wasn't quite as big as an average man, so I thought looks might be deceiving. "Dad, that appears to be one very large man you have for a mouthpiece. Is he as big in real life as he looks on the tube?"

"You betcha, that's my main man; my *black* knight in shining armor if you will. He tells me to call him GW. That's what his friends call him so I'm flattered." He spoke with the first hint of humor I had heard from him since he'd been jailed. He didn't normally use color to describe other races so I knew he was trying to ease the situation. I laughed, then I heard him chuckle also.

I repeated my original observation, "Do you, by any chance see the irony of this…one huge black man taking your side against another big black brother, and in the Deep South of all places?"

"Yeah, I love it, especially since Mr. Brown is famous in Augusta. He kicks butt. He's the defense lawyer everyone wants and he's working pro bono for me. Too bad my time is so short. I think he might have been able to get me off, or at the least I'll bet he could get me a reduced sentence. It's strange that here in the south where they have been so abused over the years, I seem to have more people of color on my side, than I had in California; there's your irony."

We spent a little longer visiting about the TV appearance of Dad's lawyer. Jerry Franks, the nationally syndicated talk show host, had asked Mr. Brown if his client was innocent. "He's as innocent as Noah Beebe was," ventured Brown. They both chuckled, along with the audience, when he said that.

Jerry went on, "Seriously, does Wallace have a chance? There seems to be plenty of witnesses who saw him pull the trigger…five times, no less! And then to just so casually walk over and sit down on the golf cart and wait for the cops to show up. He didn't try to leave the scene or do anything to help himself. You know, like wipe his prints off the shotgun. He just seemed so resigned to whatever happened. Knowing you, Sir, I'm sure you have a plan?"

"Jerry, my name is George Washington Brown and I always have a plan. Mr. Wallace lost a daughter under indescribable circumstances. She was eviscerated in broad daylight at her home along with a young man who was a friend of hers. They were murdered by Beebe in a fit of jealous rage.

"The man whom we all know to be guilty walked away. He left her blood everywhere, in his car, on his shoes and socks, in his house and yet he didn't pay for his heinous crime. Lot's of folks figured it was just a matter of time." The big man paused for effect before adding, "I guarantee that my client will never spend a day in the state pen." The police had yet to release the fact that dad was dying, mainly because only the lawyers were aware of his condition.

"That's a pretty huge guarantee you are making, Mr. Brown, is there anything you care to add?"

"No, Jerry, nothing further at this time. Mr. Wallace just wanted me to remind all of you how shamelessly the judicial system and the press have treated his daughter and his family. He now feels vindicated and I have to admire his actions, whether he did anything illegal or not remains to be seen. Remember my guarantee. "

Dad had told GW about his illness after first admonishing him to maintain the lawyer/client privilege; the same promise he had extracted from the state prosecutor. Dad didn't want anyone to know about his condition. So far he had been successful in masking it from the jailers.

He told me when I called, "I want them to think that I finally decided it was time for Noah to pay the piper, regardless of the consequences. Otherwise; my delayed revenge appears to have the trappings of an act of cowardice. "

When Dad appeared before the court to plead, GW entered a plea of nolo contendre. "No contest!" the prosecutor exclaimed. "What kind of a plea is that?' He was caught off guard, as he had been expecting a not guilty plea after watching Brown's appearance on the news. Everyone knew they were merely going through the motions for the sake of appearances.

"Work for your pay," responded GW sarcastically. He could always use the aura of a hard assed defense attorney in his business and he knew the cameras were rolling.

After the expected motions and conferences followed by a meeting in the judge's chamber, a trial date was set to start the proceedings three months from today. Dad told Brown that was fine with him.

A week later, Dad was sent to the hospital for a physical exam and then straight to the oncology ward at the prison hospital. I was surprised that such a facility existed, but it seems over the years a lot of prisoners became victims of the big C. The doctors there were insisting that he begin a rigorous round of chemo treatments. He had to call GW back in one more time to stop them.

When I received the news that he had been hospitalized, I again wanted to go to him right away, but he would have nothing to do with that. Misty wanted to travel to see him as well, but I assured her that Dad would rather she continue to work on Natalie's endowment. Things had been moving excruciatingly slow, with every department head wanting to make a "meaningful" contribution by having his statement read into the record for posterity. Hours were needlessly spent on preparing a meeting agenda that would satisfy each inflated ego.

As I stayed home and contemplated my father's life I remembered so many of the warm and loving moments from the past. Before Natalie's death there were so many unforgettable events. For years our lives had been a series of good times, laughs, and successes. Afterward, no matter how we tried to get over her death, our world was never the same. I could work up no sympathy for Beebe. I was sad for what Dad was going through, but I was glad he had gotten his revenge on that sorry piece of shit.

After Natalie was gone, Dad would often go to her grave taking a book along. He would read aloud to her. He told me she had liked "To Kill a Mockingbird" when she was younger. She identified with Scout and would act out her role sometimes. So he would read that aloud at her graveside. At other times he would take a children's book, maybe Dr. Seuss, you know, "The Cat in the Hat" or around Christmas, he would read about the Grinch, going back in time in his mind, to days when she had been a little girl sitting on his lap, giggling as she listened to his voice take on different sounds as he got into character for each scene.

His heart was broken so badly after her death. I wished that I could help him in the months and then years that followed but it was useless. The first time I heard him laugh in years was on the jail phone the day when he telling about huge Mr. Brown working for him pro bono.

My father passed away in the county hospital in Augusta seven weeks after "the incident". He had been moved there from the prison facility during his last days. Dad went peacefully and rather quickly. After he refused the chemo, he spent the last three weeks sleeping most of the time. The drugs were good, just like he wanted. He finally allowed me to visit him one last time toward the end.

I couldn't find the words I so desperately wanted to say. Tears were rolling down both of our cheeks in the little time that he was conscious. I held his hand and whispered, "You did a good thing for Natalie. I am proud of you, my father. I've always been proud of you. You've never let us down, even now with all this. May God bless you and keep you."

After his death was made public, the press, of course, milked the story for all it was worth. There was some rioting in the streets back in California. The usual rowdies in the usual neighborhoods broke out the usual windows and looted the usual stores. Things literally went on as usual.

The pundits that had defended my father's actions were reviled as "racists" or "anarchists" by the NAACP and the ACLU, along with other publicity seeking groups; many no one had ever heard of. There was weeping and teeth gnashing for poor Noah Beebe. They decried how an innocent man had been so mutilated. After all, a jury of his peers had proclaimed him to be innocent. The law had been shamefully ignored.

"Noah was cut down in his prime," a famous television minister with a viewership in the thousands, cried; literally, tears running down his cheeks.

"That's an interesting tact to take," I said to Misty, "since, during his trial, one of the defense lawyers claimed he was too old and crippled up to have the strength to kill anyone." As far as I know, no one has been able to put Beebe back together again.

# CHAPTER TWELVE

# Misty Proposes Natalie's Endowment

Misty Wallace: While Pop's life on earth was coming to an end in the prison hospital in Georgia, I had been busy trying to fulfill his wish that Natalie's murder would be more than just a sad and distant memory for a few people in the years to come. It was clear that he wanted to immortalize her memory by attaching a relationship between her name and a foundation that would allow a chosen few, future, yet-to-be-named attorneys to add a new dimension to the field of law.

My husband, Don encouraged me to do my best for his father and his sister's memory; already knowing full well I would give it my best shot because I was that kind of gal.

I had only been a professor at City University for a couple of years, but I had made a number of friends who were tenured there. I have always made friends easily. I thought it was due to my intelligence and ability to think clearly when it came to sorting out the issues. I had studied extra hard to achieve my goals; even in this modern age and in universities as well, women are not chosen as often as men for promotions. We have to work twice as hard to achieve half as much…not original but definitely a fact of life.

Don would jokingly tell me that it was because I had such an exceptionally cute ass and long legs. Maybe we both were right, I could turn on the charm when necessary, even being flirtatious at times, but when it came to being unfaithful, or hitting the sack with any of the many horny professors known for playing around, there was no chance. I was in love with my husband and nuts about his dad, only as a father figure, of course, I am a one man woman, as quaint as that may sound.

I made a tentative, kind of a mock trial, presentation to a few of my closest friends just to get their ideas on how to proceed. I began, "The motto of City University is "Fearless Investigation and Unfettered Thought". Working from this premise, I wish to propose a new endowment named after a young woman with whom you are all familiar, Natalie Wallace. The amount of the fund is nine hundred and eighty-five thousand dollars. There are a few conditions attached to the deal and the donor is to remain anonymous." It didn't take much thought to figure out where the funding originated.

I proceeded to read the requirements, as set forth by Pops, to the group. "Representation and defense of child molesters, rapists, or murderers by any recipient of this scholarship is strictly prohibited under the conditions set forth. In order to receive assistance from Natalie's endowment, the candidate must sign a contract agreeing to these terms." When I paused, I could see this had already struck a nerve within the group; and these were my friends. There was an undercurrent of low mutterings coming from the table where they were seated.

"Where's the right to choose, freedom of choice, carving out your own destiny? This stifles one's individuality immediately," were just a few of several remarks bantered about by the group. Only a couple of members of my audience gave it a chance. I thanked everyone for their time and input. The next day I made an appointment to meet with the department heads who were responsible for approving endowments of this nature. After what I had seen from my friends, I was not optimistic, but I had promised to do my best.

Some time had passed from the time of my request until an actual meeting took place, but not nearly as long as it usually took the snail paced department heads to move. Having been made aware a substantial amount of money might be involved, the wheels seemed to turn a bit faster. Since Pops had died, the furor on both sides of the issue on whether taking justice into your own hands, as he had, was ever a viable option, had mostly died as well.

The panel I was facing was made up of old white men, akin to any senate committee you might encounter on the nightly news grilling some Wall Street bankers, cigarette or automobile industry executives, asking few intelligent questions; more interested in what they themselves had to say. Unlike those industry giants who always managed to appear calm after purporting to "welcome the investigation" in front of the press cameras, later to be followed by invoking their fifth amendment rights when actually appearing in front of the committee, I was nervous and unsure of myself.

The musty odor of testosterone and old sweat from wool suits that seemed to have never been cleaned emanated from the pack of scholarly gentlemen as they eyed me with expressions that indicated a young woman, such as myself, should only be engaging their majestic selves in such manners of entertainment as only they could devise.

"Stop being a chauvinist," I reprimanded myself. "Don't read stuff into this; get Pop's business taken care of."

My presentation didn't take long and not surprisingly, the response from the board was as I had anticipated. Did I mention most of those present were members of the Central California Bar Association? Before this governing board had even agreed to attend the meeting, I was ordered to present a copy of what the proposal covered, so no one would be surprised. Each of the board members had already written their "opinion" and each was eager to present his reason for refusing to allow the endowment to be accepted.

"The very idea of establishing such a scholarship with such seemingly lofty and frivolous goals wrongly implies that members of the legal profession are not to be trusted to know how to conduct an honest defense," puffed a red faced gentleman who, we all knew, had made his reputation and fortune by defending the very clients Pops had excluded from Natalie's grant. "I refuse to be a party to such a disgraceful accusation toward my profession," he finished.

Following that pronouncement, Dr. Leonard P. Katzenberg, a very distinguished gentleman in a three piece suit that looked like it had been resurrected from the nineteen thirties, stood up and said, "This stipulation paints the whole legal defense profession with a wide brush of implied deceit and a lack of integrity. Why would we even consider the approval of such an abomination? What would the press say? Even though this scholarship grant is purported to be anonymous, we all know it comes from Ken Wallace. This in itself decries accepting the endowment. I am outraged that such a detestable article is even being presented to our august group here tonight."

Katzenberg then dropped a real bombshell by announcing, "When I heard what was afoot, I took the liberty of contacting a few of our major contributors before convening this hearing. I felt it was necessary to see how they felt about accepting such a controversial endowment.

"I was not surprised when Robert Marius, senior partner of the distinguished firm of Marius, Shufelt, & Border, told me unequivocally that his firm would discontinue their annual contribution, which is very substantial I might add, and any other support for the school of law, if we were to institute such a program. You, my distinguished colleagues, realize that many of our former students have gone on to work for Mr. Marius's firm.

"These associates too are heavy contributors to our institution; their alma mater. We cannot afford to alienate such a powerful friend for such a paltry sum as is being offered here; less than a million dollars and with such outrageous strings attached. It is anathema." Having said that he sat down abruptly, ending the debate.

The purpose of the endowment; remembrance of Natalie, was no longer a consideration, if in fact, it ever had been. The pomposity that had been exhibited in this room tonight was making me sick at my stomach, literally. I had to choke back the bile I could feel rising. I was only happy that Don had foregone attending the presentation with me. Some of these old goats might have received a lesson in reality in the form of a good old country style ass kicking from Natalie's brother.

Choking back a few tears and a lot of pent up anger; I stood up and gathered my notes along with the original copy of the proposal. Without looking at them or awaiting their permission to leave, I turned and left. I could feel them looking at that fine ass as I exited. "What a fucking brain trust!" I thought as I reached the hallway.

As Pops had requested, the money was sent in, Natalie's name, to the children's hospital and the private humane society. We didn't trust the

County to use the money as directed, wanting it to go to take care of the animals, not to be used for increased personnel salaries or diverted to some other *worthy cause* such as law enforcement. We sent the checks from the Natalie Wallace Foundation. It would seem neither organization had any problem with Natalie's name, as the checks were cashed immediately.

A lovely plaque acknowledging the generosity of Natalie Wallace and that of her family is on display today at both agencies.

As for myself, I no longer work for that outmoded institution that refuses to accept any new idea, "Ceaseless Industry, Fearless Investigation" my ass!

Do all the great young students with energy and imagination eventually turn into puffed up, self-important old men; blowhards who will not make any decision that would rock their creaky old boats?

# Chapter Thirteen

# Back in the Game

Josh: After I got my ass kicked and robbed in the Avenues of South Phoenix, I had cooled on my plan. I was still getting mightily pissed almost daily when I saw where still another scumbag cancer on society had injured an innocent young person and then copped a plea with the prosecutors resulting in yet another short sentence or even probation.

Even the terrorists caught trying to blow up skyscrapers in Dallas and subways in Washington, D.C. were only getting sentences of twenty years or so. That will make them around forty or fifty years old when they are released. I guess the sentencing judges figure they'll have gone to meet their maker, or the other guy, so the freed and prison-wise ex-con will pose no danger to them. Don't they have any concern for their children or grandchildren?

"Josh, you need to find another cause. How about the Humane Society?" Lloyd would say to me, trying to change the subject. "That would be a positive cause for you and maybe put an end to your morose attitude."

Lloyd and I still sat in the Oak Barrel bar several evenings each week; me bitching about the plight of our court system when both of us weren't giving the tree huggers a hard time. While we drank inside, the cops would sit out in the parking lot hoping for a chance to protect the city by arresting the bar patrons for having more than two drinks in an hour. "Irony?" I needed a better word to describe the way cops worked around here.

The police priority around here had turned from chasing hardened criminals and gang bangers to the pursuit of the men who liked to have a few drinks in the evening after work. This was due to the new structure of fines for DUI convictions. The amount of dollars collected has risen from a couple of hundred bucks per episode to a three or four thousand for a first time offender, while at the same time, the allowable legal alcohol level has been cut almost in half. This contradiction put in place by either a lawmaker who doesn't drink or more likely some politician with a chauffeur supplied by the taxpayer… I wonder.

I couldn't even blame the Mormons for the drastic reduction from a .12 to .07 percent allowable alcohol level over the past decade. The Feds instituted this unrealistic limit using the threat of withholding highway funds as a club over the states and cities. When I had been a cop in Riverton the allowable level had been .15.

I have to say, even though the leaders deny it, claiming they are doing it to protect lives, the cities jumped on the band wagon for the dough. Drunk drivers, rather than felons, are the target of choice for cops around here. We all had to be careful since more than two beers in an hour would get us arrested and cost us our jobs. This was another topic of conversation we beat to death on a regular basis; before leaving after too many drinks. We did keep the cab companies happy…and wealthy. Of course we had to be careful of having our vehicles stolen when all the cops were arresting a "dangerous drunk".

"Did you hear the news about Noah Beebe?" Lloyd ventured as I walked into the darkened wood paneled bar that hot afternoon.

The AC was set somewhere around sixty five degrees and the bar felt like heaven. "I'm not going back outside until October," I said. I was still waiting for my eyes to adjust to the welcome darkness after being in the sun all afternoon. Dried salt sweat stained my jeans and boots, but that was pretty normal in the desert this time of year.

Lloyd had his cold beer in front of him and it looked so good I ordered one from Brenda, who was standing at her station at the bar giving Lloyd the eye again. There is nothing like that first cold swallow of beer after a day in the sun. The dry kind of cold, salty taste is superb. If every drink of beer tasted like that first one, I wouldn't drink anything else. Good thing it's only that good for the first drink or two; I might never stop drinking them.

"No," I answered, "I've been out at the Palo Verde Power Plant checking on a dozer rebuild. I haven't seen or heard any news. What's that asshole done now? Last I heard he'd beaten up two cops in Atlanta, but his lawyers got him off...again. They claimed he was being racially profiled and everyone knew the cops in Atlanta are prejudiced, and by God, it worked! Beebe is made of Teflon; nothing sticks to him."

Lloyd could scarcely contain himself as he said, "Not this time, he finally got his, well it wasn't the law that got him; seems like he got his balls blown off along with his knees and elbows...on his favorite golf course in Augusta, no less. Who says there's no God?"

"Bill Maher for one but that's beside the point. Who? What? Give me some details on old Beebe, Lad." I was elated. This asshole had flaunted the law, the public and his victim's family for way too long. If Lloyd wasn't just screwing with me, it appeared that justice had finally been served to him; in spades.

Lloyd wasn't kidding, "Natalie Wallace's dad did it; no one is really talking about the why's and wherefore's yet, just a lot of speculation about what made him drive from California to Georgia to do the deed. I guess he decided the time had come to confront the man who murdered his daughter. Couldn't seem to get justice anywhere else, so he delivered his own."

"H'mmm," I took a deep pull of the cold beer while John Denver sang about country roads on the jukebox. That old song always brought back warm memories. Maybe it was time to reconsider the plan; just needed a new idea, maybe.

"That song reminds me, did I tell you, I ran across Jimmy Dale Baker, one of my old high school pals, last week while I was in Texas? His brother Bobby Lee's in prison in California, some place called Farmdale, in the southern part of the state. Bobby Lee and I graduated together. Guess who else is in Farmdale right now."

Lloyd ignored my question and said, "You had schools in East Texas? Who the fuck woulda figured?"

"Wise ass, you hail from Safford, Arizona and make fun of my education? I'd be surprised if you could spell 'university'."

"U N I versity," he made it sound like four letters. We both laughed at the corniness of it all.

John Denver's song and the cold beer brought to mind those times when Jimmy Dale and Bobby Lee and I had spent together as kids camping out and fishing and getting into fights.

I ordered another round from Brenda. I had told Lloyd bits of stories about growing up in a small Texas town and he in turn had regaled me with his tales of growing up in a small Arizona town run by Mormons. The intriguing thing we discovered was, while there were bars and liquor stores in Safford where the LDS leadership reigned with a heavy fist, there were no such establishments in Scurry or anywhere in Kaufman County for that matter. We had to travel to Dallas to get booze; or see our local bootleggers.

When I first told him this he remarked "You Texans were pretty fucked up. My mom belonged to the LDS church and owned a liquor store. How about that for some crazy shit?"

"*Were* fucked up?" I looked directly at him and said, "Are you shitting me? It still hasn't changed much. The only place you can get a drink around there today is at the VFW and you have to be a member to do that. You can finally buy booze at the liquor store; they just don't have any public places, like a good bar to drink in."

Over the years, I had told Lloyd about growing up in a place that seemed to be out of the thirties or forties. At school, we would get in fights behind the Future Farmers of America building which we called the Ag shop. It was set apart from the rest of the campus. We didn't call it a campus back then either, it was just the school yard. Now everything, including a business property, is called campus; guess it sounds more friendly or homey or intelligent.

Anyway, I guess all small schools had the same rites of passage. There wasn't much going on to keep us from being bored, so we would fight. None of us boys went to lunch in the cafeteria. We would all meet "out behind the Ag shop" to smoke and shoot the shit and fight.

Things would start out friendly enough, usually Leon our school instigator, would say something like, "I'll bet Josh can kick your ass, Billy Glen."

Of course Billy Glen would have to say, "No he can't, but we're not going to fight so it doesn't matter who can whip who," trying to ignore Leon and avoid a fight.

Then another peckerwood would chime in, "I'll bet you're afraid. You know Josh could kick your butt in a heartbeat!" Accusing someone of cowardice was a sure fire bet to raise one's ire, even if you didn't want to have a stupid confrontation, you couldn't let such a personal comment go unchallenged. It was worse than saying something bad about your mother...well almost.

This would go on for a few minutes; insults would then be passed between the two guys being targeted. Sure enough the fight would start; first with a push or light tap, then a half-hearted blow, and then the fists would fly. In those days there were no knives, no sticks and no kicking the other fella if he happened to fall or get knocked down.

In the end the two amateur pugilists would shake hands and have a smoke, if anyone happened to be lucky enough to have a cigarette, and life would go on as if nothing had happened. Most of us weren't big enough to inflict serious injury on one another; a bloody nose or a black eye was generally the extent of the injuries.

This same scenario went on almost every school day with the only change being who was fighting who. Leon always managed to avoid the fisticuffs, and looking back, I often wondered why we didn't all just get together, kick the shit out of him for his role as chief instigator, and just enjoy being alive. But then, maybe the fighting was part of growing up. Besides starting the shit, Leon was also the school clown and kept us laughing. No one could get mad at him no matter how outrageous his antics; he went on to become a minister.

There *were* some big old corn fed country boys like John Henry, who was all of six and a half feet tall and over two hundred pounds. He probably could have inflicted some major damage on any one of us, but no one ever dared challenge him; besides he didn't like to fight anyway.

Over time, a lot of us learned to fight behind the Ag shop in those days, figuring out by trial and error how to punch at least. Nowadays, the school administrators call the cops and put the young gladiators in jail; charged with being incorrigible. How's a kid suppose to learn how to defend himself? Maybe that's why guns and knives are so prevalent lately.

I didn't learn about gouging eyes until later when I was an eighteen year old college student. One evening just after the sun had gone down, a bunch of us were sitting on "the square", the grassy area surrounding the county courthouse where a lot of the "wild" boys hung out; we were called wild if we did anything out of the ordinary, didn't have to be really wild.

Pretty much every county seat in the South has a similar *Courthouse Square* with the mandatory statue of the Civil War Veteran out front, decked out with his pack and rifle. The plaque is attached to the base of the statue honoring the *Valor and Glory of the Soldier of the South*. Still today many of these folks still don't think the War Between the States is over. This kind of thinking is what keeps Rush Limbaugh in good drugs and Cuban cigars, as most of his utterances are taken as gospel in that part of the country.

Getting back to the story; we were drinking beers iced down in the coolers that we had in the trunks of our cars. We kept them out of sight so the cops, who would cruise by occasionally, couldn't see what we were up to. The cops wore their cowboy hats, giving us a slow knowing nod, letting us know they were wise to our doings, but they would let us be, as long as we didn't fuck up by creating any disturbance.

Most of the members of the police department had been raised around here, or in a similar small town close by, and knew how it worked. We played by their rules, when we could, so as to avoid any confrontations that would rock the boat or cause them to have to interfere. We were laughing and telling jokes; making fun of each other when any sort of opening that could be viewed as a chance to embarrass someone or make him the butt of a joke would present itself.

"What'd you do? Piss yourself?" Kenny yelled pointing to Bobby Lee's crotch where he had spilled beer earlier.

"Go fuck yourself!" Bobby Lee replied. The usual response when a wittier comeback wasn't on the tip of the tongue.

As the banter continued in a light vein among the group, I found myself in a strange predicament. Maxie Patton, one of the notable bad asses in the county at the time, was trying to bite my finger off because I wouldn't get him a beer. Maxie was a grown man in his mid- thirties. He wasn't real big, but he was known to be real tough, kinda like a pit bull.

He'd been trying to bully me for the last hour or so, figuring a punk kid like me would not stand up to him. Wrong move; as he was soon to discover because, even at that young age, I didn't take shit from anyone. When I refused to get his beer, he grabbed my left hand and sunk his teeth into the index finger at the first joint. Let me tell you that got my attention immediately, it hurt like hell. He had a good grip on it with his teeth and had already reached the bone in my finger through the flesh on both top and bottom. "This fucker is nuts!" went through my mind. Come to find out, he really was a crazy son of a bitch.

But at that time I was only concentrating on what was happening to my finger; I knew if I hit him in the jaw, my only clear shot, I would cause him to bite my finger off from the force of the punch and the angle I had to work with. Everything in my mind was suddenly clear as a bell; it was as if time was standing still because of the searing pain, I guess. I remember to this day, and that was twenty or so years ago, the intenseness of the scene.

Although I had never tried it before, I stuck my right index finger into the space between his eye and the socket. I reached all the way in until I was stroking the back of his eyeball with my finger tip. I was still clear headed and was considering popping it right out of his head, but then his knees buckled, his teeth released their grip and the fight was over.

Bobby Lee had been there and had seen the whole thing. "That was the slickest move I ever saw," he exclaimed. "I can't believe you put that bastard down. I never heard of anyone beating him before this; especially a kid like you."

I couldn't believe it myself, but I watched as Maxie stood up holding his eye. "Tough little bastard aren't you?" he muttered. I was waiting for him to come at me again, hoping he wouldn't, as my finger was hurting like hell, but he took his keys out of his khakis, walked over to his car, got in and drove away. I never had any trouble with him again, probably ashamed that a punk kid had bested him.

Bobby Lee wanted to know what I had done that had caused Maxie to go down. In the confusion he hadn't been able to take it all in. So I explained the mechanics of it all, "It's easy once you get your finger in place, touching the back of the eyeball; work it around like you're trying to dig the eyeball out, kinda like gutting a quail. I know I could have popped it out, and I was ready to if he hadn't stopped chewing on my finger."

I filed that trick into the bag of fighting tips I carried inside my head. It's come in handy more than once when I couldn't find any other way to get some asshole off me. More than one seemingly hopeless situation has been resolved in my favor when I put one or even two fingers in an eye socket. I still carry the scars from Maxie's teeth. When I happen to glance at my finger, the sight reminds me of that Texas evening so long ago. A few years back I heard that Maxie went into a hay field with a shotgun and blew his brains out; he really was a nut case.

After bullshitting about the good old days for a while and downing a few more cold beers, easing past our .07 legal limit, the talk between Lloyd and me drifted back to my earlier plan.

I told Lloyd, "I saw Jimmy Dale just last week when I went home to visit my mom. She lives in the country so I'd drive out to see her, but would get a room in town so I'd have a place to escape to when the time came. We'd spend a little time together getting along and then she would start telling me how screwed up my political views were. After a few hours of this I'd make up some excuse to go to town."

"You should be ready for that kind of bullshit when you go back home, Josh."

"I know and it makes me ashamed that I can get so upset at my dear old mom for her Southern views, but she holds onto her hardheaded views pretty well. It's just that people who think our President is a Muslim from Kenya and the accompanying nonsense that follows that line of thinking, and then defending that ridiculous position so relentlessly…well it just tends to push my buttons.

"After telling me that Rush Limbaugh was the greatest talk show host and that Newt Gingrich, the smug politician who dumped two wives because they became ill, is one of the smartest men she'd ever heard, I had to get away for a while. I drove down to the rodeo grounds where some of the guys were roping calves for practice. The Fourth of July rodeo was just around the corner and these men wanted to sharpen their skills. In another smaller arena the quarter horse competitors were cutting steers from a small herd."

"Sounds real folksy and cowboy like, but where are you going with this?" Lloyd drained his beer and ordered another one.

"I'm getting there. I ran across Jimmy Dale standing off in the dark drinking a beer. I walked over to him and pulled a half pint of Jim Beam from my hip pocket and offered him a snort. He took a pull off it and handed it back to me. We'd liked the half pints in the old days, 'cause they're easy to carry without drawing attention from any of the bible thumpers or their wives who might be in the area. We aimed to offend no one, so we tried to remain discreet. The little bottles still sufficed today."

"I am beginning to understand why your visits home are so short."

"I asked him, 'What's up? How've you been? How's Bobby Lee?' I asked him the questions in quick succession, not giving him a chance to answer any of them at first.

But when I finally gave him a chance to speak he told me, 'Bobby Lee's in some state prison in California. He's gotten himself caught three different times now on chicken shit charges and now he's serving a life sentence. *Life*, can you believe it? Even though he ain't done shit that deserves hardly any time at all…he got life; that fuckin' three strikes law they got out there can sure ruin a person's life.'"

"I was totally put out by that news. I said to him, 'My God, Jimmy Dale, I'm so sorry to hear that. I haven't seen him since the time we went in the service.'"

"Bobby Lee and I had enlisted in the Army together while Jimmy Dale decided that if he was going to get in the fighting he would be a Marine, so he went in that direction. We even tried to get the army to let us stay together, but it didn't work out."

"'What he hell did he do to wind up there?'" was my first response."

"Jimmy Dale told me 'Appears to be some kind of bogus drug bust; he thinks he was set up by the local lawmen but we can't do nothin' about it. We don't have any money for lawyers and I don't know if it would help him if we did.'"

"I asked Jimmy Dale what's the name of the pen where he's being held? I get into California every once in a while. I could drop in to see him. Guess what he said."

"No fucking clue, Josh."

"He said, 'Farmstead, in the southern part of the state, ever heard of it?'"

"I replied, 'As a matter of fact I have," with my mind suddenly racing. I was sure this was an omen and I'm not a superstitious person."

"Looks like you might be back in the game, Josh," Lloyd said with a smile. "By the way, what'd you with the five hundred bucks from you took off Lynn when 'Don't ask, don't tell' passed?

"I bought Susan that Four Peaks Amethyst ring she'd been admiring. I only had to come up with a couple hundred out of my own pocket. Good news all around," I replied with a big grin.

# CHAPTER FOURTEEN

# Josh's Target Rich Environment

Josh: Avery Evans wasn't the only scum bag on which I had set my sights at the Arizona State Pen in Florence. There were a few others I would love to have taken a shot at. At the top of my list was the guy who in 1999 killed his two year old daughter beside a dirt road in Apache Junction.

When he was caught, he told the police that he'd picked her from day care and took her to McDonald's for a hamburger. Later, as they were riding around she pissed him off by "whining too much". He yelled at her so she told him, "I'm sorry, Daddy. I'll be good." He then went to a hardware store, purchased a three gallon gas can, took it to a gas station and had it filled.

He then drove for quite a while up and down county roads looking for the "perfect spot". By the time he found what he was seeking, a dirt road out in the country, she had fallen asleep. He placed her in a ditch, still sleeping, and then he poured the gas all over her tiny body. She awoke and started crying, "No, Please Daddy" as he struck the match.

He told the cops that after he set her on fire, she had run about twelve feet in a straight line and then started running in circles until she collapsed. When her body was discovered, the plastic barrette she had in her hair had melted into her cheek. That picture stays with me a lot, especially when I can't sleep at night. I cry for that poor suffering child and the thought of her murderer sitting in prison year after year enters my mind a lot when I'm thinking about injustice.

Her father; should be another word for a person who would do that to his child, was sentenced to death…three times. Count 'em. The verdict was overturned two times before he was sentenced to die on the third attempt to convict him. I didn't bother to look up what kind of heartless shyster would defend such an animal or what kind of judge would overturn the verdict twice.

Who gives a fuck if some minor error was made during the trial? This sorry excuse for a human being admitted that he did it. I'd like to see him on the end of a big pitchfork being held over a fire. I'm not real religious, but I think the devil might be waiting for this asshole and the legal team who tried to save him…maybe preparing an extra special punishment. More than fifteen years have passed since this horrible incident took place. He is still sitting and sleeping and masturbating on death row at the Arizona State Pen in Florence. I'm trying to figure out how I could possibly slip him some really painful poison.

My next choices are a toss up. One loser in Phoenix recruited his roommate to join him as he took his girlfriend's four year old son on a ride to "see Santa". They took this trusting child out into the desert and shot him, leaving his body there in the dark cold night.

And my other choice, tied for second place, if I were able to get a chance to change his life, would be the worm that was babysitting his eight year old niece. While he was raping her, he "accidently" smothered her with his hands. Since he wasn't done, he hadn't cum yet; he kept humping her little dead body until he had satisfied himself.

After he was arrested and had confessed to the murder, he had stated matter-of-factly to the arresting officers when they asked about the post mortem coitus, "It wasn't like she was going to tell anybody," his exact words. He has gained fifty pounds while awaiting the death penalty that never seems to arrive.

These assholes are legion. I have my targets in California too. Maybe it was more than destiny; a guardian angel arriving too late, but at least finally showing up, that allowed me to help Bobby Lee meet Marcus Regan in the State Pen at Farmdale.

# Chapter Fifteen

# The Right Tool is Located

My name is Bobby Lee Baker. Since I was born and raised in East Texas, I had to have two first names. That's just the way it is. We had Davy Dean Thatcher, Billy Ray Hayes, Tommy Gene Smith, and Jimmy Paul Powell just to mention a few that attended the little school with me in Kaufman County.

Even the girls had two names, Betty Joyce Moore, Betty Jane Walker, Ima Jean Johnson, Billie Sue Peters and so on. Even state wide we had our celebrities; good and bad with two names: the infamous Billy Sol Estes, Elsie Faye Higgins of Dallas city council fame, and if you weren't given the mandatory two names when you were born, your friends, or foes, gave you the other as you grew up. While I'm on the subject, I must say I liked the name Dubya had bestowed on his mentor Karl Rove. "Turd Blossom" seemed totally fitting for a man who looks like the illegitimate offspring of J. Edgar Hoover.

Anyway with two names it's hard to be much of a success outside of the great state of Texas or at least the Deep South. Once you cross the state line to the north, well past Oklahoma anyway and to the west, people look at you strangely when you tell them your name is Bobby Lee or whatever two names you might be saddled with.

I 'm currently serving a mandatory life sentence at Farmstead state prison in California. It's not that I'm a bad person. I didn't do anything terrible or even that I am ashamed of, other than just how fucking stupid I was. I just got caught with some pot, which is considered by some, especially me, to be a wonderful natural gift from God. Well, maybe it was more than some, and it was more than just one time which was the real problem… California has this law about three strikes and it's kinda like baseball. You're out; well actually you're in for life after the third strike.

My downfall came because my dealers and my customers kept turning out to be narcs. I guess the major employer in southern California is the State Department of Drug Enforcement. Hell, I never made one legitimate drug buy or sale because I trusted these guys. You know, they looked like the real deal.

They were dirty, smelly, and had long hair and they all just seemed so damned nice to talk to. They'd get high with me as we tried out their supply…just to test it. But when I went to pick up a load of pot with a new friend, Earl; at least I thought he was a friend, from some guys and then deliver it to another good old boy, the cops were waiting for me at the end of the transaction.

This happened to me twice and both times the good old boys would be there in the courtroom, or in the backroom, testifying against me. I probably failed to mention that I'm not considered a great thinker among my peers. "Peers" is a pretty good word though. I think it means my friends and relatives. Anyhow, to say that I'm not the sharpest tool in the shed is kind of an understatement. I still have no clue as to what went on surrounding my third arrest. I wasn't even to blame that time.

As I mentioned earlier, after the third time the judge threw the book at me. My court appointed lawyer, Edward, wasn't interested in working too hard on my case, since my arrests never even made the back page of the local papers. I met with Edward for a total of about fifteen minutes over the course of the three trials. I don't know why they kept assigning this guy to me, as we didn't like each other very much. But since I had spent all my money getting to California while looking for a new start, I wasn't able to entice Gloria Allred to come to my rescue.

Anyhow, that's how I come to be here in this California prison facing life without parole.

I made some friends here. They belong to a group called the Aryan Supremes and I hooked up with them to keep the Mexicans and the black guys from kicking my ass on a daily basis. I don't spend a lot of time with them, but we cover each other's backs when it becomes necessary.

I'd been here for a few years, doing life, and I was getting pretty bored with my situation until my brother Jimmy Dale, see there's them two names again, came to see me. Jimmy Dale is a couple of years younger than me, but he's way smarter. He sells a little pot and does favors for some folks and seems to do alright. He's only been in jail a couple of times and then it wasn't for very long.

Well, he mentioned that he'd run across Josh O'Brien back at the rodeo grounds in Kaufman a month before. When Jimmy Dale told Josh where I was, it seems Josh got pretty excited. He said there was a guy he was interested in by the name of Marcus Regan who happened to be here in Farmstead. This Regan fella was also serving a life sentence. He had molested a little girl a while back and he spent a few years in the pen for it. I guess the California legal system gets more upset with pot dealers than it does with child molesters, but I'm gettin' off track here.

Seems like this guy couldn't control himself or his dick and he went out and raped and killed a couple of other young girls after he was released. He did some kind of plea deal to keep from getting sentenced to die and ended up here. I guess he had a better lawyer than me.

I later learned that this case got a lot more news coverage than mine so it wasn't too difficult for Regan to get a real hotshot attorney assigned to save his sorry ass; the same lawyer that had saved some other baby rapers and made a name for himself as a real slick celebrity type over the last few years.

I talk too much I guess, but I don't get a chance to express myself a lot in here.

Josh made Jimmy Dale a proposition about Marcus Regan. Josh always did have a strong opinion about folks who bullied or hurt others who couldn't defend themselves. I've seen Josh take on much bigger guys than he was, while defending someone who was being shoved around. It didn't seem to matter that the person Josh was taking up for, was often bigger than Josh too. The guy wasn't afraid of anyone and he hated bullies.

Josh told Jimmy Dale that he would like to see something really bad happen to Regan. He wasn't offering a contract as such, but he said there was two thousand dollars in cash that would be given to Jimmy Dale if something of value happened to this killer.

As I mentioned, I was getting pretty bored here in Farmstead, so Jimmy Dale's story got me to thinking. Now thinkin's not one of my strong suits, but I do like a little stimulation when I can find it and this seemed like something that would help pass time. I had to ask though, "Jimmy Dale, I can see you makin' out pretty good with the two thousand, but what's in it for me? You know I'm a lifer here and I don't need a retirement fund or a new car."

"Well, I figure you could use a little cash for cigarettes, pot, some pills and whatnot. Things that might help set you free for awhile, don'tcha' know? I'll throw some of the money your way…say a thousand if this fella's injuries, or whatever happens to him, warrants me gettin' paid by Josh."

"Sure, OK," I replied, "What the hell else do I have to do? Might take me a while to locate the jerk and bring this to a proper end though." I didn't shy away from violence; we fought a lot as kids back home and then later, when I was in Desert Storm I did some ass kicking there. Since my time in here, I'm what you might call a real bad ass. Not bragging, just stating a fact.

"Take your time; I ain't in no rush, although I think Josh kinda is."

Jimmy Dale said his goodbyes and promised to stay in touch. I went back to the yard and started shooting the shit with my "brothers".

"Any of ya'll know anything about this Marcus Regan character? He killed a couple of little girls and then pled out to avoid the needle. He's supposed to be here at Farmstead."

Butch Conor, the one eyed former biker, I say "former", since there aren't any bikes in here to ride, nodded at me. "Yeah, I met him a couple of times. He hangs out by himself 'cause he's afraid someone's gonna fuck him up if they find out what he did. Me and him are from the same town in Oklahoma and I knew him from there. He trusts me some, but I don't care for him. He doesn't talk about why he's here. I heard about it from my cousin."

Butch, just like most of us in here, don't take shit from anybody, but he doesn't deal it either. We had a pretty good vibe going between us over the last few months, so I thought I'd take a chance.

"Butch, let's me and you talk over there," as I pointed with my chin to a spot out of the shade that was out of earshot of the others.

"What's up, Bobby Lee?" he said.

"How do you feel about an asshole that would rape and kill two little girls just because he could?" I asked, already knowing the answer. Before he could reply I put it to him, "Would you be willing to help me deliver this Marcus dick head some pain and make him really, really sorry for his sins? Of course, there might be some payment involved that would put something in your pocket along with a good feeling for fucking this dude up...a lot."

"Fuckin' A. What's your plan? How can I help? Of course, I'm in. I already told you I don't like the sick fuck" The words tumbled out of his mouth and his eyes lit up as he spoke. Butch was just as bored in here as me.

"Introduce me to Mr. Regan. You gotta set it up first though. Say you want to introduce him to a good friend of yours. Tell him I confided in you that I raped a couple of high school girls, but I got away with it. This is yours and my secret, but I wanted to meet him 'cause I get off on talking about screwing young chicks and I like to hear other guy's stories. Explain to him that he can trust me, because I've already told you enough about my crimes to create a lot of trouble for me. He's got nothing to lose and could use another friend in here."

"Gotcha'," Butch said. "I'll get to work on it. How much dough we talkin' about here, Bobby Lee?"

"Does it really matter? I'll share whatever I get with you." He smiled and nodded.

It took a few days for Butch to convince Regan that I could be trusted to not harm him. What a dumb shit! I made up some bogus stories to relate, mostly taken from novels I had read over the years, or taken from what I imagined would have happened. I mentioned how the girls were terrified when I tied them up and ripped their little panties off and how they tried to scream thru the gag that I had tied across their mouths when I penetrated them.

It made me ill on one hand to discuss such things with him, but I was also unable to hide my own excitement, knowing what was in store for Regan. He mistook my kind of contained excitement; thinking that I was fantasizing the same as he was. As I said before, "What a dumb shit!"

Marcus reminded me of the toad from "Mr. Toad's Wild Ride". No neck, strong but squat looking. He looked as if he could handle himself in a fight, so I spent some time figuring out how to hurt him without being hurt in turn. Did I mention that I can handle myself too, so I wasn't too concerned about not being able to take him out? I just didn't want to take a chance on things going wrong. You see, after talking with this creep, I decided that Ol' Marcus had to die. Now I'm not a killer, but when I was in the Middle East I had shot a few ragheads, so death too, besides the violence, was not totally new to me. I just had never taken a life in cold blood.

The next weekend Jimmy Dale came to see me. "How's it going, Bobby Lee?" he asked. We were able to talk without being monitored since I was not classified as a hardcore criminal. I hadn't been convicted of any dangerous crimes; more like a white collar inmate that posed no physical threat. Maybe a Bernie Madoff kinda' intern…no harm, no foul, except I was facing life; I guess Bernie's in the same boat, come to think of it. We were sitting in the cafeteria at a table with no one close by. Jimmy was pretty light hearted, as he had some cash and the law wasn't bothering him much these days.

"Well, I'm doing better than I expected and it's going faster than I expected, but I want to do more than injure this asshole. I really think I want him to die."

"Wow!" Jimmy Dale exclaimed. "What the fuck? Josh just wanted this guy to be made an example out of. I don't think he had a murder in mind, although from what he told me about his feelings about Regan, he probably won't mind, just as long as it is not linked to him or his two thousand bucks. But tell me, why'd you decide to kill the prick?"

"It was somethin' he said. I think this piece of shit definitely deserves to leave this earth as quickly as possible. I feel he is going to either have an accident or he may commit suicide. I haven't quite decided yet. I'm leaning toward suicide, less of an investigation. A child killer like this isn't expected to be normal anyway. Suicide might even be something the hacks would expect," I replied.

"It's a sad but well known fact that the suicide rate in California prisons is twice as high as the national average," I said with a smile. "This could work to my advantage."

"OK, I'll tell Josh the outcome is most likely to be terminal with no footprints to lead to anyone involved. If he really objects and says he won't pay for the extermination, I'll get back to you."

Changing the subject, I asked, "How's Mom and Sis?"

"They miss you and wonder how you got yourself in such a fix. They cry a lot if I talk about you."

After a few more minutes of small talk, Jimmy Dale took off leaving me in a real state of depression. I worried about the women in my family. At least I didn't have a wife or girl friend waiting hopelessly for my return. Shrugging it off as best I could, I wandered back to the yard to swap more stories with Marcus Regan. At least that would give me something to take my mind off my troubles.

"Hey, Mark," I had started calling him Mark lately. He told me his friends call him that and he prefers it. Seemed less formal, he thought. "You got any idea where a guy could get a piece of rope? I'm on a mission to help a pal out; trade for some pills, and I need about a six foot piece. Even something hand made with sheets or socks or something will work."

Coincidence isn't a word that I use a lot, or even trust in, but it did cross my mind, "If Mark had gotten the death penalty rather than pleading out, his life would not be in nearly so much danger of ending prematurely as it was at this minute.

CHAPTER SIXTEEN

# Marcus Finds A New Friend

Marcus Regan: That Bobby Lee is such a cool dude. Not many people call me Mark, I don't encourage it. I go by Marcus Regan to most everyone, but he's pretty special. I've only known him for a few weeks but I'm sorry that we haven't been buddies forever. He says the same thing about me. We are soul mates.

He likes the young babes, just like me. He's not squeamish and it seems like he enjoys the same kind of rough sex with the little chickies…just like me. Well not quite just like me; after all I like a final ending when I'm done with 'em.

I was in the exercise yard with him the other day, I don't think anyone else in here knows what I did, except for Butch and I trust him, so the guards let me out into gen pop just like any of the other guys. They told me to keep my mouth shut about what I did for my own safety but I figured that since Bobby Lee and I were now buds, I could tell him about Becky. I needed to share it with someone. It had been two years ago, and the retelling of it made it seem like it was happening all over again.

Becky was the first of the two little beauties I'd fucked. Jenny was the last one and I got caught for doing her. That shouldn't have happened, me being caught…just dumb luck for the cops, that old lady with the dog spotting me and telling the cops about it. I should have killed her too, but that was one big damn dog she had with her. Anyhow, we were standing around having a smoke, Bobby Lee usually has smokes and he is always willing to share them with me, what a guy! So I started telling him about that day I did little Becky.

"It was getting on toward dusk out on the north beach area jogging trail. I had been scoping it out for a few weeks. I hadn't really put a plan together, just hoping something would present itself; a *crime of opportunity* I believe they call it. Well not really something, more like someone, if you know what I mean?" Bobby Lee nodded, took another puff and blew a smoke ring, and looked at me as if he were waiting for more.

"Unlike the second time with Jenny when I'd made a detailed plan; the first time I hadn't really made a plan per se, it just kind of happened when I saw her jogging toward me. She was by herself and there was no one else in sight; I couldn't believe my luck. I had picked that spot because of the woods were pretty thick here and there was this deep ravine just on the other side of the trees. There was lots of cedar and other thick brush in the ravine. It really was a good spot, 'cause it took them over a year to find what was left of her and they probably wouldn't have found Becky then if they hadn't been looking for Jenny.

I could tell that she was breathing hard and sweating pretty good as she got closer. I figured she had been jogging for a while and she couldn't put up much of a fight. I was right of course. I was twice as big as her, so I just reached out and grabbed her around her shoulders and threw her ahead of me into the woods." Bobby Lee's breathing had slowed as the story progressed.

"What happened then?" he asked.

"Well she was sorta stunned at first but when she saw what was happening she started trying to scream. The thing is, she was so scared and out of breath besides, that no sound was coming out of her...just kind of a wheezing and gasping for air kinda thing." I could tell from the look Bobby Lee had on his face, he was starting to get into the story.

"How old was Becky?" he asked. He had put his smoke out and was breathing faster than before. I liked that I had him going. Recalling the details of that day and telling about them got me worked up again too.

"I thought she was around twelve or maybe thirteen by the way she looked, so little and all, but I found out later from the papers that she was just turned sixteen. Umm, sweet sixteen! Nothin' sweeter. When I ripped off those little jogging shorts, you know the kind with a little elastic waist that barely holds them on; I saw she was wearing some kinda skimpy pink panties, the cotton kind. I really like those." I couldn't help it; I was starting to breathe faster too as I started to remember the details of that moment…moments, one picture in my mind running into another.

"She was just so helpless. She was struggling to maintain or recover, but she wasn't able to. She could barely stand as I finished ripping her clothes off. I pumped a lot of iron when I was in the pen and since I had been released I had been going to the gym, using the machines pretty regular up to that time, so I was extra strong. Wasn't much she could do and she could tell it. Besides showing a lot of fear, she looked really embarrassed because she was now totally naked except for her shoes and socks. After I had torn her tank top off and looked at those little pink nipples standing out I was about to cum in my pants. My guess is that she must have wanted it to happen in a way. God, Bobby Lee, my dick was so hard I thought it was going to explode and I still had my shorts on!"

Bobby Lee spoke, "So, she really wanted to have a go with you, you think? Even though she was scared shitless?"

"Well who knows what makes a woman tick? I think she must have been a virgin and that probably scared her too, losing her cherry and all. Didn't they make some kind of movie about what women want? By that time I didn't really care what she wanted. I knew what had to happen as soon as I slipped off my shorts and let ol' big boy out. I felt like I could squirt at any second, so I bent her over a log that was there, pretty handy for me.

I decided it would be more fun and easier to take her from behind. Her arms were kind of crossed under her and she wasn't struggling much anymore. I think she realized it wasn't going to do any good to fight it and I'd hit her couple of more times to calm her down."

Bobby Lee had turned away from me and was looking up at the guard tower. I imagine he didn't want me to see that horny look in his eyes. I could feel it in mine as I continued. My dick was hard as a rock with the retelling of what had happened to her; just like the time when it was actually happening.

"She was just lying there on her belly on that log with her creamy ass thrust up at me; still whimpering, but that didn't bother me none. I reached under her ass and grabbed that little pussy in my hand. It was wet, but I think more from sweat than anything else. I spread her legs and started to put my dick in her, but it wouldn't go. After a few seconds had passed, seemed like longer, I started cumming all over her ass. I couldn't help it! Seemed like I came forever though. My head was so fucking dizzy; I was seeing spots in front of my eyes."

"What was she doing while this was going on?" Bobby Lee asked.

"She was just lying there, real still, except her shoulders were shaking, like she couldn't stop. I was pretty damned disgusted with myself for shooting off before I even got in there. Felt like some kind of high school kid trying to get his first piece. Made me feel ashamed of myself and mad at her at the same time. She could have been more helpful. Things might have turned out different for her if she had just put a little effort into pleasing me.

Once I had come, I sat down on the log beside her hoping I would get a hard on again. She had my jism all over her butt and inside her thighs." Bobby Lee looking uneasy, his eyes kinda glazed over, turned towards me. He was trying real hard not to smile; hiding it with a funny kind of frown. He wasn't fooling me though. He was seeing the picture in his mind that I was painting for him and he was as excited about hearing about what I had done as I was in re-telling it.

I continued with the story, getting hotter as I got into it. "Bobby Lee, I kept staring at her and fantasizing, but I couldn't work it up again. I stared down at my limp dick, rubbing it but it wouldn't get hard again. She was like in shock, you know. I decided that I might as well end it then… couldn't leave a witness around. I stood up and found my shorts where I had tossed them. I fumbled around and got the Buck knife out of my pocket and snapped it open.

"You know those knives make such a solid clicking sound when the blade locks in.

When she heard the snap of the knife she looked around and her eyes got really wide. They were such pretty eyes, a real deep green, filled with tears. She tried to struggle a little, but hell, she couldn't have weighed more than eighty pounds, soaking wet, which she sorta was. I shoved her back down on the log and heard her grunt when her belly hit the log again."

I could picture it all again in my mind. I could feel my boner that I was trying to hide from Bobby Lee getting even harder. I silently remembered how it felt to reach around her little neck and put the edge of the blade against her throat and begin to slide it slowly from left to right. The blade was sharp enough to shave with. I kept it sharp like that all the time. What was the point of having a knife if it wasn't razor sharp?

Bobby Lee had grown a little impatient while I was reliving the scene in my mind. I couldn't blame him though; the best part was yet to come.

"Bobby Lee, as I cut her little throat, I could hear her trying to breathe, gurgling with bloody bubbles coming from her mouth. She made more noises, gasping, like air leaking from a big hole in a tire, as I held her down and finished cutting her; she wasn't going fast though. I hadn't cut her really deep, just enough to cause her to have a hard time breathing.

"I was watching her naked body as she was dying. Suddenly her little white butt cheeks started clenching and I'll be damned if my dick didn't stiffen up and get my attention. I spread those little twitching ass cheeks and shoved my dick right up her butt hole! Man that was the hottest piece of ass I ever had in my life. I felt like I came a quart or more while she was still quivering and hot to the touch. We went limp at the same time; man that was great."

Bobby Lee had kinda wandered away from me. He was looking at the ground and there were lines in his face that had not been there before. I figured he probably needed to find a place to go jerk off after hearing that story. I know I did.

After a few minutes, he wandered back over to where I was standing, took out his smokes, took one for himself, and then handed the pack to me. We were both breathing faster than usual. We lit up and smoked quietly for a time. He had a weird look on his face…kinda scary at first, but then he gave me a sheepish grin and said, "You really are one sick fuck." Sounded like a compliment to me, "Wish I could have been there when you were finishing her off. It's too bad we didn't hook up a long time ago. We could have had some times together on the outside." A distant look came over his face. Then he walked away shaking his head and muttering something I couldn't understand.

He told me that his brother was coming to see him tomorrow so he would be tied up most of the morning.

# Chapter Seventeen

# Marcus' Goodbye

Bobby Lee: Try as I might I just couldn't get the picture of young Becky's horrific ordeal out of my head. I kept picturing how terrified she must have been during those last minutes of her life; this pig of a human being, grunting and sweating while performing his vile acts on her little body.

Walking away from Marcus, after he finished telling his story was about the hardest thing I've ever done. He had gloated and smiled; his dick hard as he kept trying to adjust it, while I pretended to take pleasure from his rendition of what had taken place in the last moments of Becky's life. What I really wanted to do was to grab him by throat and rip out his Adam's apple, but then, maybe I wanted to gouge out his eyes first; castration with a broken bottle would have been good too, except I didn't want to touch his balls.

I decided that I had to act as quickly as I could. Having heard the story of Becky, I did not want to hear Marcus relate his gratuitous tale of his second hapless victim, Jenny and the similar sick, torturous ordeal she must have undergone. I'd looked up a few of the news articles about Regan's crimes on the computer in the prison library and found them sickening enough, without his excruciating details thrown in. I wasn't sure whether or not I could control myself not to strangle him in right there in the yard if front of the guards and other inmates if I had to listen to another of his sickening stories.

The image Regan had painted with his words wouldn't leave my mind. That coupled with the manner in which he bragged to me sweating and gloating, with his pants bulging from his excitement in reliving the crime. The more I thought about it the more it made me want to speed up my plan for his premature demise.

The suicide note was Butch's idea. It started as a joke because we never dreamed anyone would believe Marcus's death was a suicide. He'd tried way too hard to stay alive with the plea bargain, so we were just throwing the note in for laughs. Butch had done a little forgery in his past and I had a note from Marcus to use as a pattern. I told him that Jimmy Dale could get us some drugs and other stuff from the outside for a price. Just make a list and get it to me, so here I was with a sample of his handwriting, why waste it?

The note was short and simple, "I'm so sorry I have been such a hemorrhoid on the asshole of mankind." We looked at each other and laughed. "Maybe I'll be a better person in my next life. I pray that God might have mercy on me."

The last sentence came hard, associating God's name with this scumbag, but we decided, on the off chance the note was taken seriously, to put it in. It couldn't be a realistic suicide note if God's name didn't appear in it somewhere. God inevitably figures in when a remorseful suicide takes place. I don't know what made me think that; it wasn't from reading too much. You can bet your ass on that.

I met Marcus in his cell after Jimmy Dale had come by. He had slipped me a couple of pills he had hidden in his hair, just behind his ear. He explained that the pills would knock Marcus out about twenty minutes after he took them. I decided I would tell Marcus the pills were speed or some such thing to get us high. I planned to give him one and I would pretend to take the other and start acting like the pill was putting me to sleep. When the pill took effect on him I was going to strangle his sorry ass with the rope I had made. It would have been more rewarding if he had furnished the rope, but he hadn't come through with providing the *suicide* tool for me.

I think I mentioned that Marcus was a big boy, two-hundred twenty pounds or more. I guess that's why the pill didn't work quite as well as Jimmy Dale thought it would. As he started getting drowsy and the moment of truth was getting closer, I began to feel a little too cocky. I made my move just a hair too soon.

I just had to make him know what was taking place and why. When Jimmy Dale first approached me about this guy, I was ambivalent about him personally. The deal had appealed to me at first just because I was bored and it seemed like something to do. Now that I had the complete picture of what a cold blooded child molester Marcus really was, it *had* become personal to me. I wanted him to suffer for what he had done to Becky and Jenny. It didn't feel right that he should go peacefully, well sorta peacefully, in his sleep. I wanted him to experience some of the pain and terror he had inflicted on the girls he had tortured so heartlessly.

He appeared to be dozing, "Hey, Marcus, listen to me." He stirred and grunted. I had already placed the rope around his neck and had worked it thru the bars so that when I rolled him off the bunk he would choke from his own weight; hoping to make it look like he had done this to himself. "Do you remember Becky and Jenny? You're going to have a little accident for what you've done; time for you to pay, you worthless piece of shit, time to meet the devil in person."

Suddenly his eyes opened and from beneath his mattress he pulled out something sharp and struck me in the chest. He yelled "You fucking bastard!" and then fell back unconscious.

I didn't feel much pain at first, but then it was like I had been punched in the chest. I managed to roll him off the bed as I had planned and it worked. He was grunting in a sickening way…trying to breathe but unable to get any air past the rope around his neck. I had tied a hangman's knot so it wouldn't slip if he somehow had the wherewithal to grab the rope and try to loosen it.

Meanwhile I had this piece of plastic sticking out of my chest. My first impulse was to grab it and pull it out, but when I put my right hand around it and started to tug, I had a moment of clarity. Blood was flowing from my wound but at least the shiv was slowing the flow. I was kind of sitting on Marcus, keeping his arms under me so he couldn't reach the noose that was slowly stealing his life. It was a surreal moment, listening to him slip away as he groaned loudly trying futilely to get the elusive breath that would keep him alive. As his struggles ceased, he quivered slightly, and I slipped into unconsciousness.

The next thing I knew I was awake in the prison infirmary. There were tubes in my nose and my arm. I felt an uncomfortable feeling around my dick and realized they had even put a tube there. The pole next to my bed had a couple of plastic bags and a pint bottle of something hanging from hooks. Tubes running from each came together, meeting with a larger tube connected to a needle stuck in my left arm.

"Good morning, you're finally awake," a pretty young woman in a nurse's uniform smiled. "How are you feeling, Mr. Baker? On a scale of one to ten, how's your pain?"

Boy was she ever a beautiful sight, "Two, darling,'" I replied, just before I went back to sleep. I thought foggily before I blacked out that the prison did at least have some good drugs.

# Chapter Eighteen

# The Suicide Pact

Bobby Lee: By the time the hacks found me, I had almost bled out from where Regan had stabbed me with his homemade shiv. I had greatly underestimated his desire to live and his ability with the knife he had secreted in his bunk. He had missed my heart by less than an inch, but he had nicked an artery. A few more minutes of not being found, and someone else, probably Jimmy Dale or Josh would be telling this story.

Several days passed while I was sedated and strapped down; so I wouldn't tear anything loose, I suppose. I wasn't in any condition to escape, that's for sure. I seem to remember a lot of people coming by, looking at me, some speaking and asking questions that I wasn't able to understand. No one stayed long, I think the little nurse kept shooing them out.

I was beginning to have longer periods of clarity, but I didn't want to speak to anyone quite yet. After feigning unconsciousness as long as I could; I knew that I needed to get my story straight before I talked, I felt I was ready to tell my side to the cop assigned to investigate what had happened in Regan's cell that night.

He was distracted by the same pretty, dark haired nurse I had talked with after I awoke in the hospital. She wasn't giving him the time of day, but he couldn't seem to take his eyes off her; for that matter, neither could I once my vision cleared.

The cop's name was Thad something or the other. I can't seem to recall and it doesn't seem that important anyhow. I remember he had some really bad acne scars and an extraordinary large nose, laced with broken red veins. The nose also needed the hair trimmed from the nostrils. Let me tell you, he was damned disgusting to look at; all the more reason for me to keep looking at the little nurse.

Since I'd had some time to think about how to spin the unexpected turn of events before hand; I had intended for Regan's body to be discovered alone in his cell, I came up with a story that I thought might work. I figured it had a slim chance just because it was so outrageous. I explained to Thad that Marcus and I had made a *double suicide pact.*

"Double suicide pact? What in the hell does that even mean?" he asked doubtfully.

I knew I had to lay it on thick, so with a little catch in my voice, I said as sorrowfully as I could muster, "My friend Mark and I had decided that since we were both lifers, we didn't feel like we had much reason to live. It was sorta like being diagnosed with some kind of incurable disease, you know; like AIDS or somethin'…we were just awaiting the inevitable. So we decided to end it, but we were afraid that when it came down to the nut cuttin' one of us might back out."

"Really?" said Thad, not quite so disbelieving all of a sudden, but still doubtful nevertheless, "So you're trying to tell me that this was not a fight between you two, ending up in Regan's murder? Do you really think I'm that gullible?" he said this without much conviction. It was pretty vague as to whether this was meant to be a question, it didn't seem to require an answer from me, and so I didn't offer one.

"I hope so," I thought to myself. I could tell from his obvious confusion that as long as I didn't give too elaborate an explanation, I might be home free. After all, I *was* serving life in this California penal institution and even a person of average intelligence understood the psychological beat down that had to be. Thad was trying very hard to appear in control of the situation even though it was clear to me he was out of his element. I did my best to make him feel as if he grasped the situation in its entirety.

I thought to myself, "What were they going to do to me, give me a longer sentence? I already knew they wouldn't give me the death penalty for killing a child murderer. Hell they wouldn't execute the child murderer; how would it look to the public if they asked for the death penalty for me as a sentence eliminating a man the whole state had to hate? Thad didn't want to do a lot of unnecessary paperwork and no one up the ladder wanted to draw any more attention than necessary from outside the walls.

Helping him some more; easing into it, I looked him in the eye and said, "Why would I lie to you, Sir?" He seemed to like the ass kissing I was laying on him, so I laid it on some more. "I'm aware a lot of folks didn't think highly of Mark, but once you got to know him, he was really a good guy…a gentle giant. I'm going to miss him a lot. I'll probably try again to join him as soon as I can." The bullshit was really beginning to flow.

That seemed to strike a nerve in him. "Oh no, Baker, don't even think of trying to kill yourself again. You've got to find a reason to continue to live." Who the hell did this yahoo think he was, Dr. Fucking Phil?

After a while the nurse; I would soon discover her name was Mary Jane Moon, came over to my cubicle and told Thad to clear out. "Mr. Baker needs his rest. You can talk to him later. He's not going anywhere, you know."

Thad tried to protest, "I'm not finished interviewing this prisoner. He might have just committed a murder." I noticed he said this without a lot of conviction, though.

"I don't give a damn what he's done or what he's accused of, you get out of here right now!" Her dark eyes flashed as she said, "You can come back tomorrow to finish your investigation. That child killing murderer that died in his cell got just what he deserved if you ask me." She paused a moment and then added, "We nurses here at Farmdale are all glad he took his own life," then she looked at me and winked.

Seeing he was not going to win the argument, Thad tried to act like it was his idea to leave, saying gruffly, "Yeah, OK, I've more important things to do right now, anyway." Then he was out the door.

After Thad had vacated the chair next to my bed, Mary Jane gracefully sat down in the chair he had vacated and returned my stupid smile with a beautiful one of her on. I think I fell in love right then and there. I felt like a sophomore again. She seemed a little shy herself but not too much. I noticed an ugly burn scar on her left hand, which she covered self-consciously with her right.

She quickly recovered her composure saying, "Bobby Lee, I hope you don't mind me using your first name…er, names; what is it with you Texans and the two name stuff anyway? What you did was the most wonderful thing! That man, Regan, deserved what he got. Everybody on the ward is talking about it."

"That is a very sweet thing to say young lady but I have no idea what you mean. I ain't done nothin' except damn near die. How'd you know I'm from Texas?" I was laying the corn pone act on pretty thick for her. "Me and Ol' Marcus was goin' out of this life together. I really shouldn't even be here right now."

I had tried the good ol' boy routine, but I don't think I was very convincing since she was grinning at me so I changed gears and said, "Of course you can call me Bobby Lee, little darlin', what can I call you?"

That's when I found out this sweet angel's name was Mary Jane Moon. "And here you are giving me a hard time about having two first names," I said to her.

She laughed as she replied, "I'm just trying to make ya'll feel at home, only a Texan can sound like that; slow and twangy." She continued, "By the way, that's quite a story you're trying to sell, Bobby Lee, and I understand why you're sticking to it, but believe me, you've made a lot of friends here with what appears to be an assist with the early passing of Mr. Regan. A few of the usual bleeding heart people out there are trying to call it murder, but no one really gives a crap what those shitheads are saying. The more credible newscasters are putting a positive spin on your story. Pardon my gutter mouth, Sir."

"Come on; please just keep calling me Bobby Lee, no *Sirs* around here."

"There have been some people from National News trying to get in to see you, but the warden is doing his best to keep this thing quiet. He was doing a bang-up job of it until the parents of the murdered girls were interviewed this morning on all three of the major networks. You ever wonder how the same people can be on all three stations, live, at the same time? Anyway, there they were, telling their stories again about how Marcus should have received the death penalty at the time of his trial, but had gotten away with just being put in prison." She paused to take a breath.

"God, you're a pretty little thing." I couldn't help myself and she blushed and smiled at the same time. As drugged up as I was, I could still feel a stirring in my penile area; it felt good. It was then I noticed the catheter again, "Can we get this tube out of my penis sometime soon?" I turned red realizing my gaffe. "I mean do you have a male attendant or someone else who could do it?" It was becoming a real irritation all of a sudden.

I think she realized what was going on under the sheets, but she didn't seem too perturbed by it. She gave me a little pat on the thigh. "I'll ask the doctor about your tube. In the meantime I've got work to do, but I'll check back on you in a bit." She gave her butt a little twist as she walked away. I couldn't tell if it was for my benefit or not, but I was hoping.

"What the hell are you thinking, Boy?" I thought to myself, but I was feeling pretty good about my new found friend. The drugs may have helped a bit also. This was the best I had felt about life in years…love.

When she glanced back to see if I was looking, she saw I was and looked pleased that I was checking her out, "Bless you, Darlin'," I said while giving her my brightest smile.

# CHAPTER NINETEEN

# Mary Jane Moon

My name is Mary Jane Moon. I am a nurse. Chief Mathews, that is "Big Mike" Mathews, as he was known to everyone in town, had been the Chief of Police in Lewisville for years. Some say he had dirt on everyone of importance in this small city. He was the J. Edgar Hoover of his time and place, having taken the former FBI boss as his role model.

The only trait Mike had not followed while trying to emulate his imagined mentor was that he hadn't followed Hoover's semi-secret path as a cross-dressing homosexual, who publicly ridiculed the gay community. He was a much bigger man in stature than J. Edgar, but he did have the same bulldog look as his hero. He had a reputation as a man not to be trifled with. He held the reins of power in his domain and was not to be crossed.

Big Mike had driven by my house for the second time in less than an hour. He shined his spot light into my living room window each time he passed.

Ordinarily I'm not a jumpy person, after all, I work in the emergency room at Lewisville Regional Medical Center and moonlight as an EMT, but the chief had me scared, terrified even.

The nature of my work precluded dating anyone normal who worked normal hours, but a girl does get lonely. Big Mike's son, Matt was a younger, much more handsome version of his dad, tall and well built without the big gut of the older Mathews. Matt was a patrol sergeant on the city police force. Small town bureaucrats tend to look the other way where nepotism, at higher levels, is concerned. Many have sons or sons-in-law or other relatives and they might need a favor themselves one day.

Matt did have an Associates degree in law enforcement from Central Junior College, thus making him the most educated person in the department. This had made it an easier sell for Mike to get his son hired on his police force. There were rumors that some subtle pressure had been brought to bear on the city manager when he initially balked at Matt's appointment.

The push to bring him into line may have involved the threatened disclosure by the Chief of said manager's late night visits to his mistress, who also worked as the city clerk. Whatever had taken place it didn't take long before Matt was approved without fanfare. Shortly after receiving his diploma, he just showed up for work one day and was issued his uniforms, badge and gun.

In the course of events Matt and I encountered each other frequently, usually work related, when an accident or a shooting occurred. Our first encounter was at an accident on Power Road, when I showed up in an ambulance with another EMT to try to save a child who had been thrown from the back of a pickup truck. It's not uncommon in Wyoming to see unattended kids in the back of a truck while mom and dad rode in the cab.

The child's head had hit the pavement and appeared to have been forced into a sickeningly oblong shape from the impact. It was ghastly sight to look at, but at least the child was barely conscious. Matt had arrived in his patrol car, before our ambulance arrived. He was holding the child, a young girl in his arms, and though I could tell he was stricken by the whole ordeal, he contained his feelings while giving comfort to the whimpering child

I was impressed by his professional yet caring manner, since my interaction with some of the other members of the force had not left much of a positive impact on me. Lots of over-the-line sexual comments were made by the other officers when they were hanging around the hospital. All we nurses could do was to ignore their uncouth behavior so as not to encourage them. The problem was that some of the nurses encouraged the flirtations reinforcing their unwanted advances. So far, I had not been impressed by my encounters with any of the men-in-blue I had met.

After the child was delivered to the ER, I found myself standing next to Matt while we

both did our reports in the common office at the hospital. There's lot's of paperwork involved in the police and medical professions. The child was in the operating room, but her prognosis was good. We were both feeling pretty damn good about ourselves.

"Hell of a job you did out there, Girl," he said with a bright smile. I couldn't help but admire his even, white teeth. As a rule, dentists didn't receive a lot of patronage around here. Unless someone got punched in the mouth and broke a tooth in one of the many bar fights that took place in this frontier-like town, nature was left to take its course. In other words, nice teeth were not the norm on the local men.

"I noticed you handled yourself well, also." I was fumbling for words as I found myself feeling embarrassingly giddy. I had not thought much about the opposite sex since I had moved here. The crass guys I had encountered up 'til now did little to stir any feelings, other than distaste in me. Men had become something I could live without; besides I had other priorities that were much dearer to me.

Before moving to Lewisville four months ago, I had been married to a Shoshoni Indian, Danny Moon, whom I had met at nursing school in Casper. Check any statistics on the subject and you will find white girl, Indian boy marriages have rarely worked. At that period of my life, I was twenty years old and still a virgin.

I hadn't looked at the stats and it wouldn't have mattered anyway, I was in love for the first time in my life. Of course, I'd had a few boyfriends in school. We'd done some petting and a little experimentation but nothing really serious until now. I was so unsophisticated at that time in my life as I had just moved to what I considered, 'the big city" of Casper from where I had been raised, a small ranch outside of Ten Sleep, Wyoming.

My true love, Danny Rising Moon, he did not use the "Rising" as a middle name, considering it too "Indian", not that he was ashamed of his Indian blood or name, would say, "I've got to get along in the white man's world. Most of the white men hate us or look down on us so I don't want to make it any easier for them. They don't need another excuse to dismiss me."

Danny was not a big guy, he stood a couple of inches taller than me, around five foot eight, slender waist, but muscular. He rode broncs at the local rodeos in order to make enough money to continue his studies as a male nurse. He had placed in the top money in Cheyenne the year before and quietly bragged about that ride as the highlight of his rodeo career.

When I asked him, "How come you're not big, like other Shoshonis that I've seen?" he'd replied, "I think there's some Crow blood back in my family's past. Murdering rapists dog eaters! We were always at war with the Crow. Still are! They are a little people; that's why they're so damned mean." He had said this with a laugh. That's another thing that attracted me to him. Danny had a sense of humor, a trait that attracted me then and something I still look for in a man today.

He wore his shiny black hair a little too long, but not long enough to braid, as some of the other bucks wore theirs. He didn't like to be called a "buck", but I thought it was cute so he let me get away with it. His dark brown, piercing eyes, almost black, completed the package.

Danny's wardrobe consisted of tight jeans, western shirts that were not as gaudy as most, but were tailored to accentuate his nice triangular build. He finished his wardrobe off with tan deer skin boots and a cream colored Stetson hat. He looked like he was straight out of Hollywood, instead of the reservation. He made my heart race when I was with him. I never thought of him as inferior nor did I let the stares I got from the white guys when I was with him bother me. I knew I was cute and they were jealous.

He was fun to talk to when we went out bar hopping. He did have a tendency to drink too much, but we were young and I didn't give it much thought at the time. We had been dating for almost a year when we found out I was pregnant. He proposed without hesitation and I joyfully said yes; life was wonderful!

"I named her Alysha Willow," I told Danny when he came into the hospital room where I was nursing her. With a huge smile he came over and gave me a gentle hug, kissing me on the cheek.

"Sounds kind of Indian-like but it's a beautiful name for a beautiful child," he said with a proud smile.

Time passed. I finished nursing school and got a job at the hospital. I attended EMT school when I was able in order to get my certification. The town needed skilled medical team ambulance personnel and I felt obligated to help. Danny was content to coast along; riding in rodeos, doing odd construction jobs, and avoiding taking anymore classes.

Since our marriage the year before, I could see some unwelcome changes emerging in his behavior. He began to have a real problem with alcohol. Once he started he couldn't stop drinking until whatever he had was gone, all of it. If he had a fifth of whiskey or a bottle of wine, he would drink it all, fast.

"Danny, you've got to stop drinking so much," I would plead.

"I know, Mary, I'm really trying. I don't know why I can't leave it alone. Must be that Crow blood taking over," he would try to joke, but then he would burst into tears and sobbingly promise to try harder to stop. He would hold me tight; so vulnerable and contrite that I couldn't help but love him. My poor Danny Boy!

Things would seem to get better for a while, but then some friend of his would come by with another bottle and the cycle would begin again. Maybe his Indian heritage did dictate his behavior.

Drunken Indians, passed out and lying on the streets or sidewalks, were a common sight in town, especially around the first of the month when the government paychecks would arrive. In the name of helping the tribes, the Bureau of Indian Affairs had turned the Western tribes into a checker board of sovereign nations; each containing a large population of drunks.

The Indians in the northern states would freeze to death on their front porches in the winter, too drunk to open the door. Often frozen to the ground, crowbars were necessary to pry their cold bodies from the frozen pools of urine that cemented them in place. Cirrhosis of the liver and high blood pressure coupled with diabetes took another large percentage of the tribal members. Drinking and the Red Man were a bad combination.

The guys Danny hung out with, mostly Indians would inevitably gravitate to our back yard, build a fire in the fire ring he had built, and then proceed to get wasted on cheap booze. Whatever beer was on sale, usually Keystone or cheap wine, Thunderbird, Tokay, or White Port were the beverages of choice. Things would start off mellow enough, but soon their voices would get louder and louder. On most nights, after several bottles of alcohol had been consumed, angry voices would fill the night air followed by sounds of men fighting.

It was not uncommon to see a couple of cop cars parked in front of our house. Neighbors, tired of the racket, would phone in and complain. I didn't blame them, but it was terribly embarrassing for me. I felt I was acting out the proverbial walk of shame as I left the house in the morning to go to work. The only car we had was parked in the front yard on blocks with the tires and rims missing. It had been sitting there for weeks waiting for Danny to repair it.

The broken down auto often served as a guest bedroom for Danny's drinking buddies, passed out on the front and rear seats. As I walked along the sidewalk, I could see curtains being pushed aside as neighbors watched me passing by. I would be trying to hold my head up and appear nonchalant, as if nothing had taken place the night before.

Danny would sleep it off on the couch so soundly that I didn't even bother trying to wake him before I left for work anymore. I had to leave Alysha Willow with a sitter since I couldn't trust Danny to care for her, even though he wasn't working. He didn't even pretend to be searching for a job.

One of his seemingly endless friends might drop by and I had learned his priorities; taking care of Alysha Willow was not one of them. I was so damned unhappy, but I didn't know what to do. The broken promises made daily now by Danny were becoming tiresome. I felt like an old woman whose time was running out. Alysha Willow was all that kept me going. She had begun to walk and say "Mama". When I was with her, the problems of the world seemed far away, but never for long.

Danny was on his usual roll the night it happened. I was in our bedroom reading a story to our daughter while trying to ignore the din coming from the back yard.

"Apple Indian! Who the fuck are you calling an apple Indian?" I heard someone yell.

More loud voices followed as I lay in bed trying to keep Alysha from being frightened. There was a sound of someone struggling, some more and louder curses and then, "Let's get the hell out of here!" followed by more yells and strange crashing noises as several men ran thru the hedge that surrounded our back yard; then everything was suddenly quiet.

Sensing that this time something worse than usual had taken place; I ran to the door, turned on the porch light and peered out anxiously. I could see Danny lying in the fire, right in the middle of the fire, but he wasn't moving. I rushed out of the house and over to him, grabbed an arm that was not in the fire and started trying to drag him to safety. He was dead weight, literally. No one else was around to help me. The smell of burning flesh and hair was sickening as I struggled to get him free of the fire ring.

Danny had made no sound during all this time, even though he was on fire. "This doesn't seem right", I thought, in a panic, but I kept tugging until he was out of the flames. My left hand was hurting something awful. I glanced at it and saw the skin on the back of my hand had been burned away leaving a huge raw blister.

Alysha Willow was standing in the door screaming as loud as her little voice would allow. Everything seemed to be spinning around, but I was able to see the knife handle protruding from the back of Danny's neck, just above the collar of his smoldering western shirt. The point was showing where it had come out just below his Adam's apple. Suddenly there was no doubt in my mind; Danny Rising Moon had taken his last drink.

CHAPTER TWENTY

# Mary Jane Moves to Lewisville

Mary Jane: I left Casper right after Danny's death. I was not reluctant to leave this unhappy place. As Vice President, Casper's favorite son, Mr. Cheney had espoused policies that had cast a pall of distrust within me and many of my friends. Aside from all I had personally suffered there, I didn't want to remain in a city that placed such a high value on someone who held this cold man's beliefs. More and more people appeared to be leaving in each week. The hospital accepted my resignation without comment.

That's how I ended up in Lewisville. As I said, I couldn't stay in Casper any longer. The weather sucked and the memories were too painful to endure. The places we had shared when times were good, though few after our first year or so together, were stark reminders of Danny, my poor lost Shoshoni bronc buster. I left this cold and windy city behind in search of some relief.

There are some areas of this country where a half-Indian child would not stand out. So far I had not found that spot; but Alysha Willow and I kept looking. We headed further west to Lewisville. I found a job at the local hospital where I had been working for a few months when I met Matt.

As Matt and I spent more time together our fondness and respect for each other grew. The problem was, in case you haven't guessed, he had a wife. Don't judge us too harshly. Sometimes these things just happen and no one is really to blame.

Long before I arrived on the scene, Matt had found out that his high school sweetheart, Judy, was carrying his child. They had graduated from high school two months earlier. She'd hidden it from him until the beginning of the second trimester, too far along to get an abortion.

Judy had told Matt that she had gained some weight while working at McDonalds. He had no reason to suspect anything. He and Judy fooled around some in the back seat of his car, but had only gone all the way a couple of times. He wasn't sure he was in love, but there weren't a lot of girls to pick from in the small town. Judy felt the same way about her choices for boys. Matt was the most handsome boy in school and he had lettered in all the sports played at Lewisville High. He was the only senior headed for junior college in the fall.

Judy, in a calculated move, had gone to Big Mike before she broke the news of her condition to Matt. She had played them both like the proverbial Stradivarius, with uncanny precision. It had worked.

Matt and I were alone one night when he told me about the meeting with his dad. Big Mike had made his feelings clear as crystal, "You are going to marry that girl, Boy! I'll not have any bastard grandchildren roaming around town and I won't stand for any gossip about our family. You're going to do the right thing or I'll stomp the shit out of you and you'll still be getting married. We'll drive over to Wintersburg this weekend and tie the knot. We don't have time for a fancy drawn out wedding since from what Judy told me, the baby's not far away. We don't need to let this get any publicity. This could ruin my career."

Since he was a young boy Matt had always worshipped Big Mike. His dad wore a big pistol on his black leather belt. He always had black boots that were shined to a high gloss. As Matt grew older, it became his job to shine those boots and the other leather gear his dad wore.

Matt was happy to do these chores, as he dreamed of the day when he too would become a police officer like his father. All his life, he had worked tirelessly to gain Big Mike's approval; going out for all the sports available, football, basketball, and baseball, trying his hardest to excel, which he did, because he knew it pleased his old man.

When Big Mike gave Matt his ultimatum about the upcoming nuptials, he expected no argument and he got none. It wasn't in Matt's DNA to cross his father. He was upset that Judy had not come to him first, but she soothed him later that evening with the hottest sex he had ever experienced. She even gave him his first blow job…and she swallowed. Maybe this marriage thing wasn't going to be so bad after all; besides he wasn't seeing anyone else. He later came to realize the screaming orgasms Judy experienced that night were pretty much a one time thing.

He had not yet learned how cunningly Judy was able to manipulate Big Mike with the talk of "bastard children" and "public ridicule". Those were words supplied by Judy and repeated by Big Mike.

The marriage had gone off smoothly with the Justice of the Peace performing the ceremony. Big Mike had stood up as a witness for the happy couple. Later that evening in the Motel 6, as Matt tried to push Judy's head down for a repeat performance of the night before; he got his first lesson in marital bliss. "I don't feel like doing that right now," she had said as she rolled over with her back to him. "The baby's starting to kick my bladder a lot. I need to sleep."

His story brought to mind the old joke about why the bride smiles when she's walking down the aisle, "She knows she's given her last blowjob".

As things between us progressed, as we knew they would, Matt began to fill a void in my life that I had forgotten needed filling. He gave me comfort and he would bring presents for Alysha Willow, causing her to squeal with delight. That's probably a real weakness in single moms when it comes to relationships with men, be nice to my child, and I'll be nice to you. Other, more eligible men, and by eligible I mean single, didn't pursue me with the "baggage" of my half breed child thrown into the mix.

I'd decided that I shouldn't expect too much from Matt. He and Judy had a son who was now five years old. This grandson was the apple of his grandfather's eye. Big Mike spent as much time as he could spare with Little Mike. My guess was that Judy had shrewdly suggested the name in order to cement her position as matriarch in the Mathews family. Matt told me he had wanted to name his son Matt Junior but she held out for *Mike*, but then I am a suspicious bitch sometimes.

Matt had shared a lot with me in the last few months. He and his father were never as close as the bond between Little Mike and his grandfather. Matt had worshipped his father, but this strong feeling didn't go both ways.

Big Mike was pleased enough with Matt's successes at sports in high school and bragged as if he had played the games himself, but there were no hugs or any other kind of intimate father and son camaraderie shared between the two. Little Mike, on the other hand, spent hours with Matt's dad.

Once in a while when he became a teenager, a manly slap on the back had been rendered to Matt by his father but that was about it. His mother had left when he was four. He didn't know where she went or why she left. Once he had tried to question his father about it and was told, 'Shut the fuck up! It's none of your business. She never loved you or me." So he was left in the dark about his mother's whereabouts or intentions.

"What a prick!" I said to Matt when he told me that story one night as we lay together in my little house; nothing between us but the night air.

We were seeing each other once or twice a week. The sex was new and hot for both of us. We couldn't seem to get enough of each other during those early trysts. We had to work around each other's schedules. I didn't have much control over my hours, but Matt had some flexibility when it came to setting patrol hours for himself. I thought we were being discreet, but apparently not discreet enough. I was about to learn a hard lesson, in a small town such as Lewisville; secrets don't stay secret very long.

When Matt's wife called Big Mike, she was sobbing and barely coherent. I don't know who told Judy about me. Matt didn't take too much care in trying to hide what was going on, telling me he didn't care if she knew since they had been sleeping in separate beds for over a year.

Matt's cruiser parked in front of the house, or just down the street, late at night would probably be a dead giveaway all by itself. Matt didn't care about the repercussions, "If it weren't for Little Mike, I'd leave her tomorrow," he had told me more than once.

I wasn't really in the market for a husband or even a deep relationship at the time. Danny had only been dead a short time; it was more companionship for me than love with Matt. It's probably that way for most women who've had more than their share of trouble.

I was taken totally off guard when Big Mike came crashing into the house, throwing the door open and causing the glass to shatter. Luckily, Alysha Willow was at school, as it was early afternoon. I had worked the midnight shift the night before and had slept until noon. I was doing some house cleaning when he busted in.

With no preamble he spat out in an angry voice, "So you like to fuck cops!" he yelled as he grabbed me and threw me onto the couch. Besides my panties, I was only wearing a cheap flannel work shirt with the sleeves rolled up, no bra under it. I liked to be comfortable when I'm cleaning and I sure wasn't expecting company.

"Stop! What the hell are you doing?" I managed to yell at him. I knew who he was, having seen him around town, but we had never conversed. Even if I hadn't known him the police uniform was a dead giveaway. He didn't answer at first, just grunted like a pig as he continued to attack me.

While he held me down with one huge hand, he used his other to undo his belt and then push his pants down around his knees. Without missing a beat he ripped my panties off in one swift motion wadding them into a ball then using them as to muffle my screams by holding them over my mouth and nose. I felt like I was suffocating, but I continued to watch helplessly.

I was afraid to close my eyes. He grasped the front of the shirt I still had on and pulled down, hard, ripping the buttons off. With the buttons out of the way the shirt gaped open; he grabbed the back of the collar and pulled what remained of my last piece of clothing off me like he was skinning a rabbit. I was totally naked in broad daylight and totally defenseless against this huge man. I was appalled and scared shitless.

He spat into his hand and rubbed the handful of spit on his erect dick. "This will make it better for you," he said as his breathing was coming faster and heavier. His face was beet red and I hoped he would have a heart attack. My revulsion for what was happening to me was beyond description. I was in complete disbelief that I was really being raped by Matt's dad, a fat cop whom I barely knew.

When he tried to enter me it felt rough and raw. The spit he had rubbed on his cock didn't do anything for my dry vagina. Fear had caused me to clench up I guess. He backed off for a moment, licked his finger and rammed the sausage sized digit into me. I screamed in agony, despite the panties covering my mouth.

I could see his grinning face starting to turn into a grimace of sexual pleasure. "He's really starting to enjoy this," I thought through the fog that was starting to cloud my mind. His big gut began to pound me as his he drove his cock into me as deeply as he could; he had finally managed to achieve penetration. The pain was excruciating as he pounded harder and harder, crushing me under his weight. I felt like my insides were on fire and my vagina was being ripped to shreds.

I looked down and couldn't believe what I saw, my nipples were hard! What could that possibly be about? I damned sure was not turned on by this degrading act that was being performed on me. He saw me looking at my breasts, and upon seeing my erect nipples, he gave me a knowing evil grin, "You *do* like it don't you little lady? The old bull is much better than the young calf you've been letting mount you." He could hardly get the words out as his breathing became faster and heavier.

"Just let me die," I sobbed, but then I thought of Alysha Willow and that seemed to help me drift away; become disconnected, at least momentarily. The whole sordid act was probably over a lot faster that I thought, but it seemed to take forever, the grunting, sweating, pus gut pounding me made time stand still. I was in agony physically and mentally throughout the entire ordeal. I thought I would throw up at any second.

He finally ejaculated, emitting noises coming loudly and sickeningly from deep inside his big gross body; letting out a grunting moan that sounded more animal than human. After he had finished his vile act and regained his breath somewhat, he was still panting heavily. He continued to lay on me, his dead weight preventing me from being able to catch my breath. I felt that I might suffocate if he didn't move.

He finally pushed himself off with now trembling arms and stood up over me as I still lay on the couch. He stared at me with that bulldog face, his pants still around his knees. His penis had gone limp and shrunken, the head peeking out through his mass of dark pubic hair. If the circumstances had been different, I might have found his big clown-like appearance amusing. Instead, I tried to look away while my sobs continued. I still couldn't seem to catch my breath. I knew I needed a paper bag to breathe into to put an end to my hyperventilation, but I couldn't move.

He was calmer now as he began to speak in a more normal voice. "My daughter-in-law called to tell me you're a cop fucker; that you've been letting

Matt hump you for some time now. She's afraid she's going to lose her husband, but let me tell you, little girl, that ain't gonna happen! What just took place will happen again each and every day until you leave town."

He was pulling up his pants as he stopped speaking. The only noises to be heard were my sobs and his heavy breathing. He was not in the least embarrassed or perturbed as he shoved his balls and penis into his jockey underwear. After tucking his shirt tail in, he buckled his belt and made some more tugging adjustments to his crotch.

I thought it was strange at first when, I noticed he wasn't wearing his pistol, but then it hit me, he probably figured he didn't need any kind of weapon to assault a small woman. Besides it would probably get in his way while his pants were down. It occurred to me that he hadn't done this without first planning it. This wasn't simply a crime of passion, but instead it was a cold and calculated act. The realization of this scared me even more; I believed what he said about coming back.

After he'd finished putting his clothes back in place, he started talking to me again, "Now don't you be calling any of my boys at the office to try and file a complaint. The word is already out that you're a whore, especially for a guy in a uniform and your price is fifty bucks. I'm gonna consider this first one a freebie since you weren't that good. Maybe I'll leave a few bucks next time.

" If that doesn't deter you and you think you're tougher than me, I'm sure I can find some kind of illegal substance if I were to search you house; follow it up with a little pee test. I know Matt uses the stuff occasionally, and I'd be willing to bet you couldn't pass a piss test administered by your very own hospital."

On that count he was correct. Matt and I had smoked some pot he had taken from the evidence room. "They won't miss a few little baggies," he had said, at ease while we lit up.

Big Mike could see my uncertainty as he continued, "Your daughter might not fare too well in an orphanage, if you get busted for drugs. Heck, I might even adopt her myself. Raise her right, if you get my drift. Have a little brown sugar around in a few years." My heart sank; I could feel it. I always thought that was just an old saying, but I actually felt it sink into my stomach.

This asshole had thought of everything. The impact of these last words was worse than the degrading rape I had just endured. I was scared and helpless. "Just leave me alone." I could barely speak, but I had enough of my wits left to know I'd lost.

He grinned and said, "I'm going, but I'll be back tomorrow to check on you. I wouldn't be too unhappy if you were still here for at least one or two more days. I've always enjoyed new pussy and yours is mighty nice. Maybe I'll bring my handcuffs, oh… and a jar of petroleum jelly so it won't be so painful on us. My dick feels a little raw right now.

"You didn't get very wet for me. I wouldn't mind another go at it. New pussy always makes me come too fast. Maybe tomorrow that little cunt won't seem so new and I can last longer; especially if I take one of those purple pills." He was grinning now, getting into it, and I was afraid he was going to talk himself into raping me again right then. I had no strength left. It was like the time I was trying to drag Danny out of the fire, my muscles felt like jello.

I really started to cry then. "Just leave, get out now." I was trying desperately not to let him know how frightened and helpless I felt. My weakness was feeding his sexual appetite and I wanted no more to do with him.

My pleading finally seemed to work. He walked out the front door, got into his cruiser that he had boldly parked in front of my house, and slowly drove away.

Later, as Big Mike passed by the house for the second time, I nervously waited for him to get out of sight. When he had disappeared, I quickly loaded the few belongings I could carry in the car. What didn't fit would be left behind. These were just things and I could get more things wherever we ended up.

I was still shaken up, but I knew I had to act fast. I had taken a long shower, scrubbing and re-scrubbing every place he had touched me. I still felt unclean, but I worked quickly to get ready to leave.

Had it really only been a few hours since I had undergone the worst experience of my life? Even Danny's death had not affected me like this. Of course, I reasoned, this was an entirely different kind of pain. Complete and utter degradation. A thought crossed my mind, "The men who commit rape should be killed immediately; the degradation a woman feels after being sexually abused is akin to death to her. But then men had always made the laws and until women were running things, the men would continue to protect their own."

I didn't know where we were heading but I knew it had to be far from here. I had picked up Alysha Willow from the sitter on the way out of town. I had called to say I was running late. I didn't want to take the risk that Big Mike might show up again while my daughter was in the house.

I had taken the precaution of strategically placing some of my bigger butcher knives around the house in case he did show up again. I wasn't sure I could hurt the big bastard, even with a knife, and if I did manage to stop him, what would happen to my child if I were arrested? I was thankful that scenario had not come to pass.

We headed south and west, not stopping until I reached Jackson, where I hit the ATM for some traveling money. I had managed to save a few thousand dollars, at least I wasn't broke.

Two weeks later I was working in the hospital ward at Farmstead State Pen in Southern California. It wasn't the job I would have pictured for myself six months ago, but I was happy for the refuge I had found in this little town. I wasn't expecting much, just safety and solitude for my child and me.

The community was nice, a lot of Hispanic students attended Alysha Willow's new school, Benito Juarez Elementary, along with a few of the poorer white students. The more prosperous citizens of the town sent their kids to the private school. Tuition there seemed to be set just high enough to separate the classes without attracting the attention of the Federal agencies. The racial composition of Alysha's classmates helped her to feel as if she belonged and she didn't mind being in her beautiful light brown skin.

I had tried to bury a lot of what had happened, but there was a lot I couldn't shake off. I vowed to have nothing more to do with men, at least until Alysha Willow was a grown woman.

It was a year and a month later that I met Bobby Lee Baker.

# Chapter Twenty One

# Jacob "The Oak" Oakley, Attorney at Law

My name is Jacob. I was watching the morning talk show as I prepared breakfast for my girlfriend Holly and me. Our friends thought they were being ever so clever with their corny "Holly and Oak" jokes but that didn't bother us. We'd been living together for the past five years and I didn't mind cooking. My specialty was breakfast. We'd had an exceptionally pleasant evening the night before and it seemed that scrambling a half dozen eggs with chopped green onions, shredded cheese, and a few red peppers was the least I could do to show my appreciation. Screw the cholesterol, where's those hash browns?

Sausage was starting to sizzle and the pleasant smell was overpowering everything else in the house, including the kind of skunky odor of the pot we smoked last night. The smells made me feel exceptionally alive. I was thinking, "Thank the good doctors who finally managed to get medical marijuana legalized".

Since I've gotten my prescription from my golfing pal, Dr. Leonard, I swear my eyesight has improved remarkably. I stopped wearing my reading glasses after my first puff of this miraculous weed. Well, I still wear them when I read, but that's beside the point; I don't care what the AMA supposedly says, this stuff really works for me.

When I heard the name "Marcus Regan" I stopped and stood in front of the TV screen, giving my full attention to the pretty commentator, who was saying, "Regan's body was found in his cell at Farmstead State Penitentiary last night. It is not clear whether his death was a suicide or if someone murdered him. Our calls to the warden have not been returned but a press release from the prison stated, 'Regan is dead and we have no further details at this time'."

She brushed her blonde tresses aside and continued, "Another source who asked to remain anonymous has leaked that there is a 'person of interest' being interrogated in the case."

There was a picture of Regan on the screen now, the one taken when he had most recently been arrested for the murder and rape of the two teenage girls last year. He was shown being escorted into the courtroom by two huge deputies. "Those guys really should lay off the doughnuts," I thought to myself.

Next the screen flashed the mug shot of him from four years earlier when had been arrested for molesting the little neighbor girl for which he served three years of easy time. His appearance hadn't undergone much of a change between the first picture and the last other than he appeared to have bulked up later in the later pictures. He was still one ugly human being, I thought to myself, coarse features with a big head and neck. I shuddered to think of what hell his victims must have endured as he was ravaging them.

I had refused to have any dealings with Regan's attorney, Robert Marius, after the first time he defended Regan in the case of the six year old girl. He was an ambulance chaser in the truest sense of the definition. No case or client was too disgusting for him to embrace; child molesters, viewers of kiddie porn, rapists, incest, you name it. Marius would fight for his vile defendants and try with all his might to win. His firm was known to flaunt all the trappings of ethics and good taste in order to make a bigger name for itself.

How Marius got away with his slimy defense tricks was beyond me. He should have been disbarred years ago, but his political contributions were rumored to be large and diversified and on target. He didn't give a shit whether the candidate was Republican, Democrat, or Independent just as long as the money he doled out would purchase him influence.

The recipients of his campaign benevolence were careful to keep the contributions they received from him out of the public eye. The strings the pols pulled for him were always *sub rosa*. It appeared to work for him as he grew more and more famous as the go-to guy if you were guilty of a heinous or unsavory act.

Marius took some questionable cases; pro bono, but only if the client could get him some good press coverage. He lived to have his face on the evening news, but to meet his financial needs he relied heavily on the fat cat perverts who were caught in compromising positions with underage domestic help, nephews, nieces, or step children.

It was rumored that he cried in front of his law firm partners when he learned he had not been chosen to defend Michael Jackson in his most publicized case of child abuse. Regan said, while trying to hide his sobs, "That asshole he chose to save him was not nearly as proficient as I at handling these types of accusations. I offered to do it for my cost only, but Michael turned me down."

The Catholic Church had been very good to Regan over the last ten years or so, but he would only accept as clients the clergy that were *bishop grade* and above. These would-be men of God had enough clout and money at their disposal to discourage the Church from stepping in and trying to renegotiate his standard high fees. These offenders, scum to me, were what had made him the wealthy man he was today. They had become his bread and butter, and he knew all the tricks to get them off…so to speak.

Like most of the attorneys who defended child molesters and rapists, Marius would inevitably blame the victim for starters, that was rule number one in their unpublished manual. *Je accuse* was the foundation of their defense; their client was inevitably portrayed as the one who had been victimized. Bad childhood experiences or extraordinary temptation had caused him to react in an aberrant manner.

"Little Lacey's mom allowed her child to frolic in the nude, her little body glistening in the sun," was to have been used in Regan's defense, had the case gone to trial. An ombudsman acting in Marius' behalf had allowed Lacey's mom to get a glimpse of what she and her daughter would be facing, were the case to go public.

This sickening revelation had the desired effect for the defense. When the prosecutor asked Lacey's mom if she had any objections to accepting the plea deal he and Marius had devised, she reluctantly stated that she did not. She had been advised there were more tricks in Marius's bag if she did not accept the proposal. I found out about this from a law clerk I had befriended. Marius wasn't the only one with connections. This kind of underhanded chicanery made me despise him all the more.

You see it on the news interviews every week; the cries from the pundits and the wringing of hands as they raved, "Why was this animal allowed to be out of prison at all?"

"He should have been executed years ago."

"The jury that freed him or gave him a reduced sentence should all be ashamed to show their faces in public."

"Publish the names of the jurors and their addresses and where they work. Notify their employer that he has idiots working for him."

Of course this is not the proper way to expose the ignorant a-holes, but it sure seemed tempting sometimes.

Who's to blame? I guess everyone to some degree; from the self-righteous who would execute everyone to the naïve who would have allowed Hitler to live. I do my best to help keep things on a sort of even keel and consider myself an enlightened legal advocate for good; screwing with the bad and trying to help the innocent. That's why, with the more I learned of Regan's death; the more interested I became in the circumstances that led to his death.

I think it was three or so weeks later when a convict by the name of Bobby Lee Baker started making the talk show circuit from inside his cell. He was being questioned extensively about the death of Marcus Regan. The newsperson conducting the interview that I was watching kept implying that Bobby Lee knew more than he was telling.

Bobby Lee was quick and clever with his answers; I liked how he handled himself. When the questions turned to how he had come to be serving life in prison, he had some pretty good comments that struck a chord in me. He looked as if he could use my help. I decided I had to meet him.

Robert Marius had been Regan's lawyer and any enemy of either of these two was a friend of mine.

I am known as "The Oak" around the courtrooms and police departments here in California. I'm not sure if it's because of my size; I really do kinda look like a tree, I played offensive tackle for USC, or it may be that I'm such a hard headed son of a bitch. In either case, I fit the description on both counts; I'm big and I'm tenacious. I prefer to think it's the latter characteristic that gave me my nick name.

Although I had not contacted Bobby Lee Baker yet, I had continued following his case, along with the unusual death of Marcus Regan for the last week with more and more interest. I had a couple of cases that were taking some time to handle, but I kept Mr. Baker in my thoughts as I worked to clear my desk.

I had been sickened by what Regan had done to those girls at the time it happened and I was certainly not unhappy to hear of his strange demise so soon after he was incarcerated. I had disagreed with the plea deal he had copped initially. It seemed to smack of laziness on the part of the prosecutor and his department. I felt Regan should have faced a jury and been sentenced to death through the court system for his heinous crimes; even though I knew he would probably never be executed in this state.

My thought was that if Regan had gone to trial, at least a clear accounting would have been made public as to what a horrible human being he was. The acts committed on the girls would have been described in sickening detail. The proper sentence would have been handed down in accordance with the law, thereby sending a message that this kind of behavior would result in a death sentence for those who would commit such perverse acts.

But, who's to say? Maybe it worked out better this way; a message, however subtle or not, depending on your point of view, had now been sent…sex offenders might not have it so easy after all inside the penal system. What had once been a refuge for these scourges had suddenly become a place of retribution; at least in this case. The result of Regan's death and the following publicity, was at once more poignant than a decision handed down by the Supreme Court; justice had been served quickly and with finality.

A certain group of citizen activists had been crying out for Bobby Lee's head. I had to consider the irony of this, as this group who would have fought to insure that Regan did not get the death penalty, was now the very same bunch who was crying out for Baker's blood. I had little doubt that the vociferous citizenry who wanted to punish Regan's executioner could somehow rationalize the oxymoronic conclusion they had reached among themselves. "Don't kill the child killer; kill the killer of the child killer."

I have to admit his story was pretty damn weak, *suicide pact,* come on, but the fact remained Marcus Regan was dead, thus making Bobby Lee Baker a hero figure of sorts to a lot of new fans. He was especially admired by the parents of the young daughters who had been murdered. These parents had been guests on the *Today* show just yesterday, trying their best to cast Bobby Lee in a positive manner. "He was just a pot dealer, after all. Why on earth was he serving a life sentence?" was mentioned several times.

I had watched Bobby Lee on a couple of his television interviews and was impressed with what I had witnessed. He was a good looking, likable guy with the slow paced Texas drawl that while endearing to some, can be more irritating than a cat yowling to others. I was in the former group; his words came easy with a down-home kind of honesty permeating his sentences. There was, I must admit, a mysterious air that I couldn't quite put my finger on, about him; perhaps the stealthy way he moved or way his eyes seemed extra alert, missing nothing.

The second time that I saw him; Bobby Lee was appearing on the National Morning Broadcast through a remote satellite feed from inside the prison. Merry Martin, the regular host of the show had tried her best to come across as an intelligent news anchor, asking what she surmised were thought provoking and probing questions, but she had been made to look like an amateur before the interview was over.

"Bobby Lee, what was your relationship with Mr. Regan? Were you best friends or mortal enemies? A Pat Garrett and Billy the Kid sort of thing? How did you come up with this so-called suicide pact idea?"

Watching him without really wanting to be judgmental, I could tell Bobby Lee was lying through his teeth when he responded, "Mark and I...well," hesitatingly, "We were all each other had on the inside. He was despondent about what he had done to those girls; you saw his suicide note, and I couldn't stand facing a life sentence in prison any longer. We had no hope…no future left, so we decided to help each other and put an end to our misery."

Merry interjected, "Bobby Lee, what was the significance of the suicide pact? Were you afraid you wouldn't be able to end your own life? Afraid you couldn't go through with it when it came down to really…you know; killing yourself?"

Sarcastically he replied," Do you think you could end your life under the same circumstances, Lady? A dingy cell with no one you loved there beside you to comfort you?" All at once it came to me; he reminded me a lot of the character, Ryan O'Reilly in the TV series, "Oz", handsome and friendly looking, but in a subtly dangerous way.

Bobby Lee had caught her off guard. She paused for a moment, collecting her thoughts, and then she said, "There are some who say this was really no suicide at all, but a murder carried out by you with unexpected results when you were stabbed by Regan. There are also a lot of people out there who are less than saddened by his passing and are making you out to be a hero. How do you respond to this, Mr. Baker?" Suddenly becoming more formal after Bobby Lee's last cutting response.

"I guess people will have their own opinions as to what they think happened. I'd be pretty fucking…" suddenly the sentence was bleeped, but a couple of seconds too late. There was a fade out to a commercial while things got sorted out.

Merry was appalled; this sort of thing just didn't happen on the Morning Broadcast. When Merry reappeared on the screen she said sternly, "Bobby Lee, you must watch your language. After all, this is not HBO and I'm not Bill Maher!"

"You certainly are not Bill Maher," I spoke aloud to the figure on the screen.

"Sorry about that Merry; a few years of doing time can have an adverse effect on your vocabulary. Sorry too, Mom, if you're watching, I know you taught me better. I was just going to say that I've been investigated by several different law enforcement agencies, including the FBI, and found to be blameless in Mark's suicide. I'd have to be a pretty dumb son of a bitch, whoops; sorry again, I'd have to be pretty stupid if I were to tell you on national television that I committed a murder."

It was right after this statement that Merry Martin, famous news personality, really stepped on her dick, so to speak. She put on her most sincere face and waded in, "Having said that; Bobby Lee can you tell our audience how you really feel about receiving a life sentence under the three strike rule, for peddling marijuana? Do you feel the sentence is justified in your case? Will it help deter crime in the state where you are currently residing?"

That seemed to be just too much for him; he suddenly went ape-shit, yelling, "Jesus Christ, lady! Are you fucking nuts?"

The screen went blank; no more interviews with Bobby Lee were seen on television after that show. The next story to come on, after the commercial break, was about a beauty queen who fell on her ass while trying to navigate some slippery steps in spike heels. The shot showing where she fell, causing her dress to fly over her head, was shown over and over. Ms. Martin had to take a couple of days off starting right then. I've noticed lately in her broadcasts, she seems to take a little more time in framing her questions during her interviews.

Being a fancier of cannabis myself, I was intrigued when I learned that Bobby Lee had pulled a life sentence in California, of all places, for supposedly peddling pot. I spent the next three days reviewing Bobby Lee's case files including the court records.

The totally crazy sentence he had been dealt, coupled with the fact that the only persons he had been involved with in dealing pot, were undercover cops, only made me more interested in having a meeting with him. This likable young man who might be the killer of a scum bag child molester and sexual predator; well, I decided, this could well be a new and interesting project for me.

I traveled to Farmstead Penitentiary to meet him. I'm not being conceited when I say my reputation had preceded me. As is true in a lot of professions, the enforcement of the law and the trappings associated with it; the people and places that make it work, encompass a small world of their own in each part of the country. My region was Southern California; crooks, cons, cops, lawyers, and judges often interact with and watch each other.

Over the past decade I helped quite a few convicted felons; men I deemed to have been railroaded by over-aggressive law enforcement officers coupled with unreasonable prosecutors and judges with an axe to grind. I chose these cases carefully; looking for the underdog whose rights had been trampled; as opposed to the types of cases Robert Marius took. He liked the guilty guys that had money. Unlike me, Marius wasn't out for justice, just notoriety and big bucks.

When I want to show an example of what can happen in an unchecked judicial system, I need only mention the undercover narc that hit the panhandle a few years back and managed to incarcerate almost every black person under sixty years of age in a very small rural town.

It took a gutsy documentary by a major television investigative reporter to expose that pig-headed bounty hunter and the idiots he reported to. Did you know he never spent any jail time, although he caused so much pain to so many? Innocent people went to prison, lost their homes and their families while he merely lost his job.

I saw him being interviewed on TV again last year and he still showed no remorse or guilt for the lives he had ruined. I'm very surprised one of the folks he fucked over hasn't paid him back by now, in *spades*...maybe soon?

As I was saying, Bobby Lee had already heard of me. "Proud to meet ya," he said with his slow drawl coupled with that winning smile I had seen on TV. He was still moving sort of slow, from the knife wound I supposed, but otherwise he looked strong as a jungle cat, lean but muscular. Even with his injuries he moved in a stealthy manner. He looked like a man who knew how to handle himself if need be. "I have to admit when I got the word you were coming to see me, I was mighty curious. Are you here to help me, 'cause the Lord knows I could sure use some help."

I said to him, "Let's just relax and visit a while and get to know each other. Your case has gotten my attention for a couple of reasons. The first one of course is that you were the last person to see Marcus Regan alive. There seems to be a lot of suspicion in certain circles, especially pro-lifers, and by that I don't mean the anti-abortion crowd, that you might have had something to do with his demise." I could see Bobby Lee's usually alert eyes starting to glaze over, a defense mechanism of sorts, giving me an almost blank stare, with just a hint of distrust.

I spoke quickly, "Don't get the wrong idea, Bobby Lee, I'm not about to probe here. I just want to tell you that anyone who had anything to do with the death of that vile piece of shit is alright in my book. If there is more to this story than I've heard you say in public, I don't want to know it. I liked you immediately, and yes, I am here to try to help you. As far as I'm concerned the death of Marcus Regan is a non-issue here"

I could his eyes brighten and the trust in them re-emerge. There was something about this young Texan that I really "took a liken' to", as Roy or Gene would say.

"Tell me more about yourself," I said, warming up to the man who sat smiling yet unsure across from me.

# CHAPTER TWENTY TWO

# Bobby Lee Meets Jacob Oakley

Bobby Lee: After a couple of weeks in the dispensary, all the tubes had been removed from my arms and thankfully, my dick. The stitches were also gone and my scar was beginning to heal nicely. Sadly for me, I was sent back to gen pop. That was a hard day for me and I think for Mary Jane if I could read people at all. She gave me a brave smile and little peck on the cheek when no one was watching.

We'd spent a lot of time together during my stay, and there was some feeling growing between us. I would wait impatiently for her arrival each morning and she would flash that sweet smile of hers, lighting up the entire room for me. She had dark green eyes of a shade that's hard to describe, almost luminous.

God help me, I was falling in love while serving a life sentence in this joyless place. I didn't know which was worse; my life before Mary Jane being a no-hoper with nothing to look forward to, relying only on myself and my own thoughts, or the fact that I was now head over heels in love with a woman who was out of my reach, literally and figuratively. For the first time since I had been sentenced to life, I felt I had a reason to live and yet my despair was ever present.

She kept a close eye on me but, out of Mary Jane's protection, I had been interviewed by various agencies lately, due to all the publicity about Regan's suicide. The county cops wanted some publicity since the sheriff was up for re-election in a couple of months and Farmdale Penitentiary was located in the county.

The state of course had to flex their little muscle since it was a state pen after all. Even the Feds, including an FBI Agent; he said Agent Charles was his name, showed up, in their suits and ties, wearing their empty holsters and gun belts. Even the Feds had to check their guns, before being allowed inside the facility for a chat.

The investigators never stayed very long, probably missed their big pistols. I was never able to figure out the purpose of their visits, as they said little and I told them less. Oh, I talked quite a bit but it wasn't about anything real, while they were looking important by sitting and making a few notes in their little books then exiting. I suppose it made the investigation file thicker each time someone entered a new page. The thicker the file and the more it weighed probably made it look more important.

Agent Charles went through the shuck and jive of trying to be my buddy. I went along with him too, just because it seemed the easy thing to do, but I stuck to my story, adding nothing further that would incriminate me.

The biggest hue and cry was carried out by Regan's former lawyer, Robert Marius. "My client was paying his debt to society as prescribed by the law. No man should suffer the way Mark suffered." All of a sudden, it was "Mark this and Mark that" as the publicity seeking shyster put his face in front of every camera he could entice. Nothing was too sleazy for him. He had appeared on several talk shows passing himself off as an expert on protecting *innocent* criminals who had been wrongly accused! He seemed to have forgotten that he had entered a plea agreement for Regan which did not deny his client's guilt.

Lucky for me, I got a few interviews on my own and mine went better. I watched The Daily Show when I could and admired Jon Stewart a lot. We had to bribe the hacks to allow this controversial show to be viewed by us cons.

I had rarely seen him do anything serious, but I'll be damned he didn't send one of his "Chief Criminal Correspondents" around to see me and the resulting show didn't help Lawyer Marius' cause at all. Seems Stewart didn't like child killers anymore than I did. I'd had a small problem on the Morning Broadcast previously, but by then I had been exonerated, or at least Stewart didn't seem to care.

So there I was, lounging around the yard, bored shitless, when one of the guards comes over. "You're going to have a visitor tomorrow. The warden wants you to be cool or you could lose some privileges," he said very seriously.

Without a pause, I replied," What, he's not gonna let me stand around out here in the hot sun anymore? By the way who's the VIP that can get in to see me on such short notice and how come I don't have any say about it? I hope it's not another investigator looking into Mark's passing," I said more contritely.

"That high powered attorney, the one they call 'The Oak' set it up. He'll be here around nine o'clock tomorrow. Just you remember what I said; don't go sayin' anything that might piss the warden off. You've already had too much face time on TV, Lifer."

As he wandered off I couldn't help notice that the ass of his wool uniform shined like some kind of slick metal, the same kind of shine you see on the seats of bus drivers and cops in small towns. Guys that can't afford to get their pants cleaned more than once every few weeks. Jeeze, I was bored.

The Oak huh? I'd heard of him of course. He was a kind of legend among the California cons who were always looking for an angle *or a person* to use to improve their position. They were constantly searching for a way out; trying to beat the conviction that had sent them here, but I also knew that Jacob Oakley didn't waste his time on small time cons like me. I wondered if Marius was up to something, but that didn't jibe with what I had heard of The Oak. He was known as a stand up guy. Surely he wouldn't have any dealings with such a slime ball as Marius.

When we met the next day, I was edgy at first, but he put me at ease pretty quick. He was bigger than I even imagined. I'm a big fella, well above average anyhow, but he stood a good four inches above me and outweighed me by at least fifty pounds. He didn't try to be intimidating though. He seemed genuinely pleased to make my acquaintance as he gave me a big smile.

"Name's Jacob Oakley, call me Jake," he said as he held out his hand. He had a good strong grip when we shook hands. I always take that as a good sign, a good, firm handshake. I don't believe a person can fake one, even though I have met a look of old slicks who've tried. Their shake always seems to be accompanied by a phony smile; something just doesn't feel right, you know? I could sense that Jake was the real deal.

We sat down at a picnic table in the visitor area just inside the main facility entrance. There were no trees to block the view from the guard towers where the gun bulls watched what went on below.

The heavy white clouds provided enough protection from the sun to keep us from being too hot. We started to relax and make ourselves as comfortable as we could on the hard metal bench seats. I took out my cigarettes and shook one out. "Smoke?" as I extended the pack toward him.

"No thanks, I gave them up awhile back. Didn't have anything to do with my desire for a more healthful life style, just such a pain in the ass to try to find a place to light up. I found myself planning my outings around whether I could smoke there. You know, you can't even smoke in most of your friends' homes these days, without feeling like a real lowlife."

"Yeah," I agreed,"We kind of have the same problem here, but at least they let us smoke out in the yard."

"Talk about a state with influence, sometime around fifteen years ago, California stopped people from smoking in public places. Now you can't even smoke in bars in Europe! That used to be a requirement in the eighties, especially in France." He paused, "I guess a simple 'No thanks' would have been sufficient but I do like to talk, sometimes too much. Holly is always on me about it."

"Who's Holly?" I asked with genuine interest. Since meeting Mary Jane, my thoughts about women had returned, a lot. In fact and this sounds sort of fruity, but I found myself listening to the birds more and pausing to take in the sound of someone's radio when a love song was playing, I was noticing some beauty in the world lately that had been missing since my arrival at Farmstead ...plus I wanted to find out more about what moved Jake.

"She's my partner and my steadying force. We've been together for a few years now and it seems to work well. Every man needs someone behind him reminding him he is just a man. I think I read where Julius Caesar paid someone to follow him around and whisper that phrase in his ear, "Remember, you are only a man"".

There are a lot of big egos in my profession and sometimes, if we're not careful, we lawyers begin to believe the hype. Ever hear of F. Lee Bailey? His office in San Francisco was a shrine to himself and the cases he had won. In the old days it was a big tourist attraction, people standing on the sidewalk and peering in through his office window at the skull in his bookcase and the knives and other paraphernalia he had used in his many court cases. But he got greedy in his old age when he started believing what people said about how great he was."

After Jake had finished telling me about his Holly, he asked me to tell him more about myself. At first I was kinda at a loss. "Where do I start? You want childhood stuff? I grew up around Kaufman County over in east Texas and was poor like most everyone else there. It wasn't that long ago that we had an outhouse and a tin bath tub that we brought into the kitchen on Saturday nights where we all bathed in the same water. The bath water got pretty gray toward the end, when it was the kids turn to wash.

Our pets were stray, mixed breed dogs that got ran over on a regular basis. The boys and I would swim in the muddy stock ponds that we called *tanks* where we had to chase the cotton mouth water moccasins away by splashing water at them. As we got older, we would take .22 rifles and shoot them as they swam through the water with their big heads sticking up. Some fun, huh? The funny thing is I never heard of anyone ever getting bit by a snake, even though there were hundreds of them around. Guess it made us more careful." Josh nodded; a signal for me to continue, so I did.

"When I got old enough, I did a tour in Iraq and another, shorter one in Afghanistan. Compared to being raised poor in east Texas, the Mideast wasn't so bad and my practice at shooting snakes paid off. I am an excellent shot, if I say so myself, and blasting a few raghead terrorists didn't weigh on my mind too heavily after 9/11. But when my tour was up, I didn't even consider staying in the army; too much saluting and ass kissing in the service to suit me. We GI's summed it up in one sentence, 'The unable leading the unwilling to do the unnecessary.'"

"That's quite an interesting story, Bobby Lee; sounds like something out of a time warp, maybe the forties or thereabouts, but let's skip ahead. Tell me about your drug arrests upon arriving in California. Give me the details about what went down. I've looked at the court documents and something just doesn't smell right. I want to hear everything from you about what happened. If there is any legitimate way I can help you get out of here, I will, but I don't want you to waste my time with a bunch of bullshit either."

"Why are you interested in my stuff?" I had to ask "From what I've heard you're a busy guy and I'm a lifer here. I'm no big time operator in drugs or anything else for that matter. What have I done to deserve the attention of a man like you?"

He looked me straight in the eye, another trait I've always liked, and said, "I'm not implying you had anything to do with Regan's death and if you did, as I told you at the outset, I don't want to know about it, but I feel that you and I have the same feeling about what's right when it comes to bringing justice in the form of a real shit storm to ass holes who would harm children. I think if the opportunity had arisen where I could have hastened Regan's end, I probably would have done so. Let's just say that I feel I owe you one for Regan and his sorry excuse for a defense attorney, Marius," he said with a grim expression.

"Jake, I'm not a real smart man and I trust people way too easy. Even after being a convict here, I still look for the best in folks most of the time; with the exception of one dead man of course. He told me a story about…never mind, he's gone. Anyway, back to the trust thing and my first arrest." I began my story

# CHAPTER TWENTY THREE

# Bobby Lee's First Conviction

Bobby Lee: As I was remembering my first meeting with Earl Feathers at Joe's Bar in Barstow, Jake took a leather notebook from his jacket and a pen from his shirt pocket. He nodded at me with a slight smile, silently assuring me with his look that I was in capable hands. He said, "OK, Bobby Lee, let's hear what you've got."

I began, "It was hotter than hell outside and I had just rolled in from Texas via Arizona. The air conditioner in my car had given out somewhere the other side of Kingman, and I was feeling dizzy from the heat. So what do I do, but stop at the first bar I spot. It looked like a working man's place with painted over windows you couldn't see through…my kind of place, so I entered the darkened room.

"Over to the left was a beat up bar, with several beat up looking customers being served by a tall woman, with heavy arms and heavier breasts hanging loosely under a blue tee shirt. The shirt she was wearing had writing on it proclaiming 'Beauty is in the eye of the Beer Holder'. She wasn't smiling as she asked, "What can I get for you?" in a matter of fact kind of way. Like I said before, 'My kind of place.'"

"'I'll take a Coors please,' while putting a crumpled five dollar bill on the bar. I wasn't looking or feeling very prosperous. I fit in quite well with the beat up looking crowd.

"A scruffy guy dressed in filthy striped bib overalls that covered his fat belly and a tank top that revealed way too much back hair, was sitting down the bar a ways staring at me, not especially friendly like, giving me *the look* you know. His arms were resting on the bar at an angle which allowed a view of his elbows from where I stood. They were stained and crusty, a dark gray leaning toward black, probably from the ingrained dirt and grease that had been ground into them over the years.

"He was wearing an old faded ball cap that contained as much dirt and grease as his elbows. I thought to myself that he must be a shade tree mechanic of some sort. I had seen those same kinds of elbows many times back in East Texas over the years, in shops where the only hand cleaner was a pan of gasoline. Years later, the thought of them still caused me to give extra care to scrubbing my elbows each day. Funny what sticks with you sometimes. These guys always seemed mad at the world, you know? Don't wonder though; always dirty and smelly with grit in all the wrong places.

"'Scab beer!' this same guy snarled as the bartender set the bottle on the bar in front of me. I'd heard Coors called this before and I still didn't know what it meant. Something about unions I think. Although I didn't understand what he was driving at, I could feel an insult had been made toward me so I looked him square in the eye.

"'Do what?' I growled. We both knew it wasn't a question. He looked me over again, a little more closely this time and I could see by the sudden look of comprehension in his beady eyes that he knew he had misjudged me. I clearly wasn't in the shit business, I didn't give it and I damned sure didn't take it.

"He muttered something under his breath trying to save face, drained his glass of whatever he was drinking and left the bar with a half assed swagger, as if to say, 'I won'. Everyone else in the bar knew the truth; his bluff had been called in just two words.

"A guy sitting to my right spoke up, 'Hey Brother, my name is Earl Feathers, nice work,' he said with a friendly smile. He had long hair, a scruffy beard, both showing some streaks of gray .The leather vest he was wearing over a black tee shirt sported some patches sewn on by hand. The patches looked mostly like veteran stuff, but nothing that signified him as a gang member. He was sitting on a bar stool next to where I was standing. I hadn't felt at ease enough to take a seat yet, so I remained on my feet, just in case.

"Kinda hot for a leather vest, I thought to myself, but I gave him a nod letting him know I was friendly.

"He said, 'I like the way you handled yourself there, Hoss. Very understated but you got your point across. Everyone knows that Wilson is a total dick. I didn't catch your name?'

"When I told him it was Bobby Lee, he grinned and said in an exaggerated southern drawl, 'Ya'll must be from Texas, I reckon.'

"I wasn't sure if he was fucking with me or just trying to be funny so I replied, 'Sho nuff, pardner'.

"He was talking in a friendly tone, 'I'm not jerking your chain. I was raised in Deming, New Mexico. I can't make fun of anybody.' I guess he could see my puzzlement and was quick to put me at ease.

"I decided it was OK to sit down, do I did. When I had almost finished my beer, Earl ordered another round. 'Let's both have a shot of whiskey with those beers, what say? I'm buyin'.'

"'Why not?' I said. I was in no hurry to face that heat again. We started talking and drinking and then more drinking and more talking. We covered all the topics of growing up in a small farming and ranching community, hauling hay, chasing girls, trying to wrestle them out of their tight jeans without much luck. Seemed like growing up in small town New Mexico was a lot like life as a kid in the small towns in Texas."

Oak said, "That kind of world is totally unfamiliar to me. I grew up in San Francisco."

I continued with my story, "It seemed like time had flown and before I knew it the sun was setting and between the beer and the shots, we were getting pretty wasted. The guy with the ugly elbows, Wilson I remembered, had come back and stuck his head in the door, but when he saw me sitting with Earl, he must have changed his mind about coming in.

"'I've gotta be hittin' the road while it's cool,' I said.

"Earl looked a little sad, 'Where ya' headin'?'

"'I heard there's some jobs over on the coast and I need to make some money and fast. I'm about broke'" My words were coming slow on account of all the booze and as I stood up, I stumbled a bit.

"'Why don't you come on over to my place and have some dinner? You look like you might have had a little too much alcohol for you to be trying to drive tonight. You can hit the road in the morning after you get a good night's sleep.

"'My girl, Janie, is making tacos, and she always makes a butt load of them. There's plenty and it's no trouble. I'm having a good time shootin' the shit with you about old times and all. You know, most of these prunies think they're too good to talk with folks like us.'

"I had taken a liking to Earl too. He seemed like my kind of people and I've already mentioned how easily I come to trust people if they appear to be OK.

"I followed Earl in my car as he drove through town and out in the country a ways. His place was more of a shack than whatcha' might call a house but I wasn't picky and Earl was right; I really had no business driving after all the booze we'd put away.

"Janie was in the kitchen sweating over a pan, frying tortillas. It all smelled good and the swamp cooler was helping a bit with the heat since the sun had gone down. She was wearing cut off jeans, really short, and a pull over blouse and no bra. She looked to have some Mexican blood, you know, dark brown eyes, long shiny black hair, and nice slender legs. I figured she was in her early twenties and really quite a beauty. 'Lucky Earl,' I thought to myself.

"As I looked at her, Earl introduced us, 'Janie, baby, this is my new friend Bobby Lee. He's from Texas.' She seemed to be shy and looked at the floor.

"'Pleased to meetcha.' She spoke in a very low voice and seemed a bit beaten down by life, you know, a beautiful girl but not real perky. Earl didn't seem to notice as he went to the fridge and grabbed us a couple of beers.

"'Let's sit on the porch where it's cooler while Janie gets things thrown together. She doesn't like any one to help in the kitchen, you know. She has her own way of doin' things.

"'You know Bobby Lee, a guy like you doesn't come along everyday,' Earl was speaking to me as we sat outside slapping at the bugs that were buzzing around our heads. 'You say that you need to make some money and I just might be able to help,' he continued. 'We might be able to help each other, in fact. You appear to know how to handle yourself and I could use a partner on a deal I got workin'. In the short time I've known you; I can tell you're a cool dude. You seem to have your shit together.'

"'Sounds interesting, I don't have anything definite going right now. What kind of deal are you talking about?'

"He looked at me kind of suspicious like and asked, 'You're not one of those bible thumpers that thinks marijuana is a dangerous drug, are you? 'Cause if you are, we need to end the conversation right now.'

"You know Oak, I've smoked my share of weed over the years, even though Texas laws are ridiculously strict when it comes to possession of pot, so I said, 'No way Earl, I like weed as much as the next man. Have you got some?'

"'No, but I plan on getting some tomorrow. That's where you come in. I need a driver; one that the dealer I'm about to see won't screw with, a tough looking guy like yourself.'

"I think I failed to mention that Earl's a little guy, probably a hundred and forty pounds or so and not more than five seven, early forties. He doesn't look intimidating at all. 'Are you a narc?' I asked. I heard that if you ask a narc if they're an undercover cop, they have to tell you. Boy, I hear and believe some funny things.

"'Narc! Are you nuts! Janie, Bobby Lee wants to know if I'm a narc!' Earl yelled into the house. Apparently Janie hadn't heard him, I figured, since she didn't respond. I didn't notice at that time, he hadn't really answered my question. Tell me Jake, do narcs really have to tell you if you ask them?"

Jake had been quiet up to now, "Come on, Bobby Lee, think about what you're asking," he'd said.

"Earl said, 'I can put two grand in your pocket for a few hours work, but you have to trust me.'

"Before I could answer Janie yelled from inside the house, 'Tacos are ready'."

"'We'll talk about this later,' Earl said as he got out of his chair and moved inside.

"The idea of making a quick two grand sounded pretty good to me and besides Earl seemed like a good ol' boy, just like a hundred other good ol' boys I'd known over the years. What did I have to lose? All I had to do was look like a man you didn't want to fuck with while Earl made his deal. This would be a piece of cake, I thought, 'I'm in,' I said to his back as he entered the shack.

"The tacos were delicious, better than any I'd ever had in Texas, and after a few more beers to wash them down, I could barely keep my eyes open.

"'There's a little bed in the spare room out back,' said Earl. 'Why don't you get some sleep and we'll talk about our deal tomorrow.'

Jake was still listening and nodding occasionally as I continued my story.

"Janie had hardly spoken during the meal. She kept her eyes on her plate and picked at the food while Earl and I had eaten a half dozen or so tacos each, chasing them with cold beer. I complimented her cooking several times and she would say thanks in her small voice, but that was all. She didn't join in our conversation choosing to withdraw into her own thoughts it seemed.

"During the night, I heard Earl's cell phone ring several times and I heard him talking in a muted voice so I couldn't understand what he was saying. I guessed he was setting up the pot buy. The more I thought of the two thousand, the better I liked what was happening. I was starting to feel some excitement about it all but I was drowsy from the belly full of beer and tacos so I fell back to sleep pretty fast. Earl's phone calls were no longer an issue to me.

"The following morning I woke early, as I usually do, and went into the kitchen to see if I could find some coffee. Earl had a timer on the pot that had kicked in and I could smell the coffee when I entered the little kitchen. I poured a cup and sat at the table after grabbing a cold taco from the fridge. Damn, those were good tacos; even cold they were still good.

"Earl came in wearing the same shirt and vest from the night before and said, 'Good morning.' He proceeded to pour himself a cup. Looking at me he said, 'Well, what's the word, Hoss? Are you still in?'

"'Sure, why not?' I replied in my most agreeable tone. 'Let's make some money.'

"He smiled, drank his coffee with a cigarette, no food for him; and a few minutes later he stood up and said, 'Let's do it then.'

"Earl drove his car and again I followed him; this time back into town. He parked his car by the bar where we met and got in with me. We drove around a bit before turning down a dusty alley where we parked behind a wooden fence. That was one sorry assed neighborhood, let me tell you. I think almost every yard we passed had a Rottweiler or a pit bull trying to tear the fence down as we drove by. No way anyone could sneak up on a house here. I reasoned that the loud barking along with the sound of large claws scratching the wooden fences was a strong deterrent to prowlers.

"Earl told me to park in the alley behind a dumpster that was full to overflowing with assorted smelly garbage. As I did so, a weathered gate in the fence across the alley opened and a hand motioned for us to come in.

"Earl tucked a small revolver into the back of his pants trying to hide it under the shirt and vest. 'I wasn't expecting any kind of weapons being involved in this, Earl,' I said losing some of my usual bravado. Guns under these kinds of conditions tend to make me nervous; this was a lot different than being in a battle zone where everyone had a weapon.

"'Relax, Bobby Lee, it's just for looks. Everything will be fine,' he said, suddenly exhibiting more self-confidence than he had shown me up 'til now. I followed him into the yard and then over to a storage shed where four hard looking Mexicans were sitting at a table drinking beer and smoking. There was an open bag of tortilla chips and a jar of salsa on the table.

"'Hey, vato!' yelled Earl with a smile. 'Mi amigos, como esta?'

"'Bien, bien'" replied the biggest guy of the group. He was taller than Earl even while sitting down. He had a scarf of some sort tied around his head, and he sported a lot of homemade tattoos. He looked mighty dangerous to me and I began to wonder if I had fucked up by agreeing to participate in this. Everyone seemed friendly enough though. As the mood continued to lighten while banter and bull shitting continued, I began to wonder why I was even here.

"The big guy gave an Earl a canvas gym bag that had UCLA printed on it. Earl gave him nothing. Looking back, that probably should have been some sort of clue for me, but it wasn't. A few more words were passed around. No one offered us a beer or chips and we left with the bag.

"When we got back to my car, Earl handed the bag to me, saying, 'Put this in the trunk'. I stowed the bag under the spare tire figuring no one would be looking for it anyway. After I'd done that, we drove back to the bar to get Earl's car and hopefully, my money.

"'What next?' I asked, hoping we were close to being finished with our deal. Earl had been uncharacteristically quiet ever since we left the alley. He got out of my car and headed toward his, saying, 'Follow me back out to the house and I'll get your money.'

"'Cool,' I made a U-turn and started to follow him. I let him lead the way 'cause I still wasn't sure of my way around town. As I sped up to catch him I glanced in my rear view mirror and spotted a patrol car with its lights flashing. As I pulled over, two more sheriff department SUV's and an unmarked unit boxed me in. Earl had disappeared.

"'Put your hands on the wheel,' said a voice over the loud speaker, so I did just that.

"Three sheriff's deputies approached me with pistols drawn. 'Get out of the car slowly with your hands in the air!' Again I did what they ordered. Driver's license and registration were requested and produced.

"Then when I heard, 'Open your trunk,' it became all too clear to me what was taking place. 'You have the right to remain silent...'

"Later when facing the deputies who had taken a full kilo of marijuana from my car I was scared shitless.

"'If you'll cooperate, we can plea this down to a much lesser charge than trafficking,' I was told by a deputy with sergeant stripes on his shirt sleeves.

"'What do you want to know, Sarge?' Hell Jake, I was only too willing to cooperate."

"'Where'd you get the stuff?' he asked, but he didn't look like he really cared what my answer would be.

"At the jail I was led into the Sheriff's office wearing handcuffs and leg irons. The deputies must have thought I was one bad dude. Sheriff Bailey introduced himself and a Federal Agent named Byron who was sitting off to the side playing with an unlit cigarette.

"'Well, Mr. Baker, it appears you have run afoul of my deputies during your shot stay. We've got a big drug problem around here that we're trying to resolve. Can you help us out?'

"I tried to cooperate, I really did, but when I guided the deputies to what I thought was the yard with the shed, the little old Mexican lady who lived there kept saying, 'No comprende, no comprende.' No luck there.

"I even managed to direct the deputies to Earl's place. In the bright light of day, it appeared that no one had occupied the house in years. I could still detect the slight odor of tacos though. No one else seemed to notice however, so I began the journey to my first stint in the California penal system."

# Chapter Twenty Four

# Prison Friends

Bobby Lee: I continued telling Jacob about how I got where I am today, while, from time to time he shook his head in apparent amazement. "When I appeared before Judge Otis Gray, Edward, my attorney, had already advised me to plead guilty. 'Come on Bobby Lee, you were caught red handed with a full kilo of marijuana in the trunk of you car. How can you possibly plead any other way?'

"Edward could tell I wasn't happy with his advice, so to put me at ease, he added, 'I made a deal with the prosecutor, who by the way is a real good friend of mine. I guarantee that you wouldn't be able to get this kind of offer with any other lawyer representing you. All you have to do is plead guilty of possession for your own personal use and, since this will be your first conviction, you'll be out in a year, guaranteed, maybe less for good behavior!'

"Edward seemed pretty proud of himself for the deal he had struck with his prosecutor buddy. I was tempted to slap that smug look off his grinning face, but I held my temper and tried to assume the most positive posture I could muster under the circumstances.

"I knew he was right, even though losing a year of my life and being tagged as a convicted felon was not too appealing. I'd had time to think about the consequences and of course, the jail bird would-be lawyers with all their free and useless advice had instilled an even further sense of dread in me. 'This county is known for harsh drug sentences,' I was told that more than once by the several senior *law experts* who were also incarcerated in the big holding cell. If they were so fucking smart why were they in here with me?

"The court room was sweltering as we waited for Judge Gray to arrive; the small window AC unit could not start to cool the hot heavy air in the courtroom. Joe's Bar was the only place I had found in this town that was cool enough to be called even remotely comfortable. After making everyone wait a sufficient amount of time, probably to assure us that he was earning his salary, the judge entered the room, took his seat behind the bench, and proceeded to glower down at us all, both prosecution and defense.

"Sweat was beading on his high forehead as he wiped at it with a soggy handkerchief. His black heavy robes reminded me of the burkas worn by the women I had seen while serving in the Middle East. I saw a lot more of the heavy garments in Baghdad than I did in Afghanistan, but from what little I could see, the women wearing them all looked as if they were wilting. The judge had the same kind of look about him.

"'All rise'!" the bailiff ordered and that was when it hit me, 'I'm totally fucked and even my daddy, if I had one, can't help me now!'

"Edward and the prosecutor, Warren Knight, approached the bench. Knight was another one of those assholes you can spot immediately and know he's a real wormy sort; you know, like Snidely Whiplash. He was way overdressed for this hearing; vest, tie, and his black shoes were shined to such a high sheen they appeared to be made of patent leather. Quite the peacock, with his hair combed in the new style, which meant that it looked like it had not been combed at all, sticking straight up and going in all directions,  held by some kind of heavy pomade or hair spray.

"The two attorneys, the *fuckee* and the *fucker*, I called them under my breath, were all affable and preening in front of the judge. They were trying to out do each other in really kissing his ass. They hadn't had to do too much work on the case and this deal was about done. Judge Gray, dour in contrast to Frick and Frack, listened to their proposal, shook his head a couple of times then nodded and sent them back to their seats.

""'How do you plead?' he said looking at me while Edward whispered for me to stand up, but the whisper was so mumbled and low that I didn't catch what he said at first.

"The judge spoke in a voice that matched his outward demeanor, tired of it all, life, court rooms, finagling lawyers and would- be dope dealers. 'Stand up when you address the court,' he snarled. I quickly realized what Edward had been trying to tell me.

"Rising hurriedly I managed to reply, 'Guilty, Your Honor,' with a dry mouth and a nervous raspy voice. I felt like I wasn't able to swallow, choking on my dry tongue. The sentence was pronounced without fanfare and was just as the two men had agreed. I was led away to spend the next year of my life in prison. Little did I realize, what had just happened to me was the beginning of a trend."

Jacob had been listening intently and without interruption to my story as I laid it out. His frown deepened as I described the events of my first meeting with Earl at Joe's Bar, then later in the evening at the house with Janie. The house that later turned out to be deserted. I reiterated that I'd gotten pretty drunk at the bar with Earl, and then followed the booze up with the pot and tacos and more beer. I probably could have been sleeping in a barn and would not have noticed. We'd hauled ass early the next morning and my head was still pretty fuzzy.

"Sounds to me like you were set up from the get go. They were looking for a pigeon and it turned out to be you, wrong place and wrong fucking time for sure!"

He wasn't telling me anything I didn't already know, so I continued with the rest of my story, "Eight months later, I was on the streets again; early release for exemplary behavior, they told me. I had no car; mine had been taken by the cops when I was busted.

"When I asked about it at the sheriff's office, I was told by a fat deputy, 'You've gotta be shitting me pal, that piece of crap was confiscated and sold in accordance with California drug laws. Evidence seized in conjunction with a drug bust automatically becomes the property of the arresting agency. You're lucky we didn't charge you impound fees while we had it in our yard.'

"'You'd be trying to get blood out of a turnip, asshole,' I'd snapped back. He looked up with a red face and reached for the baton hanging from a loop on his belt. He rose from his wooden chair and started to come at me from behind the counter, so I made a hasty exit.

"My brother, Jimmy Dale, had sent me a couple of hundred bucks to get me by. 'I'll try to get out to California to see you as soon as I get a chance,' he had written, but I knew he was too much into his own usual funny stuff, trying to make a few bucks where he was, to come see my ex-con ass. So I caught a Greyhound to San Diego to hook up with Tom Kidd, a fellow con I met while serving out my time at Farmdale.

"Tom'd gotten out a short time before me, but told me to look him up when I made it to the outside. We'd gotten along pretty good together inside the walls. My first week in the big house, I had been jumped by a couple of Mexican mafia dudes. I'm still not sure what they wanted as I didn't have anything of value and the Mexican's weren't usually into raping men; they were probably just fucking with the gringo.

"You know Jake, I could never understand why so much butt fucking went on the in the pen. The professors on TV seemed to think it was because the cons were deprived of women. Well while I was stationed in the Mideast, we soldiers were all deprived too, but we didn't run around trying to sodomize each other. Maybe it was the guns we all carried; naw; I just never had the urge to stuff my dick up another man's asshole. I think the psychologists or whoever it is that comes up with these shit theories doesn't have a clue about what they're talking about."

Jacob looked at me with skinny eyes, "Can we get back to your story and stop pontificating about men fucking each other?" he said dryly.

"Oh, sorry, yeah, well Tom had come upon the fight just as I stuck my trigger finger into the eye of one of the guys that I had in a headlock. He was screaming and rolling around on the ground with me while I was trying to pop his eyeball out. I could feel the back of his eye and it occurred to me how smooth and round it was, just like my buddy Josh told me years ago in Texas; like pulling the gizzard out of a quail while gutting it.

"Meanwhile the other Mex was yelling somethin' in Spanish while trying to hit me in the back of the head. Little did he know that he was wasting his time trying that without a pipe or a brick. I'd been in a lot of good old fashioned street fights in the past and knew the back of my head is not my weak spot. He wasn't hurting me as I continued to fuck up his buddy with my finger, now jammed in his eye socket all the way to the knuckle."

"I didn't know you could that," said Jake with an incredulous look on his face. "That must hurt like hell."

"I guess… I wouldn't know since no one's ever done it to me. As I was saying, Tom walked over rather calmly and kicked that other fucker smack in the mouth with his Doc Martins. A few teeth went flying, along with a lot of blood. That vato curled up in a ball while putting both hands over his mouth, blood streaming through his fingers.

"It was obvious he wanted nothing more to do with either of us. The one that I had been working on now had his left eyeball dangling out of its socket where it was resting on his cheek. He was holding his head real still in order to keep the eyeball from swinging around. A sort of a whimpering sound was coming from him. He didn't seem to want to continue the fight either.

"This was my first meeting with Tom Kidd as he reached down, grabbed by hand and pulled me to my feet. 'Thanks,' I said, 'Name's Bobby Lee. What's yours?' We walked away before the guards caught wind of what had happened.

"Tom and I were pretty good buds after that. I covered his back a few times when someone tried to jump him and he had mine when someone tried to fuck with me. We'd hang around the yard smoking or pumping iron.

"I often wondered who the brain trust was that had come up with the idea of furnishing weights to cons. After a few months or years with nothing to do but lift weights, most of these guys could get out and kill the average man with their bare hands; probably come in handiny for assaulting women too, I imagine. I guess that happens more than folks know."

"Jeez, Bobby Lee, can you stay on track here?" Jacob said as he rolled his eyes impatiently. "We've got a lot to cover here and I'm due back in court this afternoon."

"Sorry, I just wonder about things sometimes. Anyhow, at the time, my hooking up with Tom Kidd seemed natural enough, but looking back at what happened later, I'm not so sure our initial meeting was as casual as it appeared that first afternoon.

"Like I told you before, Tom got out of Farmdale before me but before he split he told me to look him up when I was released. I didn't have anything else to do. I was on parole and I wasn't allowed leave the state so I took him up on his offer. Tom had told me that he had a little place in El Cajon in the seamier side of town. From what I saw while I was there for what turned out to be a very short time, the whole town was pretty damned seamy.

"Tom told me I could stay with him at his place until I found something on my own. My parole officer, a lazy prick by the name of Ben Vavra, advised me to check in with him monthly, reiterating, 'Your ass will be back in the pen in a heartbeat if you try to leave the state or miss any of your appointments with me. Let me know where you are living as soon as you find a place.' He went on to say, not very convincingly, 'I'll see what I can do to help you land a job.'

"He needn't have bothered with the job part, as I was arrested again four days after our meeting. I picked up a package for Tom at a post office box rental place in a dirty strip mall. Syringes and empty ampoules littered the sidewalk. El Cajon Packaging or something like that rented mail boxes by the week or month with no questions asked. It seems the cops had been suspicious of Tom or others who used the place and had staked it out. That was the prosecutor's story anyhow when the question of probable cause was weakly introduced by my old attorney, Edward.

"I was caught coming out the door with a package in my hand. Turns out the package contained six ounces of hash. Earlier, Tom had told me he had to go to work. 'Can you do me a favor and pick up my mail? Mom is sending me a little care package. The mail place is about six blocks down Main on the right. You can't miss it.' The fucker was right, I couldn't miss it! Again I had let trust overcome my better judgment. It never occurred to me that he wasn't playing it straight with me.

"Looking back, I kinda think that Tom might have been working for the cops all along, maybe for money or an early release from the pen, who can say?"

Jacob just looked at me and gave his head a little shake. "You had it right when you told me that you certainly are way too trusting, my friend," was all he said.

I continued with my story. "I wound up with a second conviction and another year and a half with room and board being furnished by the state. I once heard someone say, 'I'd rather be lucky than smart'. Well Jacob, as you can see; I've been neither."

Jacob scratched his head and seemed to be deep in thought. "Bobby Lee, I think I'm beginning to see a pattern here and from what I can deduce, you were being piled on for some reason. There's a lot of federal money floating around the country to fight the so-called *War on Drugs*. This wouldn't be the first time a law enforcement agency tried to get more than their fair share of the pork by rigging the arrest rate."

I began to see the point he was making. I knew things weren't right, but I didn't know about the federal drug fund.

"It's kinda like sales commissions, the more arrests made for drug crimes, the more dollars pour into the agency that makes the busts," he finished.

"Maybe I'm not as unlucky as I thought," I said. "Maybe the bad luck had a little nudge from the law. If this is true it would explain why arrest number three went down so damned smooth."

"What do you mean?"

"The second time I went in I'd had to serve eighteen months. This time I kept to myself as much as I could. I didn't need anymore new friendships after what I had gone through with the last two. Jimmy Dale had come to see me once while he was picking up some stuff in LA, but the reunion had not gone well.

"'I can't believe what a dumb shit you are,' were his first words to me.

"His words didn't help my state of mind. "'Me neither, I've been in the pen here twice in less than two years and I didn't even come close to scoring anything for my trouble. I got no money and I lost my car to boot.' I couldn't look him in the eye as I replied.

"'When you get out this time, get your ass back to Texas as soon as you can. At least leave California! I'm serious as a heart attack; this state is not for you!'

"'You're right about that,' I mumbled in a barely audible voice, as I vowed to myself not to let something like this happen to me again."

"So what did happen?" the Oak asked. "You're obviously still a guest here in the Golden State. More trust issues?" He was trying to inject some humor into the situation, but I could tell his heart wasn't in it. I believe he was starting to think I was retarded...I could understand why as I my story unfolded.

"You're not going to believe this one," I said, looking down at my shoes. The words did not come so easily now as I relived another stupid episode in my life.

"After I was released the second time, I decided to hitchhike back to Texas. I had a few bucks but not enough for a bus ticket *and* food, airfare was out of the question. I had made up my mind, the hell with the parole restrictions. I'd had enough of this fucked up state to last a life time. Let them try to extradite me from a thousand miles or more away for a simple parole violation!

"I'd only walked about a mile out of town after the prison bus had given me a ride into Barstow. I stuck my thumb out as the cars whizzed past. No one seemed inclined to pick up a lone male and the prison issue clothes I was wearing, denim over denim, didn't add much to instill confidence in a Good Samaritan.

"The overall package I presented screamed "Loser ex-convict". You can imagine my change in attitude when a car driven by a long haired brunette suddenly pulled over to the side of the highway and waited for me to run up and get in." Finally someone who could see past the clothes and appreciate my boyish good looks," I told Jacob with a grin.

"'Where you headed?' she said with a dazzling smile. Well, it was dazzling to me anyhow. So what if her front teeth were a little crooked? She was wearing shorts and a western cut shirt with no sleeves. Her breasts were also very nice. In case you're wondering, I'm a pretty quick study when it comes to checking out women."

"All we men are, if that's any consolation for you," Oakley said dryly. "Apparently the tits, legs, arms and teeth clouded your judgment somewhat?"

"Come on, I've been in the pen for the last two and a half years, not counting the quick R&R to El Cajon and I didn't get any pussy on that trip either. Of course, when the lady pulled over wearing that outfit, I wasn't thinking with anything but my dick!"

"Do I get a chance to guess? I'll bet I can tell the rest of your story from here on out and I hardly know you."

"You probably can. She told me her name was Yolanda and that's about all I ever found out about her. The deputies stopped us about five miles down the road from where she picked me up. Possession of the ounce of cocaine in the glove box and grand theft auto were the charges against me this time. I tried to tell the lawmen that neither the dope nor the car nor Yolanda was mine, but all I got from this comment was a round of laughter from the two lard assed deputies as they slapped the cuffs on me.

"'Sure pal,'" the bigger, or should I say fatter, of the two smiled, God were all the deputies around here overweight? 'We believe your story; just accompany us to the jail where we'll get this all sorted out. Sorry for any inconvenience we might be causing a busy fellow such as yourself.' I thought they would bust one of their huge guts at that one.

"These guys seemed to think everything each of them said was funny. What a bunch of assholes! I thought about running for it, but there were only irrigated fields in every direction and no place to hide. I surmised that the deputies probably could shoot pretty good, since there was no way they could chase anyone down on foot.

"I never saw Yolanda again. It was if she had never existed, maybe she never did. Probably another undercover cop, but I would never know. There I sat in the same fucking overheated court room a few days later with that worthless asshole Edward seated at my table. Déjà vu, all over again.

"After two and a half years, the only air conditioner in the room was that same small window unit I had seen on my first visit. The coke was tagged and setting on the evidence table alongside a picture of the "stolen" automobile. I felt so beaten and so stupid, I could not hold my head up to look at anyone in the room.

"Even the prosecutor was the same guy that had put me away the first time, Warren Knight, looked over at Edward and me with a mean grin. "Three strikes and your out, just like baseball," he said in a loud whisper.

"There you have it, Mr. Oakley, the whole story of my life of crime in three short Chapters. No sex, no drugs, no money, no rock and roll, just a lot of time in the California penal system for nothing.

"The only good thing to come out of all this is meeting my little nurse, Mary Jane Moon, and since that happened, my life is even more miserable. Maybe I *really* should think about suicide, whoops, scratch that. That just might the reason I was suicidal. "

"Stay off the Marcus Regan topic, Bobby Lee. We're addressing something else here. I need a little time to sort this all out, but if what I think happened to you did in fact take place, we may have you out of this shit hole by Christmas. I don't want to get your hopes up too high, but I'm really good at what I do...these kinds of crooked antics by the constabulary are right up my alley."

"I got no money. You know that already," I said doubtfully.

"I have a plan for that too. We might both do alright here. I just read over the case where the court awarded twenty million dollars to a girl up in Northern California who had been kidnapped and held for eighteen years. Seems the parole officers and the cops were derelict in their duties. Your case seems to encompass a lot more than dereliction and I plan to make someone pay...big."

I could barely contain myself as all the thoughts Jacob had planted played around in my head. Twenty four hours ago, my life was worth nothing. Today I was filled with hope and my thoughts turned to Mary Jane. Maybe we could have a future after all.

# CHAPTER TWENTY FIVE

# Jacob Prepares Bobby Lee's Appeal

Jacob: When I left Bobby Lee at the prison, we were both feeling better about the situation facing us; he, at the thought of perhaps not spending the rest of his life behind bars, and maybe even having a chance with his little nurse, Mary Jane. He told me a lot about her while we were just shooting the breeze. She sounded like a catch, if he could pull it off. I knew Bobby Lee had been dealt a bad hand, several crooked hands was more like it, and if anyone deserved a break he did. I was ready to go to work.

I was happy because I live to crush crooked cops and sleazy lawyers and other crooked assholes that weasel their way into our criminal justice system; giving my chosen profession a bad name. I still had my sights on that slime ball Marius, but he could wait…time was on my side. Right now I had something here with Bobby Lee that I could sink my teeth in and I wanted to taste some blood!

I called Holly to put her to work. "I need you to dig up all of the police reports and court records on a couple of guys; Tom Kidd and Earl Feathers." I updated her on what Bobby Lee had told me, informing her of what I was planning. Having worked with me in the past, she knew what to do. She got as big a kick out of screwing with the system as I did.

"Kidd was arrested in Barstow around three years ago and in El Cajon a year later. I think he narc'd on Bobby Lee and I'm curious if there is a paper trail tying him in with the Sheriff's Department there."

"I'm on it, Big Guy. I can tell from your voice that this case is taking you toward what you'd hoped it would be." She was my counterpart and when it came to turning over rocks to find the worms that inhabited the darker side of the law, she was superb.

She was correct about my feelings; I couldn't hide my pleasure at the thought of my latest quest, and I didn't care. I'm not good at hiding my emotions, good or bad, except when I'm in front of a jury; Holly didn't seem to mind.

"Baby, I'm taking you out to dinner tonight. We've got some celebrating to do." I could hear her giggle on the other end of the call. Her giggle, like a little girl's, always made me smile.

"I really love that woman," I thought to myself. "I need to tell her that more often." Bobby Lee's description of his feelings for Mary Jane had caused me to look inward. I had to stop taking Holly for granted; I vowed to myself to do just that.

The Firehouse Restaurant was exactly what I looked for when dining out, the smell of steaks on the grill wafting in from the kitchen, the lights were low, and some soft music was coming from the bar off to the side of the dining room. The steaks were just as we both liked them, served with the twice-baked potato and all the trimmings. I felt pleasantly full, but not stuffed, as I opened the box bearing the diamond ring. After hearing Bobby Lee's story of unfulfilled love, I decided I had to be an idiot to pass up my chance with Holly.

When she said, "Yes" with tears in her eyes, I could see that she had wanted this commitment from me for a long time. Ever since we had moved in together, I thought we had the perfect relationship, and I guess that for a bachelor like me, it was. Sex when I wanted it, help with cases when I asked for it, and no demands made on me by this wonderful woman.

It had taken a conversation with a country boy from a small town in east Texas to alert me to my shortcomings concerning my relationship with Holly. Bobby Lee was serving a life sentence on trumped up charges, yet declaring his feelings for a lady with whom he had no chance, opened my eyes.

"God bless Bobby Lee Baker," I told Holly and lifted my glass of burgundy in a toast. She looked at me with a puzzled expression as our glasses touched.

"I'll tell you about it sometime…I love you, Lady." By now there were unashamed tears flowing from my eyes also.

"You big softie," she smiled. God she was beautiful.

Before I could file for a mistrial for Bobby Lee, among other things, I had a lot of work to do. I planned to bring charges of entrapment and conspiracy against the sheriff, the state and the feds. The lawman and his minions, including the Federal officer had made a mockery of justice. Later, after my enlightening visit with Earl Feathers, I would add blackmail to the charges for the way he had been drawn into the sheriff's nefarious schemes.

Next on my list of reasons for a mistrial in all of Bobby Lee's cases was the incompetent representation he received from his lawyer. It didn't take much digging to find that Edward Peters, the court appointed attorney who was supposed to defend Bobby Lee, had never won a case before a judge during his entire career; if you could call what he did a career. Seems the only income he received, other than as a court appointed defender, was by working for real estate companies, preparing the paperwork for questionable land deals.

# Chapter Twenty Six

# The Oak Meets Earl Feathers

Jacob: After checking the records concerning Bobby Lee's first conviction I contacted Earl Feathers. Since he was involved so deeply in the case that sent Bobby Lee to prison the first time it only seemed logical to start with him. I was surprised to find he had not testified in the case because the Drug Enforcement Task Force convinced the court that it would blow his cover. The records stated, "Mr. Feathers is a paid informant. Exposing him in open court could cost him his life." According to the court records the judge bought this statement by the prosecution without question.

"Interesting," I thought to myself, wondering besides Bobby Lee, how many other poor unsuspecting drifters passing through the county had been arrested by these guys. As these thoughts went through my mind I continued reading the transcript; my query should be easy enough to research." I reached for my phone to call Holly and put her to work on gathering the info I was pretty sure existed in some obscure file.

Earl had a lot to tell me when I contacted him. I had him meet me at my office. When he arrived he came in wearing scruffy clothes, dirty jeans, some kind of motorcycle vest and heavy black boots with built up soles.

Even with the lifts I guessed he was no more than five foot seven inches tall, weighing around one hundred and forty pounds. "Not very imposing," I thought to myself, but I was reserving my judgment for a while. I try not to prejudge people; they usually let you know what they're about soon enough.

"Sit down, Earl. May I call you Earl?"

"Sure," he replied appearing somewhat uneasy.

I'd given him just enough info to spark his interest, assuring him that I was not a cop. "Bobby Lee Baker is my client and I'm doing some work for him." I had no idea how he would respond to my opener, but he didn't seemed surprised to hear from me.

"Would it be convenient for us to meet? There might be something in it for you." I had some money set aside in my office for such things. Sometimes you have to pay to get information. Anyone who ever watched a cop show knows that. That's probably one of the few occurrences portrayed in the many detective shows that's true.

After he had taken a seat across from me, I began, "Earl, I feel that Bobby Lee might have been placed in a predicament that was not of his making. Are you aware that he's serving life in Farmdale State Prison as we speak?"

I could tell by his shocked expression that this was a real surprise to him. "Shit no! I thought he was only in for a year and that was a long time ago." He seemed to be genuinely upset at my revelation.

"Tell me what your role was in setting Bobby Lee up and I'll fill you in on what I know."

I could see Earl flinch when I used the term "setting up", but he started to talk anyway.

"I liked Bobby Lee from the time I first laid eyes on him at Joe's Bar. I liked the way he shamed that fat, greasy bully in front of everyone and caused him to leave with his tail between his legs. That was a long time ago, but I remember it like it was last week. I liked the way he carried himself and I've been ashamed of what I did to him ever since, but you see Mr. Oakley, I had to make something happen; I had no choice because of Janie."

"Janie?" I asked. Bobby Lee had mentioned Janie when he was telling me his story at Farmdale. She made good tacos. From the saddened tone in Earl's voice and his suddenly downcast eyes I could sense there was something here that might fill in some of the missing pieces I needed. It turned out I was right.

Earl continued, speaking more slowly now with emotions that were suddenly causing him to choke up. "Sheriff Guy Bailey, he's the sheriff here, was growing impatient with me. It was common knowledge among those of us who smoked pot or snorted some coke that the sheriff depended on federal drug enforcement payments to in order to keep his department operating in such a manner whereby he could collect the extra money he thought he and his boys deserved.

"That's why I had to hit on a stranger like Bobby Lee. Everyone on the street here knew what kind of underhanded crap was going on when it came to the sheriff and his bogus drug busts; still is for that matter. Strangers were the only viable pigeons for the sheriff's schemes.

"I first met the sheriff and that asshole sidekick of his, Byron Ethridge; some kind of federal agent-in-charge, when they busted my girl, Janie. She'd been living with me for over a year and I really loved her. She was so young and pretty; the prettiest girl I had ever been with. You've probably already figured by looking at me that I'm not much of a ladies man. She was like the fourth girl I ever had sex with in my whole miserable life other than hookers. She caused me to come to life...to feel like a kid again.

"As our time together grew, I was unsure of what her reaction would be when I told her I loved her, but I was thrilled when she told me she loved me too. At night as she would get undressed in front of me with the lights on, I thought my heart would bust right out of my chest, every time!

"You know, I never got used to seeing her naked. It was always fresh and exciting for me. She was just as great looking when she put on those little denim shorts or a mini skirt and a tee shirt. Long beautiful legs that could drive just about any man wild... and she was with me; short, skinny, unattractive me. I'd been bullied by guys and ridiculed by the girls for what seemed like my whole life until I met Janie. She comforted me and gave me refuge from the rest of the world. I was in heaven when she was around. She made me feel like a real man.

"Her drug addiction didn't change my loving feelings for her. I tried to help her but she couldn't leave the stuff alone. The number of needle marks inside her arms and behind her knees continued to increase. Around southern California heroin use is not taken lightly and when Janie was busted in a deal gone wrong, the sheriff was ready to bring all of his weight to bear in making an example of my girl.

"I went to see her in jail. Once I was with her and saw how she was suffering my heart was breaking. We didn't have no money so she'd been assigned an attorney by the judge. His name was Edward Peters. He didn't impress me much, but like I said, I was broke; we had to accept him whether we liked him or not."

As I listened to Earl revealing his painful memories I couldn't help but see the parallel in his story and the one told to me by Bobby Lee.

Earl continued his tragic tale. "Janie and I were both crying as Peters set out to explain our predicament. This wasn't Janie's first arrest and she was facing some long hard time. She had been ratted out by an informant who had once been a friend of hers. Fine friend she turned out to be, but she'd been blackmailed by the sheriff to find drug users for him. No one can be trusted around here because the sheriff seems to have his claws into everyone who's vulnerable to arrest.

"I asked Peters, 'Do you have any sort of plan?' Our situation just seemed so fucking hopeless.

"When he said, 'Maybe one; I might have a way out of this for you two.' He had my attention immediately.

"'The sheriff just might have a proposition that will make you both well.'

"I was pretty eager when I said, 'OK, let's hear it.' By then I would have ratted out my mother to save Janie.

"The next afternoon Edward set up a meeting with the sheriff, Ethridge the Fed, and me. Janie hadn't been invited. She was still sitting in her cell. She had spent a terrible night in confinement since she needed a fix real bad. My night hadn't been much better as I sat home alone, unable to sleep.

"When we met at his office, Sheriff Bailey started the conversation, saying, 'Earl, that's sure a sweet little piece you've got for yourself. I went by her cell this morning to take a look and I'll be darned if she wasn't just getting out of the shower; mighty impressive body for such a little gal; she sure has it all in the right places. I got a big old hard on just in the short time I had to observe her coming out of the shower all wet and clean. Her skin is almost golden.'

I interrupted Earl here by asking, "Do you think he was telling the truth or was he just playing you?"

"What difference could it make, sir? He had planted the picture in my mind of him and others watching her and that was enough to cause me to agree to do whatever he wanted."

Earl, now visibly upset continued with the story of his meeting with the sheriff.

"He kept pushing, 'I'd think it'd be mighty hard to go back to flogging your dong by yourself after having tasted that fresh young pussy.' It was embarrassing to hear him speaking of my Janie like that but it didn't stop that son of a bitch Bailey from talking more and more trash."

"'What are you now Earl, around forty or so? You'll never have a twenty year old like Janie ever again.' He was giving me a leering smile as he spoke. I was getting sick at my stomach while at the same time wanting to punch him for his crude words, but that wouldn't help matters. Besides, I'm just a little guy and not much good when it comes to fighting.

"So I nodded as if I was in full agreement with what he was telling me. He knew he had me so he set the hook. 'Janie is really small potatoes to me. Oh, don't get me wrong, I have no problem with using her to make an example of how we handle heroin addicts in the county. Always looks good around election time, you know. I'd probably get some votes from them big bull dykes that work at the prison too; just for sending such a sweet young thing to them.

"'There's a lot of them lesbos working there. Who says California doesn't employ the gays?' This had caused a big laugh from both Bailey and Ethridge. I didn't see the humor at all, but again I held my tongue. 'Besides the guards, you know there's lots of inmates themselves who don't like a penis. Janie could pleasure a whole passel of gals in that place.'

"I couldn't block the horrific image he'd drawn from my mind. As I imagined what that would be like for Janie my heart pumped faster."

"Byron, here, has a boss, Uncle Sam, who likes to make the whole United States of America feel safe with this war on drugs. I ain't sayin' it's right, but it sure is a Godsend for my departmental budget, if you know what I mean.'

"I nodded still unable to respond; thinking of all that he had described as Janie's future in the pen."

"There was no lack of words for Bailey. He kept talking, 'The feds pay for results and for some reason they'd rather bust a bunch of pot heads, especially college students or other such young folks, than any other kind of drug user.'

"' Personally, I don't give a shit who we get, as long as there's funds for me and my deputies. As for me, I'm really partial to arresting drifters; guys who don't have any political clout around here. Kind of fucks things up when one of my men arrests a councilman's kid or worse yet; the kid of some banker who contributes to my campaign fund. Takes a lot of work to keep that sort of thing hidden, you know? 'Course, there's always favors to be called in when I get the right kid out of trouble, *quid pro quo*, I think they call it. '

"'Where are you going with this, Sheriff?' I asked, still not getting it."

I couldn't help but shake my head as Earl's tale unfolded. I wouldn't be surprised if snaring Janie hadn't been Bailey's plan all along, just to recruit Earl. I kept my thoughts to myself so as not to ruin Earl's train of thought.

"Bailey finally showed his cards. 'You come to work for me, Boy, that's what I'm getting at. I have some guys that can assist you in making a lot of drug busts. That puts money in my pocket and you know, shit runs down hill. I'll slip some bucks to you and, most importantly; we can give that little Janie girl a pass...for the time being.'

"His smile was pure evil as he continued, 'Earl, I'm looking for bigger fish and a lot of them. I need help and I think you and me can work together. How would like to take little Janie home today?'

"Mr. Oakley, I told you before that I'd turn my mom in to save Janie. Sheriff Guy's offer was more, much more than I had hoped for. That's the day I became a rat for the sheriff and the feds. The day I saw Bobby Lee walk into that bar, I knew he was no outlaw or dope dealer, but I was feeling the pressure to make something happen; I needed someone to give to the sheriff."

"A couple of weeks had passed since we'd made our deal and I had produced nothing of importance for Bailey. I'd ratted out a few pot smokers I knew, but he already had that info. He was pushing me hard and making veiled threats. Actually there wasn't much veiled about them.

"'I can't let Miss Janie continue to run loose if you don't give me something in exchange. I got a lot of pressure on me from the feds and the supervisors. My boys need some extra money too. The pay they get from being on the county payroll doesn't even start to cover what they need. You do get my drift, don't you? If you want to keep tapping that sweet young ass, you've got to come through for me and the boys. Justice must be served…one way or the other.'

"'Yes Sir. Got you, Sheriff Guy,' I mumbled in my most humble and kiss ass manner. Pictures of a naked Janie in prison tied to a steel bunk with big, manly looking women abusing her continued to cross my mind. I couldn't erase those images no matter how I tried to think of other things."

I reassured Earl, "That must have been an excruciatingly painful time for you. I don't know how you could stand the pressure. Why didn't you just get out of Dodge?"

"Hell, Mr. Oakley, I didn't have a pot to piss in or a window to throw it out of. I don't know how Janie was feeding her drug habit and I was afraid to ask. I knew the sheriff had his deputies and snitches watching me some of the time, I just didn't know when. He'd given me a real clear picture of what would happen to Janie if I tried to run so that wasn't an option for me.

"Ethridge had given me a cell phone with his number on speed dial. I was supposed to call him to set up a buy as soon as I made contact with a potential subject. The night I called him while Bobby Lee slept, he went right to work. He had some spics set up and ready to furnish a kilo of pot to nail Bobby Lee; the deputies were ready too.

"Bobby Lee was my first mark and he was also my last." Earl said sadly. He looked like he was ready to slash his wrists.

"What do you mean your last?" I had been taking notes along with recording our conversation. I was able to feel the fear and the anger in his voice as he told his tale, but his voice on the recorder would be much more effective as evidence, should I take his testimony before a judge.

I paused thoughtfully waiting for him to continue with his story. I could see that whatever he was about to reveal was going to be even more difficult in the telling.

Tears were starting to well up in his eyes so I gave him my handkerchief. He took it gratefully while a look of embarrassment crossed his face. After wiping his eyes and blowing his nose he began again haltingly.

"A week after I had helped the cops in setting up Bobby Lee, I came home, our real home, not the phony shack the feds had used to entrap him, and found Janie lying in the bath tub with the needle still in her arm. She was gone…dead and cold.

"Before I called the paramedics, already knowing it was too late for them to help; I decided that I couldn't leave Janie lying naked in the tub for strangers to gawk at. I lifted her wet, little body from the cold bath water and carried her into the bedroom where I wrapped her in the bed spread, leaving her head exposed.

"I lay down beside her and stared at her lovely face. She appeared to be sleeping innocently and in no pain. She seemed to be more at peace than I'd ever seen her. I said a prayer for the first time in years, asking God to forgive her for her sins and let her into heaven straight away since her life on earth had been such a tormented hell."

"My God, Earl," I uttered. I was started to choke up along with Earl as he came to the end of his narration. "That's one of the most heartbreaking stories I've ever heard. How on earth did you manage to get through it?"

"I left town the next day. I still had no money, no way to pay for a funeral and I didn't want to face that pig, Sheriff Guy Bailey. Lately I was in the habit of carrying a snub nose thirty-eight in an ankle holster. If he'd said one more vulgar word about Janie, I was ready to shoot him in his filthy mouth.

"I've wandered around the state since then; barely staying alive, but not returning to Bailey's area. I'm surprised you were able to get in touch with me; that Brad fellow you got working for you seems to know his way around pretty good. When he contacted me and told me you wanted to meet with me, I really felt a sense of relief. Knowing you by reputation only Mr. Oakley, I figured you might be trying to help Bobby Lee. I thought that this may finally be a chance to right the wrong I'd done to a guy who hadn't done anything to me.

"I'll do anything I can, testify against whoever you want if it will help Bobby Lee."

"Thanks, Earl. I think you're going to do some good here and I think Janie would be proud of you. Maybe you'll be able to pay Bailey back for what he put you and Janie through. I'll get back to you soon."

I gave Earl my card and told him to stay in touch so I could reach out to him when the time was right. I also gave him a couple of hundred dollars. He looked like he could use it.

# CHAPTER TWENTY SEVEN

# The Oak Meets With Tom Kidd

Jacob: Earl Feathers was almost a perfect witness for the case I was preparing. Aside from some of his questionable history with Janie and her drug use, he was extremely credible... he'd been forced to entrap Bobby Lee in order to keep his lady out of prison. What jury wouldn't be swayed by his story, especially now that she had died and Earl's conscience had kicked in? But I knew I had to have more than Earl's testimony to present to a judge before I could petition for a new trial.

I still needed to find Tom Kidd. Along with the relationship described by Bobby Lee, Kidd's name had come up in the court records as a material witness in Bobby Lee's trial.

Kidd was a cinch to locate as he was back in a state pen himself, not at Farmstead, thank God. He was busted for shoplifting, no shit! He received his life sentence for shoplifting a carton of cigarettes from a liquor store. He told me he didn't realize they had surveillance cameras installed. The guy was no criminal genius; this was his third strike.

When he was detained and strip searched at the El Cajon substation, he was also found to be in possession of a couple of baggies of medicinal marijuana, for which he could not produce a prescription. He was convicted for his third and fourth offenses; hard to argue with a video tape as evidence, and was sent to a state facility north of LA. At least the authorities were smart enough to realize Bobby Lee, or one of his friends, or maybe just someone who hated snitches, would shank Kidd for his role in Bobby Lee's arrest.

It was surprisingly easy for me to get him to agree to testify in Bobby Lee's defense. He was now serving his own life sentence under circumstances very similar to the man he had betrayed. Like Earl Feathers, Tom Kidd was now suffering pangs of guilt for what he had done to Bobby Lee.

"Mr. Oakley, I was bein' squeezed hard by Sheriff Bailey"…second time I'd heard that statement in less than a week I thought to myself.

"He and that Fed, Ethridge, came to see me at the state prison. I was led into a private room where no one could see who I was talkin' to. They was leanin' on me and telling me they could produce more evidence to make me stay longer if I didn't agree to help them out. I knew they weren't my friends but since they were using me I figured I might as well get what I could from them.

"The sheriff made no bones about what he expected of me. I would do what he asked and he might toss some crumbs my way. I didn't trust him or the fed, but they didn't leave me much choice. He was the only hope I had for getting a reduction off my ten year sentence and he was threatening me with more time to serve on some trumped up charge if I refused his offer."

I had been listening to Kidd's story for awhile with growing interest. He was being forthright about how he had been recruited, *coerced* was a far better word, by Sheriff Bailey. As he spoke, I was starting to have an epiphany; my mission to add the sheriff to my list of assholes that needed a lesson in how the legal system is supposed to work was reaffirmed as a worthwhile cause.

I made a note to make an appointment to see Sheriff Bailey soon. I wanted to meet him at his quarter horse ranch that I'd heard about. As I mulled that over I had second thoughts; I decided it might be better if I sent someone less conspicuous than myself to check on the place. I wanted to maintain a low profile for a while yet; it was still too early to show my hand to Bailey or Ethridge.

I considered how my nemesis, Marius, was getting real criminals off on technicalities while Bailey was putting innocent young men in prison on trumped up charges. Both men were after the same goals; money and recognition and they didn't care how they got it. These two were really starting to piss me off… as we say in legal jargon.

Earlier, when Tom and I had first come face to face, we met in an interrogation room at the facility. Kidd was in his prison denims with his name and number stenciled on his shirt. He had waited expectantly for me to speak first so when I did, I had done my best to win his trust.

I could sense that he wanted me to offer to take him on as a client. He was hoping I could do for him what I was trying to accomplish for Bobby Lee. I was being noncommittal about that aspect; so far I hadn't looked into his background much further than trying to locate him.

I began by asking, "Did your deal with the sheriff single out Bobby Lee, or were you just supposed to find someone on your own?"

"No, I had no one in mind. I didn't know who the target was until he showed me a picture of Bobby Lee. He told me that I should make friends with him. If I could do this, I would be released right before Bobby Lee's time was up, in order to set up our play. Bailey assured me this meant a five year early release for me. How could I turn that down, Mr. Oakley?"

"I'd have probably done the same thing if I were in your shoes," I replied, encouraging him to continue; not really knowing how I would have reacted to such an offer had I been in his place. I certainly would have considered it, that's for sure.

Kidd continued, "Almost everybody in the California prisons, other than San Quentin, and Folsom, is serving time on some kind of a drug charge. I don't know who's left on the outside to buy drugs. Just about every user and dealer I ever knew is serving time.

"Word is a lot of the local lawmen are getting big bucks from the feds for making these busts; doesn't seem to matter how big or small, just as long as someone spends hard time and the paperwork is submitted. The fact that the big guys who run the traffic stay out of the jail system is probably a good thing for the cops as the drug bosses keep sending more of their pawns out to be arrested. The supply of dope to be confiscated and the number of small time drug dealers to arrest seems endless. The numerous busts also help push the street price of the drugs higher."

"You make some good points, Tom," I said.

Then as he continued to speak, my suspicions about Sheriff Bailey, which were quickly becoming conclusions, were reaffirmed. As Tom talked he gave me some additional information I hadn't expected.

More at ease now he said, "When I was at Farmdale I worked for Sheriff Bailey as a trustee at his ranch. This was before him and Ethridge came to see me at the prison. The guards would take me over there sometimes. I worked on some of the ranches around Ukiah when I was growing up. I loved the work but the pay was for shit. I know a lot about horses and how to train them. I even worked some as a farrier, you know, shoeing them. That came in handy for making a few extra bucks, until I wound up in the pen.

"The warden told Bailey about me, the history of my ranch work was there in the records. He and the sheriff had some kind of deal when it came to providing free experienced help for the ranch. I was just one of several prisoners who worked for Bailey for free. Mostly cleaning out the stalls and stacking hay or painting his big white fences.

"I didn't mind though. I even looked forward to it. At least working on the ranch got me out from behind these walls for a while and I liked being around the livestock. The smells of hay and even horse shit smell were a hell of a lot better than my cell or the prison yard. Bailey's got a registered quarter horse stallion over there that cost him over fifty thousand bucks. He's a real beaut out of the Doc Bar linage. It's said the stud fee's between three and four grand, depending on who you are or who you know.

"I don't figure any cop's wages, even a sheriff's is good enough to pay for a spread like that. Can't say for sure though, since we just recently heard the chief of police over in Bell makes over four hundred thousand dollars a year." Kidd thought for a moment and then seemed to come to a conclusion, "But that's probably not real common, otherwise everyone would be trying to break into law enforcement jobs instead of working outside of it. Maybe he's gettin' some of those federal dollars too."

The more I talked with Tom, the better I liked him. I couldn't help but notice how alike he and Earl and Bobby Lee were. They were just good old country folk; a little rough and very naïve, who had been dealt a very bad hand it seemed.

"A lot of good guys seem to be inside while many of the bad guys seem to be on the outside," I couldn't help but commenting to him. I tried not to show the pity I was feeling for him.

He was just another small town cowboy who had gotten busted the first time while driving a pickup truck load of Mendocino County's largest cash crop south. Other than the prison garb, he could be any young fellow from anywhere in rural America. "Such a waste," I mused sadly. I was reminded of how the worst offenders were on the outside of the prison walls.

I'd gotten all I needed from Tom Kidd for the time being. His story backed up what Bobby Lee and Earl Feathers had both related to me. I told him I would be getting back with him to discuss his testimony as soon as I could get a trial date set. Tom's story about Bailey's ranch caused me to be more intrigued than ever about that operation.

"Keep our conversation to yourself please, Tom. I don't want Bailey or any of his deputies to get wind of what we're doing. Something bad, an accident or whatever might happen to you or Bobby Lee. If anyone comes around trying to pressure you, tell them you're my client and the client-attorney privilege applies. I'm going to instruct the warden that you are not to speak to any law enforcement officers unless I am present. I'm also going to tell him that Bailey is not to know that I came to see you or he might be appearing in court as a co-defendant."

He smiled at me hopefully and said, "Am I really your client? Do you think you might be able to help me too?" Finally he'd laid his cards on the table.

I suddenly made up my mind, saying, "Tom, I'm not going to lie to you. That's not my way. You're now my client and I'll draw up a contract and keep it on file in my office. I don't know if I can help with your sentence, but since I'm already in a similar area with my other case concerning Bobby Lee, I'll do what I can for you." I said it and I meant it. "This is one fucked up world!" I muttered.

I left the prison with a couple of new quests facing me. I felt a little like Don Quixote, wondering if I was tilting at windmills…but after a moment of considering it, I thought not.

# CHAPTER TWENTY EIGHT

# Call From Deputy Johnson

Jacob: With the information I had retrieved so far from police reports and court records, I felt I was building a pretty good case to petition the court to grant Bobby Lee a new trial. The story was firming up to be as he had described it to me. The only weakness I could see was that my key witnesses consisted of Bobby Lee; himself a three time loser, serving life at Farmdale. Then there was Earl Feathers, who was good, but; as the prosecution would frame it, "He had been living in sin with a now-deceased junkie, twenty years his junior," and that might not set well with some jurors. Lastly, I had the cowboy, Tom Kidd. He was what appeared to be yet another professional convict with no history of veracity. He'd lied to his new *best friend* while serving with him in the pen and then set him up for a phony drug bust.

I knew deep inside that my client and his witnesses were good men at heart and were telling me the truth, but that didn't mean I could convince a jury of what I felt. I was uneasy and in doubt about just how to proceed. I was in dire need of a strong witness with no history of illegal activity; an honest cop would be nice; and in this county extremely rare it seemed.

It was about this time I was handed a real gift; Ellie Johnson, that is Deputy Ellie Johnson. I was in my office running a little late, so I was the only one there when the phone rang. Reluctantly I picked it up. I was supposed to pick Holly up in less than half an hour.

"I'm trying to reach Jacob Oakley, the attorney," I heard a woman's voice say.

"That's me, what can I do for you?" I told her speaking rather abruptly.

"I understand you're working on a case surrounding a drug bust that took place in San Bernardino County a few years back. I believe that I may be of some help to you."

I suddenly was aware that my efforts at keeping my name out of the investigation until I was ready to make my move had apparently failed.

"Where'd you hear that?" I replied suspiciously, my tone was not friendly. Was this some kind of setup? I had no idea who was on the other end of the call.

"The buzz at the cop shop for the past week has centered on a number of requests being made by some attorney's office for this info. I guess someone heard you had been over at Farmdale talking to Bobby Lee Baker and put two and two together. Am I off base here?" Her tone was inquisitive and much friendlier than mine, but businesslike nonetheless.

I was caught off guard. What fucking cop shop was she talking about? "May I inquire as to whom I'm speaking? Why are you calling me?" I was curt with my question.

"Sorry, Sir, my name is Deputy Johnson. You may call me Ellie or Ms. Johnson or even Deputy Johnson if you prefer. I work for Sheriff Bailey, but his ideas of enforcing the law and mine are not quite the same. Is Bobby Lee Baker really your client and are you trying to help him? I hear that you're an honest attorney; a rare breed I must admit since I haven't met many so far."

She certainly had all of my attention and quickly at that, "I can't discuss this with you over the phone." I so wanted this to be real. "Is there someplace we could meet? You have my undivided attention, young lady." I wasn't sure if this was a setup, nothing had been what it appeared so far when it came to Bailey, but if Deputy Johnson *was* legitimate my prayers would be answered. I had to take the chance of meeting her and I wanted it to be soon. I am not a patient man once I start on something this important.

"Anywhere outside the county is fine with me. I'm off shift for the next two days. I could drive over to your office tomorrow if you're going to be available?" She sounded a little doubtful.

"I'll make sure to be available. You might be just the one person I've been looking for. How's ten o'clock sound?"

"See you then, Mr. Oakley," and she hung up.

I took a moment to let what had just happened sink in. Was fate stepping in to lend me a hand? I left the office feeling a little lighter in spirit but still not sure. I don't much believe in fate and what had just taken place seemed too good to be true.

# CHAPTER TWENTY NINE

# Deputy Ellie Johnson

Ellie: Being one of the few female deputies working for Sheriff Bailey, it had taken a lot of courage for me to take that first step and call Mr. Oakley, although after all I had witnessed, I felt I had no choice. Most all the cops in the department seem to know The Oak, at least by reputation. He's recognized as a champion for the little guy, but only the "good" little guys. So far as I know, he doesn't represent sleaze bags and makes no pretense about it. The good deputies; one's that I trust, who've had dealings with him, or know someone who has, respect him. At the same time, the cops who tend to make bogus arrests; cops like my boss, fear and despise him.

However, lots of cops, just by the very nature of their profession, dislike defense attorneys, usually for good reason. Often, just like the way Ohio State hates Michigan and vice versa or how Phoenix Suns fans hate Kobe, cops and defense lawyers are natural enemies.

Negative remarks, "Fucking shyster" and "Ambulance chaser" were a couple of the more common epithets being tossed around the office as of late when the rumors started flying about Oakley checking out what had happened to Bobby Lee Baker. These remarks came mostly from the old timers; sergeants, detectives, and other cronies of Sheriff Bailey; the ones making the big bucks and driving the fancy SUV's. Sheriff Bailey's inner circle, the chosen few, as it were.

These were the deputies that wore hand made Lucchese boots sent directly to them from the factory in El Paso, where the molds, patterns of their feet, were kept in the store room, allowing the boots to be ordered over the phone while guaranteeing the fit would be just right. These men knew how to go first class; sporting heavy gold chains around their necks, Rolex watches on their wrists and diamond solitaires on their pinky fingers. To say they were "ostentatious" was an understatement. They wore all this shit shamelessly, as if no one could figure out that something just wasn't right; you can't dress like a cowboy pimp on deputy's pay.

Only once did I see the sheriff react adversely to the crazy shit that was going on within the department. Lieutenant Sherrow had shown up at work one morning with a diamond solitaire stud in his left ear lobe. It must have been at least a full carat. When the sheriff spotted it, he came unglued. He called Sherrow into his office, and with a beet red face that we could all see through his office window, in a booming voice that could also be heard outside the office, read him the riot act.

"We don't need to draw this kind of attention to ourselves and the department! You look like a fucking gay peacock. Don't you have any sense at all? And while I'm on the subject, tell the rest of those yahoos to cool it. You look like a bunch of cowboys from the set of Miami Vice! Shape the fuck up and look professional! You're going to blow our whole operation with this kind of crap...maintain a low profile, Sherrow."

Sherrow sullenly removed the stud then and there while Bailey glared at him. Deeply chagrined, the lieutenant left the office and slunk out the door like a dog that had been punished; jaws tight, never once looking up. After that day most of the bling was only brought out for social occasions or at the bars during happy hour. However, the two hundred dollar Twenty X Beaver Stetsons remained part of their everyday uniform. Even the wrath of Bailey couldn't put a stop to the deputy's addiction to the wearing of the expensive cowboy hats.

I'd been to the deputy's happy hour a couple of times at Manfred's Legal Ease Bar when I first joined the department. Attendance, after shift, seemed a requirement in order to be accepted by the other deputies. I don't go there anymore.

Manfred, he only had the one name; like Kramer, was a former cop from the Valley. He'd been shot in the pancreas and in the stomach a couple of years before he was supposed to retire. The night of the shooting, he'd responded to a call involving an irate husband who was beating his wife.

Upon arriving at the scene he attempted to intervene. It was then that the husband pulled a thirty two caliber revolver and emptied it in Manfred's direction. Although Manfred caught two in the belly, he managed to kill the husband and accidently wound the wife at the same time when a shot from his 9MM passed thru the husband hitting her in the ass.

The surgeon at the ER removed half his stomach and a quarter of his pancreas that had been punctured by the .32. Following an investigation by Internal Affairs, he was offered an early retirement, partly due to his disability and partly due to the wounding of the wife's posterior...and pride.

Manfred had been advised by the medical specialist on the case to never drink another alcoholic beverage as his damaged pancreas couldn't handle it. Contrarily, Manfred took his savings and bought a bar in this desert town! He wanted nothing else to do with the big city and the shit that went with it so he moved inland searching for a more peaceful life by opening a bar that catered exclusively to law enforcement personnel...go figure.

Manfred's was the only bar in town that the cops and their cronies frequented. In fact, his was the only bar within sixty miles that offered such sanctuary away from civilians and their bullshit. When I first heard about Manfred's semi-private club, I assumed this exclusivity must drastically limit the number of clientele the place attracted. I'd failed to take into account the number of Highway Patrolmen, drug enforcement officers, border patrolmen, city cops, and deputies that liked to have a drink out of the general public's eye. Even the city and county animal control officers drank there.

Manfred's also served as a hangout and refuge for various court personnel, clerks and lawyers. Both defense team types and prosecutors could find refuge there. It was sort of a demilitarized zone. These adversaries seemed to get along much better in the bar than they did in the court room; maybe someone should introduce the concept of making an open bar available during trials.

Many of the cops I've known over the years have the morals of a feral tom cat. They work weird hours and have unexpected court appearances, so their wives have no idea what they're up to at any given time. Besides being a hot spot for singles, Manfred's was a good place for those guys, and gals, who had little respect for their wedding vows, to hook up.

The young ladies who work as dispatchers, typists, and the other less romantic jobs inside the legal system, usually relegated to women, are pretty easy pickings for these experienced womanizers. The bling, the uniforms and the bullshit that flowed from these egotistical blow-hards would entice the unsuspecting girls as they listened, with wide eyed admiration. These "studs", as they viewed themselves, were great at embellishment as they regaled anyone who would listen with accounts of the fights they had won, shootings they had been involved in, and other sundry cop crap bull shit meant to woo and impress these gullible young ladies.

It's not unusual for the new hires, most commonly young, naïve girls straight out of high school or community colleges, to become enamored of these slick talking cockhounds who are continuously trying to add another pubic scalp to their sexual trophy case. Once the girls are used a few times, usually badly, they either grow to like what is happening to them or, if their morals were instilled by a stricter upbringing, they become disgusted with themselves or their suitors and move on; sadder but a hell of a lot wiser.

It was definitely a man's world that I had walked into, both on duty in the Sheriff's Office, and off duty at Manfred's. The first time I entered the dark bar accompanied by our daytime dispatcher, Patty, who had promised to show me the ropes, there was the thick fog of cigarette smoke filling the place. I almost choked as I asked her, "Doesn't anybody know that there's a law against smoking in public businesses in California? This place looks like an opium den, or at least how I would imagine an opium den would look."

"Oh, that's true, Ellie, there is no smoking allowed in public establishments, but you do realize this *is* a cop's bar and they make the rules. Who you gonna' call, more cops?" she said with a laugh. She reached into her purse and pulled out a pack of Virginia Slims, shaking one out for herself before offering me the pack.

I shook my head and looked around. She put the cigarette in her mouth and lit up, inhaling deeply. There was an old antelope head mounted on the wall at the end of the bar. It must have been hanging there a long while as there were thick, dusty cobwebs running from one horn to the other. It also appeared to have a bad case of mange. "Very attractive," I thought to myself.

As my eyes wandered around taking in the rest of the place I was becoming even less impressed with my surroundings. Through the thick smoky haze I could see dozens of pictures hanging on the walls. They were mostly of cops; groups of cops in uniform, photos of what must have been more cops dressed in baseball shirts and caps. The photos were interspersed with small shelves that held a shit load of cheap trophies, each one topped by individual little baseball players, little bowlers, or little skeet shooters.

I guess I've been in worse places, maybe in Tijuana or some other such city, but at the moment I couldn't be sure. I could see no reason to hang around this joint. It didn't seem worth the effort just to garner a few brownie points with a bunch of men who held no interest for me.

I hadn't been there more than five minutes, trying decide how to make my exit as subtle as possible when I hear, "Hey Ellie, are you a virgin?" I turned toward the sound of the voice ready to bitch-slap the classless jerk, who was giving me my first crude welcome to the bar.

I saw that it was one of the big mouthed sergeants from the city police force. I don't know how he knew my name, since I didn't know his. I decided to let it slide as I headed for the door. While I was ignoring that asshole, another cop I didn't know walked over and gave me that tired old line, "Hey gorgeous, if I said you had a beautiful body, would you hold it against me?"

"Get the fuck away from me, Dickhead!" I growled without thinking. I realized that my response wasn't any cleverer than his stupid attempt to make an impression on me, so I left quickly, keeping my mouth shut. That was my first visit to Manfred's; it should have been my last. I guess I'm a slow study sometimes.

On my second visit, at the incessant urgings of Sam Crist; a young deputy who had been assigned to be my partner the first week I was on the job, things didn't go any better.

"Come on, Ellie, give it another chance," he'd wheedled. "You just caught the place on an off night."

Against my better judgment I gave in and returned to Manfred's one more time. This is a pretty damn boring town after all and the only people I had met had been in law enforcement. I thought about going to church, just to meet someone who wasn't in the business, but I kept pulling the midnight shift on Saturday and Sunday morning.

When I finally got off work after wrestling drunks and breaking up fights, I was just too exhausted to think about getting cleaned up, changing clothes and going to church. It didn't hold that much appeal to me anyway when I considered it fully. I remembered sitting through hundreds of boring and confusing sermons as a child and then as a teenager, at my parents insistence…boring. The only fun I'd had was sitting in the back row with Joey Gerardo, reading the suggestive titles in the hymnals, such as *Oh Why Not Tonight?* and giggling while the preacher droned on about hellfire and damnation being the reward for lustful thoughts and deeds.

This time I ordered a drink from the bartender, a draft beer, thinking if I had to leave in a hurry, I wouldn't have wasted money on a more expensive drink. Ordinarily I would have ordered a dirty Absolute martini, but they cost five bucks and I didn't have five bucks to spare. I hadn't received my first paycheck yet so I had to make due for two more weeks on the meager savings I had scraped together.

The bartender had just set my drink on the bar when a tall, good looking guy walked over and stood beside me. He was decked out in a George Strait cowboy hat, pin striped western cut shirt, starched jeans and tan boots. All in all, he was one good looking son of a bitch, I thought to myself, but something just didn't seem to be right with him. The look in his eyes was just a little off; like he was here in the bar, but his mind was off in space. "Drugs? Speed maybe?" I wondered, as I looked away, letting him know I was not interested in him.

He didn't take a seat on the empty bar stool to my right, choosing instead to stand in the space between the empty stool and me. He was way too close and I was uncomfortable with his bold nearness. He brushed his leg against mine and gave me a knowing smile. Trying to ignore him and at the same time, discourage him, I looked straight ahead. There was his face in the mirror behind the bar, looking back at me with a smirk that seemed to imply he knew something that I didn't.

"Can I buy you a drink, honey?" he asked boldly. There was definitely something about him that put me off.

"No thanks. I'm here with a friend," hoping that would discourage him.

I looked down the bar to my left where Sam was chatting away with the newly hired blonde clerk from the records department. He didn't see me, as I tried to get his attention by giving him a hard stare, *the look*. He was too taken with the perky little boobs pushing against Blondie's thin blouse, as she seemed to hang on his every word. He wasn't looking around, focused entirely on the up thrust breasts staring back at him.

"Fuck!" I thought. "Looks like another unpleasant evening in this shit hole. Girl, when will you ever learn?" I was starting to feel pretty stupid about then.

The obnoxious stranger turned toward me again. Without a word he reached over and stroked my right breast with his hand! "What the…!" I yelled without thinking. I am not a small woman. I stand five feet ten inches tall and I weigh around one hundred and fifty pounds on a good day.

Besides being a weight trainer, I had gone through college on a basketball scholarship I'd kept in shape in the off season by learning kick boxing and doing palates. I didn't become a cop to be fondled by some asshole like this guy. I saw red instantly and came off my barstool while instinctively punching him below his breast bone, at the same time I brought my knee into his crotch with all my might.

He tried to scream, but he couldn't as the blow to his solar plexus had driven the wind from him. He was gasping on the floor and holding his nuts with both hands. I hoped I had driven them up into his stomach. Sam finally stopped talking to the blonde and walked over to see what had happened.

"Well, I'll be damned," he grinned, "If it isn't Johnny Wise Ass lying in a pool of shit."

His name *was* Johnny Wise I later found out, and he *was* rolling around on the floor in a puddle of beer, spit, and other wet stuff, spilled or tracked from the bathroom into the bar. As he struggled in his pain, no one offered to help him to his feet. In fact, no one seemed willing to offer him the slightest assistance; just derisive laughter in abundance. The crowd, now aware of what had taken place, well, part of what had taken place anyway, had gathered round. Everyone was cracking up at the pitiful sight of him wallowing in the muck.

"I've got to get out of here before someone calls the cops!" I said a little too loudly. But as he continued to roll on the floor, I couldn't help myself; I gave him another hard kick right in the ass. He was starting to get his breath back and he let out a moan as I kicked him one final time in about the same spot. My footprints were on the seat of his pants.

There were more guffaws all around as Sam, laughing also, said, "Relax Ellie, we are the cops. You won't see anyone sticking up for this dickhead, except maybe his uncle. That boy is never gonna learn, I guess. He is sure misnamed, but maybe you should refrain from kicking him in the ass anymore for a while." I stepped away from the man on the floor. The fancy shirt that had formerly looked so nice and crisp was now filthy with tobacco juice, mud, and God knows what.

"Looks like Old Johnny Boy finally met someone who wouldn't take his shit! Good for you Ellie."

I hesitated before asking, "What was that about his uncle again?" I didn't like the sound of that as I suddenly sensed things might not be as simple as Sam seemed to think they were.

"Johnny Boy is the son of the Sheriff Bailey's little sister, Nora. That's why he hangs around in here. But even the sheriff can't get him a job with any of the cop shops, though he sure has tried. He was a deputy for a little while, but he got drunk in the patrol car and ran into a school bus, one of the short ones. Sheriff Bailey pulled a lot of strings to keep him out of jail but he had to let him go from the force. Even the sheriff couldn't let that episode go unchallenged. Bailey came close to losing the last election because of nephew Johnny Boy's antics."

"Am I in trouble, Sam?" thinking how it didn't take me long to fuck up.

"Probably not, but be ready for an ass chewin'. As you probably know, Bailey's got no kids and he's kinda' adopted Johnny, even though he's a real piece of work. Johnny helps the sheriff out around his ranch sometimes. I guess that's where he get's his spending money, 'cause nobody else in this town will hire him." Sam continued to grin as he talked about the hurting Mr. Wise.

That was the last time I was ever in Manfred's Legal Ease Bar.

The next morning when I came on duty there was a note in my box to see Sheriff Bailey. With some trepidation I walked down the hall to his office and knocked on the door. He could see that it was me through the glass as he motioned me in with a wave of his hand and a stern expression on his face.

"I'm as nervous as a knocked up nun," I thought to myself and then had to suppress a giggle as that silly thought crossed my mind. I wasn't about to take any crap for defending myself against someone who had been so brazen as to touch my breast the way his nephew had…not without my permission anyway. I decide who gets to take such liberties.

Bailey must have sensed my resolve as he watched me. His countenance seemed to soften some as he spoke, but his expression belied his words as he said, "I hear you had some trouble in Manfred's last night. Appears you were getting your period or something and took it out on my nephew. Wanna tell me about it?"

I was speechless and taken off guard, but only for a moment. "Period my ass! That misogynist son of a bitch grabbed my tit without so much as a how do you do. Nobody and I mean nobody gets away with that shit with me! You should be happy I didn't haul his ass in and charge him with sexual assault! In fact, Sheriff, if you want to make an issue of this, I'll go arrest the cock sucker right now and bring him up on charges!"

I was pretty sure my face was bright red, but it matched my state of mind right then and I didn't care. "Period"…that was the pat answer for every ignorant man who ever saw a pissed off female. "Fuck him and fuck them!" I thought to myself as I waited for him to respond.

"Whoa, simmer down there deputy." It was evident he hadn't expected such an outburst from me; being new on the job and a woman at that. I probably shouldn't have used the SOB thing since Johnny was his sister's son, I thought, but the shoe seemed to fit.

"I just wanted to get your side of it." Apparently he had forgotten the "period" reference he had just made that set me off. I was still mad as hell but I decided to play ball and let it pass.

"Well now you have it and if we're done here, I'll get to work."

"Sure. You go on ahead there. Be careful, deputy."

I turned and left his office without looking back. Again the realization hit me; the number of ignorant men with asshole tendencies in high-level positions is legion. At least the innuendos and sexist remarks from the other officers seemed to cease after that…guess they didn't want my knee in their nuts.

# Chapter Thirty

# Jacob Meets Deputy Ellie Johnson

Jacob: As we'd agreed when on the phone, Deputy Johnson arrived at my office promptly at ten the following morning. Ever since I had gotten the call from her the day before, my outlook took on the aura of a sunny day in the Napa Valley wine country. Little did I know how at the time how her story would impact so many players; some in a good way, others not so much.

As Ellie entered my office I was pleasantly surprised by what I saw. She wasn't what you'd call a stunner but she *was* easy on the eye. She was tall and athletic, like a tennis player. She appeared to be strong physically and as I stood up and shook her hand, her firm grip told me I had been correct.

Ellie had a strong jaw, but not in a manly sort of way. This gave her a look of determination, sending sort of a "Don't fuck with me" message. Her bright hazel eyes exuded a superior intellect that took both my office decor and me in at a glance. From her expression I felt she approved of what she saw. We both recognized the professionalism in one another immediately.

I don't have the usual attorney's "Envy me" wall displaying such trappings as diplomas, bogus awards, and letters from, and pictures of, local or national politicians. The ones cherished by so many of my fellow attorneys, with the phony grins on their faces shaking each other's hands or hugging like brothers.

I figured that most people who entered my office would realize that I wouldn't be allowed to practice law in the state of California if I hadn't graduated from an accredited law school and then passed the bar. Such unnecessary displays seemed redundant and self-serving to me.

It's been my experience over the years, the more of this crap a person had on his or her wall; the less effective they were at their jobs. The old adage about baffling them with bullshit seemed to be the rule. "How can you say I don't know what I'm talking about? Look at my wall! I'm somebody to be reckoned with." Bunch of crap if you ask me, I preferred the picture of the ocean that was on my wall to a bunch of pieces of important looking certificates and photos.

"Hello there," I smiled as I opened our conversation trying to put her at ease. She appeared a little nervous, but not too much. I wanted us to get started on the right foot. "I'm Jacob Oakley and I'm very happy to meet you."

"Deputy Johnson, but you can call me Ellie. Do I call you Mr. Oakley or 'The Oak' as you seem to be known in a lot of public circles?" she said with a warm smile.

"*Jacob* is just fine, Ellie. That's what my friends call me and I think you and I are going to be friends. Have a seat; can I get you some coffee or a soda?"

"Diet Coke or Pepsi, if you've got it, thanks." She'd brought along a briefcase which she placed on the floor beside her chair. I didn't want to rush her so I went over to the little refrigerator I keep stocked for clients and pulled out two Diet Cokes. I opened the tabs, handed her a can and sat down at my desk and took a sip from mine. I was trying my damndest to play it cool with this lady.

She began, "I'm one of only three female sworn officers on the county sheriff's force of thirty five deputies. I'm still at the same rank I was when I went to work there five and a half years ago, even though I have a Bachelor's degree in Law Enforcement.

I've taken all the tests and attended the classes required to maintain my status as a professional law enforcement officer as required by the state. I don't want to sound like a whiner, Mr. Oakley; I mean Jacob, but the glass ceiling, for lack of a better term, is defined by Sheriff Bailey's fiefdom."

"I'm sorry to say this, Ellie, but that seems to be more the norm in your chosen profession than in most others. It's a sad thing too, since most female law enforcement I've dealt with are superior to their male counterparts."

Happy for my encouragement, Ellie continued to speak of her career at the SO as I wondered where this was leading. She went on to tell me of the incident involving the sheriff's nephew, Johnny Wise, and the meeting with Bailey that had followed. This had happened over five years ago, and yet it seemed she was still being punished for her insolence.

"You're probably wondering what this has to do with your investigation, while at same time wondering why I stayed on the job for so long." She could see the questions forming by the look on my face. She was a savvy lady alright.

"I'm not a quitter; never have been. I'm determined to make a success right where I am as a deputy. I've made a lot of friends on the force in the past five years, ones that I have chosen. These are honorable professionals unlike Sheriff Bailey and his hand-picked toadies.

"I could go somewhere else, to another department, but the job I started five years ago isn't finished. I want to make things right! I want to change the image of the Sheriff's Office. When I heard the rumor of what you were checking on, I thought this might be an opportunity; the chance I've been waiting for."

"What things are you talking about making right, Ellie?" Her motives were starting to become clearer as she spoke.

She continued," I live in a modest condominium and drive a three year old Ford Focus. Sometimes, if I have an unexpected expense, I can hardly make my mortgage payment and my car payment. At the same time Lt. Sherrow and a half dozen other sergeants are living in style. These guys, Bailey's select few, drive new pickups and live in fine homes. Homes fine enough that they are not close to being affordable on a deputy's pay, no matter what his rank."

"You think most everyone in the department is dirty?" knowing the answer before I asked.

"No, not all of us, but enough to create big problems. Look, I've witnessed the unsavory methods used by Sheriff Bailey and his federal crony, Agent Etheridge, while keeping my opinions on their lack of ethical behavior mostly to myself. There are still a few of us in the department who want to do something to stop him, but until I contacted you, we've been stymied. The deputies who aren't on the inside with Bailey don't want to rock the boat. These days everyone needs to keep their job.

"Who *do* you contact to try to bring down the strongest law enforcement officer in the county? He's got a lot of influential friends; at the local level. The board of supervisors loves him because he brings in extra money and freely spreads it around. There's never a deficit when it comes to the SO's budget. There are surpluses every year!"

"Surely you can go above the county level to bring him down?'

"You have to understand," she said with mild exasperation, "Bailey reigns supreme in the southeastern part of the state. His influence reaches to the state capitol and Ethridge covers Bailey's ass with the Feds. With what's at stake here, I sometimes fear for my own safety.

"Should Bailey or one of his men get wind of what I have found or what I'm doing by meeting with you...well let's just say they aren't strangers to ruining a person's life. If they'll set up a man, a complete stranger, like Bobby Lee Baker, and condemn him to life in prison by framing him with three bogus drug busts, there are probably no limits to the punishment they would bring to bear against someone they felt had crossed them; someone who might put their extravagant lifestyle at risk, besides I'm already on the sheriff's shit list."

"Who's Bailey's contact in Sacramento? Do you have any idea?" I was thinking this good ol' country sheriff had a lot more on the ball than I had given him credit for.

"I don't know if the guys there are dirty or just stupid. Each year he sponsors a hunting trip to Colorado. He's taken the Director of the State Department of Investigation or his assistant the last four years in a row. I don't know where the money comes from; his pocket or some government slush fund, but no one from the state ever comes in to audit us. Money talks, Jacob, and Bailey has a lot to say."

"There's got to be more going on than just getting bounties from the Feds for the pot busts, don't you think? I mean, from what you're telling me, we're talking a lot of money here. Hunting trips, SUV's, a horse ranch, payoffs to his men. I'd say we're looking at a million or more dollars a year for which he is not being held accountable.

Ellie picked up the briefcase from where it had been resting on the floor and set it my desk. I waited while she took a key from her shirt pocket and unlocked it.

As I waited, she removed some legal size envelopes from the briefcase. On one was written "Lt. Sherrow"; on another was" Photos of Homes and property". There were seven envelopes in all, each of the remaining five had someone's name printed on the outside.

"When the sheriff impounds a vehicle in a drug bust, the owner never sees it again. I believe the same thing goes on when a stolen vehicle is recovered. The owner's not contacted unless the vehicle has been burned or totaled, at which time a report is filed. On the other hand, if it is saleable, one of Bailey's men takes it to a chop shop in East LA where it is sold for cash."

"How do you know this? This doesn't sound like something many people would know about."

"Like I said before, I've made a lot of friends at the SO. Just because I quit going to Manfred's, the local cop bar, doesn't mean others stay away. When the booze starts flowing and the stories about who is the biggest swinging dick start, there is always at least one braggart that talks too much. Sorry, I didn't mean to use offensive language."

"I'm not offended. I couldn't have stated it any more clearly myself *and* I get paid for *my* words," I replied with a smile. She really did have it together.

"Ellie, I can see this thing is a lot bigger than I anticipated but my main concern at the moment is obtaining a new trial for Bobby Lee. Can you shed any light on how the game Bailey played on him was accomplished?"

"Of course, Bailey and Ethridge and a few others set these busts up. Bailey gets around $50,000 from Ethridge's drug bureau for each conviction. There's a special task force within the department that sets things up. They use blackmail or sometimes if they can't persuade someone to work with them, they will plant drugs on the guy they want to use, threatening imprisonment if he refuses to play along. The targets are set up carefully, guys without money or influence; maybe someone with a past prison record and no credibility. They look for men, and women, who have no friends close by to come to their aid. In order to not kill the golden goose they have to keep these bogus arrests under the radar

"Bailey used Earl Feathers to trap Baker and then he set up Tom Kidd to entrap Bobby Lee again after he got out. The sheriff already had collected for on him once and he knew Bobby Lee was an easy mark; no money and no contacts.

"Bailey then persuaded Kidd to buy in by offering him a shorter sentence. Did I mention that the warden at Farmstead also accompanies the sheriff on his hunting trips periodically? They also do a lot of fishing in down in Baja together. Whenever Bailey wants an early release for someone, it happens. If he wants someone to stay longer, he can make that happen too. That's how Kidd managed to leave prison before Bobby Lee."

Wow, she had brought a lot to the table for me to consider. Changing the subject, I asked Ellie, "What's in the envelopes you brought?"

"You can keep those to peruse and maybe help build your case. There are photos and addresses of the deputy's homes and pickups that I told you about, along with receipts from various car dealers where the sheriff's guys paid cash for their vehicles.

"I guess I kind of misled the salesmen by implying that I was investigating a stolen car ring. They were really cooperative when I flirted with them a little and hinted that I might be buying a new Taurus soon. I do like that new Taurus, don't you?"

She smiled coquettishly, showing a less businesslike and more feminine side than I had seen until now. She was giving me a small glimpse of this softer side she had used to get the info she wanted from the gullible salesmen.

Very cute and very effective; probably would have worked on me too, I thought.

"There's some papers in there from the chop shop and some deposit slips from a bank in Mexico. Don't ask me how I got these. I only hope you can use them as evidence. If not at least you have a starting point to find something you can use legally."

231

"Ellie, when the time is right, can I count on you to testify for Bobby Lee? From what you've told me, I know there could be some danger for you if you agree. I want you to know I appreciate what you brought me and I'd understand if you don't want to risk anymore than you have already."

She gave me *the* look, "I'm not doing this just for your client, Jacob, even though he was railroaded. Of course I'll testify for you, but you've got to help me out here also. I've given you enough information to start an investigation against my boss. I've told you of his contacts, but I know a lot about you too.

Besides what I've heard around the office, I checked you out on the internet and you have a reputation. They don't call you "The Oak" for nothing. I want you to help bring Bailey and his crooked deputies to justice. Oh, and after that, I want his job; the first female sheriff in the county. You help me and I'll help you." She flashed that sweet disarming smile again but I could sense the underlying steeliness within her. It was clear to me that she was a tough lady.

Ellie's request seemed reasonable to me, so I said, "Why not? You seem pretty capable to me. I think you would make an excellent sheriff. If as you say, you've checked me out, I guess you're probably aware that the State Attorney General and I are old classmates and have worked together in the past. I'm pretty sure that he doesn't hunt or fish with Sheriff Bailey." This was not a question. She smiled and nodded.

Ellie and I had spent a little over an hour together and in that time, much to my satisfaction, I learned a lot more from her than I had anticipated. I decided I needed to find out more about where the good sheriff got the money he needed to operate his enterprise. I placed a call to Boyd Reynolds so he could pay a visit to the horse ranch. I had a feeling there was a lot more than horse semen being sold from there.

# CHAPTER THIRTY ONE

# The Oak Sets His Sights on Bailey

Jacob: I started my investigation of Sheriff Bailey right after I had wrapped up my meeting with Deputy Ellie Johnson. Having secured her agreement to testify for Bobby Lee and against Bailey assured, I was feeling elated; no more Don Quixote, more like Robin Hood.

I had put Boyd Reynolds to work to see what unsavory facts he could discover about how the sheriff did business. Boyd had retired from the LAPD after twenty years on the force. With the city's generous retirement policy, that made him forty-five when he hung up his badge. After he retired it hadn't take him very long to get bored with watching Rockford and Magnum reruns. To maintain his sanity, he started his own private investigation business.

Over the years Boyd had made a lot of friends…on both sides of the law. When he'd been on the force, he didn't arrest people for petty shit. The way he figured it, possession of a little pot or even recreational cocaine was not justification enough to ruin a person's life; especially in California where much more serious crimes than possession of a small amount of narcotics were occurring hourly.

In his last years on duty, when the DUI laws became so harsh that good people could lose their jobs and sometimes their homes as a result of a conviction, he was cautious when deciding to make an arrest. Of course, he wouldn't let someone who was obviously a danger to himself of others slide, but he also didn't harass the guys who were able to control their vehicles after downing a few beers or cocktails.

Many of his fellow officers looked for easy DUI arrests knowing the exorbitant fines levied by the courts would make their supervisors happy. The *really* lazy officers would park outside drinking establishments, bars, late in the evening. It was easy for these cops to pick out which cars had been there longest as the officer would cruise by the bar and make mental notes or jot down license numbers for future reference. They would return later to stake out the bar, sorta like the practice of shooting deer from a tree stand; not very sporting as far as Boyd was concerned.

An arrest would be imminent if the bar patron turned out to be the least bit over the legal limit; regardless of their ability to control their vehicle. The new alcohol limits didn't leave much room for a guy to get away with having more than two or three drinks in an evening.

"Probable cause" as an excuse for a stop was never an issue; "You swerved" or "You made a wide turn" were the two most often cited reasons for forcing the unfortunate bar patron to stop. It didn't matter that no infraction had actually occurred; the cop making the arrest was always right in the eyes of the law. The judges and the prosecutors had heard the "wide-turn" story with little variation hundreds of times and never questioned it. This was considered normal procedure when it came to "probable cause".

As I said before, Boyd's style had gained him a lot of friends over the years, since he was not in the habit of being an overbearing asshole; in or out of uniform. These various relationships had served him well in his latest career as a private investigator. He was able find out things that no cop on the force ever could. He'd done a fair amount of work for me previously. The fees he charged were fair and his work was exceptional…and thorough. In fact, he was working for me now, part time, studying what Robert Marius and Marius' latest clients were up to. "The city never sleeps, Oak," he told me when I called to ask if he had time to lend a hand.

His response brought a laugh from me. "What the fuck does that even mean, Boyd? The city never sleeps?" I asked derisively.

Without missing a beat he replied, also with a laugh, "I have no idea, but it sounds pretty cool, don'tcha' think? I saw it on some movie."

"I guess; if you say so. I still don't get how it relates to your business, but if you like it, who am I to judge?" I took some time to tell him about Sheriff Bailey and my suspicions about his nefarious dealings. I also let him know about my interest in trying to help Bobby Lee and why I felt it was important to try to see justice served.

"First of all, I need you to nose around and see if Bailey's truly selling the cars he confiscates. See what you can uncover and we'll go from there. I also need you to take a look at the infamous quarter horse ranch. I'll get you some more details on how best to approach that, later. Right now concentrate on the car scam. Call me when you have any news."

"You bet. I'm already on it, Oak."

# CHAPTER THIRTY TWO

# Return to Farmstead
# to See Bobby Lee

Jacob: My conversation with Deputy Johnson, Ellie, had given me a lot to think about. After she left my office and I had finished my call to Boyd Reynolds to get him lined out, I sat back in my chair to reflect on what had just transpired. I jotted down a few additional thoughts about how I could go about slamming the gate on Sheriff Bailey's assorted illegal activities. I had to analyze if I would able gather enough evidence to build a case. I realized I didn't know what all he might be into nor did I have any idea how many different agencies and criminal elements might be in cahoots with him but I was determined to find out.

Just to cover my bases I placed one more call to Buddy. Buford Hollins is the Attorney General for the state and has been for three terms now. Only his closest friends call him Buddy. He's been "Buddy" to me since we were in law school together.

There was no answer when I called his office, so I tried his cell. He said, "Hello, Oak." Sometimes caller ID is not a bad thing since he would take my calls almost anytime.

I jumped right in, "Buddy, I need to pick your brain about Sheriff Bailey over in San Bernardino County. I think he's involved in shady shit and I might need your help in an official capacity if I get in over my head."

"Gee, Oak, I know he's got a lot of powerful friends around there in his home county and in Sacramento, but that's all I know about the guy. I've heard a few rumors, but my office is too busy these days to follow up anything that is not solid. What do you have? Anything I can hang my hat on?"

"Well, for one thing, other than you Buddy, I don't have a lot of friends in the capitol. I guess I don't always fight for the proper causes or donate to the right candidates. But putting all that aside, I think Bailey has aligned himself with a crooked Fed on the narc squad by the name of Byron Ethridge. I need you see what you can find in his background. I also think Bailey is running a couple of other scams, but I have to get more info before we can make a move. I've got Brad Reynolds nosing around for me. If there's something going on that would be of interest you I'm sure Boyd will find it. "

Buddy chuckled before asking, "You and Boyd make quite a pair. Are you still after Robert Marius? Don't answer that one. How'd you get into this deal, Oak? You're usually fighting for some lost cause involving a miscarriage of justice against one of your clients by some real or imagined authority figure. It's strange to see you trying to put someone away for a change. Are you getting more mellow in your old age?"

"I *am* working for a client; a young fellow that was railroaded by Bailey. I found this other stuff, this dirt on Bailey, by accident. My main concern is freeing my client of course. I may also need your help with that issue as well, but that's later on down the road. If I can cast Bailey in a bad light by discovering something solid to use against him, it will make my work in freeing my client a hell of a lot easier."

"You know that you can count on me, Oak. Just keep me in the loop and I'll do what I can. You know I appreciate how you've always shot straight with me and having you as a friend has done a lot for my credibility with the voters and the honest state officials over the years. We have no trust issues and if I can help you nail a crooked public official like your sheriff Bailey; legitimately of course, it's always good for some positive press at election time. No one likes a crooked sheriff. I'll se if any of my staff have any info that will help you with your case."

The next day I placed another call to Boyd Reynolds. "Boyd, I think it's time for you to bone up on your knowledge of quarter horses. Buy yourself a hat and a pair of boots if you don't have a pair already and go visit Sheriff Bailey's ranch.

"Unless you can come up with a better story I'd say just tell the foreman you've got a mare you want to have bred. You're looking for a stud with Doc Bar lineage which Bailey's stud has. Mention that you heard about the ranch from one of your friends in the business and you want to take look at Bailey's stallion. You're shopping around and looking at several candidates for a sire for your mare. While you're there, try to look around and see if you can spot anything strange. See if you can get a tour of the ranch while you're at it, but above all, don't mention that you know me.

"At first my plan had been to visit the ranch myself, but I don't want to arouse Bailey's suspicions. Rumors about me are already circulating around the SO, but there seems to be a lot more to his operation than I first thought. Ever hear of the "Cowboy Mafia" thing back in Texas in the eighties? Drugs were being transported by cowboys in horse trailers. It turned out to be the biggest RICO bust in history. This kinda smacks of the same kind of deal."

Boyd replied, "Can't say as I have. Cowboy Mafia? Nope. Can you tell me what I'm supposed to be looking for? Do you think Bailey is ballsy enough to have marijuana actually growing in the alfalfa fields or just bales of it moving on trucks or something more subtle? Give me a clue, Oak."

"I wish I knew, but I'm not sure. I'm suspecting that drugs are being shipped in and out from there; a distribution center maybe. There seems to be a lot of money changing hands within members of his staff and his cronies. When that's going on, drugs or some other illegal commodity is usually close by. Just keep an open mind; getting some pictures fo the place are probably out of the question."

"OK, you're the boss. I'll be on my best Sherlock Holmes behavior; different type of hat is all."

"Right! I'm off to Farmstead to visit with Bobby Lee. I'll catch you later, "I said hanging up.

While following up on a few leads and checking records, I hadn't been out to see Bobby Lee for awhile. I wanted to reassure him that I hadn't forgotten his case and I was giving it my full attention. Maybe there was something he had remembered since our last talk that could make our case stronger.

When I got through the security gate at the prison and met Bobby Lee, we walked together to our picnic table and sat down. It had rained earlier, but now the sky was clearing. Even on the prison "campus" the air smelled fresh and clean; giving the feeling of possible new beginnings in the wind. He seemed happy to see me. I say "seemed", but that was an understatement; he could hardly contain himself.

"What'cha got for me? Good news? Come on, Oak, give it up!" He was acting like a kid waiting for Santa.

"Slow down, Bobby Lee, I told you this could take awhile, but trust me; I believe we are making some progress." I didn't want to tell him about Ellie yet. She and I were sworn to secrecy at this point. Too many things could go wrong. Holly was still gathering info on the case histories. I was confident that Holly would come up with what I needed. It all just takes time.

Years ago, when Holly and I were just getting to know each other, she had used a series of words to describe herself to me: a dreamer; bold, curious, spontaneous, intuitive, fearless, brash undaunted, genuine, and strong.

"That's a lot of good characteristics for such a little thing as you," I had told her laughingly.

"Just you wait and see," she'd replied sweetly smiling at me with eyes full of self-confidence.

Since that time, I'd learned that she was indeed everything she had claimed to be and more. *Tenacious* was the trait that I had come to think of most when it came my turn to offer a description of my fiancé.

Bailey's office was being very uncooperative about supplying the crime report folders his deputies had turned in regarding the cases against Bobby Lee. I had thought the sheriff couldn't know for sure that I was involved, but I was beginning to imagine he had a good idea of who was behind the requests. Especially since Ellie had contacted me unsolicited; someone inside the Sheriff's office must have tipped her off.

We weren't surprised by the SO's reluctance to come up with the material we had requested, so we continued to press on with obtaining the court records from Bobby Lee's three trials. "Go get 'em, Holly, but be careful. Sheriff Bailey seems to have a lot of friends in high places," was all I could say.

I had been lost in thought for a moment and I could sense the lad was getting impatient with me so I said, "Bobby Lee, Tom Kidd told me that he worked on Bailey's ranch a few times when he was in on his first rap. Did he ever talk to you about anything strange or anything that appeared to be out of the ordinary going on out there?"

I could see him frown at the mention of Tom Kidd. He didn't know about the pressure Bailey had brought to bear on Tom to make him throw his new friend under the bus. He took his time reflecting on my question and then I could see that he had thought of something. I planned on talking to Kidd myself later in the week, but since I was already here, I figured I could use this visit to maybe glean a little more info about Bailey's dealings.

"Jeez, Oak, why are you talking to that asshole? Kidd is the guy that got me sent up on the second charge. If it weren't for him, I wouldn't be in the fix I am now. Shit!"

I gave him a little time to cool down and then I explained the offer Bailey and Ethridge had made to Tom about reducing his sentence, "Tom feels very badly about what he did to you. He's willing to testify in your behalf when the time comes. You might want to consider what you would have done under the same circumstances…a five year sentence reduction is a big temptation. Remember Tom didn't know you until Bailey approached him. It wasn't like it was personal. "

I could see the wheels turning but he wasn't buying my whole spiel. "I don't think I would ever treat a friend of mine like that, no matter what." I couldn't help but admire his ethics; the code of loyalty he exhibited toward his friends was rare indeed.

To reassure him I replied, "I understand where you're coming from, Bobby Lee, and I can't say that I blame you for your ill feelings toward Tom, but it might help your case if you can you remember any of your conversations about Bailey's ranch?"

At least he was heeding my words as he spoke, "Tom said it was a really nice ranch, beautiful horses and all, alfalfa fields and white fences with several barns filled with hay. He did mention that it was strange the way the hay trucks would arrive with a load of hay, drive to one of the barns to unload, then go over to another barn and pick up another load of hay from there.

"When the trucks left most of them were still loaded with hay. He said he didn't give it much thought at the time, but he did admit that it sure did seem strange when he thought about it later. 'What the hell are they feeding their livestock?' he'd said."

I had seen an e-mail a while back where the drug runners in south Texas were using hollowed out hay bales to smuggle drugs in from Mexico. I thought at the time how clever the system was, since loads of hay are hauled all over the country with no apparent rhyme or reason as to pick-up point or destination.

Alfalfa is hauled from Arizona and California to New Mexico, Texas and other points north and east. I wondered to myself if the good sheriff might be using his trucks to make deliveries while at the same time securing evidence to be planted on his soon-to-be prisoners. The arrests were a double bonus for him as it kept suspicion away from his operation while putting money in the coffers of the sheriff's department with the rewards paid by the Feds. It seemed to me the sheriff had become quite an astute businessman.

Sheriff Bailey had built a reputation as a hard liner against drugs in his bailiwick, much in the same way Sheriff Joe of Maricopa County over in Arizona had built a reputation as a tough guy on illegal immigration. No one would ever suspect either of these upstanding paragons of law enforcement of breaking the very laws they were sworn to uphold.

Their actions had kept them above reproach for years. "Maybe not so much anymore, Mr. Sheriff," I thought to myself.

I glanced at my watch and realized it was time to go. Time seemed to fly by when I was working on something that interested me, as this case did. I realized it was too bad that time did not zip by the same way for my new client as he waited for me to do my job. I told Bobby Lee he would hear from me soon. We shook hands as we parted. He was impatient, but who could blame him? The wheels of the bureaucracy are oiled with glue.

# CHAPTER THIRTY THREE

# Tom Kidd and the Skunk Odor

Jacob: I phoned ahead to the prison to set up my second visit with Tom Kidd. I talked with a clerk in Admin who told me he did not have the authority to allow me to see Mr. Kidd. I explained about lawyers and clients to him and told him I'd better have a positive answer real soon, "This is Jacob Oakley and if you don't want to be visited by a shit storm real soon you'll have the warden get back to me...quickly."

A few minutes later, I received a call from the warden of the minimum security prison where Kidd was serving his time. This prison was not run by the state, but was one of a chain of several such private facilities located in Colorado and Arizona in addition to this one in California.

These facilities were owned and operated by a family out of Utah. The lessons learned by the younger members of this family while on their missions for the Church must have stuck. The young entrepreneurs had convinced the collective governors of three states that it was cheaper to hire *the family* to house prisoners than it was to incarcerate them in a state prison. Despite several recent news stories that publicized the financial records covering expenditures over the last several years and belied their claims, the governors adamantly stuck by their guns in defending their decisions to continue utilize these private institutions.

"We can't afford to build more prisons in Arizona. What else can we do? I have no choice," Arizona's governor had stated while campaigning before the last election. Her irrational reasoning must have worked on the fearful voters; she was re-elected by a landslide. The fact that she was affiliated with the party in power helped to cover a lot of her shortcomings.

Three murderers had recently escaped from their compound in Arizona, killed a couple of tourists, and left egg on the face of the governor and the family, but not enough to remedy the situation. However; the violent acts had raised a lot of questions.

The press had been relentless, not only locally but nationwide. It had been the top story on CNN for more than two weeks. Law suits against the state were being threatened by the family of the victims. The prison owners and the politicians weren't in the mood for more negative publicity, so a gag order had been issued to the various wardens at each private institution.

Warden Ellis let me know in no uncertain terms, he was not going to be pushed around by "some fancy hotshot lawyer". He continued in a very agitated voice, "The Family has put out a strong memo holding each individual administrator personally responsible for any glitches or bad press. I can't afford to take any chances that might imperil my job. This is my life! I have a family to take care of and I'm not risking my career to help some drug addict."

"Easy, Warden, I'm not pushing anyone around. Mr. Kidd is my client and you know, as well as I, that you can't keep his attorney from seeing him. I'll be out this afternoon just as I informed your secretary a few minutes ago. By the way, Mr. Kidd is not a drug addict." Warden Ellis hung up without further comment.

Tom was waiting for me when I arrived. He had been placed in an interrogation room of some sort and when I saw it I just shook my head at the guard and said, "This won't do. I'm not about to confer with my client in a place where our conversation can be recorded."

He tried to reassure me by sort of bowing and saying in a placating tone, "Oh, Sir, we know better than to try something like that. Warden Ellis just thought you would be more comfortable here by yourselves." I could see the camera in the corner of the ceiling. The big mirror on the wall was so obvious that I merely nodded my chin toward it and smiled.

"We'd like to conduct our visit in the picnic area, please."

The guard was less condescending all of a sudden, as his tone changed, "I gotta call and get an OK. It ain't up to me." He didn't like his authority challenged; like I cared what he thought. I had seen his kind in many government venues over the years. He had his orders and this was creating an unnecessary pain in his ass, I could tell. He gave me what he obviously considered to be a menacing scowl, to no avail.

Stone faced I matched his tone, "Make the call. Tom and I will wait."

Fifteen minutes later we were sitting at a picnic table outside. The day was a cool and pleasant one, typical of most days in Southern California, so we picked a spot where the sun was shining on us. Tom took out a pack of cigarettes and lit one up before we began to talk.

I waited for him to give me a signal before I began. He blew out a stream of smoke and looked at me with an open trusting expression. He too was waiting so I spoke first. "How are they treating you, Tom? Anything funny going on? Has the warden or the sheriff been by to see you?"

"Naw, not much going on here Mr. Oakley. Things don't change much inside these places. You makin' any headway with Bobby Lee's case…or mine?" he added hopefully.

"I think so. I'm finding a pattern of less than ethical practices on the part of Sheriff Bailey. That's why I'm here. You told me that you had been to the sheriff's ranch a few times, but you didn't tell me anything about the operation. Bobby Lee said you mentioned something strange with the hay trucks?"

"Oh yeah, they'd come and go but they seemed to be always loaded with bales of hay. Round ones, the big five hundred pounders, and sometimes just the regular two or three wire bales. Seemed kinda' crazy when I thought about it at first, but then I figured they must be tradin' oat or grass hay for alfalfa or somethin' like that."

"You told me you've been around some drug operations up in Mendocino County in the past. Anything strike you as similar about what was happening at Bailey's ranch?" I gave him some time to consider my question.

"Skunk! There was always a real strong skunky odor everywhere even though I never saw one. The smell overpowered the horseshit even. I didn't think about it before, but it could have been some really strong that pot I was smellin'."

"Good job, Tom. I kind of suspected there must be something like that going on." We shot the shit for a little longer as he told me how day to day life was pretty boring in the new facility. Finally I told him, "I've gotta run, but you've been a big help. I'll see you soon, hopefully with some good news about your case."

"Really? That would be great, Mr. Oakley." He could barely contain himself. More soberly he asked, "How'd Bobby Lee take it when you told him you'd talked to me?"

"As you can imagine, Tom, he didn't take it too well at first. I had to explain your situation and your offer from Bailey. He seemed to be in a better frame of mind toward you after that. By the way, call me Oak."

CHAPTER THIRTY FOUR

# Visit to Sheriff Bailey's Ranch

Boyd Reynolds: The Oak needn't have worried about whether or not I had the boots, Stetson, or the knowledge of quarter horses. Since I retired from the police department and took on the private investigator shtick, I've tried to become grounded in a lot of areas. My good friend Ken Evans had schooled me long ago about the basics of the cutting horse culture.

Ken had started by telling me some of the history of the breed. Tilting his hat back and sipping Wild Turkey on the rocks he gave me the lowdown. "The first true quarter horse was Old Sorrel and was owned by the King Ranch in south Texas. He'd been purchased in 1915 and was originally used on the ranch as a work horse to cut or separate individual cattle from the herd to be branded or vaccinated. The breed, also known as cutting horses, had come into it's own with the creation of the American Quarter Horse Association in 1940. Old Sorrel was registered with the association that same year.

With great detail he brought me up to current day events. "Doc Bar had been foaled in 1956, after his sire, a quarter horse stallion, was bred to a racehorse; a thoroughbred mare. Doc Bar turned the quarter horse breed completely around. Quarter horse competitions soon started taking place all over the country. Prices for the animals and the stud fees have soared. Doc Bar's offspring were in huge demand. They became some of the most valuable of the quarter horse family and still are today."

I learned that over time, raising and showing quarter horses has become an industry unto itself. I had met Ken in Vegas a few times to watch his horse, Skip Jo Doc, perform at the Tropicana Arena where hundreds of horses would compete against each other for the title of World Champion. Once chosen as champion by a team of judges, the winner's stud fee would increase dramatically; enough that the owner's financial life would also undergo a huge change for the better if he wasn't already rich. It was sorta like winning the lottery in some ways. The prize money wasn't bad either.

Skip was never a finalist, but he usually paid the expenses for the trip with the prize money he won. That was good enough for Ken, as this was merely a hobby of his. Skip and the other quarter horses were a joy to watch perform. When we'd seen enough of the cutting show, which ran twenty-four hours a day for five days and nights, there was always another good show going on inside the casino away from the arena.

The cowboys and the gentlemen ranch owners would be crowded around the dice tables. There would be lots of yelling and laughing, whooping and hollering, as it were, from the men wearing the big hats and colorful boots with their spurs still buckled on. The pit bosses and the other casino employees looked on nervously; even the old casino hands weren't quite sure about this crowd.

An occasional fight would break out; but hell, these were cowboys and fighting was part of their mystique. Casino Security would come and break up the altercation, quickly separating the antagonists without calling any cops. The casino bosses knew these boys spent way too much money in the gaming areas to allow something like a little fisticuffs to interfere with business. In a few minutes everything would be back to normal, or as normal as the place could be when hosting this rowdy group.

I had no qualms when it came to passing myself off as a gentleman cowboy. I set up the visit to the G-B ranch just as Jacob advised. I placed a call ahead to verify that the sheriff wouldn't be around. Jacob had made it clear it wasn't yet time to brace the sheriff.

"G Bar B, leave a message and we'll get back to you," was the greeting on the answering machine.

"Yeah, this is Boyd Grayson from up north." I didn't want to say Boyd Reynolds just in case someone had heard of me. "I have a place just out of Alturas up by the Oregon border, where I raise a few horses. I own a very exceptional mare; well I think she's special anyway, and I want to have her bred to a comparable stud. I hear that you've got a stallion bred out of the Doc Barr line that has the characteristics I'm looking for.

"I'd like to get her bred in the next month or so and I was wondering if I might take a look at your stud if that would be OK. I'm going to be in your area for a few days." I left my cell number along with the phony name. I didn't think anyone would recognize my real name and connect it to my profession, but you never know. When it comes to lawmen or crooks, and Jacob had implied this bunch might be both, this can turn out to be a small world. I wasn't in the habit of taking chances.

An hour or so later my phone rang, "This is Gary Goodman, foreman at G Bar B. You left a message about a mare you want serviced?"

"You bet, Gary. I was in the area on business and I've heard about your stud from some friends of mine that follow the circuit. They've seen your horse work at some of the shows. They tell me he's a magnificent animal and might be just the sire I'm looking for."

"As I said in my message I left on your machine, my mare is very special and I want to breed her to an equally special stallion. Since I was in the valley I wondered if I can come take a look at him." I didn't see how this could arouse any suspicions, since horse breeding was the purported business being conducted at the ranch.

There was a slight pause as if he might be checking his calendar; then suspiciously he asked, "Who are you again? I know most of the breeders around and I can't say as how I've ever heard of you."

"Name's Boyd Grayson; I've got a little spread up in Modoc County, down by the Pit River. I'm not really well known in horseman circles. It's more of a hobby with me. In fact my mare is one of the first horses I've acquired.

"I retired a while back, left San Francisco, and now I need something to keep me busy. When I first retired, golf and fishing were OK for a while, but let me ask you Gary; could you be satisfied just whacking a little white ball around a pasture day after day? I wanted something a little more stimulating. Besides, I think I can make a few bucks off the horses while I'm enjoying myself."

I waited to see if my answer would allay his suspicions. It must have worked, as he responded, noticeably friendlier now, "Yeah, I know what you mean, Boyd. I never could understand that golf shit either, other than maybe the nineteenth hole or maybe the pretty girls driving the drink carts." He seemed to stifle a giggle at what he'd just said.

"Tell you what; can you come by around ten in the morning? I should have my chores done by then and I'll be free to show you Mr. Bailey Bar. You can see for yourself that he's really something…just like your friends told you. We can put him through his paces with some steers. I was planning on giving him a workout anyway. He's getting' a little fat and lazy here on the ranch with not much to do other than mount the pretty mares that come to see him."

"That sounds fine with me. Will the owner be around in case we need to negotiate the price?"

I could feel the change in his voice going from warm to cold rather quickly. "Sheriff Bailey's got other more important things to do that keep him pretty busy. He leaves the runnin' of the ranch to me. The fee is five thousand dollars and it's non-negotiable." His voice took on an edge, hardening as he told me this. I wasn't sure if it was that I sounded like a cheapskate or that I had insulted him by implying he didn't have the authority to put the deal together.

He'd given me my answer about Bailey not being in attendance, which was my purpose in asking the question that seemed to set him off, so I made amends quickly. "No sweat, Gary. I didn't mean to cause offense. If what I have heard about your stud is true; the price sounds fair enough to me. I wouldn't be much of a horse trader, though, if I didn't try to save a few bucks, now would I?"

That seemed to put him at ease again. I heard him chuckle. "Greenhorn horse traders… gotta love 'em. Of course, Boyd, no offense taken. It's just that I'm in charge of the horses. No one else; not even the boss, tells me what to do when it comes to them. Bailey takes care of marketing the hay and entertaining his big shot guests. You're not the first to ask for a deal and I'm sure you won't be the last. See you in the morning then, by the way do you need directions out to the ranch? "

I didn't, but I didn't want to do anything to make him suspicious. "Sure, how do I get to your place from Barstow?"

"It's not far from where the Lone Ranger and Tonto used to hang out. You got a pen and paper?" The ranch was about sixty miles from town and he spent a couple of minutes telling me which roads to take. I thanked him and hung up. Then I called Jacob to bring him up to date.

Jacob answered on the first ring with a light hearted tone indicating he was in a good mood. "Oak must have discovered something good," I thought to myself.

When he heard my voice he said, "Hey Boyd, how'd you make out? Are you going to see the ranch? I might have a little more info as far as what you should be on the lookout for."

His good mood had yet to rub off on me. "That would be nice, since you haven't given me shit to go on so far," I answered sourly.

My surly attitude didn't seem to dampen his good mood as he replied, "Don't be that way, Amigo. If I haven't been as informative as you think I should be you have to realize that there's a lot here for me to sort out. I just left Tom Kidd at the *renta-prison* and he described what appears to be a major drug operation taking place there at the ranch. Seems like it might be a distribution center or something like that. Pot for sure and whatever else…is being transported on hay trucks and probably other Trojan horses, pardon the pun."

"Sorry, can't pardon that. It's too fucking corny, pardon *my* pun," I said.

"Tom says he saw a lot of trucks coming and going, some loaded with hay and others pulling horse trailers. Come to think of it, those horse trailers full of old hay and horse manure would be the ideal vehicles to put false bottoms in. They could also be used to transport the stuff that sells for big money than pot in small quantities; meth or coke."

"I'm meeting the foreman at ten o'clock tomorrow. I'm told Bailey won't be there so you can come along if you'd like."

"Let me think about that for a minute…Naw, you can handle it. I don't want to take even the slightest chance that might alert the sheriff to the fact that he's being watched, especially by me. Let's meet day after tomorrow at my office." With that we ended our conversation and I began to make a plan on how to reconnoiter Bailey's operation.

I arrived at the entrance to the ranch early the next morning. I wanted a chance to reconnoiter the area before I met with Gary. I was hoping he was busy with his morning tasks. If questioned, I would just say I had misjudged the time it would take to make the trip out here to the ranch.

A sign resembling a small billboard announced:

## G-B QUARTER HORSE RANCH

### GUY BAILEY, OWNER        Mr. Bailey Bar, at stud

The long narrow lane that served as the entry way back into the ranch itself resembled something from the old Southern Ante Bellum plantation days. Huge pecan trees lined either side of the stamped concrete drive forming a huge canopy over the *faux* brick pattern; providing a very shady and serene atmosphere. The drive led straight up to the single story adobe main ranch house about a hundred yards off the rural black top road. Any resemblance to the Old South ended here. Santa Fe architecture and furnishings dominated the area around the house.

It was a sprawling affair, covering at least four thousand square feet, built around a courtyard filled with bougainvillea, blooming bird of paradise plants, and dozens of other flowering plants that I couldn't begin to name, but I could appreciate their colorful beauty.

I could see a good sized pond, three acres at least, with weeping willows set back from the edge. There was even a small dock running out into the clear blue water. A small Boston Whaler with an electric motor was tied there. Other than a large aerator pushing a fountain of water high into the air, it all looked very pastoral. Dimples appeared on the surface of the pond caused by what appeared to be a school of large fish feeding on a swarm of insects.

White wooden fences that looked as if they had been freshly painted surrounded the entire eighty acres or so that made up the ranch. There was no barbed wire to be seen; only the more expensive wooden fencing. Either the horses here were too valuable to risk the damage that could be inflicted if they were to become entangled in the wire or, more likely, from what I had learned of the man, Bailey probably liked the ostentatious display of wealth, associated with the thousands of dollars worth of fencing. Sorta like some fat cat buying a King Air rather than a Beech Bonanza, which would have served him just as well, to carry him fifty miles to his office each day.

As ten o'clock neared, I followed the road around the house toward the stables where I could see a pen full of skinny steers chewing contentedly around a rack filled with alfalfa hay. Next to that pen was the enclosure where the teaser stallion stood with his head up seeming to watch everything going on.

His hide was covered with scars, some healed and some still fresh, from kicks and bites he received from the mares he had tried to service while preparing them to be mounted by Mr. Bailey Bar. Poor teaser gets the mare all excited and then when she's ready to receive him, he's led away, kicking and neighing loudly, while the stud walks in and mounts her without a fight.

Looking toward the beat up stallion I said, "I'll bet you'd like to kick the shit out of Mr. Bailey Bar, wouldn't you? You do all the work and he gets all the action. Concentrate on the job at hand, Boyd," I reminded myself. As I slowed down the unlucky stallion looked at me and neighed.

Off in the distance I could see two large hay barns surrounded by fields of alfalfa. There was no way to sneak up on the structures, as the alfalfa was cut short. I could make out one road with a chained large metal gate that led to them both. The road then became a circle while providing a drive thru loop that allowed the big trucks and trailers to pull into and through the barns. Either barn could accommodate an eighteen wheeler stacked with a large load of hay. A couple of men stood outside the closest barn appearing to do nothing but keep a look out. I didn't see any weapons, but then I wasn't close enough to the men to be certain.

I was sitting there in my car watching them when I heard someone approaching.

"You must be Boyd."

"And you must be Gary." I shut off the engine on my rented car and stepped out while grabbing my hat off the seat next to me. I turned to face a lean and hardened cowboy that seemed to be made of tanned leather and sinew. Dressed in jeans that were covered by chaps' worn slick from years of work, he looked like something straight off the set of Monte Walsh…Lee Marvin or Jack Palance, only not quite as hard as those two had appeared in that movie.

I noticed that there was a certain gentlemanly softness about him that I couldn't quite lay my finger on. His black felt hat was dusty and sweat rimed. The old boots he was wearing were stained green around the soles from the alfalfa and manure he tromped through. The heels were run down on one side while the spurs looked as if they were from much earlier times and had seen lots of use.

Gary was just less than six feet tall; he probably weighed in around one seventy and looked to be between forty and fifty years old; his sun lined face made it hard to tell at first glance. "Capable," I thought to myself would be the one word I would use to describe him. He was the kind of guy you would immediately like but I had to wonder if he was he one of the bad guys? Time would tell.

# CHAPTER THIRTY FIVE

# Boyd Meets the Deputies at the Ranch

Boyd: Gary and I stood around making small talk and drinking diet Cokes while one of the cowhands was getting the stud saddled. Gary had a beat up ice chest in the back of the ranch pickup that we were leaning against as he smoked a Virginia Slim and drank his pop. The chest also contained cans of Coors that looked pretty good, but I stuck with the pop as it was still morning. While we were making small talk five Mexican steers were herded into a larger arena where they milled around in a corner pressing against each other nervously waiting.

I was keeping an eye out for anything suspicious that I could report back to Jacob; didn't appear to be much going on other than a ranch hand running a tractor off in the distance. He was pulling a hay rake turning windrows in one of the hay fields, taking his time. The smell of freshly cut alfalfa was pleasantly heavy in the air.

It was easy to see why Gary had been so proud of Mr. Bailey Bar. As he entered the arena with a rider on his back, even I could see that this was a magnificent animal. His muscles rippled as he walked toward the band of steers, fully alert. His color was a handsome dark gray, while the roached mane gave him the air of a bad ass marine drill instructor with his military haircut, if you can imagine giving human attributes to an animal. I tend to do it often, especially if the animal has a personality. The stud made quite and impression as he stood there impatiently.

When he spotted the huddled steers, he appeared to go into a semi-crouch, getting lower to the ground. His nostrils flared as if he were smelling their scent. His ears pricked up and then moved forward as he moved toward the bunched steers, looking like a stalking tiger, totally focused on his prey. As the rider laid the reins across the cantle and gripped the saddle horn to show the horse could work on his own, he easily cut a steer from the herd, forcing him toward the other end of the arena. Afraid now, the steer tried to get back to the protection of the herd, but Mr. Bailey Bar had no intention of letting that happen.

The stallion's eyes appeared locked with the steer's, anticipating every move the frightened animal was going to make before he knew himself what he would do. Mr. Bailey Bar would get so low his chest would almost touch the ground, and then he would spring right or left to block the steer's escape. The horse, a true athlete, was so light on his feet that he hardly seemed to touch the ground. Even though he stood fifteen hands high and weighed around thirteen hundred pounds, he seemed almost gazelle-like. After a few minutes, the rider took the reins and pulled the horse around, letting the relieved steer return to his friends.

"What do you think? Hell of an animal, isn't he?" Gary said with pride as the horse approached.

"Bet your ass. I don't know if I've seen anything like that since I saw Handlebar Doc win the world championship in Vegas." I could see that Gary was pleased with my unfeigned admiration.

As Gary and I were watching Mr. Bailey Bar strut his stuff, I saw a Ford Bronco with a sheriff's decal on the door cruise through the area, driving past slowly while checking out the horse show. The two deputies inside appeared nonchalant, barely giving me a glance, as they cruised down toward the big barns. I made a mental note to get that information to Jacob as it seemed strange for them to be patrolling the horse spread.

When Gary's cell phone rang, he looked at the caller ID and said, "Sorry, I need to take this."

"Sure, go ahead."

"Yeah, this is Gary, what's up, Boss?" He listened for less than a minute, looked at me in a funny way, frowned and then walked a few more steps away...

I could hardly hear what he was saying but I did catch, "Yeah, Grayson, Boyd Grayson, from Alturas; wants to breed his mare."

Then he said in a louder voice," No shit! OK." He folded his phone and put it back in the carrier, now giving me a cold stare.

"Anything wrong?" I asked, knowing damned well there was.

He didn't answer; just looked over my shoulder as the Bronco returned and parked behind my rental car. The two deputies got out of the vehicle, one finishing up a phone call, and then they both looked knowingly at one another as they started over to where Gary and I were standing.

"You Grayson?" the taller of the two asked. I noticed that his name tag said he was Greg Smith. The three stripes on his sleeves plus the insignia on his collar indicated that he was a sergeant. He wore his hair too long for the Stetson on his head. It just didn't seem to give the effect of professional lawman that he seemed to be trying to achieve. He looked like Owen Wilson from that western he was in with Jackie Chan, I thought to myself.

"Yes I am and I must say I'm impressed with all I've seen here," trying to keep it light.

"Bullshit, Cut the crap! We ran the plates on your vehicle and then called the rental agency. It's rented to Boyd Reynolds, who it turns out is some kind of private investigator out of LA. You want to try again? This time tell me what the fuck are you doing on Sheriff Bailey's ranch, nosing around. Who are you working for and what do you expect to find?"

The sergeant was starting to look pretty damned grim. I decided to change my opinion; he didn't look like Owen Wilson anymore; looked more like Owen's ugly brother all of a sudden.

Fuck! I hadn't expected this. I hadn't even bothered to make up a cover story in case I was found out. It never entered my mind that this could happen so fast. Groping for an answer I said, "I'm working for a jealous husband, can't tell you his name, client confidentiality you know. He thinks his wife is screwing around with one of the cowboys here. The guy who, seems to have a lot of money, hired me to find out if it's true. He's no spring chicken," I added.

Sergeant Smith was looking at me dubiously but I could tell that I had piqued his curiosity. I figured I'd created a reasonable diversion when he asked, "Which ranch hand are you checking on? You can tell us that much. It's no secret that this is a randy bunch of young cowboys for sure and there are a lot of bored housewives out here. The old men have the money and the prestige, but these trophy wives do get horny, especially when they see these skinny young ranch hands showing off their asses in their skin tight jeans."

"Great!" I thought to myself. "He's buying it." The only ranch employee whose name I knew was Gary Goodman's. I had noticed earlier that he wasn't wearing a wedding ring. Since he was a ruggedly handsome cowboy the odds were pretty good that he was screwing at least one wife in the neighborhood. I took a chance, "There's this elderly fellow with a pretty little wife living nearby, again I can't name names, but he seems to think that Gary here is porking his pretty little wife." This had to work. My fabrication had all the elements of a good and believable story...sex and money and beautiful woman.

Sergeant Smith and his partner both started laughing at the same time. Gary looked down at the ground, scuffed his boot in the dirt in a chagrined cowboy kinda way, and with his face bright red, headed for the barn without looking back.

I started laughing along with the deputies. All of a sudden we were all buddies, in on a common joke at Gary's expense. I could feel the camaraderie building among the three of us. I felt pretty good at having avoided exposure, all at Gary's expense.

Suddenly Smith, tears running down his red face, stopped laughing quite so loudly and pulled this big old service revolver that looked like Dirty Harry's .44 magnum, from his holster. "You're under arrest, Reynolds." He was still snickering.

I almost lost it at the sight of the pistol leveled at me. "Come on fellas, I wouldn't hurt your pal, Gary. I like the guy. I understand how pussy can really mess with a man's mind. Hell, I get in trouble over it all the time"

"Well Brad, here's the deal; everyone in the county knows that Gary is queer as a three dollar bill. Not even the dumbest son of a bitch in the state would suspect him of having a liaison with his wife. His heroes are Rock Hudson, Tab Hunter and the cowboy on the Village People. What are you really doing here, podnuh?"

Jeez, what an idiot I was. I thought of Bogey's line from *Casa Blanca*; of all the cowboys on all the ranches in the whole southwest, I had probably picked the only gay caballero within a fifty mile radius, well twenty miles anyway, *not that there's anything wrong with it.*

"What's the charge?" I asked, not bothering to answer his question.

"That's what everyone asks," replied Smith with a sly grin. His partner, a typical pus-gutted doughnut hound with bright red hair, had not said a word so far. He seemed to have forgotten his name tag. "Trespassing for starters, but I have no doubt we'll find more to charge you with as we go along; I mean continue our investigation."

"I had an appointment with Gary. I'm not trespassing."

"Grayson had an appointment. No one gave Reynolds permission to be here. Rusty, check out Mr. Reynolds's transportation for anything suspicious." At last, the deputy had a name, does it speak I wondered?

My question was answered soon enough.

"Hey Sarge, you gotta see this!" I heard Rusty yell as he was bent over appearing to be searching under the seats. He pulled out something that I couldn't see from where I was standing.

I had anticipated this. "I have a permit for that pistol," I said; just a little too cocky.

Smith met Rusty half way between my car and where I was standing. Taking the package from Rusty, he turned and came back toward me, looking more confident than I suddenly felt. "I guess you probably have a prescription for this half pound of Mary Jane? I suppose it's medicinal?"

"No one calls it 'Mary Jane' anymore you dumb shit." Where the hell did that come from? I had spoken the words without thinking. Now the implication of what Smith was holding started to become clearer; my turn to be framed.

"Now let's not start throwing nasty names around at each other Brad. Bad things can happen if you should decide to resist arrest. Looks to me like you have more than enough for your personal use. Mr. Reynolds, along with trespassing you are under arrest for possession with intent to distribute; assume the position, please."

Smith put the cuffs on me and led me to the Bronco. "Get in," he said giving me a boost into the front passenger seat. I gotta say it's pretty fucking hard to get into one of those SUV's while your hands are cuffed behind you.

"If this is going to be a long trip, I need to pee," I said.

"You're just going to have to hold it, pal." The laconic Rusty had spoken once again as he slammed the door and walked toward my vehicle. Since I had left the keys in he ignition, he started it up and sat there waiting.

Sergeant Smith slid under the steering wheel and started the engine. Picking up the radio he said, "Unit 33, back in service. Tell him we have the package from the ranch. We should be back at the SO within the hour."

As we left the ranch, I could see Rusty following in my rental car. He seemed to be singing along with the radio.

The line "What a fuckin' nightmare!" came to mind as we headed toward town. My full bladder was starting to really occupy my mind, causing a major distraction. At least it helped take my mind off my current predicament with the deputies.

# Boyd Goes to Jail

Boyd: The ride to town seemed to take forever. My bladder seemed about to burst from the moment the ride began and it grew steadily worse as the trip unfolded; should never have drank that Diet Coke. It was all I could do to keep from pissing myself, but the thought of the embarrassment of arriving with a wet crotch was more powerful than the pain I was experiencing.

I tried using a different tact with my driver to relieve my discomfort by speaking nicely, "Come on Greg, let's take a pee break; please."

"Shut the fuck up and don't call me Greg. It's Sergeant Smith to you." That ended what little conversation we'd had.

There had been no point in denying ownership of the pot found in my car. Sergeant Smith and I both knew that it had been planted by Rusty. After what seemed like hours, but probably was only around fifty five minutes, we arrived at the sheriff's office. I exited the Bronco, again needing Smith's help to keep from falling on my ass. My dignity had all but disappeared. I really needed a bathroom.

I knew I should keep my big mouth shut but I just couldn't. "You guys may think you look pretty macho in these SUV's but when it comes to patrol car duty, they're pretty fucking impractical."

Smith gave me a wolfish grin and said, "I wouldn't know about that since I don't wear handcuffs when I'm driving or riding in one." As it turned out, Smith could be as big a wise ass as I was.

We had parked in an alley on the south side of the Sheriff's Office where a side door was located. A sign on the door proclaimed "Authorized Personnel Only". Smith punched in some numbers on the keypad beside the entrance, releasing the lock, and pushed me inside.

"May I please relieve myself? I'm dying here. I promise not to try to escape." I couldn't remember when I had been in such pain. I wasn't sure if my bladder hadn't burst during the ride. Can bladders really burst? I wondered.

"Sure, turn around, but don't try anything stupid. You're already in deep shit, Reynolds. Didn't anyone tell you that this is the wrong county to be caught in while trying to deal drugs?" He removed the cuffs and placed them in his belt. We both knew that he wasn't expecting an answer, so I didn't offer one.

We were standing in a long gray concrete hallway that extended to the back wall of the building. I could see the solid steel cell doors toward the end of the hallway. Everything was gray, even the floor. It looked like someone had found a deal on surplus Navy battleship paint. The booking room was on the right as Smith led me to the bathroom. We entered together and I proceeded to the urinal as quickly as I could. Smith stood off to the side of the urinal as I finally relieved myself.

"This is better than sex" passed through my mind. I felt like the stallion, Mr. Bailey Bar himself, taking a big horse piss. Relief was coming at last, I could now turn my thoughts to more important things, like "How the fuck am I going to get out of this?"

Looking over at Smith, I did it again, "You seem awfully interested in what I'm doing, Sarge. You got anything in common with your ranch buddy Gary? You guys spend time in the bunkhouse together?"

"Keep it up with that smart mouth of yours and I'll give you a free lesson in some offensive moves with a night stick," he replied with an evil grin."

I could tell this wasn't his first rodeo. He appeared a little too eager to make me pay for my lack of respect. Well it wasn't my first rodeo either. I decided to use a little discretion so I said, "Yes sir," and zipped up.

As we left the john and returned to the hallway I saw this tall female deputy looking me over. I gave her a smile and a wink, but she didn't acknowledge either, as she turned away totally disinterested, or seeming to be anyway, Smith made a rude comment to her as she walked away. She continued to walk away, ignoring us both.

"Too bad, Baby, I can't see why you wouldn't be turned on by a strange middle aged man headed for lock up. Where's your sense of adventure?" This time I didn't say the words out loud, I merely played them over in my head. She looked like she was more capable of kicking my ass than Smith was.

"This way," muttered Smith, guiding me toward the cell block and away from the booking area.

"What about my phone call? Haven't you ever heard of Miranda?"

"Yeah, he's the sorry assed greaser who raped a girl in Phoenix and got off on a technicality. I heard they found his body full of stab wounds in an alley off South Central a few years back. As I understand it, they never did find out who did it. Too bad, I pray for his soul every night before I go to sleep." Sergeant Smith really was starting to develop a sense of humor.

"You crack me up, Sarge," I said sarcastically.

"Don't push it, Slick," he replied more menacing than ever.

I was placed in a small, dark cell in the very back of the facility. Graffiti covered the damp walls. I wondered how the inmates had gotten their hands on writing instruments. The odor of strong industrial disinfectant scarcely masked the heavy odor of piss and shit and stale vomit.

"I thought our cells in LA were bad, but this one looks like something I would imagine would be found in Morocco."

Smith looked at me with a sudden interest. I could see he thought I was a real easy mark. He appeared to be exploring a weakness he had just discovered, "You spend a lot of time in jails do you, Reynolds?"

"Yeah, I hope to shout," I said out loud. "Asshole", I thought to myself. "I retired from the LAPD about five years ago."

He had not expected that as his look of triumph quickly changed. When he ran the plates on the rental car, he had found out my current occupation, but it seems he hadn't checked beyond that.

I asked again, "How about that phone call?" I started to feel more apprehensive. I was in their power and no one knew where I was. Of course, Jacob had been aware that I was heading out to the ranch this morning, but I hadn't talked to him since yesterday. He had no way of knowing that I had been taken into custody by Bailey's deputies. Our next appointment wasn't until tomorrow so he had no reason to worry if I didn't contact him.

"The sheriff will see you shortly. You'd best have the right answers for him. No more of your wise ass remarks. Sheriff Bailey don't take that kind of shit...not even from retired LA cops."

He locked the door behind me and strode off leaving me with my thoughts and the offending jail smells. "Fuck me!" was the only coherent thought I could muster.

# Chapter thirty Seven

# Ellie Phones Jacob

Ellie: As I saw Sergeant Smith leading his prisoner down the hall to the cell area without bothering to book him, I grew suspicious. I had heard the call over the radio from Smith about picking up the package at the ranch.

"Mornin' Deputy Johnson, how's it hangin'?" Smith had said when he saw me. His prisoner looked embarrassed at my obvious displeasure. I walked away without responding to the dickhead.

When I first heard the call from unit 33, the thought crossed my mind that this was probably just another dope deal or some sort of money exchange. Bailey's boys were always talking in what they considered code over the radio. It didn't take much to figure it out after a few weeks…packages, loads, bales, boxes, bags; geez, give me a break fellas, a real bunch of clowns. I seemed to be the only one getting it though. No one wanted to mess with the status quo. Bailey continued to run a successful operation in spite of the lack of ability in his men.

But what caused me to take a special interest in this particular "package" was this was the first time a package had shown up as a person. Smith had made of a point of letting the sheriff know that the package had come from the ranch and that raised a red flag.

Jacob had mentioned that he was sending a PI to the ranch to look things over. "Could this be Jacob's man?"

When Smith came into the break room and got a pop from the Coke machine I wanted to hit him but instead of giving in to my emotions, I asked him nonchalantly," Who's that guy?" I was hoping not to arouse his suspicions.

"Don't you have a report to write or some coffee to make?" he replied sourly.

"Misogynist," I thought to myself. Look that up in the dictionary and there would be a picture of Smith and his men. These guys never change in their attitude toward women unless they thought they might get laid. Fat chance! At least as long as I was viewed as the "little woman" or "bitch" or even that most offensive of words,"cunt", I would not be suspected of being intelligent enough to rock their boat. That was some consolation, but not much.

"Have a nice day, Asshole." I said and left the building.

I drove a few blocks before stopping at the Circle K where I went in and bought a bottle of water while checking to see if I had been followed. I wanted to make sure no other deputies were around before I stepped into the phone booth to call Jacob.

I picked up the sticky phone with some trepidation. When I put it to my ear, the smell of the mouthpiece was enough to make me gag. Dead crickets and June bugs covered the floor of the booth and crunched under my shoe soles. "Yuck! Screw this," I thought to myself. I put the phone back on the cradle, deciding I would rather risk my cell phone being monitored than to risk hepatitis or whatever disease might dwell in that huge Petrie dish.

Jacob answered saying, "Hello Ellie, what's happening? You OK?"

"Yes sir, I'm fine but I've got a quick question for you; did you send your investigator out to Bailey's ranch this morning?"

"Why yes I did. Boyd was playing gentleman horse rancher to see if he could spot anything funny going on around there. What makes you ask? Did you see something?"

"One of the sheriff's flunkies, Sergeant Smith, brought a guy into the SO. He put him in an isolation cell in the back, not in the tank as we normally do with arrestees. He didn't book him either, just took him straight back to the cell. When Smith called in over the radio, he told the dispatcher to advise Bailey that he was bringing in the *package from the ranch*."

Jacob sounded concerned as he asked, "Was this guy around forty-five and wearing boots and a Stetson? Scar on his left cheek? Kinda handsome for a guy that age?"

"That's your man, he even gave me a wink as he was being led to the cell; interesting guy in a strange way," I told Jacob, wondering what his next move would be. He didn't make me wonder long.

"That's Brad, Ellie; I'm going to make some calls that will stir things up. I'm fed up with Sheriff Bailey's play. It's time to make a move. Does anyone at the office suspect that you're talking to me?"

"I don't think so, but I was the only one that asked Smith about his prisoner. That might make him wonder."

"You be very careful. I can't stand the thought of anything happening to you. You're a very brave lady. Thanks for your help in all this and for the help you will give down the road. It might be a good idea if you took a vacation for a few days; out of town even."

"I can take care of myself, Mr. Oakley. You do what must. You've got my cell number. Call me if you think of anything else I can do to be of assistance."

Ignoring Jacob's warning, I decided to stay close to the office in case someone tried to move Jacob's man. He was kinda handsome for an older guy...forty five, huh?

- Chapter Thirty Eight

# Enough is Enough: The Oak Makes His Move

Jacob: As soon as Ellie and I finished speaking I placed a call to Buddy Hollins, "Attorney General's office, how may I help you?"

I recognized his assistant's voice and said, "Jude, this is Jacob Oakley. I need to speak to Buddy right away!"

"Why hello Oak, it's been a while since we've seen you. How've you been?" She and I had known each other for years; since she first came to work for Buddy after being an irreplaceable member of his election team. I had found her to be a very resourceful lady.

"I'm fine Jude; well not really. I need to talk to Buddy right away. There may be a life at stake, literally."

She picked up on my urgent tone this time saying, "Buddy's not available right now, Oak. He's in court and I don't expect him back until tomorrow."

"Shit! Sorry, Jude. If he checks in please tell him I need to talk to him right away….tell him it's about Sheriff Bailey." I hung up trying to think of what my next move should be.

"Screw this!" Casting caution to the wind, I called Bailey's office. I had to make sure Brad was not harmed.

"Sheriff's Office, what's the nature of your call?" The person on the other end of the line was all business.

"This is Jacob Oakley and I wish to speak with Sheriff Bailey." I too was all business.

"The sheriff isn't taking calls right now," The voice was more curt now with no offer to take a message.

"Please convey to Sheriff Bailey that Mr. Oakley is holding on the line and that if he doesn't take my call I will be showing up with the state police in less than an hour. I'll hold thanks."

I heard a click; I wasn't sure if I had been placed on hold or if I had been disconnected so I waited. I had held for at least two minutes and was about ready to hang up when he came on.

"This is Sheriff Bailey, what's this about the state police? Are you making some kind of threat against this department? I don't take this sort of thing lightly, Sir! I've heard of you and your arrogant attitude toward law enforcement officers. That shit won't fly with me. I don't care who you are." He paused to take a breath.

I wasn't in the mood to exchange pleasantries either. "I'm looking for a constituent of mine, Boyd Reynolds. I have reason to believe you are holding him illegally. Is he in your custody, and if so, what are the charges?"

He took a more professional tone saying, "Nobody here by that name. Someone is giving you some bad info, pardner. Now I'm a busy man who serves the public in my county. I can't be wasting my time with some big shot lawyer who doesn't pay taxes here so I'll just say goodbye to you Mr. Oakley, and ask that you don't call here again."

I could tell his dismissal of me was a bluff so I quickly said," Does the name Bobby Lee Baker ring a bell? How about Tom Kidd or Earl Feathers? Are you and your Fed pal Ethridge still using fucked up entrapment schemes to imprison innocent men?" I waited to see if he would slam the phone down or take the bait.

He did, hook, line and sinker, "I don't know what you're talking about. Those guys you just named were drug dealers pure and simple. Feather's woman was a junkie so he helped us out voluntarily to protect her and get her help. It's not my fault she died."

He seemed to be searching for something more to say in rebuttal to my outburst, "Now I get it; Mr. Oakley, eh? I know someone has been trying to get Baker's arrest reports; is that your doing? Well, you're barking up the wrong tree, Pal." There was a nervous tremble in his voice that belied his confident reply.

"Oh come on Bailey. I've been talking to a couple of your disgruntled deputies that are pissed off because you aren't cutting them in on the action," I calmly lied. "I have copies of some of your private files supplied by these informants; deputies that work for you but are helping me."

He didn't answer and the silence lasted too long so I took a chance, "I know about your drug smuggling on the ranch and how you use the hay trucks to mask your actions. I called Buddy Hollins. That would be the State Attorney General Buford Hollins to you, and told him what I know. We have aerial photos of your operation and have tailed some of your trucks to their destinations," continuing to fabricate the story that I was sure contained several grains of truth.

"You know Sheriff, there's a lot of good old boys in the pen awaiting your arrival. They're anxious to pay you back for all the shit you've pulled on them. How many are there, you reckon? Never mind, further investigation will probably tell us a lot, don't you think?"

"You have no proof of any of this you suit-wearing cock sucker!" It sounded like my bullshit story was being taken seriously so I dove in and elaborated.

"I guess you'll be Bubba's bitch, taking it up the ass for a while. Maybe if you're really good to him, you know lick his cock after he's done, he may protect you, at least until the guys *you* fucked catch up with you when he's not around." I surprised myself with my own use of such base vulgarity, but it felt good.

I continued," Once this story hits the press, you'll be world famous, well maybe not world, but at least you will be a household name in the Southwest The name Guy Bailey will be synonymous with corruption in the field of law enforcement and misuse of power. In the future, when a public official gets caught with his hand in the cookie jar, the press will say, 'He pulled a Bailey'."

I felt I had presented a pretty good case so I concluded with, "Now do you want to tell me where you're keeping Boyd Reynolds?"

"Fuck you, Oakley!" he yelled vehemently. He hung up.

I ran out of my office while dialing Jude again. When she answered, I yelled, "Get word to Buddy that I'm on my way to Sheriff Bailey's office. It's a forty-five minute drive for me. See if he can get in touch with the state police and have someone from that department meet me there. I can't wait; I believe that Boyd Reynolds's life is in imminent danger.

# CHAPTER THIRTY NINE

# Boyd Tells of His Encounter With Bailey

Boyd: "Come on Reynolds," Smith had said, pushing me along the hallway toward the cells. . As we moved closer, we passed a sign stating, "NO FIREARMS BEYOND THIS POINT'", so I was pretty surprised when the sheriff himself entered my cell a little later, holding a cocked .44 magnum in his hand. I could tell it was the sheriff by the four stars adorning his collar.

For some reason one star is not enough bling lately to designate leaders of law enforcement, even though the next lower rank in the chain of command is usually a captain or a major; no stars on those guys. Oh well, it makes them easy to spot when they are in front of a camera. Maybe one star might not stand out enough; there I go again. It was probably better that I didn't point out that Wyatt Earp had only worn one star.

To say Bailey was extremely upset was like saying Hurricane Katrina was a strong wind, but please…don't get me started on that fucked up fiasco. He looked at me and said, "Ex-cop, eh?"

I thought to myself, "This is it Boyd me lad!" There was no way to jump him but I knew I had to try; I was dead either way and I hated to go down without a fight. I was gathering myself for the attack which I knew to be futile, when he suddenly lowered the pistol to his side.

He began to speak with great emotion; on the verge of tears, "All my life I've tried to do my best for my community. I protect the good people and stand as a human shield between them and the scum that would destroy our way of life. Those losers I dealt drugs to would have gotten them from someone else if they didn't get them from me."

He was really getting into it now, like making a campaign speech, but going in a strange direction. "I kept the money in the county. The fed's money went into the county coffers and the money I made off the drug deals was used to provide jobs for good men as law enforcement officers; an honorable profession. Those men Oakley mentioned you know Baker and Kidd and others like them that I have put away would have gone to prison anyway. You can't entrap an honest man; I truly believe that. These guys were rotten before they ever met me."

Suddenly he seemed to view me as a friend taking me into his confidence; he looked at me expectantly and pled, "As a former law enforcement officer, Reynolds, don't you agree? You know you have to work outside the system, making up your own rules as you go in order to be effective. "

Looking for a way to keep from getting my ass shot off, I quickly agreed, "Sure, Sheriff, you had the best interests of your fellow citizens at heart." He was rambling on and I wasn't about to say anything to upset him further, especially by disagreeing with him.

Bailey grew silent for what seemed to be several minutes. It became uncomfortable as I tried to appear smaller and unintimidating. I was sweating now and my heart felt like it would jump out of my chest…what next?

"I can't take this anymore. I can't face the humiliation. I've had a good life and folks should remember me as I was. Fuck you Reynolds and fuck Oakley too!"

As he raised the pistol from his side it became level with my face for a moment but then continued upward as Bailey placed the barrel in his mouth and without hesitation, pulled the trigger.

The sound was horrendous in that small concrete cell. Blood and brain matter covered the upper half of one wall, causing it to appear as if the wall had been sprayed with really wet pink and red plaster from an industrial texturing gun. My ears were ringing; other than that I could hear nothing.

Three deputies rushed in with guns drawn. Sergeant Smith viciously hit me across the mouth with his revolver. I felt my teeth shatter as I fell to the floor, stunned. Then I was being kicked and stomped. I tried to scream, "Stop you fucking idiots," but what little air I had in my lungs went whoosh past my broken teeth and bleeding lips as I took a boot in the stomach. The combination of the two blows rendered me totally incoherent.

"Enough! Stop it, right now!" I heard a woman shouting orders in a commanding voice that made it apparent no nonsense would be tolerated... I managed to sneak a peek and saw the same female deputy I had spotted earlier in the hallway. In her right hand she held a cocked pistol.

No sooner had Smith taken another free shot at my ribs with his boot, not his pistol this time, than this magnificent lady officer hit him behind the ear with a leaded sap she was holding in her left hand. He went to his knees as the remaining two deputies looked at her in disbelief. I was happy that that the kicking and hitting had ceased.

# CHAPTER FORTY

# Jacob and the Attorney General at the SO

Jacob: When I arrived at the sheriff's office, about forty minutes after I hung up the phone from my conversation with Jude, it looked as if every SUV belonging to the sheriff's department was parked haphazardly in the wide street in front of the place. About a dozen more cruisers and patrol cars from other agencies were parked off to the sides of the street. There was a small corridor, barely wide enough to drive through that had been left open to the main entrance. An ambulance was backed up to the entrance with it's lights still flashing.

A cordon of grim deputies blocked the entrance. I tried to get past them by saying, "I'm a lawyer and my client's in there."

"Fuck off, buddy, lawyers are the last sons of bitches we are letting through today." that from an overweight giant who looked like he might have been a sumo wrestler in his younger days.

"Who makes uniforms that big?" I wondered as I was turned away.

I joined the crowd of onlookers, waiting and wondering what was going on. My feelings of frustration were growing as the excruciating wait dragged on. Was Boyd OK? Was he taking a beating? I'm normally accustomed to being in control of a situation and this unnatural feeling of helplessness was driving me nuts.

I couldn't believe my eyes as I watched my old pal Buddy Hollins, followed by a caravan of state police cars, pull up and park in front of the SO next to the ambulance. He jumped out and looked at me as I stepped forward to meet him.

"Hey Oak!" He smiled as he greeted me. He could see my confusion. "Jude found me shortly after you called. She said you sounded seriously upset. That's not your usual style so I figured the situation must be grave. What the hell is going on here anyway?"

"I have no fucking clue. I can't get in to see, but from the number of cops gathered here, the shit must have hit the fan. I'm really worried about Boyd though." I couldn't mask my concern and I didn't bother trying. "Bailey's guys took him into the building a long time ago."

"Open a path for me, Captain," Buddy said; addressing the senior state police officer who had driven the car Buddy arrived in. The captain made a sign to his men. Six of them formed a wedge and shoved their way through the crowd. Buddy and I brought up the rear.

Once inside, the foyer appeared to be in utter chaos. The officers and staff along with what appeared to be a couple of reporters with cameras, were pushing each other and yelling; pandemonium reigned.

"Let me have the bullhorn," Buddy ordered his second in command. From out of nowhere a bullhorn appeared and was handed to him. He raised it to his mouth and said firmly, ""Everyone shut the fuck up! Now! I'm State Attorney General Buford Hollins and I am taking control." Other than a few murmurs toward the back of the hallway, the area grew quiet immediately.

"If you have no official business in here, get the hell out! If you do have business here, sit down and shut up. I will talk to any one of you who can shed some light on what the hell is happening here. Now…who's in charge, besides me?"

No one moved for a moment, and then I spotted Ellie in the sheriff's private office. I could also see Boyd and a couple of other deputies in the office with her. By the determined look on Ellie's face, I could see there was a lot of tension among the occupants.

"Talk to her," I told Buddy. "She's the deputy I told you about. Her name is Ellie Johnson"

Officers started shuffling out of the building. The city cops were exiting enmasse followed by a few of the SO staff but there were still a lot of people milling around; too many to suit my friend.

"Secure this entire area with evidence tape," Buddy directed his captain. "No paperwork leaves here until I give the OK...lock it down."

"Yes sir," the captain replied. He turned to one of his sergeants standing beside him. "You heard the man. Get the tape and get some men in here to secure the area. Start herding the pack outside. Get names of witnesses and any other pertinent info you can."

Buddy and I entered the office to speak to Ellie. "Where's Sheriff Bailey?" Buddy asked her without any preliminary greeting.

Her jaw had been locked in a look of determination but it softened as she answered Buddy. "Bailey's dead; looks like an apparent suicide but we'll need to take a closer look at the scene. My efforts have been focused on keeping these jerks from doing further harm to Mr. Reynolds." She nodded toward the two deputies who had been trying to look menacing, but not doing a very good job of it since our arrival. It was easy to see that Ellie was in control.

Boyd looked terrible as he tried to give me a grin through his broken teeth and bloodied lips. His clothes were filthy and torn. He literally smelled like shit and my heart went out to him.

"Sorry my friend. I shouldn't have let you try this on your own." I felt guilty as hell and angry at the deputies that had done this to him.

"My job," it sounded like he was trying to say, but it came out, "Muh yob". I felt even worse as I eyed him more closely. He was in bad shape.

"Let's get him to the hospital first thing. He needs medical attention," I said, stating the obvious. "By the way, Boyd, nice boots," I tried the joke to put a lighter spin on things but it fell flat.

Boyd gave me a thumbs up along with what seemed to pass as a smile. It was hard to determine what feeling he was trying to convey. I could tell the pain was starting to kick in and I feared he might be going into shock.

Buddy looked at the deputies and snapped, "You guys get out of here. Do it now!"

The look that passed between the two deputies spoke volumes. There was surely a ton of incriminating information in Bailey's office they did not want the Attorney General to get his hands on—too bad.

Buddy then said, "But don't go too far, fellas. I may have some questions for you. In fact you can just about bet on it." The two officers were visibly shaken, but they had no choice about leaving. They started out the door.

"Keep and eye on those deputies, Captain." He turned to another of his state sergeants and said, "Get Mr. Reynolds to the hospital. Use the ambulance parked out front. From what Johnson says, the sheriff won't be needing it. Take a couple of your men with you to make sure he is not accidently harmed," he said without his usual humor while giving Smith and his side kick a hard look.

The cell where Bailey's body lay, with most of the back of his head missing, had been cordoned off, awaiting the arrival of the coroner and his staff, I supposed. At least that part had been handled professionally. Upon arrival, these individuals checked in with Buddy before beginning their work. There was no doubt in anyone's mind who was in charge now.

The Attorney General, Mr. Hollins was handling every step in a totally professional manner, leaving nothing to error. His experience in the courtroom had taught him to be aware of the traps that could be laid by his opponents and used against him months later when the case moved to trial.

When he had lined out the crime scene staff in the cell and returned to Bailey's office, he didn't waste time, "Now let's start checking these files and notebooks. I'm looking for names and payments."

Sergeant Smith had been standing just outside the door of Bailey's office holding an icepack against his head. When he heard Buddy's orders, he tried to re-enter. "You can't be going through official sheriff's department files and private papers without a search warrant. You don't have any authority here. This is county business," he protested.

For the first time since he had entered the building, Buddy flashed his famous smile. From inside his jacket, he pulled out an official looking document. When unfolded it was clearly a search warrant. "Issued by Judge Cameron from Sacramento. We've been watching you boys lately. We've had an informant in your department for a while now feeding us information about drugs, missing cars and illegal arrests. You can't always trust everyone to be a bad guy, just because you are. Hopefully, Deputy, you've nothing to hide. Now get the fuck out of my way."

Thus began the investigation that would change the lives of many people; some for the better...some not so much. I smiled to myself as I thought about Bobby Lee and Tom Kidd.

I was anticipating that Buddy would uncover enough evidence to prove my clients should be freed. I was looking forward to delivering the good news to them.

# CHAPTER FORTY ONE

# Ellie Gets Promoted

Following the public revelation of Bailey's suicide and the many unlawful dealings surrounding him and certain deputies, a panic began to grow within the County Administrative offices.

The supervisors knew that not only the budget for the sheriff's office, but other departments not connected to law enforcement, relied heavily on the money acquired through Bailey's actions. The money the sheriff had brought in was siphoned off regularly for pet projects near and dear to each board member. Fully fifty percent of the Sheriff's budget had been paid for by federal drug agency dollars. Since Bailey's suicide and Buddy's findings, RICO had confiscated all of the sheriff's assets, leaving nothing in that particular account for the county supervisors to glean.

The County Chief Financial Officer had been visibly shaking when he presented the budget report, requested by the supervisors, at a quasi-legal private meeting. The board members were shaken even more when they discovered their greatest fears had come to pass. A bill increasing property taxes by twelve percent, the maximum allowed by law, was immediately introduced and passed unanimously in emergency session by the board of supervisors.

The public outcry caused by the airing of the story, which was on practically every news channel in the state, outlining how innocent men had been entrapped and sent to prison by Bailey, precluded local law enforcement from continuing involvement with Federal Agent Ethridge's group.

It wasn't long before an official letter from the DEA was delivered to the acting sheriff, Ellie Johnson, stating that Agent Byron Ethridge had been reassigned to a top secret operation in another part of the country. In other words, no one could find him or any of his team members. The Feds had simply disappeared and would not be replaced locally. The letter cited fiscal constraints as the reason that there would be no further assistance from the Federal Government in this area of drug enforcement; not is this part of the country anyway.

In another emergency session the board had decreed that Ellie would continue in her new capacity as acting sheriff until the next general election scheduled in two years. They simply did not have enough money to call a special election at this time.

Some members had voiced concerns that one of the senior officers might contest their decision until Ed Williams, the county attorney, pointed out the obvious, "Most all of the senior deputies are under indictment by the state attorney general and are either suspended or on unpaid leave, awaiting their day in court.

These senior Sheriff's Department officers that you are so worried about are most likely headed for jail. At the least; they will no longer be employed as law officers in this county. We have yet to hear from all of the victims of Bailey's actions. Nor have we heard from said victim's lawyers for that matter. It's my understanding the hungriest lawyers are still crawling out of the woodwork. They smell the dollars at stake. The liability we are facing could very well bankrupt the county."

Williams went on to point out, "Ms. Johnson is the only experienced officer left on the force who holds a college degree. Her reputation has been beyond reproach and her assistance to the Attorney General in exposing the corruption that has prevailed in the Sheriff's Office for years has proven to be invaluable. She seems to be a badly needed breath of fresh air."

"But she's a woman!" Supervisor Harold Dean, an old timer who had been a board

member for twenty some odd years, snorted with obvious disdain. His face was puffy and white yet netted with broken red veins and his jowls quivered. This year, it was his turn in the traditional rotation, to serve as chairman of the Board of Supervisors.

"You sir have made a brilliant observation, once again. She is indeed a woman!" Williams retorted, his voice heavy with sarcasm. "Frankly, I for one, am sick tired of these strutting roosters in the sheriff's department. These *men* have made our county the subject of ridicule and set us up as an example of what can happen when lawmen are allowed to operate with impunity."

The County Attorney was getting into his summation mode as he continued. He was also managing the difficult feat of seeming to look each board member in the eye at the same time while condemning practically everyone in the meeting room who dared to disagree with him.

"We've all known for years that something was not quite right with Bailey's operation, but we were so happy with the money he put on the table that we refused to question him. He had that big assed ranch that he loved to flaunt and his officers lived in finer houses and drove nicer cars than you or me.

"While this was taking place, not one of you, or me for that matter, dared question where these dollars were coming from. We turned a blind eye to Bailey, not wanting to cut off the flow of cash the county was banking. We must now admit that we all share in the responsibility for this whole fucked up mess and we can't allow it to ever happen again."

Josephine Wilcox looked properly shocked by William's language but she held her tongue. She was younger than Dean, but not much. After a moment she said, "I move that we ask Deputy Ellie Johnson to fill the position left vacant by the tragic death of Sheriff Bailey."

"Second," from a member at the end of the dais.

"All in favor say 'Aye'" ordered Chairman Dean surprisingly without dissent this time... He seemed to realize that William's proposal was the only logical choice...woman or not.

The vote was unanimous. "I'll inform Deputy, I mean Sheriff Johnson, of the board's action," Williams said. "You've made the right decision. Maybe the first intelligent move made in this room in quite a while."

"Now see here young man!" Dean blustered, clearly offended once more by County Attorney's words. "You work for us and you'd best show us the proper respect we're due!"

"Bull shit!" Williams shot back. I'm an elected official, just like you. You know I'm right and if you don't show some balls about illegal activities in the future, I'll tell the whole county what a buffoon you really are. I too work for the people of this county. I don't answer to some pompous old bastard like yourself." With that said Williams got up and left the meeting.

# CHAPTER FORTY TWO

# Aftermath

Jacob: The notes and records I had received from Ellie, plus other records obtained by Holly had been delivered to Buddy shortly after Sheriff Bailey's death. The investigation initiated by Attorney General Hollins, after he had seen the information, created quite a sensation in the news and on the street.

Once the word was out that Bailey was dead and Buddy had his secret records, there began a mini-exodus of law enforcement officers, not only from Bailey's office but also from departments in nearby cities and states in the Southwest.

The secret, and not so secret, bank accounts were quickly emptied as the *usual suspects* headed south…way south, across the border. Several of the offices formerly occupied by small town sheriffs and police chiefs and detectives were vacated while administrators were left scratching their heads and wondering what had happened. Their worlds had turned upside down.

The FBI and DEA only lent their slow and reluctant support to the investigations after public pressure was applied. There were some real surprises revealed as far as who was involved; especially in higher echelons. Requests for extradition of suspected felons sent to the Mexican government and other Latin countries concerning these expatriates fell on deaf ears.

This lack of cooperation from neighboring countries came as no surprise to most of those involved in the investigation. These fleeing gringos brought money with them; lots of money. They had made friends in high places over the years through their various dealings. Drugs coming into the states undoubtedly had ties to powerful people south of the border. Bailey had been correct about one thing, if he had not supplied the drugs to the people around here who wanted them, someone else sure as hell would have.

Through our coordinated efforts, Buddy and I had succeeded in having the sentences of Bobby Lee and Tom Kidd reversed. There were unverifiable reports that each of my clients had received a substantial amount of money from the Golden State for their troubles. There had been no point in trying to get reparations from the county, since the biggest source of revenue there had taken his life. The Board of Supervisors had filed for bankruptcy two months after Bailey's demise.

One thing I did adhere to, that my fellow attorneys knew as Rule Number One, was to go for the deep pockets. If you're going to sue for money, it is a waste of time to sue a person or entity that was destitute. I knew that going after the county for reparations was a waste of time.

As their attorney of record, I am not at liberty to divulge what I know about the money the two men received. I will admit that both Bobby Lee and Tom insisted that I take at least ten percent, a very modest fee when you consider what most of these ambulance chasers charge. We also set aside enough money to cover Boyd's dental work. He now has a beautiful smile. He recently told me Ellie liked a bright smile on a mature man.

I placed the money I received from my two clients in a college fund for my yet-to-be-born child. Holly and I had gotten married following the hearings. We exchanged vows on Catalina Island, honeymooning there in secret in order to avoid the press. Unlike many of my colleagues, when it comes to my personal achievements, I try to avoid the press and the publicity that goes with it.

I found it interesting; however, when I read in a series of articles published in the California Law Review in the months following Bailey's death, more than fifty inmates at Farmdale State Prison had been released. These were men who had been arrested by Bailey and Ethridge and other similar sting operations in the state over a six year period. Justice had finally been delivered to both the good guys and the bad guys. I could now turn my energy back to trying to do something about my nemesis Robert Marius.

# CHAPTER FORTY THREE

# Robert Marius Comes to Jesus

Robert Marius: I was sitting in my office when my private cell phone rang. I have two, one for business and this one for friends and family. I only give this number to my really close friends and family. The caller ID showed it to by my daughter, Stephanie. "Hello Baby Girl," I said automatically. Her calls were the high point of my day.

A man whose voice I didn't recognize said," How's it feel, Bob?" Definitely not Stephanie on the line.

Immediately surprised then suspicious, I growled, "No one calls me Bob unless I give them permission. How did you get my daughters phone?"

"Hey, Asswipe, I've got Stephanie and I'll call you whatever the fuck I feel like calling you. Do you want to waste my time by standing on ceremony, you pompous prick, or do you want to cooperate and see your daughter again?" His voice was heavy and unpleasant. "Me and the boys need money. According to the papers you just made a shitload of it. The story of your latest victory in court is spread all over the news. We don't follow the news much, but your good fortune was hard to miss."

My heart sank, "Bullshit you don't have my daughter!" I said trying to sound confident but, failing miserably as I suddenly feared the worst. How else could this rude bastard have gotten her phone?

"Check it out, Bob. I'll get back to you in a half hour. By the way, don't even think of calling the cops. There's a bag in the front seat of your fancy assed car. Stephanie's undies are in the bag. Pretty sexy stuff for such a young lady, don'tcha think?" He hung up.

Stephanie, my little girl, we had just celebrated her fourteenth birthday last week. I had spent a fortune on new outfits for her. She's a tiny thing, but beautiful, a little blonde doll, just starting to blossom. Even as her father, I couldn't help but notice how she was starting to develop into a lovely young lady. It had bothered me a lot lately when I considered how quickly she was growing up.

She's always been a straight A student and wise beyond her years; often questioning me about my work and my clients. When she pressed too hard, I would change the subject or talk around her questions. I couldn't tell her about the types of clients I represented. I would tell her in my best oratorical tone, "The constitution of the United States guarantees that my clients are entitled to the best defense possible, and I am the best, Honey." I failed to disclose to her that the charges levied against my clients were often of a terrible nature.

"I know that you're the best, Daddy," she would say, giving me a peck on the cheek and snuggling against me as we sat on the couch, reaffirming my credo that I was doing the right thing in providing all the nice things in life for her. She served to make my life seem worthwhile, allowing my conscience to be eased in spite of how I made my living.

How can this be happening to me, especially right now? Five minutes ago, I had the world by the balls. I had just collected my largest fee ever, high six figures, after finishing the most publicized case of my career. I had made money and gotten good press at the same time. For the first time in my years of courting the press, I felt I may have made a mistake by being too much of a public figure.

Due to my skilled efforts if I must say so myself, Heinrich Richmond III, heir to one of the largest cosmetic companies in the world, had gotten off with a slap on the wrist. He'd paid a substantial amount for my services, but I'd proven to be worth every penny to him. Even as I represented him, I was shocked at how he could treat women so shabbily. Considering that the fortune he had inherited was amassed solely by money spent by women throughout the world, made his behavior seem stranger yet. However; his attitude toward the fairer sex, was not my concern. My job was to have him exonerated, regardless of what type of terrible crime he might have committed.

Heinrich Three was facing up to twenty years when he came to see me. Actually I had sought him out, but that would have appeared unethical if it was made public. It was alleged he had used the so called *date rape* drug on several young women he'd picked up in local nightclubs. He was said to have secretly dropped the pill in their drinks before taking them to his home where he had molested them.

When leaving the clubs the young ladies would appear to be intoxicated so no one paid much attention to what was occurring as he steered them into his car. This had been going on for some time until one brave victim had finally come forward and filed a complaint.

The prosecution not only presented pictures from the security cameras in several clubs showing him with the alleged victims; the police had videos that the dumbass had stashed at his home. He had recorded himself committing various sex acts on the nude comatose girls while he smiled stupidly into the camera.

"What a fucking douche bag!" I thought to myself when I heard about the videos, but he was *my* fucking douche bag, and he was very, very rich; I went to work doing what I do best.

Lucky for me, or I should say us, the search warrant issued to obtain these videos had been applied for and executed without following proper procedure. I had petitioned the court that since the purported victim had been video taped on several previous visits to the club while drunk, before she had met my client, she had established a record of drunkenness.

Therefore her word alone was not sufficient cause for such a warrant to be issued. I easily had the Heinrich tapes ruled inadmissible; citing several cases that set precedent against unlawful search and seizure. When I had finished making my case, the only two people in the courtroom who were not visibly enraged and disgusted were Heinrich and yours truly. Oh well, that's just part of the job.

I felt no remorse about my role in freeing Heinrich; I did my job. It wasn't my fault the prosecution had fucked up. The case was dismissed for lack of evidence. In addition to throwing out the tapes, the girl who filed the charges had let too much time elapse between the time the purported crime had been committed and when she called it in. She was unable to prove she had been drugged or raped. No rape kit had been proffered; therefore, in the eyes of the court, the crime never happened.

I love the American jurisprudence system. It's made me a rich man; one to be reckoned with. That cowboy lawyer out of Wyoming who spent so much time patting himself on the back in his book for never losing a case is quite the blowhard. It's not that difficult for a smart attorney to win every case if he picks and chooses carefully.

The judge angrily gave Heinrich a stern lecture about the law and forcing women to have unconsensual sex, but it was obvious that the scolding fell on deaf ears. My client was having a hard time keeping the smile off his smug face while the judge spoke. It was the same stupid smile that we'd seen in his home videos. I tried my best to get him to display proper decorum, but it was in vain. The guy was a piece of work for sure.

I was happy as I had been paid in advance. I don't trust these rich kids. Their word is for shit. Hell, if they were honorable and trustworthy, I wouldn't be sitting in court representing them.

I, Robert Marius, am the senior partner in the firm of Marius, Shefelt, and Border. Our firm specializes in defending clients who have been charged with dangerous crimes against children. When I first decided to enter this lucrative field it was with some misgivings, but as I studied the competition, it was apparent there were few firms that would get down in the dirt and rub shoulders with these creeps. Besides, the multitude of clients was mindboggling. Seems like at least twenty percent of the male population preys on children and young women.

There were a couple of firms in Dallas and one in Chicago that specialized in these unsavory clients, but here in California my firm was without peer when it came to defending these creeps.

Most lawyers who were willing to take on these disgusting clients and their cases were not very good at the job. After all, if they were good litigators, they would be expending their energy and talent defending less odious clients; clean guys like Bernie Madoff and the late Kenny Boy Lay. They would be keeping their hands and reputations clean while toting up all the billable hours they could accumulate, hopefully no less than sixteen and no more than twenty hours per day.

When I was first starting out in this field of endeavor, I had considered trying to get 1-800-MOLESTER as my office phone number. I figured it would be a catchy way to attract new clients. It seemed like a good idea at the time. However, in retrospect, I guess it's a good thing the number had been assigned to someone else, not as "MOLESTER" let me add. I soon learned a more subtle approach worked better. No need to draw undue attention from the gentler citizens. As it turned out, word of mouth has turned out to be much more effective when it comes to getting the word to my type of clientele.

As senior partner in the firm it fell on me to instruct our new fresh faced crop of newly hired law school graduates each year. I had grown to look forward to sharing my knowledge with this next generation of defense attorneys. There were many things to be taught that were not covered in a conventional law curriculum.

I would begin each of the seminars in the same way with my standard opening statement. I had constantly improved upon it over the years as my experiences in the courtroom sharpened my ability to deal with the system. I had dubbed it our *Mission Statement*. "It is the duty of our firm to protect those individuals charged with heinous crimes. Our clients are stigmatized at the very outset of the trial when the accusations of child molestation or rape are levied against them.

"Not many large or prestigious firms want to take such cases for obvious reasons, but I feel these individuals, who are alleged to have endangered children or other hapless persons, deserve the same rights as those accorded to individuals accused of robbery or murder. We, at this firm, have been a beacon in the area of human rights for many years.

"We have managed to achieve this status by endeavoring to find ways to discredit the child's testimony when we are representing a client in the court room. As you are aware, children are often mistaken in what they perceive might have happened to them. These young minds can be coerced into making false accusations against adults, often mistaking innocent gestures for something else. It is my duty and yours, to bring to light these mistakes in order to protect our clients."

I would pause at this point in my presentation to see if anyone would refute my hypothesis. Sometimes the doubters would later be quietly asked to seek employment at another firm. I felt it necessary to weed out the naysayers early on. We had to have a positive staff in order to succeed. There could be no room for self-doubt that could jeopardize the firm's mission.

"Jot down these words and phrases then commit them to memory. Learn to let them roll of your tongue as if you were quoting passages from the bible. The first of these, which can prove invaluable, is *'coerced confession'*. If your client is so stupid, I mean to say, so confused as to implicate himself in a crime, the confession is obviously 'coerced'.

"He either did not understand his Miranda rights…if they were indeed read to him or, more likely, he was under duress; intense pressure from the harsh and undisciplined treatment meted out by the brutal, untrained cops. Surely he did not understand what was happening. It is imperative that the confession not be admissible or you've lost your case at the outset through the actions of your client. It might be prudent to invoke the Fifth Amendment against self incrimination at this point.

"Your next move could be to beg for "mercy" from the court for your *remorseful* client. This would be the time to cite his willingness to cooperate, as evidenced by his *tearful* confession. You noticed that I emphasized the two most important words here. You should role play this defense technique with your client before trying it in front of the judge. The remorse must appear genuine. You should point out to your client the areas where he can improve his performance while you two are alone rather than making an irretrievable or embarrassing error by failing to properly prepare, thus losing your case in front of the jury.

"Should your client have difficulty in producing tears; and this is often the case, tell him to think of his first dead puppy when he was a child or some other sad thought along those lines. I doubt that thinking about his victim will produce the desired results. Toothpaste or a dab of soap secreted under a fingernail and then rubbed into his eyes at the proper moment will produce realistic tears." I would give my young colleagues a moment to absorb the point I was making; one must always have a back-up plan.

"Another useful term is *'incensed'*. The client, and you as his friend and confidant, is either *incensed* or *outraged* by the fact that such audacious charges have been brought against this good citizen. *'Family man'* is a good character description, as is *'pillar of the community'*.

"Remember though, you must be extremely careful when using some of these descriptive terms as they can backfire on you if it should turn out that he obviously lacks the virtues you are trying to bestow upon him. *Caution* is key. Should the prosecution produce witnesses that contradict the picture of your client that you are trying to portray, your credibility will be shot. Once that happens, you have lost the case.

"The statement that your client is *'incensed'* cannot be disproven, yet definite character traits can be shown to fabricated through reliable witnesses who know your client and can testify to his unworthiness. Don't underestimate the intelligence and resourcefulness of the prosecution team when it comes to digging up dirt on your client. You must take measures to insure you are not taken by surprise. There is a lot of truth in the old saying, 'Never ask a question before a jury if you don't already know the answer'.

"Let me reemphasize here, it is your responsibility, and your duty to check out your client's background before presenting his character description as a possible defense tactic. You may be using others to research your client's background, but it is you and you alone who must prepare and present the case."

A lot of these terms were not unknown to my students of course, but it was my belief it never hurts to reaffirm the tried and true phrases that have proven effective over the years to be solid defense techniques when they are brought to bear in order to sway an unsophisticated jury. And when it comes down to it, I only have to convince one juror my guy didn't do it. The prosecution must convince them all in order to win his case.

My lecture continues, "Without fail, we *'welcome the investigation'* and we are *'happy'* to be given this opportunity to exonerate our client. We are *'looking forward'* to our court appearance in order to reestablish our client's good name.

"When appropriate, your client is first and foremost the victim of a *'witch hunt'*. 'The police have ceased the search for the real criminal or criminals who actually committed the crime and have and zeroed in on your client', oblivious to the all other evidence pointing to his innocence.

"Remember how Scott Peterson's attorneys used that as a defense tactic over and over again until it became apparent that even the best defense attorney in the state could not cover up Peterson's deceptions. On the other hand, this tactic seemed to work well for OJ.

"The Juice was anxiously awaiting his release from jail so he could find the real culprits. If you remember he searched pretty near every damned golf course in Southern California and Florida for the murderers when he finally got out." There was another round of laughter from my students.

"When using *witch hunt* defense it is imperative to point out how the cops are trying to pin the crime on our innocent client. This can be blamed on 'laziness and/or incompetence on the part of the police department' and it can also be due to 'public pressure brought on by biased news reporters' who are crying for your clients head.

"Though not a necessarily a derogatory term per se, the word "cop" implies a certain lack of professionalism when pronounced with just the right inflection. Like when people refer to us lawyers as 'shysters' or doctors as 'sawbones'; it dispels the aura of the profession. Practice saying 'cops' in front of your mirror at home until you find the facial expression and tone that work best for you." Inevitably at this juncture of the class, I would see several of the class silently mouthing the word, "Cops," while making strange faces.

By this time, even the brightest in class; those who thought they already had the all answers, would get that spark in their eyes that showed the light had come on. "This guy has stuff I can use." I would then continue with the next phase.

"While we're on the subject of our police officers, this would be a good time to point out the benefits to be gained by discrediting cops on the stand. There will come a time when you will encounter a police officer on the stand whose testimony is becoming damaging to your case, at which time you can say, sternly, and I must emphasize very sternly but with an undercurrent of doubt, 'Remember Officer Jones, you are still under oath', as if you believe he has just uttered a lie.

"When you enunciate each word very slowly and emphatically with a certain air of disdain, you can create a feeling of distrust or doubt about his credibility that can descend like a cloud over the courtroom. The jury will automatically wonder about, and possibly have doubts, concerning the veracity of the officer's testimony without realizing that it was you who created this doubt."

I would then move on to the next topic, *guilt*. "If you think your client is guilty, and if you are any kind of attorney worth your salt, you will know if he is, here are more guidelines. You don't care if he is guilty; really, you are merely there to be his attorney, to offer your professional and unbiased counsel.

"Under no circumstances do you allow a guilty client to take the stand! It is the duty of the prosecutor to prove beyond a doubt that your client is guilty. Do not help him make his case by putting your client in a position where he will have to answer difficult questions. It is not your mission to prove your client is innocent. Until the prosecution can prove otherwise, it is assumed under the American Jurisprudence System, the accused; your client, is innocent.

"This age old rule is sacrosanct and it is the foundation on which our legal system rests; 'Innocent until proven guilty'. Don't ask your client if he did it or not. This knowledge could come back to bite you in the ass, as the attorney/client privilege does not exonerate you if it becomes public knowledge that you suppressed evidence or perjured yourself. If he tells you he's guilty, you can't very well stand in front of the judge and swear he is innocent. There are some things you just don't want to know…for your own protection.

"If your client takes the stand and is lying, even the most naïve juror will usually be able to detect the charade. So just don't put yourself and your client at risk by allowing the prosecution to ask him dangerous questions that can damage your defense.

"I have noticed that over the last few years it's become easier to manipulate the wording of the burden of proof when making a summation to the jurors. The accepted wording in the past stated the proof of guilt must be 'beyond a reasonable doubt', but this has been revised lately by certain defense lawyers to be interpreted as, and spoken to the jury as requiring the burden of proof to be, 'beyond the shadow of a doubt'. This slight wording changes the meaning completely. If you are able to get it past the judge it is possible to place a whole new burden of proof on the prosecutor.

"On the other hand, if your client is innocent, which is rare indeed, you may place him on the stand without fear unless he is a real mess. W.C.Fields once said, 'you can't cheat an honest man'. All kidding aside, this statement by that old rascal will carry over into your profession because it is hard for an honest man to be deceitful. Again, even the simplest of jurors can recognize honesty much easier than he, or she, can recognize deceit."

Once during a class one clean cut lad raised his hand and asked, "Are you telling us to ignore the fact that our client might be guilty of a terrible crime, Mr. Marius? Shouldn't we look for a plea deal in such circumstances, rather than practice dishonesty?"

I told him patiently, "You're not listening, Son. You don't know that your client is guilty! He hasn't admitted anything to you because you haven't asked him whether he or not he is guilty of committing a crime. It may be the elephant in the room, but it must continue to be ignored. Trust me on this. You don't care whether he did it or not. You must not care. If you do care about such details, you should go apply to the county or state prosecutor for a job. Do I make myself clear?"

He gulped, "Yes sir; crystal clear."

At the time this conversation occurred, I jotted down a note. I wasn't sure he was meant to become one of us here at the firm. I didn't need to ponder it for long, as the young man turned in his resignation that afternoon.

Our firm does suffer from an unusually high attrition rate, especially once the younger attorneys have children of their own. They seem to project their work situation into their personal lives fearing the same criminal acts perpetrated by their clients could befall their child. I have never let that cloud my thinking when deciding to take a case. You can't take this job personally.

I would include several topics in this discussion. I call it a discussion although I did most of the talking. After all, what could they teach me? "It is to your advantage as a defense attorney, that the average juror does not like authority figures. Bear that in mind when you have a police officer; pardon, I mean when you have a *cop* on the stand.

"More often than not, the jury you stand before will not be composed of the uppermost strata of society. I don't mean to belittle our jurors nor do I wish to sound superior to these good folk, but more often than not, intelligent men and women; professionals such as yourselves, who have the means and the connections to avoid the arduous and time consuming burden placed on them by jury duty, do not serve."

When I make this statement and I see some doubters in the group, I merely say, "If you don't believe this, let's see a show of hands. How many in this room have served on jury duty?" It is rare indeed if even one hand is raised.

Then I say, "Let's see a show of hands from those who have avoided serving by using an excuse such as being too busy with class schedules or some other conflict of interest. Be honest now." This request generally gets a positive response from at least twenty-five percent of the audience; thus proving my point.

"It's ironic I know, since these same people who dodge jury duty are the ones that howl the loudest when an especially repugnant criminal is found 'not guilty'. I'm not being critical of you, even though you are included in this group; as I am just as guilty as the rest of you. My standard excuse has always been that, as a practicing attorney, 'I cannot, in good conscience, pretend to be unbiased. Due to my circumstances and professional training, I can't help but root for the defendant.'

"Speaking to the situation of poor performing jurors, these good citizens who complain fail to make the connection that the fault lies with them for failing to do their civic duty. But let me emphasize, the failure of these *intelligencia,* for lack of a better word to describe those who will not serve, is good for us prosecutors. In fact it is better than good; it is the foundation of our firm. If the majority of jurors were above average you would most likely today be sitting in the offices of a different, and I must say, less successful firm, rather than here at Marius, Shufelt, and Border.

"Moving along now I would like to note that it is useful to question procedures used by the police during an investigation; and use these to your advantage. If it appears that I reference the OJ case a lot, it's because there are so many lessons to be learned from the innovative tactics used by his defense team.

"In the Simpson case the blood samples taken at the scene of the murders proved to be worthless as far as the jury was concerned. In their minds, the samples had been tainted when they were placed in paper bags by the 'rookie' female investigator at the scene; 'Rookie' being the key word when describing the investigator. This one word was thrown out in order to cast doubts on her ability to be professional. Look for such words or phrases when preparing your case.

"And sorry ladies but facts are facts; adding 'female' to the rookie's title was a subtle way of pointing out the inability of the officer to do a professional job. Remember when I told you about the innate distrust many jurors have against cops? Well, a lot of older men, and even some older or uneducated women, have the same mistrust toward women whom they perceive to be putting on airs by working in a career meant to be reserved for males. Ladies, please; don't blame me and don't blame society for their prejudices. Use these ignorant beliefs to your advantage; they're free and often hold the key to helping win your case.

"Here's another lesson to be learned from that particular trial. The 'paper' bags in question were the same types of bags that had been used for years, but the defense made it appear that this was an outdated and unreliable method for collecting evidence in our modern age. To further discredit the investigators, the defense made a huge deal out of the fact that the samples were not delivered to the lab until the following morning.

"Now you and I know this was all smoke and mirrors, but it worked for OJ. The samples were not tainted and it didn't matter when they were delivered to the lab. Even the chain of evidence was brought into question because of the time delay.

"'My God, this evidence was placed in the trunk of the car!' cried the defense As if it really mattered where the evidence was placed in the vehicle. Through the combined efforts of the seasoned defense team, these crafty attorneys were successful in discrediting each and every standard investigative procedure in the eyes of each juror. Every step taken by the investigators, no matter how meticulously they worked, appeared to be handled incorrectly.

"All of the officers involved, without exception, were made to appear incompetent, and in some cases lazy or dishonest, even though each step of the investigation had been done in accordance with established police department procedures. The important thing is the jury bought it. To put it succinctly, they were baffled by bull shit. Later on in the case, even the science of DNA was discredited by one of the Dream Team members. Again the jury disregarded science in favor of a good show."

"Isn't that the same lawyer that has been using DNA for quite some time now to get his clients freed?" a young lady had asked.

"Ironic isn't it?" I replied. "But then irony appears quite often in our line of work, just try to use it to your advantage. This particular defense attorney, through thinking outside the box, invented an entirely new field of endeavor. It has made him a rich man along with bringing him a lot of publicity.

"Our clients are always innocent. If they happen to be found guilty, there has been a *miscarriage of justice* and we will be seeking a new trial on grounds yet to be disclosed.

"Charges levied against our clients are *alleged*. This sets up a foggy aura of innocence and implies the charges just may be a result of gossip, innuendo, or at least a mistake of some sort. The cops are unsure of their case. Be on the lookout for technicalities that can be used to suppress evidence or result in a mistrial. Try to create doubt in the juror's minds. Mistrials are good for your case for a variety of reasons. At best, you have a chance the case will not go to trial again, and if it does go to another trial, you have obtained good insight as to what the prosecution has planned to present against your client.

"The next topic on the agenda is one of the best and most simple defense techniques you have at your disposal, '*blame the victim*'. Let me tell you about a case I had a few years back concerning a former client."

I would then tell them how I had defended Marcus Regan after his first arrest. I was careful not to disclose his name or the fact that he went on to rape and murder two girls after his early release. I occasionally experienced some twinges of conscience about my efforts in securing such a light sentence for his first offence, but not enough to stop me from taking his next case in regards to the murders. He still deserved a fair trial and since I knew him best I felt I should step up. At least, under the deal I cut with the DA, I made sure he would not be released to kill again.

"I was defending this client against charges that he had fondled a young girl who lived next door to him. As it turned out, the mom would let little

Lacy swim nude in their pool and then dry off by frolicking in the yard, still nude; oblivious to my client relaxing in his own back yard, separated only by a few hedge plants and a low broken wooden fence.

"Since some *alleged* fondling had taken place between my client and this eight year old child, I was not able to get him off without some punishment. However, he did receive a greatly reduced sentence. I believe he ended up serving three years, after my presentation at the hearing. I contended that the temptation of seeing Lacy playing in the nude caused my client to act out certain desires brought on by viewing her wet and naked body so close by. Had she not been so available, my client wouldn't have been tempted to break the law. She had been partially responsible for my client's aberrant behavior by enticing him with her nakedness." I could tell my young audience found this one a bit hard to grasp, but I continued.

"If you look hard enough, there is usually some blame that can be attached to the alleged victim. In this case, you have to ask, 'who really was at fault here, and who was the victim?'"

Seeing doubt in some of my listeners, I would add, "Couch it in these terms; who's to say my client's life might have taken a completely different and more positive turn had he not encountered this uninvited nude girl in his back yard? Lacy's mom must take some responsibility for placing this temptation in my client's path. I can tell you the mom was not happy with my reasoning, but we were able to reach a plea deal with the prosecution that we could all live with."

I could still see a degree of doubt in the faces of a few members of my class. This distasteful case was probably not the best example to present to the new kids, but they needed to be introduced to the innovative methods used by our firm to win tough cases. If they couldn't face the distasteful ones in a class setting such as this, they had no chance of making it in a real courtroom setting, defending much more reprehensible characters than Marcus was at the time I took him on.

"By the way '*naked*' is another word to add to your arsenal of words meant to inflame and stir the blood of jurors. You might have found yourselves somewhat titillated by my description of little Lacy playing nude in the grass. Don't be ashamed or uncomfortable; it's a perfectly natural reaction. I used this visual to impress on you that words are important. The use of proper words, calculated for effect, are what help us to win the difficult cases."

It would be here that I would reel them back in by putting an ethical spin on the way our firm operated. I had to make them feel that choosing to work with me was the correct career move. I would accomplish this by repeating a creed I had committed to memory. "We at Marius, Shufelt, and Border do our utmost to present and maintain a strong, honest and united front for the public to see. We are a solid established law firm and constantly work to maintain that image.

"You will not see the partners doing self-serving commercials on TV, nor will you see our faces on billboards staring arrogantly down from on high. We have eschewed such ridiculous macho animal or professional football team names such as Legal Tigers, Law Lions, Ethical Eagles and other such nonsensical titles.

"I've often wondered about what would happen if some new firm comes up with *Sharks* or *Jets* for a name. Would our profession then stir thoughts of '*West Side Story*'? I tried to sing, "When you're a Jet, you're a Jet all the way."

I could often count on this corny action to get a chuckle from my young protégés. I could feel them relax as they let my words sink in. I could almost hear them thinking, "Maybe this was not such a bad deal after all. Maybe Mr. Marius is right. Someone does have to defend the underdogs. Better ten guilty men go free rather than one innocent man serving a sentence for a crime he did not commit."

As the end of my presentation neared, I would try to end on a high note. "We, my partners and I, have been content to receive our publicity the old fashioned way, through legitimate news articles, regardless of how biased these stories can sometimes be. We accept that we may not always get good press, but we do get press nevertheless. We are looking for justice for our clients, nothing more, except billable hours of course. Which leads me to the most important lesson I can teach you; get the money up front." This too was usually good for a laugh.

I would wrap up the presentation at this time, feeling pretty good about what a great job I had done, again.

These methods I presented had been gained through hours of experience in the courtroom and had served me well over time. I was at the top of my game. I was the Ari Gold of defense lawyers on the west coast. At least I had been until that terrible phone call.

As soon as I put down the phone, I headed out of my office at a run. At the same time I tried to call my wife to see if Stephanie was with her. "Please God, please let her be home!" There was no answer from Cindy so I left a message for her to call me right away.

Just as I entered the parking garage, my phone rang again. I answered it with a trembling hand. The same voice I had spoken with earlier said, "Hello Bob, did you find my package?"

I felt a chill run through me and I suddenly felt weak. My limbs felt like they were filled with water. I dropped the phone and watched in dismay as it hit the pavement. The battery fell out from the impact as it landed, sliding under a parked car.

"Shit! Fuck!" I cursed loudly as I got down on my knees trying to recover the battery and the phone. I had to get down on my stomach, since I couldn't reach the battery, and crawl under the car far enough to retrieve it. Old grease, dirt, and oil stained my crisp white shirt and thousand dollar suit but that was the least of my concerns at the moment.

I finally had the battery in my grasp and inserted it back into the phone. As I hurriedly neared my red Jag, the weirdest thought suddenly occurred to me. This was such a pretentious machine. I wondered what ever had possessed me to buy it. I always lock the car before I went to the office and I could see the door was slightly ajar; someone had broken in. My fear grew stronger as I realized this was some bad shit happening.

The plastic Wal-Mart bag was lying on the driver's seat. Fearfully I picked it up and looked at the contents. My mouth fell open I'm sure when I saw the small white bra on top of the blue bikini panties. I was reminded of how Steph had been bugging her mom about getting some thong panties, but Cindy had remained adamant about not giving in.

"Who would you want to show those to, your boyfriend?" Cindy asked, only half seriously.

"Oh Mom, all the girls in school are wearing them."

"How do you know? Do you girls show and tell each other what underwear you are sporting? Sounds kinda gay to me honey. We'll get you some sexy bikini panties, but you can't show them to anyone." They had worked out a compromise, so far. Cindy was a good mom who did most of the detailed work of raising our daughter. I was just the sugar daddy.

Looking more closely, I could see a piece of what appeared to be some sort of cardboard about the size of a postcard. It turned out to be an old style black and white Polaroid picture. I wondered that such film was still available for those relics as I turned it over and stared in horror.

Of course it was my little girl! She was lying on her back, on a double bed, wearing only the bra and panties I now held in my hand. Her legs were spread and her eyes were closed. I was unable to determine from the poor quality of the photo if she was merely asleep, drugged or dead. I started to gag and then I threw up. Vomit splattered my pant legs and shoes as I puked on my fine leather seat.

Clarity was slow in returning but I hit the speed dial for Stephanie's cell as soon as I had regained some composure. My hands were trembling as I nearly dropped the damn phone again. It was answered on the first ring.

"Bob? What the fuck happened? I thought you hung up on me. That's not very nice, you know?" He sounded testy.

"No I didn't hang up. I dropped the phone by accident. You startled me." I was scared and angry at the same time, but I didn't want to show either emotion to the kidnapper. I was trying hard to remain calm so as not to give him a hint of how I felt. I had to play it cool. I felt so fucking helpless!

"I guess you found the bag," more of a statement than a question.

I nodded and then realized he couldn't see me. "Yes, I have it. Please don't harm my baby." I was on the verge of tears and unable to disguise the tremor in my voice.

"Oh, Bob, Bob," he sounded resigned to deal with a distraught father, "She'll be OK…for a while anyway. You didn't call the cops did you? That could change the whole picture…for all of us."

"No, no cops. No one. What do you want? What's your name? Who the hell are you?"

"Bob, Bob, slow down. You don't get to ask the questions. I'll tell you all you need to know soon enough." He was remaining calm, emotionless and calculating. He sounded totally in control as if he was no stranger to this kind of situation. I grew more fearful and then I began to hiccup, big painful hiccups. I hadn't had the hiccups since I was a kid.

"Shit!"

"Do you have access to a pen and paper, Bob?"

"What?" between hiccups.

"Come on, Bob, it's not a hard question. Can you fucking write, Dip Shit?" He was beginning to sound upset.

Again I nodded without thinking and then remembered I had to speak, "Yes, I have a pen right here." I pulled out my gold Cross pen, giving it a twist but not sure if I could write anything with my trembling hand.

"Here's a number, write it down." He rattled off eighteen numbers, which I did manage to copy down. Due to my shaking hand, the figures were barely legible when I was done. "Now read them back to me. We can't afford any fuck ups, Bob. Stephanie's life depends on you getting everything just right. Just do as I say and she'll be returned to you, unharmed. Otherwise, the picture in the bag should give you an idea of what might happen to her if you do something dumb."

"The numbers I just gave you are to a bank account on Grand Cayman." He then gave me the name of a bank and the electronic address. "You've probably deposited some of your own money there over the years. I understand you give a discount to your clients who deal in cash.

"Shit, this could just be an intrabank transfer for all I know. They might just pull the money from your account and put it in mine." I didn't answer. I was waiting for the other number. "Two million," he said calmly, as if he had read my mind.

"Are you serious?" I almost screamed. "No, you can't be! I don't have that kind of money! Maybe a couple of hundred thousand at most." Then I said without thinking, "This is all a terrible mistake," a line I had so often used in court to justify an unjustifiable action by one of my clients. What the fuck was this guy thinking? My mind raced as I tried to take stock of how much money I actually had and how much more I might be able to lay my hands on quickly.

He didn't seem to take a breath before replying. He'd been anticipating my response. "Don't bullshit me, Bob!" His repetitive use of my name was starting to get on my nerves. "I've been following your career for some time now. That house of yours, out on the point, is worth a hell of a lot more money than what I'm asking for the safe return of Stephanie."

The way he spoke her name so casually unnerved me. I was suddenly at a loss for words; a condition that up until then was totally foreign to me. When I didn't answer him immediately he yelled into the phone, "Don't piss me off by underestimating my intelligence, you arrogant fuck!"

"No, please, I'm not implying that I'm smarter than you. You must know that my house is mortgaged to the hilt. In fact, with this market I'm upside down in it." I was pleading now.

Still cold as ice he replied, "Two million, Bob, I'm not playing games here. I'm not one of your shyster buddies that will cut a deal with you. Speaking of what I *must* know; we both know you have partners who will help you. You've got assets and cash squirreled away too. Your kind always does. Two million dollars, firm, no more bullshitting me Bob, the money or Stephanie's cherry, what'll it be?"

Those last words jolted me back to the real issue here. My daughter, not the money was at stake. "OK," I said resignedly, "How long do I have?" He had me by the balls and we both knew it.

"Take as long as you need, Bob. The boys and I aren't in a hurry. Just remember, the longer we have that little beauty lying around on that bed with nothing on, the more impure thoughts will enter our minds. After all, she's not our daughter and we don't have any other women in the house right now. She looks pretty fucking delicious and boys will be boys, Bob."

When he finished that sentence, my stomach suddenly felt as if I had just drunk a half gallon of warm curdled buttermilk. I probably would have puked again, but there was nothing left to heave. Still holding the phone to his mouth, I heard him call out loudly to someone who must have been in another room, "One of you guys bring me a beer and don't let me tell you again; stay the fuck out of the girl's bedroom!"

After a moment I heard him take a long gurgling drink from most likely was the beer bottle, followed by a loud belch. "Excuse me," he said, drawing the word *excuse* out so it sounded like "excuuuuusssse me". He started to laugh. "Sorry I'm so crude, Bob. I never finished high school, much less college, so I didn't learn about proper manners like you probably did."

I was silent, awaiting any further instructions. He took his time and seemed to be thinking, then he said, "By the way, Bob, can I count on your to represent me in case I ever need a good mouthpiece? It won't be for this transaction, of course, because you're never, and I do mean never, going to reveal what's transpired between us. I have friends who know where you live and I'm sure you wouldn't want to do this twice. It would put such a strain on little Stephanie, not to mention your feelings. We could even get that cute little wife of yours and have a real gang bang, if you know what I mean.  From the way you keep gasping for air, I don't think your heart could take this type of excitement again.

"But seriously, Bob, should I ever find myself in need; would you be there for me? I know you like to represent the hard cases, the one's that seem impossible to win. After this deal, you could probably use the money too. I'll sure be able to pay you won't I?" I could detect the cockiness in his voice now, savoring how clever he thought he was being.

I wanted to tell him to go fuck himself, but I didn't answer. This guy was really nuts and I was scared for my daughter. He continued, "I know you're a good 'un cause you got one of the boys here off a few years ago. That's what brought you to my attention. Ol' What's His name, you know I can't tell you his Christian name, well he's not really a Christian anyway, said you insisted on cash in advance to take his case, a lot of cash. Oh, he said to tell you he wants it back…with interest. Then I'll be damned if he didn't see your face on the front page last week. It said you collected a huge fee from Richmond the Third.

"Heinrich Richmond, now there's an asshole who really deserved to pay, didn't he? Hard to believe that you, a father of a beautiful little girl like Stephanie, would work so hard to get such an asshole released. Anyhow; a big hullabaloo was made about how much money you got, 'undetermined substantial amount' was the wording in the paper as I recall.

"We figured 'undetermined substantial amount' must mean a whole shit load of money. Were we right, Bob?" Not waiting for a response from me he continued, "Now, thanks to you, that rich fuck walked away free and me and the boys will be rich, too. Doesn't that just give your crusader spirit a big lift? Everyone's a winner; well almost everyone, Bob. Richmond's victim probably didn't feel too good about the outcome, but as they say, 'Shit happens'. Let's hope Stephanie is a winner too. She has the looks of a winner, a real thoroughbred."

Stephanie's abductor was starting to sound as if he was getting drunk and bored as he neared the end of our conversation, "You have my number, Bob. My banker will call me when he receives the wire transfer. Remember, Bob; don't try to pull any funny stuff—no cops definitely. The police are not your friend. From what I hear they probably all hate your guts anyway; just for all the shit-heels you've put back on the streets.

"We'll be keeping an eye on you, and Stephanie too, of course. She's real easy to keep an eye on…maybe too easy if you understand what I'm sayin'. By the way, the money you send will only be in that account for a couple of minutes before it goes somewhere totally untraceable. Just do what I told you and everything will be fine." He hung up then, leaving me in the depths of fear and despair.

Three days later I managed to get the money transferred to the offshore bank. These had been three of the longest days of my life. Horrible scenarios continued to play in my mind; Stephanie, naked, being gang raped and sodomized by a bunch of filthy biker types. I couldn't erase these violent and disgusting pictures from my thoughts and I couldn't sleep. I pictured the worst villains I had ever seen in the movies lying with my daughter. I was a wreck.

I had given Cindy all the Vicodin I felt she could safely take, without it killing her. She was in a much worse state than me. I was busy gathering the money, so that task offered a bit of a distraction at least. Cindy had wanted to contact the police, but I put my foot down and told her that course of action would undoubtedly end with our daughter being tortured and murdered.

During these sleepless nights I had a lot of time for some serious soul searching. I came to realize that I had spent the last decade or so defending the sort of scum who preyed on children and young girls; girls like my Stephanie. I had dedicated my life to protecting the rights of men who would do her harm if they had the chance; men like the unnamed animal who was holding her hostage. How could I have been so greedy and callous? I had rationalized my actions and justified them by pretending I was upholding the constitution; defending men in need. What bullshit!

I had often asserted to my critics, "I swore an oath on the bible, a holy oath. This is my duty," I had lied to myself and others all this time. I now had to face the truth; there is no attorney oath in any state or country that says it is OK to lie and cheat to gain your client's freedom. We at the firm, under my steady hand, had hidden under the guise similar to the military's "Don't ask, don't tell" rule. If we don't ask our client if he's guilty we must, as I had so often instructed my protégés, assume his innocence. The pain I was enduring now was obviously the same pain visited upon the parents of children who had been harmed by many of my former clients.

"I am a worthless piece of shit," I played that self-deprecating line over and over in my mind.

I had prayed to God to protect my darling, innocent daughter, "Please dear Lord, I know I deserve nothing, but for my little girl's sake, please, please, deliver her to me unharmed; or if you can't do that, at least send her back to me alive." I said this same prayer dozens of times over the three days, with little variation.

An hour after the money had been transferred; I was now almost, penniless and no doubt would be in debt for the rest of my life, my cell phone rang. It was Stephanie's number on the caller ID. My heart was pounding in my ears as I said, "Hello?" expecting the worst.

"Daddy, come and get me." It was her sweet voice on the end of the line. Surprisingly, she seemed unperturbed.

"I could hardly speak, "Where are you honey? Are you OK?" still fearful that this might not really be happening.

"I'm at the Dairy Queen. You know the one, across from the high school."

Again I asked, "Are you OK, sweetheart?"

"Sure Daddy, come and get me now, please." She still didn't sound the least bit frightened or upset. I took this to be a good sign but I was still consumed with doubt; what had they done to her?

I rushed out the door to my car. Cindy was sound asleep, passed out from the drugs, so I left without trying to wake her. I had to get to Steph as quickly as I could. When I arrived at the Dairy Queen, something like five minutes later, I spotted my little girl sitting under a canopy at one of the tables that was placed in a grassy area.

She was eating a burger as I pulled up. I could see a large milkshake cup on the table in front of her. Everything seemed fine, a picture of Americana; pretty teenage girl, Dairy Queen burger and a strawberry shake. I felt the tears start to well up in my eyes. She was clad in an old fashioned tie dyed tee-shirt and a pair of too-large plaid Bermuda shorts, neither of which I had seen before. "She's beautiful," I thought as I jumped out of the car and ran over to her.

"Stephanie, are you really OK?" I asked again, holding her tightly. I hadn't seen any signs of apparent physical abuse as I ran toward her. "Thank you Dear Lord," I silently breathed.

She shook me off and stepped back. "That's too tight, Daddy." She seemed happy and healthy enough. I looked her over again for any cuts or bruises... nothing.

"Honey, tell me what you've been up to for the last three days," I demanded, still fearing she might be suffering from shock. She just appeared too damned calm for what she had been through.

"Well, Daddy, like it was kinda weird. I was on my way home from school when these three women in a red Mustang convertible stopped and asked if I knew where the library was. It's like, right on my way home, you know. When I told them I lived just down the street from the library, they offered to give me a ride if I would show them where it was.

"Everything seemed safe enough. They were all like young and pretty and seemed very nice so I got in the back seat with the one called Lee. She was drinking a coke and offered me one from a little ice chest they had in the car. I took a couple of sips and that's all I remember about the ride.

The next thing I knew, I woke up in this strange little house. Was it really three days ago?" she asked. I led her over to the car and told her to get in but keep talking.

She still appeared a little groggy but other than that she seemed fine as she told me, "Like it seemed like I never really woke up the whole time I was there, Like, they kept feeding me and giving me drinks when I did wake up, but then I would fall asleep again. I think we watched some videos or movies but I don't remember what they were."

We arrived at the house and went in to wake her mother. Normally, the overuse of the word "like" by Stephanie and her friends would drive me up the wall; today I was like just so happy to be hearing it again.

I was so grateful to have Steph back and so relieved she had not been harmed but I couldn't help but wonder what all of this had been about; the kidnapping, the ransom demand, the women in the red Mustang, and the asshole on the phone who kept calling me Bob. Somehow the whole surreal episode didn't quite appear to be what it had seemed at first.

Things became clearer a few weeks later when I saw an article in the Living Section of the Sunday paper. The title of the piece was, "Local Battered Women's Shelter Receives Anonymous Donation of Two Million Dollars." I recognized the name of the shelter as the one that Jacob Oakley had helped found and currently directed. I didn't bother to read any further and strangely enough, I wasn't all that upset at the time. I mean I wanted to kick the shit out of him for what I figured he had put me through, but he is a really big sonofabitch, after all and he *had* given me a lot to think about.

Later, when I'd had time to consider what had taken place, I thought about calling the cops, but I knew it was hopeless. I hadn't filed a complaint; still afraid the guy on the phone would keep his promise of a revisit if I reported what had taken place. I still had thought they were really bad guys until I saw the story in the paper.

The cops would surely want to know why I had waited so long before making a call to them. Furthermore, I didn't want Stephanie questioned about what had happened. I was not going to allow *anyone* to upset her ever again. That fucking Oakley, though; he'd been a pain in my ass for years, always critical of the way our firm worked…maybe someday I will find a way to pay him back…judgmental cocksucker!

Oakley's play, if it had indeed been his doing, I still couldn't be sure, did result in a major change in my life. My partners and I no longer take on clients who have committed crimes against women and children. I offered no explanation other than just that it was time to change direction. The partners seemed relieved at my decision. The money had been good, but I'm sure their conscience must have suffered while defending some of the creeps we had taken on as clients at my insistence.

My family and I live in a smaller home, much smaller than the one on the point. I now drive a white Ford Focus and I'm happier than I've ever been in my life. I do want a bigger car though; not another Jag, but at least a Taurus, as soon as I can make a few bucks. But first I have to repay the men who loaned me the money for Stephanie's ransom.

I seem to be spending most of my time these days defending politicians who have made mistakes that are considered illegal by certain prosecutors and state or county attorneys. My new clients are a lot alike as they seem so surprised that their actions are questioned and result in appearing before a judge. "We welcome the investigation" is still our credo.

When Cindy asked about this new line of work, saying it still sounded unethical, I replied, "Come on, Honey, I am a defense attorney; you can't expect me to go to work for the government, and the honest citizens have no need of my services. I've gotta make a living for you and Steph."

I'm discovering, happily enough, that there is good money to be made from these clients. Although they are sleazy for the most part, they are saints compared to what I was dealing with before.

Most of them seem to be well heeled and eager to pay with little haggling. My partners and I have just been retained by the entire city council, mayor, city manager and chief of police of the small city in southern California that has received so much recent notoriety concerning the outrageously high salaries they had given themselves. His honor, the Mayor was shown speaking in broken English, and I quote, "If ju wanna get good help, ju gotta pay for it." It's shaping up to be an interesting case for which I'll need to use some of my sharpest skills. I welcome the opportunity!

## CHAPTER FORTY FOUR

# Heinrich Calls Marius Again

Robert Marius: While I was waiting for the hearings to start on my city council case, I was surprised to read that Heinrich the Third made the news again when one of his potential victims turned out to be an undercover cop. Officer Evelyn Rodriquez feigned the standard reaction Heinrich anticipated when she pretended to consume the drug laced drink he offered her. He'd seen her across the room from him at the Neon Lounge, marking her as his next *conquest*. Later on a TV interview, I could see why he had taken the risk. Officer Rodriquez, it turns out, was a beautiful brown skinned beauty with long black hair and dark Spanish eyes.

Heinrich noticed that she didn't appear to have really large breasts as she was willowy, but what she had seemed fine enough for him. He had given her his best smile as he asked the cocktail waitress to deliver a drink to her; he gave the girl a twenty dollar bill and told her to keep the change.

When the drink was delivered, the waitress leaned over and whispered something to the unknown Latin beauty that caused her smile also as she looked his way. Heinrich took this as an invitation. He arose from his bar stool and walked over to her table.

"Hello, I'm Heinrich Richmond, may I join you?" and he was off. They chatted about the usual stuff, music, the quality of the drinks and other small talk. When Evelyn excused herself to go to the powder room, he slipped the drug into her cocktail. Upon her return she appeared to take a deep drink. Being a little tipsy himself, Heinrich failed to notice when she held the glass under the table she tilted it so it spilled quietly onto the carpet. He was extremely pleased when she appeared to succumb to the effect of the drug so quickly.

He had to practically carry her to his car and load her inside like a sack of potatoes. She was almost totally passed out, unable to speak coherently, long before they arrived at his house.

He pulled a little blue pill from his jacket and popped it in anticipation. He was anxious to consummate this meeting.

As I watched the news that evening I tried to imagine Heinrich's surprise at the turn of events. Even though she was not very heavy, he had struggled to carry her up the stairs to his bedroom. He wasn't in the best physical shape; besides being a heavy smoker, he ate and drank what he wanted and hated the thought of exercising.

He was out of breath by the time he reached the bedroom; dizzy from the drinks he'd consumed earlier and then by the strenuous climb he had just completed. It was all he could do to throw her across his king sized bed. He'd then set up his cameras, and started to remove his clothing. When he looked down past his paunchy belly, he was pleased to the pill had kicked in. He could just make out that his dick, though not impressive in size, was as hard as he had ever seen it. He looked in the big mirror at the foot of the bed for reassurance.

As he looked at his reflection, he was smiling in anticipation and still breathing hard from the exertion of carrying her up the stairs. The thought of what was about to take place added to his heavy breathing. He looked at his heaving white gut and chest with mild disgust. "I've got to get to the gym soon and get back in shape. This is killing me!" he thought.

He was totally naked as he began to remove Rodriquez's outer garment, a short one- piece dress that he easily unfastened and slipped over her head. She was wearing tight gym shorts and an athletic bra with what appeared to be some kind of padding, under her dress. "This can't be Kevlar, can it? What the fuck?" Her choice of undergarments had puzzled him at first; as he was accustomed to a skimpy bra or no bra at all and thongs instead of panties on the young girls these days.

Any further question about her choice of underwear flew from his mind as his eyes greedily took in how perfect her body was. Her stomach was flat and her skin was a smooth, warm golden invitation. A veritable feast for his hungry eyes, he said out loud, "My God, Baby you might just be the hottest chick I've ever fucked!" As he prepared to remove her shorts he spoke again "I might even have to eat that little pussy." He'd confided in me that this act, performing oral sex on the ladies, was not something he normally enjoyed. He'd rather receive than give; selfish in all aspects of his life.

When she suddenly jumped off the bed and threw him to the floor, handcuffing his hands behind his back, it was an astonishing moment for him; something totally unfamiliar to a spoiled rich man who was usually in control of the situation. "What the fuck! Get these handcuffs off me, right now!" He could not fathom what was taking place in the imagined refuge of his very own bedroom.

"Shut up, you filthy pig! You are under arrest. Consider yourself Mirandized, you slimy mother fucker." Detective Rodriquez tightened the cuffs until he cried out in pain.

"Please, you're hurting me, please, can't we work something out? I have money, lots of it. Don't you know who I am? " The reality of what was happening caused his head to start to clear. He had the presence of mind to note the situation didn't do anything to the drug induced erection. Even in this strange turn of events, the drug kept his penis at attention; what an embarrassing situation for the man who answered to no one until this moment.

The backup cops had been waiting just outside the house for Rodriquez's signal. Heinrich was quickly hustled from his bedroom by several large police officers. When he arrived at the station, having been hauled there, still naked, in the back seat of a squad car, he couldn't believe his eyes at the size of the crowd of reporters and paparazzi awaiting him.

It was obvious they had been alerted well ahead of time, probably by one of the investigators who wanted to make sure Heinrich was *exposed* as the pervert he was this time. The officers wanted to take no chances of more technicalities arising that might be used to free him this time.

Two large uniformed police officers perpwalked his sorry naked ass from the car into the station in full view of everyone. No one had offered him even a towel to hide his nakedness or his stiff dick standing up and slapping his fat belly with each step. The howls of sustained laughter coming loudly from the exuberant crowd, along with what seemed like hundreds of camera flashes, appeared; as exhibited by his chagrined and embarrassed countenance, to a have more devastating effect on him than the fact he had been arrested for attempted rape.

Heinrich's hands were still cuffed behind his back preventing him from shielding his face or his aroused sexual state. He had been known to brag that his imported "get hard" pills were the strongest money could buy. His claims appeared to be true.

Someone from the crowd of reporters yelled, "That's a pretty persistent erection you've got there, Heinrich. Maybe you could do an ad for television, like that Bob guy with the shit eating grin who sells those penis enlargement pills." It was a Kodak moment, literally. The pictures that appeared in the press the next morning were priceless, but not nearly as good as those that appeared uncensored on the internet.

Come to find out, his arrest had happened during a sting operation that apparently targeted Heinrich and some other misogynistic pigs that were suspected of emulating his predatory methods in the local clubs.

His first call had been to me. I have to admit I was not surprised, as I had already seen the pictures. I had to stifle a chuckle at the thought of them pasted all over the headlines and on the local TV news channels. I was very happy that I was no longer taking such cases. This one would be a bitch to defend.

"You've got to help get me out of this Marius. Did you see those horrible pictures? My civil rights have been violated!" He was indignant about his arrest while being as polite and condescending toward me as he could manage under the circumstances.

"I was set up by this Mexican cunt. I'm not sure she's even really a cop. You've gotta see what kind of dirt you can dig up on her. These charges cannot be allowed to stand. You know how to do it, Marius, use 'entrapment' or whatever you have up your sleeve. I thought she was a prostitute or a coke whore. You got me off the last time. You're good; I know you can work your magic. I'll double your fee, cash, in advance… your call." He was desperate; as well he should have been. I don't think even I could have helped him this time.

Since my recent ordeal had changed my life, I had no intention of touching this case, quickly demurring, as I had promised myself… and God that I would. I wasn't even tempted by his offer of a big fee, as poor as I currently was. The picture of Stephanie, lying passed out on that bed in her undies, crossed my mind again; as it often does, reminding me of my new vows.

"Sorry Heinrich, from now on you're going to need to find someone else to pull your nuts out of the fire." I smiled to myself as I realized I had made a joke. From the looks of those pictures, you might need some help I mused but I didn't say so aloud, again smiling to myself.

"I don't handle these types of cases or clients such as you anymore." I could have berated him and his piggish behavior, but to what avail? I kept my thoughts to myself. He was up to his ass in alligators already.

At first, he sounded shocked, then angry, "What'd you do, find Jesus all of a sudden? If that's the case, I want the money back that I paid you for representing me before. You're supposed to be my attorney and my friend." I could hear the desperation beneath the anger in his voice as the arrogance that had been his trademark subsided with the sudden realization that, for once, he was on his own.

"I *was* your attorney but I was never your friend you sorry mother fucker," I stated; finally running out of patience with this rich spoiled asshole. "The money you paid me is gone but I wouldn't return it, even if I still had it. I earned it and almost lost my soul in the process.

"You need to be taken off the streets for the crimes you've committed against women, you low life piece of whale shit. I hope you rot in prison so you can't harm any more innocent girls." I hung up on him then. The more I thought about my new direction, the more I started feeling pretty pleased with myself.

I continued to follow Heinrich's story, out of curiosity, watching as his machinations failed, one after the other. After going through several councilors, he had finally settled on one of the attorneys who had defended Scott Peterson. I guess he figured that someone who was so devoid of morals as to work so hard and expend so much extra time and energy fabricating wild scenarios in order to try to free a person who had murdered his wife and unborn child, would find Heinrich to be a breath of fresh air.

Unfortunately for Heinrich, not even his high powered attorney was able to introduce enough innuendos about how such a huge miscarriage of justice by the illegal and outrageous use of entrapment, had prejudiced the jury against his client; thus stopping the wheels of justice from grinding fine and true.

For once, money was not a deciding factor in the outcome of the trial; even though a lot of it was tossed around. There was nothing plausible brought before the court that would justify the charges against Heinrich to be dismissed, although dozens of reasons to declare a mistrial were presented on Heinrich's behalf at the seemingly endless pretrial hearings. The judge wasn't buying it. Requests for a new and less partial judge as well as requests for a change of venue were summarily denied.

Before the case was finally heard, a team of four high priced defense lawyers had been brought on board, but unlike the other famous "Dream Team", this effort was to no avail. An intelligent jury was seated, against vehement outcries from the defense, especially when a potential juror who showed signs of being able to think for himself was seated after being deemed acceptable by the prosecution.

The defense had run out of their allotted strikes early in the selection process because an inordinate amount of those citizens who had been called to jury duty for this particular case seemed smarter than average.

It only took a short time by current standards; about eight months, for the trial to begin. In record time, less than a month, despite all the objections and expert witnesses proffered by the defense, the case went to the jury. Two hours later, the verdict was returned; "Guilty," spoke the jury foreman in a firm voice.

"Was the verdict unanimous?" asked the judge.

"Yes, your honor," was the reply from the foreman.

Of course the defense demanded that the jury be polled, but this just stalled the inevitable. All the jurors had voted for a guilty verdict.

Heinrich immediately posted bond, since sentencing would not take place for at least six months. His attorney's were immediately appealing on the grounds that the jury had not deliberated long enough. There were also questions as to Heinrich's mental stability; after all he had been given everything he had ever wanted since he was a child. He didn't understand the concept of being denied anything...up to and including sex from an uncooperative female.

"He could not be held responsible for any of what had taken place with regards to Officer Rodriquez. Mr. Richmond is the victim here; there's been a *terrible mistake*," this from the famous expert psychiatrist I had relied on so many times before, Dr. Jameson who never failed to deliver. This time his testimony proved to be no help for the defendant.

The dream team of attorneys Heinrich had assembled, not to miss any opportunity to play out the drama, also declared that the jury pool had been tainted by *prosecutorial interference*; a term heretofore unknown even to me. I did have to admire their tenacity and inventiveness, however.

After understanding he probably didn't have a chance at being exonerated, Heinrich took his money and fled to Mexico before the sentencing date arrived. He's has not been heard from since...officially.

The Mexican government, through their various spokesmen, has stated several times, "We have no knowledge as to the whereabouts of Senor Richmond. We are cooperating with the American authorities one hundred and ten percent in their search for this sick and potentially dangerous criminal." All the releases are identical, word for word. They don't even bother to rewrite their more recent comments.

"Bull shit," was my instant reaction, each time I saw this repeated update being played with little new information provided. At least the young women frequenting the clubs around here have one less asshole to fear. However, the pretty senoritas south of the border probably are not so lucky since it is doubtful that Heinrich will ever change his behavior until someone takes his life.

# CHAPTER FORTY FIVE

# Coming Home to Texas

Bobby Lee: Mary Jane, Alysha Willow and I were heading home to East Texas. I found myself growing nostalgic as I took in the familiar sights and smells. Smells have always been a vibrant factor of daily living in the heavy humid air of the South. Besides the dead skunks every few miles, the odors of cow manure, mixed in with the dew or rain moistened wet pastures, even has a pleasant smell; rich and strong and reeking of life. I think it must be what the beginning of time must have smelled like when the first creatures crawled out of the mud.

While I was stationed overseas during Desert Storm, I had often let my mind wander back home, southeast of Dallas to the good times I'd spent there as a youth. It seemed the unpleasant memories of the hard times associated with growing up there, and there were many, rarely entered my thoughts while I was in the Iraqi desert.

Hauling hay had seemed like such a hard chore before I joined the army. Remembering the smells of the fresh cut Bermuda grass or alfalfa waiting to be loaded on the hay truck seemed like heaven to me when I was away. I blocked out the times my buddies and I would puke our guts out because we got too hot under the steaming Texas sun. There was no such thing as going home just because we were sick. The hay had to be gotten in as soon as it was baled. There seemed to always be a rain storm off in the distance, usually headed our way; rain caused the hay to rot.

It seemed easy to overlook any of the other unpleasant memories such as the heavy, hot and humid air that would beat me down. The sweat soaked boots and gloves and wet ragged jeans. The deep bloody scratches on my forearms at the beginning of the hauling season before the skin had gotten so tough, as it would later in the summer, that nothing but a strand of baling wire sticking out of a bale could bring blood.

When I would lie on my cot and visualize these memories of home, all I would remember was the cold beers at the end of the day after the work was done. I'd remember the sounds of the field lark singing or the Bob White quail whistling and wistfully think, "God, I wish I was back in Texas right now loading a truck with hay or driving the John Deere, raking windrows". Amazing what crosses the mind when one is homesick in a distant place.

I had the same kind of memories when I was in the pen. I'd forgotten about the snakes and the flies and the chiggers. Now I was on my way home with Mary Jane and Alysha Willlow. I wondered if they would be as happy to be here as I was happy to be coming home. Considering all we had been through out west, I couldn't imagine that we would be unable to find a better life and happier times back here…bugs notwithstanding.

As I drove along the farm to market roads, it seemed that little had changed. The romantic visions I had entertained while I had been away slowly evaporated somewhat in the reality of the East Texas countryside where small spreads exhibiting bone deep poverty were continuously displayed alongside the more prosperous farms and ranches.

But I was enjoying the hell out of driving my new Ford King Ranch Edition pickup through the countryside where the only vehicles I'd had in years past were real pieces of shit. I was listening to Willie singing "On the Road Again"; joining him in the chorus. Mary Jane had been playing around with her new wireless computer when I heard her let out a low unladylike kind of grunt.

"Did you just snort?" I kidded her.

She looked embarrassed as she said in a quiet voice, "I was just looking at some older editions of the Lewisville News on-line and something caught my eye. I lived there once, you know. Anyway I read where Big Mike, the Chief of Police, had a massive stroke. Looks like it happened shortly after

I left. They say his mind seems unaffected, but the article says he's lost control of all his limbs. He can't even feed himself."

"Too bad; did you know him very well?" There was something strange in the way she spoke of the man; nervousness perhaps.

"I met him once but we weren't close," she replied. She seemed to settle back in the seat and then relax more. A slight smile slowly appeared on her face. Mary Jane had continued the habit of self consciously trying to hide the burn scar on her hand when she grew nervous or uneasy. I saw her covering it again now and sensed something was disturbing her.

"Are you sure you're OK?" I asked again.

"Sure; it's nothing important," but I could tell there was more here than she was letting on.

Maybe someday she'd let me in on what memory was stirred by her discovery,

I thought to myself as we continued on our way. There were still many things we had to learn about each other. I knew I loved her deeply and she appeared to feel the same toward me. We had shared some personal feelings and stuff on the drive east. When I had been released from Farmdale I visited her right away at her little apartment in town.

It had taken a while for The Oak to settle my accounts with the state. He'd said something before about bureaucracies and glue; I was beginning to understand what he meant.

While I waited for the check to arrive, I'd made quite a nuisance of myself by hanging around Mary Jane's apartment. I moved slowly in my courtship. I could tell she'd had some bad experiences, probably from men; isn't that always the case with a lovely lady?

It seemed that my patience with her and Alysha Willow; I walked the child to school and back home each day, had worked wonders. When I finally received the check from the state, my first action was to deposit it before California ran out of money and tried to give me an IOU. My second move was to ask Mary Jane to give up her job at the prison and come to Texas with me.

"Are you sure you want to make such a commitment so quickly?" She had asked quietly. "You haven't met any other women in a long time. You don't want to rush into something without thinking it through, do you?" I couldn't tell if she was referring to me or to her own uncertainties.

I looked at her with a naked expression of pure and aching love for her on my face, "You entered my heart the first time I looked at you in the hospital after I came back from the dead. You've been there ever since. I love everything about you, even that burn scar on your pretty little hand that you seem to want to hide all the time. You are everything I could ever want for a companion, even wife, if you'll marry me. I'll treat Alysha Willow as my own daughter; I already do." I had run out of words for the moment so I waited for her to speak.

She hesitated for what seemed way too long for me. My heart started to hurt. Had I moved too quickly? Then she spoke the words I had been waiting for, "Bobby Lee, I'm going to trust you and take the chance. As crazy as it sounds, I've come to love you too, and if it means I have to move to Texas, I'll risk that as well." She threw herself into my arms as tears ran down my cheeks. I wasn't even embarrassed by them.

What had this woman done to me? We left two days later. I convinced her that was all the notice she needed to give before quitting her job. Who knows what terrible things could happen to a pretty little nurse in a prison hospital from one day to the next? I didn't want to risk it. This state had brought me no joy, except for bringing Mary Jane into my life.

I was still heading east as Willie began singing "Angel Flying Too Close to the Ground".

I had purchased every CD Willie Nelson had in the Texas Truck Stop just east of the state line. Other than the sad ending his words seem to fit the occasion perfectly. Bless his heart. He's a national treasure that's for sure. Wish the cops would stop bugging him about smoking pot.

We'd spent the previous two nights in Dallas at the Adolphus Hotel. As a kid my cousin Beau and I had walked along the sidewalk in front of this famous landmark, never daring to enter such a fancy building. I remember a huge Black man wearing a long overcoat and a fancy red cap standing at the entrance; intimidating both Beau and myself without ever giving us so much as a glance. He was no longer there when Mary Jane, Alysha Willow, and I arrived.

Wood panels dominated the interior of this richly decorated antique building built at the beginning of the last century by Adolphus Busch. Now that I had enough money to spend the night there, I decided why not? The girls had loved it and it was a great way to introduce them to Texas.

Mary Jane, Alysha Willow and I spent a day at *the* State Fair which was being held at the appropriately named *Fair Park*. For me, the Fair and the revisit to the Museum of Natural History was a real treat; taking me back to my childhood. In those days there was no admittance fee to the museum or the aquarium, so when my buddies and I went to the Fair and had blown what little bit of money we had managed to scrape together by picking cotton, we would retreat to the cool dark interior of this magnificent museum.

Looking back I realized that we country bumpkins were pretty easy pickin's for the carnival barkers who promised us prizes for busting balloons or tossing a ring around a coke bottle. We were usually flat broke by eleven in the morning on Rural School Day and the bus that we rode to get to the Fair didn't leave until around four. We had a lot of time to kill, so the free displays of stuffed animals in the museum were great. The air conditioned building was like a refrigerator to us country lads.

As the three of us entered the cool darkness I could see that most of the dioramas were unchanged after twenty years. The black bear family that had been there when I was a kid, was still looking at the little red and black snake they had found when they had ripped the old log apart. It was a nostalgic time for me and a new experience for Mary Jane and Alysha Willow.

After checking out of the hotel and heading toward our new home, it was very noticeable how the landscape had changed from what we had seen on the plains of West Texas to the rich blackland fields and oak woodlands around East Texas. We passed at least a half dozen Dairy Queens between Dallas and home. Alysha Willow had already learned about Mini-Blizzards along the way and would throw a small tantrum each time the big red sign appeared if I drove past without slowing down.

The landscape was dotted with large spreads and ranch style homes with wrap around verandas. Interspersed between these pretentious spreads were shanties that were gray-brown from weathering. The yards in front of these shacks had no vegetation since they were used for parking the rolling stock. Seemed to be the poorer the house, the more old cars there were parked in the yards. Some of the vehicles looked like they were operational, while others were rusting, their tires flat and rotting. Most of the windows in the rusting vehicles were cracked or broken from rocks thrown by the kids or the result of BB gun practice by those rural lads lucky enough to own one.

Many of these shacks had not seen a coat of paint in years, if ever, and seemed to defy gravity by continuing to stand. Some wore a covering of tarpaper that had been tacked over rough sawn lumber. The tarpaper hung down from the sides of the houses in strips. Old age and wear and tear from the winds had taken its toll. Seems no one ever thought of tacking the shreds up with strips of new one by two's…or replacing the siding with newer tarpaper, or better yet, shiplap or aluminum siding. It was difficult to believe that these dilapidated structures were still inhabited, I mused. They had changed little from when I went to school here.

The yard dogs were still present at all the houses, rich or poor. These ubiquitous extended-family members seemed to reflect the status of their owners. The fatter ones, at the well kept homes, lay under the tall oak trees, hardly looking up as a car passed. The less fortunate mongrels, victims of unlucky sperm I guessed, with their ribs showing, would run after the passing vehicles, barking and snarling, as if they could bring the car down and dine on it like a pack of lions devouring a wildebeest.

As I drove along I realized even more acutely that little had changed in the four years I had been away. The biggest change it seemed was that the dogs at the home place were not the same ones who occupied the space under the front porch before I left.

The house I had called home had been built close to the road where the cars whizzed by at sixty miles an hour; the posted speed limit in these *residential* areas. The dogs, cats, chickens, and sometimes kids would wander into the traffic. This close proximity to the road seemed to be a prerequisite for laying out home sites in East Texas. The cotton would be planted almost against the sides of the dilapidated houses. Lawns were nonexistent around these poor excuses for homes, while the fancier spreads had acres of grass around them that had to be mown by tractors pulling mowers. Sometimes I would spot a patch of land set aside to grow vegetables. There was corn, okra, tomatoes, and various melons waiting to be picked.

There were few concrete driveways and with forty-eight inches or so of rainfall each year, a lot of the time the yards would be wet and muddy. Folks dropping by to visit would park along the roadside to avoid being mired in the black mud that could suck a shoe off if you stepped in a really soft spot.

This closeness between the houses and the road, coupled with speeding rednecks, created a high attrition rate among the "house cats", not to be confused with the feral ones, and dogs. At any given time there was at least one dead dog lying on the roadside every few miles; having misjudged the speed of the cars they were trying to take out. I remembered it was not wise to get too attached to your pets. The attrition rate due to vehicle mishaps was staggering.

The carcasses would swell quickly in the summer sun and maggots would infest the rotting mess. When I was younger, while bicycling along the country roads, I learned to move to the other side of the highways so as to avoid the sight of maggots feasting and the horrific odors emanating from the rotting carcasses. The dogs alone weren't the only sacrifices lying on the altar of asphalt; bodies of possums, skunks, coons, rabbits, various species of snakes and armadillos were also abundant.

When Mary Jane saw her first armadillo lying dead, but not too damaged, along the highway, she had exclaimed, "What the hell is that thing, Bobby Lee?" We must have passed a hundred dead skunks and rabbits by then but this was the first armadillo so far.

"Wait," I said slowing down and making a U-turn and going back so she could get a better look at this strange sight with its little piggy nose and armored shell. It closely resembled a miniature triceratops without the horns.

"Yuk is that thing for real?" she said, making a face.

"Oh yes, we've got lot's of strange stuff in these woods, Baby." She gave me a doubtful kind of look, like maybe she wasn't quite ready for this new country and the creatures that inhabited it.

Mary Jane sat beside me in the front seat while Alysha Willow slept in the back. "Bobby Lee, this is pretty country all green and with all the big trees, but it kind of smells like something died or is rotting, fecund mud. The air feels like it weighs more than water; it's sure not California." She was starting to sound a little despondent. I couldn't blame her. Rural Texas takes some getting used to.

"You're right about that," I replied. "But we're out of prison, both of us, and we've left an ugly Chapter of our lives behind. Just wait 'til you see the farm Sis found for us." My little sister, Loretta had been selling real estate since she got out of college. She said she had a deal on the old Talbert place just out of town. "If it's as pretty as I remember, and I'm sure it is; I helped build the main house while I was in high school, you'll be tickled to death. The air conditioner will take care of this humidity. This hot air only lasts about four or five months then you freeze your ass off the rest of the year."

"Oh Bobby Lee," She said as she gave me a trusting smile.

I said a silent prayer of thanks for my fresh start on a new life in an old familiar setting. "Thank you, Jesus. God bless us everyone."

# EPILOGUE

**Bobby Lee:** Mary Jane, Alysha Willow and I are back in my hometown in East Texas, It's a little town called Scurry just six miles from Kaufman. We're pretty close to Dallas, so if we get bored here on the little farm I just bought with my 'California Winnings", it's just a short drive to the big city. Neither of us wants anything more to do with California and those crazy fuckers out there. I do appreciate their money however. At night the lights of downtown Dallas can be seen off in the distance. From where I sit on the veranda, I think their glow reflecting off the clouds makes it as beautiful as any city in the world; but then I might be prejudiced.

Sometimes at night when I come home from visiting my friend Jack over in Rockwall, I cross the bridge over Lake Ray Hubbard and see the light house across the lake. It's a beautiful sight but at the same time, it reminds me of the guard tower on the wall in Farmdale Prison. I realize that California in my rearview mirror was the best sight ever.

I wonder about Tom Kidd sometimes. After The Oak squared me away about how Tom had been coerced into setting me up, I began to forgive him. He hung out with me a little while I was waiting for my cash. He had to wait for his award too and when he got it, I'll be damned if he didn't go to the government auction at Bailey's ranch and buy the Bailey Bar stallion. He told me he got it for nearly nothing and was going back home to start raising quarter horses. I wish him all he best.

I was looking forward to seeing my brother, but Jimmy Dale, who I always figured was the smart one, managed to get his ass arrested outside Tucson; at a funeral service no less. He was passing through a small town on his way to pick up a little shipment from one of his Jack-Mormon herbalists and was driving past the local cemetery. He noticed it was a military service where a marine was being laid to rest with the honor guard present.

Seeing the Marine honor guard standing beside the coffin touched Jimmy Dale, you know Semper Fi and all that. Marines seem to never get over having been in the Corps. We army vets, on the other hand, are just happy to be back in the civilian world.

Out of respect for a fallen comrade Jimmy Dale pulled his car into the cemetery joining the small group of mourners; he had some time to kill before picking up his pot and being a veteran, he figured it was the least he could.

There was a hush over the solemn service as the flag was being removed from the coffin, folded and presented to the mother of the fallen soldier. Suddenly a group of people, definitely not members of the service, who had gathered about two hundred feet away, started screaming anti-gay remarks about how God hates queers. The taunts grew louder and uglier; asserting that the death of this young man was a just punishment for America for allowing gays to live in this country. The signs the protesters carried were vile and had nothing to do with Christianity.

Well Jimmy Dale and a handful of other vets that were in the funeral crowd paying their respects to the fallen Marine, took this action by the obnoxious demonstrators rather badly. Two guys who were standing alongside Jimmy Dale were wearing black leather vests with a lot of patches on them signifying they were Viet Nam vets; *Legion Riders* was on one of the patches.

The two weren't young men, Viet Nam was a while back after all, but they looked capable of kicking some ass. Later I saw their pictures in the paper and they looked pretty damned intimidating. There were some cops standing around but they made no move to quiet the offending group of zealots. Seeing that no one else was willing to take any action, Jimmy Dale and the other two guys started toward the boisterous group of agitators. No words passed between them; the three men seemed to be of the same mind.

The loudest of the group was a white haired old geezer who appeared to be the leader. He kept yelling, "It's God's will, it's God's will! He deserved to die!" This seemingly crazed old man was carrying a sign that had been stapled on to a three foot long wooden grade stake, with *"God Hates Queers"* written in large red letters. The stake was about an inch and a half wide and a quarter of an inch thick.

Jimmy Dale and the two angry men who had joined him seemed to have the same idea simultaneously. Zeroing in on the old dude while the rest of his group looked on, suddenly aghast at what was happening, the three men acted decisively and in unison. The crowd of self-appointed Christians appeared to be more noisy than brave when it came to encountering physical violence. I don't know what the hell they were expecting, desecrating the funeral service of a fallen Marine like these fools were doing was just asking for a royal ass-kicking.

Anyway, the old fart with the big mouth, Phillips, or something like that was thrown down, by Jimmy Dale. His pants were pulled down around his ankles by the other two vets. Skid marks on his white boxers were visible to all of the onlookers.

According to the news report, what followed appeared to have been choreographed, although it all happened spontaneously in a very few seconds. Jimmy Dale grabbed the sign from the old mans hand and was trying to stick the sharp end up the guy's wrinkled ass when the police finally sprang into action.

"I was trying to bury it, but the cops jumped in," he told me. This unexpected and violent act by Jimmy Dale had caused the cops to finally spring into action; wouldn't you know it. Backup was called and Jimmy Dale and his new friends were taken to jail. I guess he was lucky he hadn't purchased any illegal substances before the altercation…nothing incriminating was found in his car.

Jimmy Dale was charged with aggravated assault, reduced from an initial charge of attempted murder. The reduction in charges only came after a large hue and cry from Veteran groups around the state.

The County Attorney, not a veteran himself, had defended the more severe charges at first by saying, "The law must be served"; but when threatened with being recalled by the huge number of Veteran's groups in the state, he backed off and reduced the charge. Jimmy Dale and his two accomplices were the only ones incarcerated. Ain't this a funny country?

This particular group of protesters was from some church in Kansas that claimed to be Baptists. Turns out they're more like a group of polygamists, a cult, mostly inbred and not really affiliated with any organized religion. Even the Southern and Missionary Baptists disavow any connection with these crazy fuckers. They preach a lot of hate; especially toward gay people. They are not a very loving or Godlike organization.

Their shtick seems to be traveling around the country disrupting military funerals and adding more pain and suffering to the families of America's fallen soldiers. The dead soldiers don't even have to be gay. Until these nut cases met Jimmy Dale, no one had confronted them with anything other than words.

According to the law, I found out, as long as the protestors stayed at least two hundred feet away from the funeral service, they could say or do anything they pleased. They probably won't be coming to any more military funerals in Arizona after this incident.

When I got the news from Mom, I called on my old friend Jacob. Turns out he had a lawyer pal in Tucson who just happened to be a lieutenant colonel in the National Guard. Through his efforts, and additional pressure brought to bear by the state Veteran's groups, he managed to get my brother a pretty light sentence. Jimmy Dale should be out in another four months. This time I had the money to pay for the lawyer and the hefty fine levied against my brother. Financial circumstances and friends in the right places can make a lot of difference when it comes to balancing the scales of justice.

Anyhow, I ran into Josh at the class reunion, our fifteenth, that was being held in the high school gym; no open bar at these functions. A country style pot luck was being held along with the reunion, of course. There was lots of fried chicken and ham, mashed potatoes, home grown green beans cooked with bacon, potato salad and scalloped potatoes covered in melted cheese with the brown crust on top. You just can't have too many different potato recipes at these kinds of gatherings.

The desserts alone covered one six foot long table that had been set up at the end of the row of tables of similar size holding the rest of the spread. The amount and types of food were kind of amazing when you figure there were only twenty seven people in our graduating class. But all their friends and relatives came too along with other school alumni. It didn't matter what years they attended the little school. There was no shortage of delicious home cooked victuals at the event.

Josh and I went back for seconds before hitting the dessert table. We were so full we could hardly breathe so we took a break from stuffing ourselves, although I kept eyeing one more golden brown drumstick. He was still living in Arizona and I hadn't been home for very long, so we both had been away for a long time without the real good food that can only be found in the South.

Since there's no booze at these events, heart of the Bible Belt and all, we had a good talk that wasn't overshadowed with stupidity by us being drunk. In spite of living in a dry county and being underage a lot of the time, we'd managed to drink ourselves silly a bunch of times when we were younger. We'd had a lot of great conversations on how to fix the world with the help of the Pearl or Bud influence. This time we were sober.

After polishing off the last of his pecan pie, Josh says to me, "Ain't this a hell of a note? What started out as me wanting to teach a hard lesson to a guy at the state pen at Florence, Arizona ended up getting you sprung from a life sentence in California and made you rich at the same time. I got an ass whipping from gang bangers in South Phoenix and that murderer Regan ended up dead, good news, bad news. I guess the Lord works in mysterious ways."

I paused before answering; reflecting on what he'd said, "Josh, you started the wheels turning when you sent Jimmy Dale to talk to me at Farmstead. I can't thank you enough, even though you had no idea things would work out the way they did. Too bad Jimmy Dale's in that state pen in Florence and not here with us to enjoy this spread, but he tells me he should be out in another few months if he doesn't fuck up in there."

"That's something I'd like to discuss with you, Bobby Lee. There's still this unfinished business with Avery Logan. He's the guy I started out after when I came up with the idea of trying to find some justice. It gnaws on me that he's still living such an easy life. I keep thinking of that teenage girl that Logan blasted between her legs with a shotgun and how her life has been ruined. He's sitting around the pen in Florence doing dope, jacking off and getting fat. I hear he's made himself right at home there."

Josh paused, seemed to gather his thoughts and then went on, "The baby rapers and other such scum bags at the state pen appear to have formed some kind of alliance to protect each other from the rest of the cons. Sometimes, though, one of them strays from the pack and gets pretty fucked up by the men that still have a sense of justice toward these worst types of criminals; even though they are in prison for other offences themselves. It reaffirms my faith in my fellow man when I hear a bank robber or car thief has worked over a child molester inside the walls.

"The state keeps those stories quiet, but I still have contacts inside that keep me posted. Problem is, none of my guys want to take the chance of getting in trouble or else they don't have the balls to do what needs to be done. I can't stand in judgment of them but I could use some help from someone on the inside like Jimmy Dale."

I told him that I'd not heard about that sorry-assed buddy system of child molesting maggots watching out for each other, but I was flying out to see Jimmy Dale next week for a visit. "Gonna take him some of this kind of food to remind him why he should stay on track."

"I'm asking one favor here, Bobby Lee." Josh's expression was one of bitterness and anger mixed with compassion for the girl whose life had been ruined. "Jimmy Dale can't personally get involved with any retribution against Logan. Considering your questionable role in the Regan suicide, even the dumbass prison cops would have to suspect that was too much of a coincidence; for two brothers from the Lone Star State to be involved in the deaths of two child molesters, even though the crimes occurred in two separate states."

"Whatever are you talking about?" I asked innocently, but I couldn't help sharing a smile with Josh.

"You've got some money, I've got some money. If Jimmy Dale could find a friend on the inside, a real bad ass kind of friend with nothing to lose, a lifer like you once were; maybe this friend would have a family on the outside that could use some financial help?"

"Josh, did this Logan guy really shoot that little girl where you said?" I asked.

"Yeah, she was fourteen years old. He thought it would destroy his DNA after he raped her."

"What a sorry piece of shit. I'll see what I can do, I promise."

A month later, I received a short newspaper clipping in the mail. It was in an envelope with no return address. It was postmarked "Florence, Arizona". The clipping read, "Murder/Suicide in State Pen". The story went on to say, "Two convicts serving twenty years to life in Florence for crimes against children were found dead in the cell they shared.

The article went on to say, "Investigators released a statement saying that Avery Logan and Thomas "Junior" Thompson, who had been cellmates for the last six months, apparently got into an argument and fatally stabbed each other with knives they had fashioned from pieces of metal taken from the license plate manufacturing shop.

In a strange turn of events, after inflicting a lot of damage over what appeared to be an extended knife fight, it seems they managed to stab each other in the heart simultaneously. No other suspects are being questioned and the case is considered closed."

I forwarded it on to Josh, again with no return address. I mailed it from Dallas with a note enclosed, "Don't worry about the money, it's taken care of. A friend."

Last week there was a sympathy card from Josh in my mail box. Four names were printed inside with this message, "I don't mean to appear greedy but is there any chance these residents might meet up with the two that went before?"

I thought to myself, "Could be," as I smiled and placed the card in my pocket.

The last time I talked with Josh, I told him he should look up Jacob Oakley when he next visits the Golden State, "I think you'll find you have some common interests. It's rumored he pulled a real coup on a well known slime bag defense attorney a while back"